SAVE THE
LAST
Piece

by Clare Solly

Text copyright © 2023 Clare V. Solly All Rights Reserved
Published by Hidden Cat Publishing

ISBN 979-8-9890172-0-1 (1st edition paperback)

This book is dedicated to Paola and Lecinda.

Although you are no longer with us, your belief
in my dreams was implicit.

Chapter One

S heer panic has overtaken me. Every pore is leaking, drenching my shirt. Pungent stress sweat wafts from my armpits. Even though the ceremony is over, there are five hours left of this wedding. Plenty of time for disaster.

Twenty minutes behind schedule might as well be twenty days. Two hundred and eighty-one wedding guests are migrating at the speed of icebergs in winter from the third floor to the twenty-first. Even with my tersely polite suggestions to "take the elevators upstairs," they won't move any faster. Dressed in thousand-dollar haute couture, the bejeweled Louboutin-ed wedding guests refuse to squeeze in together. Most guests are out-of-towners—obvious from their personal space requirements and refuse to ascend in groups of more than four. With minimal guests ascending in the slow elevators of this hundred-year-old hotel, everything is in slow motion, except my racing heart.

If the tension caused by the turtle-like speed of the guests isn't enough to have me on the path to a migraine, a non-stop stream of text messages will be. Question after question just keeps coming. And there is nothing I can do or say to make any of it better. The stress level is so high today, you'd think the president was attending. I feel helpless as I stand near the elevator bank trying to move the immovable.

No matter what you see in movies, or even when you attend them, events are smoke and mirrors. Hidden behind the glamour is manic precision and tension. Weddings are large emotional parties filled with buttercream and over-obsession. In New York, the scale of these events is massive. Most of the time, the bride or the "hostess" has never hosted a party of this scale in her life, and yet her family is throwing thousands if not millions of dollars into making it amazing. Which is why wedding planners exist. To make everything beautiful, breathtaking and memorable. And of course, every good planner has an even better assistant.

Enter: me. My job is to solve any problem without showing panic... and I mean any problem. I feel like I get extra points on each event if I can make everything seem easy and as if it were a joy to execute. Imagine me as a beauty queen crossed with a firefighter. I literally smile, wave, and look pretty while I put out various fires. I'm not joking. Thrice in the last five minutes glass, water, and lit candles have gone flying. The grandeur created by the candle-filled hurricane vases lining the St. Regis marble hallway keep getting kicked by champagne-sipping guests crossing down through the Louis suites. Each time another clank-crash of glass sounds I stifle a sarcastic yell of L'chaim! Instead, I refrain and only point another staff member toward the pool of wax, broken glass, and water.

When people ask me about my job they assume it's full of enchantment and romance. At this point in my career, nothing is glamorous. Especially after dealing with event attendees who think that they can do anything they want at any time during the event. Nowadays, I envision the guests as a herd of well-fed geriatric cats with an aversion to movement. Although truth be told, I wouldn't want to move if I were being fed shrimp that are each the size of an infant's fist, black sparkling caviar that was one hundred and forty dollars an ounce, hundred-dollar imported French champagne, and unlimited top-shelf liquor.

With a deep breath, I channel calm in this sea of unmoving wingtips, stilettos, and silk, and never-ending text messages from the panicked wedding planner, and her other assistant, Sarah. We are currently brainstorming how to work through running late. The overtime rates on this venue could purchase a fully loaded luxury car with leather interior and all the bells and whistles. Including a personal driver. Sarah is in her test run as Event Manager and is feeling the heat. I have managed over fifty weddings, and have gotten to the point where I can see places we could gain time back in an instant. That confidence took a long time for me to build, but I can make a split-second decision on anything at a wedding these days. Sarah isn't there yet. She needs to figure it out on her own while the pressure is piling up and tension is running high. It sounds mean, but honestly, there is no other way to learn the skill. You can't win in dodgeball if you don't face the firing squad. Sarah is currently in the hot seat.

Our upcoming season has several double-booked weekends which means our small team will need to divide and conquer. Sarah is to manage some, and I will run others. If today's test run goes well for her, I get to be in charge of events on my own. Something I've been waiting for as long as I've had this job. But before I get ahead of myself, today I was to "observe" her and give feedback later on ways she can improve.

Today's plan is failing. In the operatic miserable way. So far today is running as if Sarah has never worked a wedding at all. In the past week I had coached her through everything for today. And she has the experience of ten weddings under her belt. But even with experience and preparation, she was terrified. I believed in her, however she didn't believe in herself. On our final prep call last night, I told her whenever she was second-guessing herself to text me. That was a mistake. Around seven this morning texts started coming at me every forty-five seconds from Sarah panicking. Mixed with unnecessary reminder texts from

3

Zella, as she keeps asking about things that I have either already taken care of or they're on my radar, the buzz of my phone every ninety seconds has made my jaw so tense I could give the Tin Man a run for his money. It's an intense pressure. I'm used to it, but Sarah is not.

Sarah's sheer terror stems from working for our boss. Ahem. Sorry, I mean the founder and CEO of Tremaine Events. "Madame" as she is called behind her back, who dubiously signs my paychecks, while complaining she pays me too much. Gizella Tremaine, or "Zella" as she prefers to be called, would burn anyone with death rays from her eyes if they called her "boss," or "ma'am." It's true. I've witnessed this many times. Zella is one of the most sought-after event planners in New York City, or so she tells every client who calls her to plan their big day. At first, I drank the Kool-aid and thought Tremaine Events was the best event company in town. Don't get me wrong, Tremaine Events is a highly sought-after, premier company in the five boroughs – even if Zella will really only work in two, and sometimes in Connecticut or New Jersey if the fee or client profile is high enough. But don't tell anyone I said that—Zella to any potential client or referral saccharinely "always considers every client and wants to make sure that the chemistry is the best before a contract is on the table." Chemistry. Ha. More like logistics and economics. But I digress.

Where were we? Ah yes. Zella micromanaging via text from whereabouts unknown; Sarah panicking up on the twenty-first floor with the bandleader and head waiter putting pressure on her about when to start the music and serve the first course; and me sweating like a nun in a cucumber field, while trying to herd the guests upstairs. Oh, how I want a calm moment to breathe right now. "Breathing is for Mondays," Zella always replies when I say I need a

4

breath. I roll my eyes to this exchange in my head. Mondays after events are supposed to be our days off, but they rarely are. Planning is never-ending. Especially between March and October, otherwise known as "Wedding Season." I step around the corner, close my eyes, and partially to spite Zella and partly to calm myself, and I take a deep breath.

Then genius strikes. I now know how to clear the room. Jumping into action, I dash over to the jazz quartet and tell them to cut the music. Then I wiggle my way through twenty people to cross ten feet to the bar and tell the bartenders they are closed and to refer anyone requesting a drink to head upstairs. Then I have the waiters stealthily remove the shrimp and caviar. All without guests noticing. All while answering the continual barrage of texts.

In a record seven minutes I got every guest up to the ballroom. Meanwhile Sarah got wine service and dancing music started. Zella, who had only been an omnipotent presence via text for the last hour, resurfaced laughing with the bride and groom. They came toward the third-floor elevators. She must have been schmoozing, excuse me, "seeing to their needs before going upstairs, giving them a calm moment before being congratulated on looking magnificent and being newly wedded." She says this so often, I have it memorized. The woman is a better actress than most Broadway actors I know who have had long term contracts. Her whole song and dance is a well plotted play. I honestly don't know if she likes the planning so much as she likes the pageantry.

To be fair, she has trained me well to be a supporting actor for this performance. In fact, a wedding is a pop-up one-day show that I have become incredibly good at. Long hours of planning and replanning help to lay the groundwork for our twelve to fourteen hours onsite. Anything can go wrong at any time, and it usually does. The trick is to fix it or smooth it over so the bride and groom never see it and have the best day of their lives. A meticulous eye and a cool head are required. A flower petal out of place or a mispositioning of a name card could derail perfection. It sounds dramatic, but I can't tell you how many times one person noticed, told the bride, and then she's upset about it for the entire evening. Extravagance like this has to also be perfection. Once I rearranged the escort cards fourteen times because of incorrect spacing. Three hundred cards readjusted fourteen times. I still have nightmares.

I know you're thinking most of the weddings you have been to the details weren't that important, they were beautiful and that you would notice if things went wrong. But that wasn't the case. Like a duck on the water, you saw only the smooth sailing, but under the water the legs of the duck kept paddling. In the background, we don't stop moving either. Good events are well oiled machines with things like the cake delivered to the venue just at the right time so it doesn't have to go in the refrigerator, but also can sit out for five hours before it's cut—this way the icing doesn't melt, the cake doesn't get dry and it's delicious. Placement of the final flower two minutes before the guests walk into the room, all while the lighting designer is figuring out how to wash the room in a romantic light to highlight the work of the decor team.

Oh, while I'm talking about light, candles are a terrible idea. Sure, they look nice, but they have to be lit at the very last minute and very carefully because they melt quickly and tend to blow out. Try lighting two hundred candles as fast as you can, I've gotten it down to five minutes.

Basically, for everything to look like it's easy and no work at all, a pre-established wedding itinerary timed down to the minute, that took weeks to prepare will ensure perfection and precision in everything in the hour's guests are present. Sheer choreography of everyone on site is required so the day runs as smooth as possible.

Speaking of running smoothly, the twenty-two minutes we are now behind have me sweat soaked and hands tied. In order for everything to stay smooth tonight we need to get that time back. And there are twenty-two unread texts from Sarah, one for each minute we are behind. The band wanted to start the first dance, but the bride and groom were missing.

During cocktail hour the bride and groom had disappeared, which Zella had been texting about. Zella had finally found the couple in the back room doing shots with the best man and the maid of honor. Ben, the photographer from Precision Studios, had also found them and snapped photos of the drinking. Zella vehemently commanded through more texting that I would need to email Ben on Monday to request those shots not go into the online photo album. The groom's parents are both sober, and the bride's mother is a devout Presbyterian. To put out this fire, I have already started to compose the email to Ben while I've been waiting.

"Putting out fires" should be a special skill on my resume. Actually, I don't just put them out, I anticipate them, run and throw myself on them, preventing the flare up the moment a spark happens. Many brides after their wedding have said something like, "Wow, this was an easy night for you, my wedding went so smoothly." I will always smile and agree even though I managed to solve or deflect dozens of issues during their party.

My current fire is the photographer, not only for taking the alcohol dousing photos, but absorbing all the time to get the iconic photo: the couple alone in the candle lit hallway

7

sharing an intimate glance. Or a kiss. Very romantic. Very hard to get during cocktail hour while it is crowded, the iconic shot is taken after the guests leave cocktail hour before the décor crew dismantle all of it. Now is the time. I take another deep breath while channeling as much patience as I can muster.

I text Zella that the hallway is clear, as I hide in the elevator alcove. She texts back that they're coming, so I can't move. There isn't a better place for me to go, as if I step out, I will be in the hallway, and in the picture.

My annoyance was rising. With one hand I smacked the button to keep the elevator in the bank. The St. Regis is after all a working hotel, and we are not the only ones requesting elevators. With the other hand I keep texting Sarah who is now dealing with guests playing with the sword that the St. Regis brought out to cut the cake. She also is getting complaints from guests that they weren't getting photobooth prints. It is all I can do to hold back my quippy text covering both the swordplay and the photobooth of "Avast me hearty! Sing to them in a princess voice that 'someday their prints will come.'"

As I pace the six-foot square space of the elevator alcove, my shoes squeaking on the marble, I feel imprisoned. Every click of the camera feels like one more brick of anxiety piling up on my shoulders. I check my watch. We are now almost thirty minutes behind. If we have any hope of getting back on schedule: the kitchen has to serve dinner before the best man can do his twenty-minute speech complete with slides and a flash mob. I needed to get the bride and groom upstairs to start their first dance. This would calm Sarah, and would hopefully curtail her stress filled texts, chirping every thirty seconds asking the ETA of the bride and groom.

I text Zella:

ZT we need to get the B&G upstairs.

We use shorthand as much as possible. "ZT" being Zella Tremaine and "B&G" being bride and groom. We've used shorthand so much, autocorrect does it for me.

BUZZ. Sarah to me:

Photobooth operator says they only purchased the digital package. But guests don't want to just email pictures to themselves.

BUZZ Sarah again:

But he says that if they agree, he brought the printer.

BUZZ Sarah again:

But it will cost an additional $300.

DING. Elevator. I hit the button.

BUZZ. Zella to me:

WAIT.

Zella operates in a life of such intensity that everything is all caps.

BUZZ. Sarah to me:

WHAT DO I DO?

Great. Now Sarah is in all caps. She WAS learning something from Zella. I rolled my eyes.

BUZZ. Sarah to both Zella and me:

Bandleader wants to know when the bride and groom are coming?

BUZZ. Sarah to both:

Do we go into a new dance set?

BUZZ. Sarah to both:

They're playing with the sword again.

BUZZ. Sarah to both:

The guests.

BUZZ. Sarah to both:

Not the band. The band doesn't have the sword.

BUZZ. Sarah to both:

9

Any word on the ok for the extra charge for the photobooth?

See what I mean? Sarah needed to chill. I was just about to text her that when:

BUZZ. Zella to both:

Natalie, why aren't you handling this?

Zella had probably forgotten that I wasn't running things and didn't realize I was in the elevator alcove waiting.

BUZZ. Sarah to both:

It's ok ZT. I'll figure it out.

BUZZ. Sarah to just me:

Sorry.

DING. Elevator again. I hit the button.

Squaring my shoulders, I decide to take the reins. Sarah was ready, but the girl needed to breathe.

Me to Sarah:

STOP. One problem at a time. Have the Maitre 'D take the sword back to the kitchen until the cake cutting at 10:30. Tell the band it will be ten more minutes and to play another dance set. I'll confirm on the printer, but it's probably a yes. Take care of the band and sword. By the time you're done, I'll have an answer.

BUZZ. Sarah to just me:

Ok. Good.

BUZZ. Sarah to just me:

Thanks.

Me to Sarah:

Breathe. You've got this. I believe in you.

Me to both:

ZT can we get a firm yes on $300 more for photo booth prints?

Why is it when you need an answer it takes an eternity to get one. Ellipsis from Zella. Those rippling three dots indicating a text is on its way are probably the most irritating things in the world. My impatience is spurred on even more with the irritating click of the camera and the ding of the elevator. So I do the unthinkable. I peek my head out.

"GET OUT!" The loud hiss is flung in my direction from a doorway across from my hiding place. I shrink back into the elevator alcove as my phone buzzes in my hand.

BUZZ. Zella to both:

YES.

I really hated it when she wasn't specific. From experience, I knew that if I screwed up or read into a text she had sent, it would be my fault later. Luckily, I had learned to ask a precise question, so I could show her the proof later. My text asked for a firm yes, and she gave one to both Sarah and me. I take a screenshot, for good measure. Then I text Sarah:

[Thumbs up emoji] *photo booth prints. I'll try to get B&G upstairs in 5 min or less.*

BUZZ. Sarah to just me:

Thanks.

BUZZ. Sarah to just me:

How do you do this each time? The pressure is killing me!! I'm sweating like I'm wearing a puffy coat on a humid summer day!!!

I smirk to myself.

Me to Sarah:

Magic deodorant. And DEEP BREATHS.

More silence. Irritated that the photographer was still snapping, I really wanted to hurry things along. I wonder if I should peek my head out again?

DING. The elevator again. With all the irritation I am feeling, I smack the button.

In an effort to be productive while I am a glorified elevator operator, my head spins through how to get the schedule back on track. Over the last three months, I had spent many grueling hours going back and forth over today's schedule with care and precision. Normally I would use my amazingly timed, comprehensive outline Zella and I had perfected. So many venues and vendors complimented us on our schedule.

Even though we rarely strayed from our wedding equation, Zella always wanted to edit my work. We had built a good skeleton that allowed for cushion time for delays such as this photography moment, missing bridal party members who are supposed to give a toast, or a serve out of a course that took too long.

Unfortunately, this bride's favorite hobby was micromanaging. She wanted the timing of the evening to be tighter, with a long dance set at the end of the night after the cake is cut. Big mistake. Huge. Once the cake is cut, everyone leaves. It's the cue to depart. Insider tip: if you want people to stay all night, wait as long as possible to cut the cake. Now we have no choice; we will just have to push back the cake cutting.

I smile to myself and relish being right. Last week this bride screamed through her cell phone at me, in one of many bridezilla moments I'd dealt with. She insisted I kept screwing up her wedding schedule. So, I was not about to tell her that we were behind schedule right now. If we had just stuck to my original plan, we would be fine. If the bride asks, I will let Zella tell her. Usually in the moment, everyone gives complete trust to Zella and "her timing." Or really, my timing.

If I just could get them all on the elevator and upstairs, I could coach Sarah how to get this all fixed. I said a silent prayer that they would come through the door in the next sixty seconds before Sarah texted me again.

DING. I pressed the button for the elevator.

Barely nudging my head out of the alcove door my voice comes out in a sing-song tension, "I'm holding the elevator, just let me know when you're ready."

"GET. OUT. OF. THE. SHOT." Irritation spewed from Zella with the brutality of Attila the Hun. This tone means there might be a beheading soon. Morbidly curious, I peek out with my head again. A waiter scurried down the hall in the opposite direction.

BUZZ. Sarah to me:

It's been ten minutes. Extend the dance set again?

Just as I was about to send my reply, the photographer burst through the elevator alcove doors towards me. With militaristic precision Ben whipped the camera lens toward the bride and groom with paparazzi-like nonstop snapping pictures.

Plastering a beauty pageant-worthy smile on my face, I punched the button for the elevator again and the doors open immediately. Thank goodness for the little things. Gazelle-like Ben jumps into the awaiting elevator. Immediately followed by the groom with hair as slick and shiny as his shoes. A crimson-colored pocket square to match the color of the bridesmaids' dresses and the invitations, blossoms from his chest. Complaining about his tie not being straight.

To myself I think the tie is straight—the man wearing it is questionable. That later discovery would be for his gym bunny bride, currently clinging to his arm and tottering behind him in her four-inch Jimmy Choo's. Surprisingly she is calm and unfussy for the first time in six months and is beaming in her white lace and silk twenty-five-thousand-dollar Monique Lhuillier that came complete with its letter of authenticity. Years in the industry and I'm still confused about what one is supposed to do with a certificate of authenticity for a wedding dress. Does it get framed and put on the wall next to a college diploma?

Speaking of confused, the willfully blind couple, solely focused on appearance, hops into the elevator. Oblivious that they are still the center of attention, she yanks up the bodice of her dress while he fixes her flyaway hair. Camera clicking continues catching it all including the couple simultaneously baring their teeth to check for food. This Discovery Channel primate documentary moment is one we see in some form at every wedding. It never ceases to make me bubble with happiness. I have a small collection of what I called "documentary wedding pictures" in an album in The Cloud saved for when I needed uplifting. This would be an addition.

My phone buzzes again. I don't even have to look to know it is Sarah. "Um, Zella?" I say with a strained smile and a nervous titter, "The band is wondering if they should start another dance set, or if we are on our way?"

"Yes. We should go," Zella coos with authority as if the brilliant idea had just come to her. Those four words spoken in her origin-less haughty accent is enough to urge the most stubborn to move. She glides onto the elevator as if she is one of the most important guests. In her mind, I guess she always is. Stepping back, I don't get in the elevator. I know Zella loathes it when we both are on the elevator with the client at the same time. She always says too many crew is overwhelming, although I know differently. Besides the capacity of the elevator is six people, and the wedding dress takes up space for two. I am happy to wait.

As if I am a ride host for a children's theme park, I smile and wave. "I'll see you all up there!" I say feeling like I am almost in the clear as the elevator doors close.

Just then Mick Anders, the head of the St. Regis Event department, in his freshly tanned, million-dollar smiling way, eases past me and onto the elevator. Mick immediately hits the door open button, and the doors retreat to their casings.

"There's enough room," his voice like a delicious cognac flirtatiously wafts through the air. "Join us." He beams at me.

"Nah, it's okay," I say, "I'll get the next one," blushing a bit as I step backwards. Although it is a tiny glint, I catch Zella's approval. But then the unthinkable happens: the bride and the groom cheerfully shift to make more room.

"There absolutely is room," the groom joyfully expresses, as if my presence in the elevator would make everything more perfect.

Confused, I wait for an objection from Zella. Everyone keeps smiling at me through the open door. Time ticks on. I will the elevator doors shut so I won't have to make the choice. No objection comes. Mick then hits the doors open button. I wince a smile and step toward the threshold.

Suddenly, "NOOO!!" vehemently echoes through the air.

Everything goes into slow motion. As my foot crosses into the car, a hand comes toward my chest. Zella's eyes are crimson with angry disapproval. Then THWACK. Her hand strikes me squarely in the sternum. My breath and balance are knocked away. Adrenaline and survival mode kick in. The marble floor of the St. Regis was not something I wanted to fall on. Heaving myself upright, I try to regain my balance. I overcorrected and start to fall into the bride. Her face of terror sears my brain.

To avoid falling into the dress, I twist and try to veer left to fall on the wall of the elevator. But I gauged the

15

distance incorrectly and wobble toward the groom. With no other choice, I topple out of the elevator.

During my human pinball routine, a barking cackle echoes through the vestibule. Zella's famous laugh makes me panic more, but also seems incredibly wrong for this situation as my knees and hands slap onto the marble floor.

Pain sears through my body, and not wanting to register any of it because I don't want to ruin the bride's day, I shake my head to get rid of the laughter and the pain, hoping it is just in my mind. But I doubt it is.

Stupefied, but trained both by Zella and my theater education I know the show must go on. My phone buzzes impatiently with yet another text from Sarah, unable to refrain from having a massive anxiety attack seventeen floors above. I crawl on my knees to clear my feet from the elevator, trying to say as undramatically as possible over my shoulder, "I'm fine, just go on without me!" Plastering on a smile, holding back tears, I reassure, "I'm totally fine!"

The barking laughter had stopped, and Zella says with a dismissive wave, "She's fine. Let's go." And she smacks the door close button.

My knees throb. The doors ding shut. The elevator ascends. Taking a deep breath as I lean back on my feet, I gather my wits and assess for injury. I slowly stand up and regain my stability. The fall replays in my mind. Zella's cackle echoes through my head. She was regularly hurtful and insensitive, but this was a new level. My phone irritatingly buzzes again with a text from Sarah. I do the unthinkable: I ignore it.

For three years, I had been available 24/7, obedient under impossible circumstances. I had walked out of dinners and parties to answer her calls; I had given up weekends; I had even ordered photo albums from airplanes when I was heading on vacation. I put up with being yelled at, ignored, and thrown under the bus to brides and vendors by this woman. But being literally thrown to the ground was a new level of abuse. Sure, this job seemed glamorous, but I had given everything to a woman who just shoved me out an elevator and laughed as if I were entertainment. But what could I do about it? I had been saying for months under my breath that I needed to walk away from this job. This was after years of feeling daily like I was going to be fired.

But I was done. This was the last straw. I couldn't just quit in the middle of a wedding, could I?

Chapter Two

So how did I get here? Cue the glamorous movie montage with a great hit song. I know I'm being theatrical. I'm an actor turned event manager: theatrical is in my makeup. The Hollywood version of my rags-to-riches story would portray me as a bright, shiny recent college graduate brimming with promise. This story starts moments after graduation, lucking into the position of a lifetime with an elite wedding planner. Naive and starry-eyed, suffering the trials of her first job, the heroine touches the heart of the audience but still brings a bit of humor for the rest of us on her path to success.

Here's the unpolished truth: I'm a struggling actress in New York City, midway through her 30s. Not enough movies feature middle-aged women. There is a pocket of experience the world is missing out on. I'm imperfect, jaded, and always on the lookout for lucrative but not soul-crushing, flexible jobs. From the outside, I'm a dreamer and a hot mess. I'm an artist. My hobbies include worrying about having a stable job and panicking about paying rent.

Tall and buxom—that's the nice way to say I need to lose weight—and rife with experience and talent, I'm still a little naïve. This late onset naïveté seems to be a constant among my friends, and actually for loads of people here in New York. Which makes sense. People come here to follow their dreams. I have heard New York referred to as Never Neverland more than once, because we come here with childhood dreams, and try to maintain them and our agelessness. For seven years I've lived in The Big Apple. I've lived here just long enough to be jaded but I still love this stinky brutal city. My resume includes part time jobs like catering waiter, coffee machine demonstrator, receptionist, sample sale clerk, Broadway theater usher, and babysitter to name a few; my experience is a veritable monetary patchwork quilt that I'm still piecing together while trying to pursue acting as a career. My agent says any day now.

Interestingly, I got the event job through theater. I had booked my dream role of Paulina in Shakespeare's A Winter's Tale that paid very little. Performances conflicted with shifts at the jazz club where I worked nights, and I hated the job anyway, so I quit. Add to my monetary woes, my five-year nanny gig was coming to an end as Levi, my ward, was getting too old for a nanny.

Enter Amanda. We met during rehearsals in New York City's West Village. I met my boyfriend Sam, during that same production. He's another story that I'll get into later. My role paid a small stipend which allowed me to pay rent but when the show closed, I needed a job. Amanda mentioned early on in the rehearsal process she worked for a wedding planner. When I asked about working for her company, she said she would give me a call if they were hiring. Then I thought working for a wedding planner would be awesome for two reasons. One, I loved weddings and two, although the event industry and theater seem totally unrelated, they both deal with putting on a show. Well, three reasons: both are filled with drama, gay men, and illusion. Coincidentally, much like my life. But Amanda didn't seem too hopeful about it at the time, so I forgot about our conversation.

A Winter's Tale closed, and I went back to the grind of auditions, nannying, and waiting tables. Months later, on a blustery day in March, Amanda called.

I was just released from a crazy audition—they were setting Romeo and Juliet in Africa on the South

Africa/Mozambique border. The audition was such a workout that I felt too hot to wear too much even though it was a brisk day, so I was shrugging out of my coat. My phone rang as my arm was halfway out of the second sleeve. Fumbling to answer, I caught the call on the third ring.

I answered with a melodious "Hello!" both from being pumped with endorphins from the work I had done in the audition, and blissful at seeing it was Amanda calling. She responded back in her light Colorado drawl that she tried to cover, and it ended up sounding like she was from Massachusetts by way of England. After exchanging pleasantries, Amanda told me her news: the event company she worked for, the prestigious Tremaine Events, had a demanding upcoming season and needed to bring on a new assistant. I was ecstatic!

"You'll basically be a gopher at events," Amanda explained. Then there would be light filing, running errands and a little computer work during the week in the office. It was part time, but paid decently, and was flexible. Amanda sold the job even more, mentioning we were usually fed the four hundred a plate dinner at the events. I'm a curvy girl who wishes she were a size four but likes eating enough that she's a size fourteen. Good food is always a clincher.

Without hesitation, I jubilantly accepted!

"Great! Zella will want to meet with you for a brief interview at her Flatiron office. When are you available?" Amanda asked.

Flipping through my calendar, I offered Monday at 1pm or Tuesday at 10am.

"I'll check with Zella and will text you the one that works best!" Amanda said. We said our goodbyes and hung up. I smiled as I ran to the subway to catch the train I heard approaching.

Just making it on the subway, I also got a seat. This day was magical. I just had a kick-ass audition, and had a potential job—one that would allow me to audition, and would allow me into elite parties and events that I had only fantasized about attending. Even the voice in my head got high pitched and excited.

By the time I reached my tiny Harlem studio apartment that was barely enough square footage to house my boyfriend and me, Amanda had texted back asking for Tuesday at 9am. I groaned. Not a morning person, I loathed committing to anything of consequence before 10am. Before I could send Amanda a cranky response, she beat me to the punch apologizing that Zella was booked both of my available times and "surely I could make 9am on Tuesday work." This adjustment, if this were a movie and not a story about my life, would have been a sign: uh oh, here it begins. But in real life it seemed a simple change. I texted back to confirm, even though a 9am interview meant getting up at the crack of 6:30am to make sure I was showered, made up, caffeinated, coherent, and on time.

Monday night, the eve of the interview, I planned to go to bed early. When I climbed into bed at 11:30pm I couldn't sleep. Sam had gotten home late and we finished a bottle of wine and the latest episode of this dragon show we both got hooked on, to celebrate my interview and to commiserate that I didn't book the African Romeo and Juliet—the rejection email arrived during the day. I couldn't stop yawning during my getting-ready-for-bed routine. Sleep usually comes easily for me but my brain wouldn't shut down. My excited brain spun in anticipation; my body tossed and turned. Chipper chatter was on a loop in my brain: I love weddings—I love champagne I love the romance of a wedding. Beautiful flowers. Beautiful people. I'm great at taking care of people and helping them stay calm. I'll be great at this job. There is something so magical about a flower-drenched room and couples surrounded by their friends all filled with champagne and hope. I really want this job. I hope I get this job. Weddings make life seem more livable—I really hope I get this job and she likes me and—UGH! Go to sleep, Natalie!

Around 1am I gave up and took melatonin. Induced sleep had to be better than no sleep at all. The last thing I remember was that my phone said 1:45am. When the buzzing and blaring sounds came from the direction of my nightstand, I thought I had only been asleep for five minutes. Groggily, I pulled the comforter over my head to mute the sound and tried to cuddle toward Sam. A few moments later I realized Sam had already left to teach his early morning fitness classes.

Finally putting it together that the annoying beep was my alarm, I sat straight up in bed, wide awake. Full of excitement and terror, I rushed around my apartment. Sam had already set up the coffee for me, so I hit the button. Sweet Sam, always taking care of me!

Putting in my contacts, I rethought my outfit choice. Amanda hadn't mentioned I should wear anything particular. Wracking my brain to think about what I saw that wedding planners wore on those pseudo-reality TV shows, or what JLo wore her planner movie I decided to go classic. I grabbed a black pair of slacks and a black blazer out of the closet I thought would be appropriate. They didn't quite match in color, but it didn't matter if I broke it up with my sapphire blouse. It was my power audition shirt, and I felt good about the outfit.

I hopped into the shower. Deciding it was necessary, I did a clarifying facial mask and shaved, even though it was thirty degrees outside, and I picked pants. Mentally, I reviewed my entire wardrobe. The black blazer made me think of Katie and I smiled.

When I first moved to New York, my friend Katie advised me, "update your wardrobe to have mostly black clothing. Real New Yorkers wear black. A simple black blazer and a pair of slacks is a must. You'll blend—it's like urban camouflage."

Now I have one black blazer and one black jacket: they're rarely used. Honestly, I have never understood all black. Sure, black gives a skinny illusion, but I'm still me. Every inch and curve is still there. Added bonus: I look bland. And at six feet tall, I have never blended in, so I just felt boring wearing all black. Besides, I didn't have to worry about blending in here in New York. Everyone was busy rushing somewhere or looking at the sights. We ignore each other.

As the water rushed over me, so did the realization. Screw the black. I needed to wear something truly me: a grass green blazer, and a knit navy dress with a paisley print with an empire waist and flared skirt with pockets. The dress made me feel confident even though it showed more leg than I preferred. My mom always said, if your tush isn't showing, you're allowed in public. Case in point, The Naked Cowboy. After the outfit was on, I felt mildly self-conscious, and cold, so I added leggings. I threw on gold ballet flats and some long teardrop gold and green earrings to tie everything together. I felt funky and classy all at the same time.

The clock read 8:10am. How did it get so late so fast? I grabbed my purse and down-filled coat and dashed out of my apartment. On the street I pulled up directions to Zella's and headed to the subway. I had mapped the directions on three different apps five times each on my phone. I didn't want to be late for something this important. Each app said that it would take me approximately twenty minutes to get to my destination. I gave myself forty-five, because subways aren't reliable.

Good thing I planned ahead. One delay after another detained me. Full of anxiety, five minutes before I had to be at my interview I got to my stop. I ran four blocks. My feet slammed on the pavement through my ballet slippers. My lungs exploding from the lack of air. All makeup and deodorant I had put on was now gone. A trickle of sweat ran down my neck and back and gave me a chill as I entered the building.

Yanking off my coat and dabbing my forehead with a napkin I had in my purse; I ran to the doorman's desk waiting for his attention. I caught my breath and checked the time. It was 8:58. If the elevator was fast, I would still be on time. A shaved-bald black man behind the desk just stared intensely at the computer screen in front of him. I waited. He stared. I waited longer. He stared at the computer. I willed him to look up at me.

"Um, hello?" I said after what seemed an eternity of time.

"Just a second," he said gruffly.

"Ok," I said annoyed.

Anxiously, I waited. Then I looked at the time on my phone. It was 9:05.

"Uhh…" I said again nervously, and to remind him of my presence.

He still ignored me.

"I'm so sorry," I continued with sticky sweetness, "but I was due for an appointment with Gisella Tremaine five—"

He abruptly stood kicking the chair he was sitting in back as if he were about to jump over the desk and tackle me, he reached for the phone and started tapping buttons. "Why didn't you say you was going up to see Miz Tremaine?" he asked me accusingly in a light foreign accent, as if it were my fault he was ignoring me. "What did you say your name was?"

"I didn't but, uh, um, I'm Natalie Luna, I have—"

"Hello, Miz Tremaine it's Dominic downstairs. Nancy is here for her appointment." He paused for a moment, and I tried to tell him my name was Natalie not Nancy. He ignored me. "Uh huh. Sure, I'll let her know and I'll send her right up," he said as he hung up, and looked up at me with a squinting eye and pursed lips. "Miz Tremaine said to tell you she doesn't like tardy people, and the next time you're late, I'm not to let you up, hear me?"

"But I—" I started to explain he was part of the reason I was late, but it seemed fruitless. He continued to glare as if to drive the point home, and then in a tiny nod over his right shoulder he indicated the elevator. "Fourteenth floor, take two lefts out of the elevator. 1402."

The elevator opened as I got to it. Just as the doors were closing, I could swear I heard Dominic sarcastically mutter, "Good luck." I wondered what he meant.

As the elevator ascended, my confusion and frustration turned back into anxiety. A sour body odor smell hit my nostrils as I raised my arm to put my phone in my bag. I tried to convince myself as the last few floors ticked by, I would be the only one who could smell it. Just in case, I would remember to keep my arms down and I would remain a safe three feet from anyone else. If I could help it.

A ping sounded, and the doors opened to a murky forest green hallway. Two lefts Dominic said, so I stepped out of the elevator and went left. There were no doors, so I just kept walking. The hall turned to the left and I followed, starting to wonder if I should have left breadcrumbs. My tension and nervousness mounted. I came to a door that said 1402. Two pairs of shoes were on the outside of the door—one was a pair of sensible black Tieks flats, and another was a beige pair of Miu Miu lace up ballet flats with a gingham bow. A thousand dollars in shoes were mindlessly left outside a door. Wondering if I should take off my shoes before I knocked, the institutional gray metal door suddenly opened.

"Natalie!" Amanda shrieked as she reached out to hug me.

I hugged her with my elbows at my sides to keep my smell and sweat to myself. She stepped back and pointed at my feet, "Take off your shoes, and come on in. Make yourself comfortable," she said before she disappeared into another room. I quickly slipped off my shoes. My feet demanded a pedicure, embarrassment crept out. My feet were dry. Chipped purple polish only remained on some of the toes. It was March, my feet had been hidden in boots for the last six months was my excuse; I hoped no one else would notice.

Closing the door behind me, I then turned around to see a breathtaking loft space. High ceilings gave way to windows that were almost ceiling to floor. The view of Madison Square Park was the centerpiece. All of the furniture was low, minimalistic rustic in aluminum or gray tones. Curated and chic. An overstuffed gray mohair sofa stood on steel legs. The quilted leather "L" shaped chairs stood at attention guarding the sofa on both sides. An oversized hammered steel coffee table adorned with a horn handled magnifying glass sitting on a set of three hardcover books, the top one with a giant bottle of Chanel No 5 on the front. Every piece from the throw pillow to the walnut bowl that disguised the remote controls was placed perfectly.

Behind me was a gigantic thirty-foot shiplap island that besides housing a sink and a stove held a large flat screen computer. Above the stove dangled copper pots that were so shiny, I wasn't sure if they had ever been used. Glass cabinet doors revealed any number of stemmed wine glasses. Heavy wooden stools lined one side of the island. A fridge, a wine fridge and a set of knives magnetically hanging from the wall gave me the idea that Zella must entertain in this space.

A giant rectangular gray marble topped table stood in the middle of everything, with cross-back chairs surrounding it on all sides, gathered like gossiping schoolgirls. A gigantic vase of at least fifty gigantic white peonies sat in the middle, each with a streak of blush or purple acknowledging they were real. They were fully open and were emitting a lush scent into the room casually. Behind the table on one of the walls was a four-foot-high Warhol lips, framed in a brushed aluminum. Authentic. The painting hung just above a giant distressed aluminum desk that looked a bit like an old airplane wing. Eight neat piles of papers sat atop. Sticky notes were scattered about like it had just struck midnight on New Year's Eve. An oversized modern wingback chair upholstered in the same sofa mohair sat near the desk. It was very homey for an office.

I was about to take another spin around the room to better take everything in, when a purring voice from behind me said, "You must be Nancy."

When I turned, I got my first look at The Zella Tremaine: planner extraordinaire.

Honestly, I was disappointed: I was expecting Auntie Mame. Instead, Zella seemed like a regular upscale New Yorker. Her bobbed blonde hair glowed like a halo around her tanned, bronzed face. Her makeup was perfectly minimal and gave the illusion she had no makeup on at all. Barely any age lines showed on her face either from a regimented skin routine or Botox. Either way, her face was perfect with striking features. She wore a chic black crochet top that lazily draped down to her waist over black calf-leather pants that looked as soft and comfortable as a pair of well-worn sweatpants. She looked hip, opulent, and comfortable all at the same time. She was in all black—maybe I did wear the wrong thing.

Finding my stunned voice after taking her in, I gently corrected her, "Yes, hello, I'm Natalie." I looked to Amanda nervously, wondering if it was all right to correct someone of my own name.

"Natalie," she purred slowly in a deep voice making my name sound like NAH-tuh-Lee as she circled around me like Shere Kahn. Her face softened as she stopped in front of me. She looked me up and down, halting on my toes, then stopping again at my fingers, and then back up to my eyes.

Zella continued, "I always want my girls to be polished, I don't care if your fingernails are painted blue, as long as they're manicured and clean. Except on the rare occasions when we stuff invitations."

I flexed my fingers and held them out and glanced peripherally at them to confirm. I sighed with relief to find that at least my fingernails weren't chipped. I looked up to see Zella's eyes resting again on my feet. I tried to tuck my toes under. She pursed her lips and was about to say something when from her desk her cell phone rang.

Amanda rushed to the desk, as if it were the SID room's ring for Madame President. Zella adroitly reclined her arm from the elbow balletically for the phone to be placed into her hand. Amanda expertly placed the phone that was bleating a rhythmic carousel sound into Zella's awaiting palm and while doing so, Amanda slid her finger across the phone's screen, starting the call and whispering, "It's Christopher." My jaw dropped in awe of the choreography. Would I have to be that good?

Placing the phone up to her ear, Zella purred into it, "Chrissy, darling, what's the gossip?" The last word sounded like "Gaaah-sip."

Although Zella seemed to be distracted by the call, she continued to look me up and down, observing everything. She scrunched her nose as if she smelled something disgusting. I hoped it wasn't my armpits. Finally, she took her intense gaze off me and went to sit on the cashmere sofa and let out a barking laugh. I, of course, took the laugh personally.

"She likes you!" Amanda whispered excitedly ushering me to the table. Nervously, I kept my arms locked at my sides. I put my purse on the chair next to me as I sat. I pulled out a pen and my leather-bound notebook that I used to write musings. Okay, the real story in the office supply store months ago the notebook spoke to me, and I thought if I had the notebook, inspiration would come. I purchased it, put it in my bag, and carried it everywhere. Usually, the notebook got in the way when I was trying to find my keys or lip balm. Today, it was my savior.

"Well done," Amanda said, impressed. "Zella always wants everyone to have a notebook to write everything down. Word of advice, don't rely on your memory—things come rapid fire here and you'll get instructions for twenty things at once."

"Great, I really want to be good at this," I confessed secretly hoping my seeming preparedness would make up for my toes, and my colorful outfit, and my mild tardiness.

My thought was interrupted by a purr from the couch, "Girls, Christopher needs resources for socks with crowns or gnomes on them—he is doing a bat mitzvah and needs them ASAP."

"Write that down." Amanda said quickly as she jumped to grab her own notebook and pen by the computer.

Zella appeared to my left, and I tried not to look up at her. She looked towards her desk and continued. "We also need to find—"

She rattled off more things: a décor meeting needed to be set for the Nichol family, a tasting needed to be set with The Pierre for Marina Adams and her parents—we also needed to find out if the groom would indeed be attending, a comparison of photography pricing and options was needed, a pantone color was required for an invitation that matched the bridesmaid dress swatch that was in a bride's folder, a napkin sample needed to be messengered over to—not a lot of it made sense to me. The list went on. I wasn't sure if I even had a job yet, but I just kept up my scribbling frenzy, just in case.

The room went silent. Looking back over my list, I realized I scribbled so quickly, I couldn't read one of the items. "Um, Ms. Tremaine, what was the fourth thing—"

"Call me Zella. DON'T TALK TO ME."

My head snapped up to see Zella tapping on her phone. Shit. I'd been here for fifteen minutes, and I had already screwed up. My toes, my armpits, my outfit, and now talking.

Amanda beside me soothingly said, "If she isn't looking at you, don't talk to her. If you need to ask a question, wait until she has stopped doing something and then you can ask her." She said as she shifted her eyes to my list. "Which one are you missing?"

"Um," I looked down at my list. My handwriting looked like get Milliken crumbs for A. "Whatever she said between the photographer comparison and the cake vendor sketch."

Amanda looked down at her notes, "Oh, that—don't worry about it, it's for the Adams wedding," Amanda explained, "They want to have a milkshake and cookie passed on the dance floor, but the bride doesn't want the cookies to crumb, so she wants me to tell the caterer not to over bake the cookies." Then she said under her breath, "Like the bride will really notice, she will probably be drunk or too tired by the time the milkshake and cookies are passed, if she even eats the cookie—she's so skinny and still wanting to lose ten pounds, so she probably won't eat anything anyway." Amanda sighed, "The delightful demands of clients!" Sarcasm oozed from her, then she became perky and said at normal volume, "I've already reached out to the caterer and let them know, and John the manager said he would make sure that the cookies wouldn't be crummy."

As I started to scribble out my gobbledygook note, Amanda's whisper stopped me. "I wouldn't just disregard it. Make a note next to your note saying that I did it and put today's date. Just in case you're asked about it later. And you'll most likely be asked about it later. Zella tends to ask questions and expects whoever is nearby to know the answers. From now on, it's your job to know anything and everything," Amanda said, giving me a knowing look. "Now, let's work out the rest of this list."

She clarified a few things for me, and some things she said she would deal with. So many of these tasks were foreign to me, and I had no clue where to start. With my past experience, I thought that I could do or figure out almost anything. An overwhelming feeling of not wanting to screw up took a permanent seat in my mind. Tonight, I would be spending a lot of time researching the industry.

Many of the tasks terrified me so I took the sock research task for Christopher. In thirty minutes, I had found ten styles, five each. I sent screenshots and website links through my personal email to Zella's work email to review and forward.

Amanda tackled the rest of the tasks. When I was done, I didn't know what else to do, or if I was even needed to stay any longer. So, I sat and waited. Zella was clicking away at her keyboard. Then she picked up her phone and tapped a text, sighing. Heeding Amanda's warning, I waited to see if Zella would look up at me. She went back to her computer until her phone dinged, and her attention went back to the phone's screen. "Amanda—" she said and then looked up in my direction, "Oh, you're still here. Well—"

Amanda came rushing from the bathroom frantically drying her hands on the tiniest guest towel, "Yes, Zella?"

Zella looked back and forth between us both, as if we looked like twins and she couldn't decipher who was who. "Amanda," she said, looking again at me, but handing the phone to Amanda, and finally turning to look at her. "Christopher was pleased with the sock choices I sent him. Good work. Harold wants the cake tastings to be next Saturday, can you answer him back since you set it up," Zella commanded and then strode the room to me.

Zella looked me up and down again, and matter-of-factly she said, "I like you. You're tall. You'll be great for event days because I'll be able to find you in a crowd. I'll start you at fifteen an hour, and after a trial period we can see if you're ready for more responsibility and a raise."

Without allowing me to answer, she turned on her heel saying, "we're done," and walked back to her desk. Once more she looked at me and said while she was dialing on the landline, "This job will open a lot of doors for you." Then without saying hello, "Corey," she barked like a lieutenant, "why are the fucking hors d'oeuvres on your latest quote

32

different from the ones approved at the tasting?" She continued to give whomever Corey was a verbal spanking. Amanda walked over to me, took me by the arm and walked me to the door. We both stepped outside the apartment, and she let out a deep breath.

"Wow, she really likes you. I could tell because she put you to work right away." I started to put on my shoes while she continued, thinking with Zella's dismissal, Amanda couldn't be more wrong.

"Really?" was all I could say.

"Yeah, you were fantastic. I'll call you later today to figure out when you'll come in next. And check your email—I'll send you some paperwork. You did a great—"

"Amanda!" an upward lilting command came bellowing out from the apartment.

Amanda looked toward the door with her hand on the knob, but said to me, "You know how to get out, right?"

"It's a bit of a maze but I—"

"Ah-MAHAAAAAn-duh!"

"Great! I would walk you but—," she said urgently and whipped her head back at me. "Gotta go. The Adams wedding is just around the corner, so this week is crazy." And with that she slipped back in through the door and was gone.

33

Chapter Three

Waiting for the elevator I quickly processed my crazy interview. I checked my phone and saw I only had twenty minutes before pick-up time for Levi, the boy I nannied for the last five years.

A ticker tape with the fastest options to get uptown flashed across my brain. Once again in a mad dash, I took off toward the subway. I didn't need the gym with all this sprinting around town.

Levi was thirteen and protested being picked up after school on Tuesdays. Although I knew that he secretly loved to see me. It was my only regular day with him anymore. His parents, Suzanne and Ira adored me, and were continually thrilled that I was always willing to help and didn't flinch at any task they gave me to do. But at thirteen he had become self-sufficient, especially the days he rode the school bus home.

However, Tuesdays were busy days. This semester Levi had a trumpet lesson, session with his private tutor, and baseball practice. Both Suzanne and Ira worked late so I still met Levi after school and usually put him to bed. And although they were getting more lenient, his parents still wanted him to have a chaperone for days like today.

Luckily, I was only a few minutes late and Levi and I walked over to Lincoln Center for his trumpet lesson. As I was texting checking in with Suzanne if she needed me to run errands while Levi was in his lesson, a text from Amanda buzzed.

Zella would like to know when you will be in next. Can you do Thursday at 9am?

Excitement poured over me. I did it!!! I got the job! But yikes!! Nine in the morning again? I inwardly groaned at the early hour. One of the perks of nannying was that I didn't start until 3pm.

You don't have to dress to impress on Thursday. You can wear comfy clothing.

Amanda texted. I wondered if she could hear my thoughts of hatred towards waking up early.

Resigned, I knew 9am wouldn't kill me. Plus, I really, really, really wanted this job.

Sure. I agreed via text.

Amanda texted back:

Great. I'll be there so I'll give you the lay of the land.

I responded:

Awesome. My notebook and I will see you then!

I'm not ashamed to say I jumped up and down in the middle of Lincoln Center for a good sixty seconds like Rocky Balboa. I was that excited. This job could turn into a career and at the right moment of my life, too. So many thoughts flooded my head, I didn't even notice when Levi was standing in front of me petulantly with his trumpet case dangling from his arm. "Earth to Natalie—it's time to go," he looked irritated, and then his face brightened. "Ben said I didn't have to practice this week since he will be gone next week."

"Well, that was nice of Ben to let you off the hook," I said. "But you still have to practice bud, sorry. I'm sure mom and dad will want to hear you play!"

"Ugh! Fine. Let's go." He said, a bell curve of emotions that started out mad and then was like nothing happened.

Admiring the way Levi could just toss away something frustrating; I hopped up from my seat and took Levi to baseball practice. After dropping him off, like usual I ran to the grocery store and met him at the subway after practice. After that we headed to his apartment. Levi started homework and I headed to the kitchen to put away groceries and make dinner.

My phone dinged, as I was putting away the groceries.

Hi my love! How is your day? When will you be home?

The biggest smile lit my face. Sam, the love of my life. No matter how inane, his text messages were a sunbeam, the kind that suddenly peek out from a cloud or hit your face the moment you walk outside. Sam was always so giving, I often quietly doubted if I deserved him. I'm aware that I sound mushy and not just a little co-dependent, but he made me feel wonderful. Sam might just be perfection personified. I basked in the glow as I texted back:

Hi love! I'm GREAT! I got the wedding planner job!!! And I should be home by 8:30.

After sending the text, I turned on music and searched for meatball ingredients, continually checking my phone, waiting for a reply.

With his crazy schedule lately, we didn't call and text as often as we did when we first were dating. We were living together, so I told myself it didn't matter. But I would be lying to everyone if I said I wasn't disappointed.

Singing along with the music, I made meatballs, washed my hands, and lit the stove to simmer the sauce. Levi came to have his homework checked and I abandoned my phone. Half an hour later I returned to check the meatballs and my phone. The meatballs were almost done, and Sam had texted me twice.

Congrats babe! Headed out with work friends, I'll be home around 9.

And the second that came in almost twenty minutes after was:

Love you.

With a sigh and a smile, I started to compose a text message back, but nothing seemed right to say. I wanted to be funny with a "well, you should" or a sarcastic, "isn't that your job?" I also had thoughts of being mushy. Or maybe I should send him something super sexy about what I wanted to do to him when he got home. I ended up replying simply:

I love you, too.

Smiling, I went back to hang with Levi. Suzanne came home about thirty minutes later, and after a quick debriefing, she handed me cab money. With a hug to Levi and grabbing my coat and purse, I headed out the door.

Levi, Suzanne, and Ira lived on Riverside Drive. Sam and I had moved in together in East Harlem last month. So I had negotiated for cab fare for my Tuesday evening trip home, as taking the cross-town bus, and then catching the train home took me almost an hour. In the elevator I sent Sam texted:

Hi love! Headed home now. What is your ETA?

It was a nice night, so I thought I would walk to Broadway to catch my cab. By the time I had reached the third block, he texted:

Having fun. Ok to stay out longer?

I was irked; I really wanted to tell him about my eventful day in person. But I also didn't want to be that girlfriend who demanded time from her boyfriend. It seemed that once we moved in together, we saw each other less. But I also knew that Sam was vying for a promotion at work, and he had to work and schmooze after hours.

He was a group fitness instructor for Spark Gym—one of the biggest fitness companies on the East Coast. Sam had big dreams of creating his own classes and health programming. Although he never said it out loud, he hoped to someday have his own reality television show that would help people lead healthier lives. He wanted to make an empire of fitness, not only so he could touch the lives of others, but so he could bring healthy living to those who needed it but couldn't afford it. Sam was headed toward his dreams, and I wasn't going to hold him back.

I texted him back:

Okay. Sigh. I wanted to tell you about my crazy interview. But have fun. You home tomorrow?

Since there was no rush to get home now, I pocketed the cash that Suzanne gave me—I'd use it to order Chinese delivery when I got home. The crosstown bus pulled up right as I got to the stop. Once I was settled into a seat, my phone rang. A picture of Sam's face graced the screen, and I swiped to answer the call.

"Decided your friends aren't as exciting as your girlfriend?" I asked with a haughty laugh.

"Ha! Yes. Of course, no one is as important as you are to me." Zing—my heart flew when he said things like this, even if it was in sarcastic rebuttal. "So, tell me about this job, babe."

Excitedly, I launched into it, "She put me to work—it was crazy. And don't even get me started on my armpits—I got there two minutes late and I stunk to high heaven. I spent half an hour looking for socks with gnomes or crowns on them. I feel so out of my league with this job. I'm heading home now to do an internet search on the industry."

"Aww, babe," he replied. "Well, it sounds like a great opportunity! I mean how many people can say they work for a wedding planner?"

"None. Other than Amanda." I paused, remembering my moments of terror earlier. "Do you think I'm out of my league with this?"

Sam answered right away, "Nah! I think you've totally got this. You're my details, girl. Who is the one who always notices the editing mistakes in movies? Who randomly sees a pair of shoes and can find where to purchase them and at a discount? Who is the best at diffusing crazy situations? You."

Always my cheerleader since the first moment we met, Sam always reminded me about my finer points.

"Yeah, you're right," I said, not believing it.

"Babe, I'm totally right. You'll be great for this job."

My bus seemed to nod in agreement as it bounced over a pothole then jerked to a stop. Looking up I saw we were at Lexington Avenue.

"I love you so much. You always make me feel better. Thank you," I said. "My bus just stopped at the 4/5/6 and I need to hop on the subway. Talk to you later?"

"Of course, babe. I'm always here if you need me. I need to get back to the Spark crew anyway. We have some great ideas we are bouncing around. Mark is here and he is really impressed with my ideas."

"That is great, love!" I replied, finally getting excited about something other than Sam himself. I knew Mark was some big head honcho. "Go knock him dead!"

"I will. Bye babe!" He started to end the call and quickly reminded me, "text me when you get home."

"I will. I love you."

"I love you more."

The phrase "I love you more" made me feel like I won a lottery, complete with prepaid taxes.

Sam and I met in the same show where I met Amanda. It was probably one of those kismet things. I was meant to do that show because it would open doors for me—wow I sound like Zella right now. I mentioned earlier I'd tell you how Sam and I met.

You know those relationships that seem too good to be true? That was me and Sam. Maybe it was because Sam and I met in a way that only happens in movies, or maybe it was that we just fell into pace with each other, it all seemed too easy. And I ignored that feeling because it was so nice to love and be loved. I was truly fortunate to have found him, and I promised myself daily that I would do whatever it took to keep us together and happy.

He had met my eyes when I walked in late to our first rehearsal of A Winter's Tale and I found out shortly after that we would end up being love interests. Sam came up to me when we took a break and said something so perfect, which from anyone else would have sounded like a line. But when the Greek god of a man, standing at least six inches above me, bounded over like a puppy to my side and said, "I think I've been waiting my whole life to meet you," what do you say to that? Let alone how do you not fall for him instantly. Spoiler alert, I totally did. We had drinks after rehearsal, exchanged numbers, and have talked every day since. We even moved in together shortly after. It was partially necessitated by his lease ending and my roommates moving out. Everything with Sam was always too perfect.

Remembering our first meeting had me in a dreamlike trance and made me almost miss my stop on the subway, but I got out just before the doors closed. Mild panic sank in as it always does when I exit a train quickly, that I had left my phone. Feeling around for it I found it again and I looked at my phone screen. I had pulled up the photo from that first night.

Today was an amazing day, and Sam, who was always inspiring me and pushing me to do more, was part of that. Then my stomach grumbled to remind me it needed attention, too. I pulled up the phone number of Red Star—I had it saved the first week I lived in this apartment, because Chinese food is a necessity—and ordered a feast of General Tso's chicken, Veggie Lo Mein, extra steamed veggies, and fried rice plenty for leftovers or for Sam. I also ordered extra fortune cookies, a gal can always use all the fortune she can get, even when everything seems perfect.

Chapter Four

Fortune seemed to have truly smiled on me. Zella not only gave me a job but threw me into the wedding world right away. Amanda, having promised Zella that I could handle myself in high-pressure situations because she knew I could with a theater background and having several professional shows under my belt, helped me through the first wedding.

"I want you to shadow me. Find Amanda if you can't find me," Zella shouted the instructions over her shoulder when I arrived. The warehouse today's wedding was at had been converted to a dance space and an event hall.

Running after Zella, I was enamored with all the activity in the room. There were hydraulic lifts going up and down. One with a man working on lights, another with two people hanging some sort of floral garland. Catering team members were flying by with trays and bowls of prepped food that was headed toward the kitchen area to assemble and heat. Tables were being popped up and put into place.

"Make sure you put masking tape down before you tape anything to the floor," a man shouted from behind me to the entire room. "No other tape is allowed."

"Tape leaves residuals on the concrete floor," Amanda said from just to my left when puzzlement crossed my face.

"Now," Zella had stopped and turned around. I almost skidded right into her. "Wow, you are tall, aren't you?"

"Yes." What else was I supposed to say?

"You will be great at this," Zella started.

In disbelief that she already knew I was talented I started, "Thank–"

But she cut me off as she continued, "I'll be able to find you anywhere." She looked me up and her nose scrunched. "You're not wearing that? Are you?"

"No, I–" I looked down at my body. I was in a pair of bright blue leggings with a stretchy shirt dress in a bright pink, topped with a blue cardigan. Comfort, with a touch of chic. I also wanted to wear something that I could get messed up just in case I had to crawl around anywhere. Amanda had warned me on our prep call last night.

"For tomorrow, bring your suit, but show up wearing something you don't mind getting a little dirty. Sometimes I have to crawl around on the floor during event set up for all kinds of reasons," she'd told me.

"Got it," I said. "Can it be anything I want? Or should it be all black, too?"

"Hmm, come in something bright, so when she sees you in your black, you will look extra chic," Amanda said, knowing I loved to wear all kinds of color, the complete opposite of Zella's aesthetic.

At our pre-event walk-through, Amanda jumped in to support me, "Natalie had to take the subway from uptown and didn't want to get dirty before the event. I suggested it. Also, Zella, she's in a black suit that you approved, as we didn't have time to get her fitted for your uniform yet. Do you need to see the picture again?" Amanda already had her phone out of her pocket and was flipping through photos to show the one I had sent her earlier this week. They had agreed that as long as I was in an all-black suit or black pants, blazer and blouse, I would be appropriate enough. Apparently, the uniform was a sort of tuxedo that I would become well acquainted with later.

"No. I trust you," Zella said, waving a hand over her shoulder. Then she shouted at one of the men in the air,

"Larry, what are you doing? Is that what we discussed? Because it doesn't look like it." And she was off.

"Come, follow me," Amanda said as she walked off toward the kitchen, a smile on her face.

A few steps behind Amanda, I said, "Do you really think it's ok that I wore this?"

"Yes. Stop being nervous. Zella can smell it a mile away. Like I said yesterday, it will make you look chicer when you're in your blacks. If you showed up in the blacks, you would have been all over the floor, gotten dirty, and she would keep telling you your outfit didn't match in color. This way she sees you just as the guests are arriving and can't say anything in front of the client."

"Smart." I said just as we stopped abruptly at a circle of the catering staff.

"Hi all, I wanted to introduce the Tremaine Events team," Amanda waved as we walked by. The circle opened and let us both in. "I'm Amanda." A few people waved. "I'm sure you all know or know of Zella," the entire group winced, "Yes, she's running the show tonight. But if you need anything find me, or the lovely Natalie," she motioned to me. I looked around the circle, smiling. Pretending I knew what the heck I was doing.

A tall curly-haired guy with icy blue eyes gave me a wink as my eyes met his. It was disconcerting. He was tall and handsome and directly across the circle from me. Blush climbed my cheeks, and I faked a cough so I could look down and hopefully hide my blush. I took a deep breath and then looked up.

"Hey, Natalie. I'm Dave, your captain for tonight," a brunette with his hair combed back and his tuxedo shirt unbuttoned reached out his hand to me. "Let me know if you need anything at all, ok?" He smiled and then turned back

44

to his team. "Great team, you know your assignments, let's get going. Family meal in twenty."

Everyone moved off to their stations, except the curly-haired guy. He looked younger than me. I would guess late twenties. His white button-up shirt was done up except for the collar. His black tie was tied, but loose. A crooked smile graced his face when he walked over to us. "Boss, we did an inventory of the glasses and we're missing two trays of highballs."

"Thanks, Matt. Make sure you note that on the paperwork and remind me at the end of the night. I'll make a call to the rental company and see if they're coming back and can drop more off if they are."

"Will do." He nodded at Dave, then turned to Amanda and me, nodding and saying our names as he was walking away.

"Ladies, did you want to go over the run of show since we're here?"

"You read my mind, Dave," Amanda said, whipping out some tri-folded paperwork out of her back pocket. "Here Natalie, I brought you a copy," she said, handing me a page. "Dave, did you need a copy?"

"No, I've got the one you emailed out last night. So, unless it's changed–"

"Nope. Great. Ok, so at seven on the dot, we're having the bride and groom walk in," Amanda continued to point out to Dave any major moment in the evening ahead, and he noted when they needed champagne glasses and to whom. When Zella and the bride, the soon to be Mrs. Keller, wanted food served, and when they wanted to do cake cutting. Dave nodded and asked a few questions. The whole back and forth took about three minutes.

"Great. I've got it. I'll see you ladies later," Dave said as he walked off.

"Wow, that was breathtaking," I said to Amanda, my compliment completely heartfelt.

"Just wait," Amanda said. " you'll be able to do that soon." We turned, and Amanda picked up her phone. "Ah, Zella wants you. The cake is here, and she wants you to help place it. The layout of the floorplan is on the back of your itinerary." I flipped the page over and she pointed to shapes. "This is the DJ booth. Here is the sweetheart table. And the cake goes here. Because it's buttercream, it needs to go into the fridge, until right before the guests arrive. So go get the cake, have them show the lighting designer, Larry, what it looks like, then bring it back here to Dave, and have his team put it in the walk-in fridge until 6:30."

I repeated all of this back to her.

"Right. Now, where is your cell?"

"Uh, it's in my purse back with my suit."

"Keep it on you. Literally, keep your eyes on it at all times. And be ready to run and problem-solve. That is what this job is. If you're asked to do something, do it. If you're asked to make a decision, text first, but just make a choice. I'm going to start a group text now for this event. Always answer texts as fast as you can, if you have an actual answer, and especially if you're name is on the text, got it?"

"I think so?"

"I'm sure you do. Text if you have questions."

Dashing off to get my phone I met up with the cake person and carried out my mission. My cell phone was going off constantly, and at least twice I was on the floor picking something up or helping find a cord.

It was magical how this space transformed. When I walked in, it was a concrete floor and industrial walls, and

46

now at 6:30 there were blue and white lights slowly moving all around the room giving the feeling of a soft breeze. The DJ was playing a contemporary jazz pop artist doing a cover of a Frank Sinatra staple. His desk, for lack of a better term for it, looked like it was wrapped in delicate gold leaf. It sat in front of a shimmering gold cloth that had been stretched from floor to ceiling to cover up the back wall. The fabric was an opaque version of the tablecloths that hid the door to the kitchens and storage rooms that were off to the back. It also allowed for a pass-through for anyone wanting to get from one side of the room to the other without snaking through all of the tables. This, I assumed, was partially for the catering staff to be able to deliver food to the other side of the room more easily without crossing the dance floor.

The round tables that were spaced all around the room seemed to shimmer with their champagne sheer tablecloths, gold flatware, making the room seem opulent and warm. Who knew flatware could warm a room. Large column vases that were probably a foot around that were flaked with gold and glimmered held thousands of white orchids spraying out of the top and gracefully falling all about like they were floral fountains. Clear round back chairs were placed by a gold charger rested with a menu, personalized with each guest's name in calligraphy at the top on a buff handmade paper, designating exactly where every person was assigned to sit.

The smell of baked bread, brown sugar and fresh greenery wafted through the room. The entire room felt soft and opulent. If heaven had a waiting room, it might look like this.

A few people scurried around making last-minute touches, tying a bow, clipping a stem, shifting a light, moving a fork, so everything was perfectly placed. A white dance floor had been laid in the center and had a monogram of the bride and groom's initials pulling everything together.

As I gaped around and tried to take it all in, I knew one thing. I was in love. Head over heels in love. Theater seemed to have been a passion before now. But this. If I could do this every day for the rest of my life, see rooms transformed like this, I knew I would do anything, and I mean anything to be able to make this magic happen.

"Hey, the cake–" Amanda's voice came up from behind me pulling me out of my intoxication.

"I just asked them to roll it out. The florist–"

"Decor."

"What?"

"They're not florists, they're decor designers." Amanda corrected me in a delicate way.

"Ah, ok. The decor team wanted to put fresh flowers on it. They're over there now, waiting for it to come out."

"Great. You need to go get dressed," Amanda said as she looked me up and down. "Bathrooms are over there," she nodded to the doors across from us over by the large garage doors, and I ran off to change.

"Hey," I asked just a few steps away. "Where are they doing the ceremony?"

"Oh, they had it at a church a few blocks away. They'll be coming over soon. Zella left a bit ago to go over there, but this event had two teams. One here, and one at the church." I must have looked disappointed because she said, "Don't worry. You'll do a ceremony in two weeks."

Smiling, I turned and jogged off to get changed. The magic I felt was just carrying me on a cloud. Even though the last four hours had been a whirlwind, the next four were even faster.

Guests filed in, milling about in awe of the spectacle. I was to point them to their tables, using a list of all the guests and the floor plan Amanda had given me earlier. After everyone was seated, Zella came out of nowhere, and grabbed me by the wrist, pulling me after her.

"Come, I need your help with the bride and groom." Her head whipped back to me, "I need you to listen, and not talk, got it?"

With no idea what she meant, I nodded and followed quickly after, not letting her abrupt tone and condescension bother me.

She whipped back around, and somehow her finger was right at my nose. "Don't give me a reason to fire you today, make sure you are professional at all times."

Not knowing what to say to this, other than, "Got it," I did and kept following her. Wondering what would constitute being fired. Before I knew it we stopped in front of two well-dressed people.

"NAH-tuh-Lee, this is Melissa and John Keller, our bride and groom. They are just about to be announced into the room and then are going to do their first dance. When they're done, I want you to meet them on the dance floor with champagne glasses." Zella's tone changed a little. I would come to learn later that this was her dissatisfied tone. "They want to do toasts right after they dance. All the toasts. Can you make sure Dave knows? Dave is the–"

"Captain," I said, finishing her sentence. "Can do, Zella. Anything else?"

"Go," she said, shaking her head.

Turning and starting to jog off, I mouthed to the bride, "You look beautiful!" She returned with a "Thank you," and Zella hollered at me not to run.

I had taken one step into the kitchen when one of the caterwaiters saw me and asked me, "Natalie, what do you need?" She knew my name. I was floored. I mean she had been at the meeting, but still to have someone remember my name that had met me once was kind of amazing.

"Dave." I said, looking all around for him. He appeared, as if I had summoned him.

"Hey, Nat, can I call you Nat? What can I help with?"

"Sure. Um, Zella sent me. They want to change the toasts. All will be on the dance floor right after the first dance."

"Not a problem when is the–"

Beyonce's Love on Top blasted from the speakers, and then the DJ announced, "Please welcome for the first time, Mister and Missus John Keller," followed by raucous applause. I stepped back out of the kitchen to see the lights swooping all around and watched the bride and groom dance to the middle of the dance floor.

"Um, now," I said.

"Not a problem. Follow me." We walked to the bar. Dave pointed at one of the bartenders, "Kyle, I need two champagne glasses to the dance floor right after this song," he pulled out his copy of the Tremaine Events itinerary, and a pen. I did the same, pretending I knew what was going on. "So," Dave said, "I'm assuming they're moving all toasts now," he looked at me.

"I feel like that is safe to assume," I said, still having no idea what I was doing and pretended I did.

"Great. Matt," he hollered without looking up. It was the guy from earlier who waved at me. Dave kept talking to him, "I need a best man glass, then a maid of honor glass, then two flutes for the parents of the bride. Kyle, take them the two glasses when this song ends, and standby with the tray. You can go out when the DJ goes to get the mic."

Shoot, I thought to myself, Zella didn't mention anything about the DJ. Was that my job? I had no idea. I looked out to the dance floor and everyone beaming beatifically at the bride and groom as he spun her around and then dipped her. A sea of phones were up snapping shots, and video of the newlyweds as the photographer seemed to be waltzing counterclockwise, I knew the song and estimated that I had about sixty seconds until it ended.

I scurried as quickly but as discreetly as I could from the bar, through the tables, ducking from any pictures I could, and across the back of the dance floor around to the other side of the room to the DJ booth. I had about thirty seconds left of the song and spent most of that trying to get his attention. When he finally acknowledged me, I waved the itinerary at him. He gave me a signal that he needed a minute. My eyes got very wide, and I guess that finally signaled to him that there was an issue.

"Hey, what's up? This song is about to end."

"Yes," I said glaring at him. "I know. Zella said the bride and groom want to do toasts on the dance floor right after this song."

"Crap. Why didn't you say something sooner?"

Rolling my eyes at his back, as he turned away from me, I said, "I just found out," trying to be nice at all times.

"Fine. Here," he shoved a mic in my hand. "It's not on. Before you hand it to them, flip the switch on the bottom and wait for the green light to come on, ok?"

"Wait. I'm taking them the microphone?"

"Unless you want to introduce them and work the booth," his hands waving over several serious-looking instruments and a computer. I gave him a confused look because he didn't have a turntable. I realize this is the technology age, and that all music is digital, but it was still a shock not to see traditional records.

"Well, too late, there is your cue," he said as he faded the music and pointed to the dance floor. "Ladies and gentlemen," he said, talking into another mic he made magically appear. "Put your hands together for Melissa and John Keller, our bride and groom, who would now like to say a few words."

I don't know how I knew, but I waited for Kyle, the caterwater, to start walking onto the dance floor from his side, and I walked on from the opposite side, and we reached the bride and groom at the same time. Melissa grabbed both glasses and waited for me to give the mic to John before she handed him a glass. Kyle and I walked off the floor together and I walked back to the bar.

My phone buzzed.

Zella to the group:

Good Natalie.

Trying not to analyze or feel like I was just being petted like a dog, I took a breath for what seemed the first time in five minutes. Dave walked back over to me.

"Nat, I've got all of the dinners firing, but they're holding on bringing out the salads until after the toasts." I nodded and made a thoughtful pursing of my lips, like this was the perfect solution. He continued, "I've got my staff positioned," he pointed around the periphery of the room with his pen, low and behind his paper to point out the waiters that were poised with champagne bottles. "They have instructions to do refills during the toasts, but as soon as they've filled for the last toast, they're headed into the kitchen and will standby to drop salads. Then they'll take dinner orders."

"Got it."

"Will you still want this timing for dinner to be dropped, or will it change since we're not doing the toasts in between salad and dinner?"

My mind raced. Not wanting to make it apparent that I had never done this before, I picked up my phone. "I think we'll do it immediately after, but let me check with Zella," I said and quickly tapped out a message to the group.

Me: *Zella, catering is asking if you want dinner dropped right after salad. Dave says he's firing entrees.*

Amanda: *Do we want to do a dance set in the middle so they can clear?*

Zella was typing according to the annoying rippling ellipses.

Amanda: *ZT I'm on my way to DJ. Nat, stay with Dave.*
Zella: …

I watched the three dots from Zella start and stop and start again. I looked around the room to see if I could even see her. I couldn't.

"NAH-tuh-Lee," Zella's voice came from out of nowhere and made me jump. "Where's Ian?"

"Ian?" I asked dumbly, trying to remember everyone I was introduced to today, and not remembering Ian.

Dave reached out a hand to Zella. "I'm Dave, the captain for tonight's event. Ian is on a different project today."

"Wonderful." Zella said thick with disdain. "NAH-tuh-Lee said dinner is ready?"

"Yes, ma'am," Zella cleared her throat at being called ma'am, but Dave didn't seem to notice. "Yes, when Nat let me know we were shifting the timeline, I asked the chef's to get dinner ready as well."

"Will it ruin the food if we hold onto it for twenty minutes?"

My phone buzzed.

Amanda: *ZT DJ says he can do a dance set.*

Zella hadn't picked up her phone, but I crossed my hand over my arm to nonchalantly show her the text from Amanda. She glanced down at it.

"I'm sure we could hold if needed," Dave said with something like mild fear.

"Good," Zella purred. "I knew I liked you, Dave." She pointed at him like acknowledging he was right. He took it as the sign that he was to head to the kitchen. "He's an idiot," she sighed looking onto the dance floor and the best man who was giving a speech. I wasn't sure if she was telling me that Dave or the best man was the idiot. She turned to me and nodded toward my phone. I raised my eyebrows. "Take care of it," Zella said and then turned and walked off.

"I guess that means we're doing a dance set?" I said to no one then tapped a message to our group text saying, Zella wants a twenty-minute dance set between salad and main course.

When that excitement was over I thought the chaos would cease. The rest of the night had me running in different directions to do different things like prep the favor table, get the father of the bride a drink, make sure the cake topper was put in a box for the bride and groom to take home with them, and make sure that all of the wedding gifts and cards, got into bags and stuffed into a cab with the mother of the bride. Even though I was constantly moving, it still felt like I was running back and forth through heaven.

After the last of the guests had left, Zella pulled us all together. There were two other gals in all black that I had seen running around.

Amanda leaned over to me and whispered, "They were the ones doing the ceremony. They hardly work with us, so I'll introduce you next time."

"Ladies, this was a great event. Thank you all for your hard work. The client was very happy, and you'll see it in your checks, because they didn't bring cash. Take cabs home and send me the receipt, and I'll reimburse you for up to twenty dollars. Amanda, I'm taking off, show NAH-tuh-Lee how to close up."

"Will do, Zella." Amanda said and then tapped me on the forearm to follow her.

"We have to wait around for the next hour to make sure all of the vendors are out of here. At this venue, overtime kicks in after an hour, so we have to make sure we keep things moving. Basically, we get paid to sit here for another hour.

Although I would love to tell you that I was disenchanted by watching all the beauty be deconstructed, I was not. In fact, I might have been more in awe to see how the party, which had taken at least four hours to set up onsite, and probably more in preparation before anyone was here, was completely torn down and moved out within a quarter of the time. Amanda left me to watch shortly after.

"Just sit here and relax for a bit until the rental company starts to come take the chairs. I'm going to change, and I'll switch with you. If anyone comes over to ask you a question, just answer it." And she was gone before I could ask her how I should answer said questions. I sat there and puzzled over that for a bit and jumped when I heard the warm rumble of a man's voice next to me.

"Good job, new girl." The handsome, wavy-haired bartender was standing next to me with a bottle of water extended to me. "Water?"

I looked up at him, mildly confused.

"It's good to hydrate at these things. Otherwise, you'll feel like you're hung over tomorrow." He sat the water down, and before I had the chance to respond, he walked away as someone hollered, "Hey, Matt."

Drinking the cool water and watching the beautiful destruction happen, I once again couldn't believe my luck in getting this job. It was a full-on performance with a set and leading actors and everything. I remember the moment, and this thought so clearly. This job was worth any sacrifice, and I was ready to do whatever it took to stay in this business.

I was so naive.

Chapter Five

It was an understatement that I was feeling all the challenges that come with a new job. Zella was just short of certifiable all the time when we were alone together. She would go from blissful to pissed in two seconds. I would ask questions and she would fly off the handle at me. I was trying to learn how to do my job, or even understand the entire scope of my job. These were both impossible.

I knew she would be hard to work for. I knew that this job would be challenging. I knew that I had promised myself that I would work hard, so I could deserve this job. I didn't realize that every moment I worked for her would feel like I was a breath away from getting fired. I know a lot of people say that in their first few months, but honestly, I felt like I was a moment from getting fired almost every day for three years.

The office was a hurricane zone. Zella would tell me to start one project, then immediately pull me to another because she said it was more important. Thirty minutes later I would be chastised for not finishing the first task and questioned if I had the ability to multitask and focus. Unsolicited, she told me at least twice that I might have ADD, and she understood if I needed medication. Pulling me from one task to the next without letting me finish any one thing. And this went on all day long. If things weren't finished, I was expected to stay and complete it no matter how many hours I was scheduled to work.

Even though I was supposed to be part time, I had worked four eight-hour days in a row. Although I knew I didn't deserve to be treated like this, I still felt like I needed to rise to the challenge to make her happy.

After this hectic week I was exhausted and knew I shouldn't indulge in an evening out, but I wanted to see my friends. The City That Never Sleeps makes it difficult to see friends. Although the nickname for New York originally was about the continuously glowing lights, I think the name actually meant all of the dreamers that immigrated to this city were continually working non-stop and often were too busy for a social life. Take Ginger for instance. An actress friend who made her living babysitting two girls a couple days a week, bartending four days a week, and representing a small batch whiskey company. We broke plans as often as we made them, and usually ended up on the phone drinking coffee together on opposite sides of town.

Bennett, a fantastically gay Californian that I had met on the west coast had moved east to pursue a film career. Once he got here, he realized he really wanted a family. Dabbling in the real estate industry, Bennett became one of the top sellers for the company and gave up his acting dream for the picket fence dream.

Jordan had also left the performing world. She was the roommate I had before I moved in with Sam. An opera singer with a big, gorgeous voice, Jordan had bad luck. She would audition often but rarely booked anything. She went back to school to learn coding, and upon graduation immediately booked a six-figure job, which was more money than we had collectively made in three years. I hadn't seen Jordan since moving day; there just hadn't been time.

When Sam told me that Ginger, Jordan, and Bennett were all meeting us for drinks, I was ecstatic. All of my people in one place. We were out for the evening, and it felt great. Sam had invited some of his friends from Spark to join us too.

After working overtime for Zella, I ended up meeting Sam at the bar instead of going home to change first. He and his colleagues were already there, having come to dinner directly from Spark Gym. The admonishment from Zella about weight, and meeting Kate, Fiona, and Nick who worked out for hours a day as their profession, made me question my beer and fried cheese order choices. But I wanted fried cheese and beer. The gym group were dressed in chic workout clothing and looked as if they belonged in a smoothie bar or fitness magazine instead of this dark pub. When our food arrived and I saw that they all ordered fried bar food too, I felt so much better.

"Babe, don't let my job and work friends make you think any differently of yourself. I love you and I think you are stunning," Sam said into my ear as he stealthily patted my butt. I looked into his eyes and kissed him. He snagged a quesadilla wedge off my plate and smiled at me, still making eye contact, and shoved the whole wedge into his mouth. I rolled my eyes and laughed silently.

"Natalie," I heard a shriek in stereo. At that moment Ginger and Jordan walked in together. They both elbowed their way through the quickly filling bar to the long table we had occupied. I stood and gave them both giant hugs. Sam stood and hugged Jordan. They met on moving day and had shared a craft beer she made as Jordan was clearing the fridge. I introduced Sam and Ginger who had not officially met although they had hollered hellos to each other through the phone. Just as we were finishing our hugs, Bennett walked in and worked his way to our table.

After introductions all around we resettled. Our friends literally took sides. Bennett sat next to me with Ginger and Jordan across. Kate and Nick sat across from Sam, and Fiona sat next to him. Next to me, Sam put his arm around my waist. He turned to chat with his friends, and I turned to mine. One more reason for me to gush about Sam: he liked physical touch. All my past dating partners seemed to hate this. Sam and I always touched each other whenever we were together. I loved how we couldn't get enough of each other. I was a little jealous of the slim, beautiful girl sitting next to Sam, but neither seemed interested in more than what to do for their next classes—apparently, they co-taught something that sounded like recess for adults. Plus, Sam was paying me plenty of attention. He gave me a peck on the temple when he went to the restroom, and a couple of times gave a stroking massage on my lower back, so my worry subsided.

It was so wonderful to see my friends, but as the evening waned, our group thinned. Jordan and Bennett were the first to leave declaring they had early mornings. Through an alcoholic haze, I remembered I did too. I had only had three beers at that point, I think. Oh, and we did a round of shots. Who's idea was that? My brain told me it didn't matter. It was my party, and another hour at the bar wouldn't hurt.

Kate and Fiona left not long after Jordan and Bennett—they were sharing a taxi as they lived in the same neighborhood. Ginger and Nick stayed, and the four of us kept drinking. Nick is really great and exactly as Sam described. I had been hearing a lot about him lately. He was Sam's mentor in the fitness program and talked Sam into running a marathon with him. Ginger's whiskey company was sponsoring the marathon, so the conversation switched to that. After that I don't remember much. At some point in the fun, I looked at my phone and saw it was 1am.

"Sammo, I have to go home," I slurred and looked at him dreamily. "I have to be at work in seven hours, and that means I have to awake in five hours, which means that I'll get four and a half hours of sleep if we leave now."

He smiled that gorgeous smile and looked at me with laughter and love shining in his green eyes. Taking my face with his hands he leaned in and deeply kissed me. I heard an aww from Ginger.

"Alright, babe, I'll get the check," he said a bit huskily and then dotted another kiss on my nose as if to punctuate his task.

As Sam rose to find the bartender, Nick said loud and overtly flamboyant, "He is a real catch." I turned my head from watching Sam to Nick who was also watching Sam predatorily.

"You're telling me. He's mine, all mine," I said, raising my arms to the sky as if I was a winner on a game show.

Nick turned to me and started to say something, but then shook his head, laughed, and threw back the rest of his vodka and diet tonic. He pulled cash from his wallet and tossed it on the table.

He stood and I'm pretty sure he flexed his muscles as he bent to grab his backpack and said, "Let Sam know I'll see him tomorrow. And if I owe him more than that," he pointed to the twenty, ten, and five dollar bills he had tossed on the table, "I'll give it to him later. At the gym. After our class." This last he said pointedly toward me. I tried to puzzle through his tone in my alcohol haze, but Ginger interrupted my thought.

"Wow, that queen was really trying to say something," she said as she watched him walk out of the pub. "Whatever." Her tone changed from accusatory to happiness, "Natalie! I'm so excited for you and this talented

61

job. It's great to have a steady thing outside of theater and babysitting, right?"

Ginger and I used to babysit for families that lived in the same building. It was great because we could "visit each other for sugar" a few floors away. But Levi's parents had moved to a different building a year ago so Ginger and I saw each other much less.

"Ugh," I groaned, "So niiiiice. I mean, to be fair, Suzanne is an angel. I'm extended family at this point. But to have the ability to go to fancy weddings is lovely. Ginger, I'm so lucky! I really hope I'm good at this job. I mean, it's a lot of work. I mean a lot. And Amanda says I'll be babysitting brides, and the glamour will fade… and my boss..."

Sam returned, pausing my sloppy gushing. "We are all settled up. What's this?" he asked as he pointed at the thirty-five dollars that Nick left behind.

"Nick's contribution to the bill, and here's mine," Ginger handed a wad of what looked like only ones and fives, probably tips from bartending.

Looking around the bar for Nick, and then looking down, puzzled at the money on the table, Sam was jarred out of his stupor when Ginger scooped up the money Nick had left, added it to hers, and shook her full hand of money at Sam. "Here! It's all yours!"

He paused again, and then reached for the money and took it. I had no idea what was wrong with him, he looked very concerned. I wanted to ask him why he looked upset, but everything was very fuzzy. And I suddenly realized I had to find my scarf that magically disappeared from my hand. I probably should have registered Sam's look of concern.

As I had my butt in the air looking under the table, Ginger said, "It's right here."

"What is?" I said blankly forgetting why I was in a forward bend.

"Um, you're looking for your scarf, right?"

"Here I'll take it," Sam said. "Come on, babe, be careful there," he said, assisting me to stand. Fitness instructors are always good at that.

We all walked out to the street together, Sam called a car service on his phone, and then hailed a cab for Ginger and held the door for her as she stepped in—she was headed across town. I reminded myself how lucky I was watching this tableau. Our car pulled up right as Ginger's drove away, and he helped me in, and I snuggled into his shoulder thinking how smart I was to set my alarm for the morning before we went out.

Chapter Six

And then the blaring happened. The irritating beeping that sounded like a petulant electronic toy bird kept chirping. TWEET… TWEET… TWEEET… It echoed through my skull. Somehow the ridiculous bird scared away the luscious cake that I was just about to eat. As my dream disappeared, I flapped my arm out to silence the sound. A clatter to the floor brought me to the surface of consciousness. The sound kept going, and I registered it was my alarm that was now blaring at an annoying level. Jumping out of bed and crawling almost completely under the bed, finally I retrieved and silenced it.

By the time I had turned the alarm off, all the movement was enough to wake me. I cursed my alarm. And then it hit me: I was going to be part of planning a perfect and magical wedding and would be meeting a bride today. Waking up early and fighting a massive hangover was worth it. Something in me always snapped back to a hopeful, even blissful, mindset when I remembered I got to play with brides and flowers. And I got paid to do it.

I jumped out of bed and into the shower—I knew I needed coffee, but if I didn't shower first, I would regret it. My stomach lurched a little, and my temples pounded. Why did we stay out so late? And why did I drink that last beer? Ginger was a minx getting me to have one more. She didn't get hangovers, and neither did Sam, my boyfriend. He swore he was not a morning person either, but was already up and out. Evidence to the contrary. If he were still here, I would curse my job and snuggle back in with him until my hangover was gone. Sometime next week. Instead, I sighed and assessed my physical and mental state, and then jumped in the shower.

The warm water rushed over me, hopefully taking the pounding in my head down the drain with it. I indulged in the memory of my first audition where I met Ginger.

My second week in the city, I was following my dreams. Half in disbelief that I had relocated across the country all by myself, half in delusional excitement, I entered the audition hall. The dream that brought me to the city was that today could be my big break to Broadway and stardom. Fame and fortune were just down the hall, I could smell it. Well, I could smell the dance class that was just ending. But my dream couldn't be that far away.

Chuckling at my dreamy younger self, I cringed at the memory of how I cheerfully tried to make friends with the monitor of the auditions. She guarded the sign-in sheet, looked at me like I was an escapee of the mental ward, and harrumphed at me when I asked if I could borrow a pen. At that moment my hope sank a little. After writing my name down on line 239 and being told to take a seat, I turned to the room where two hundred and thirty-eight people were crammed, doing all kinds of stretching and silent vocal warmups. My hope plummeted. A bright face smiled at me from across the room and motioned to the empty chair next to her. I took a deep breath and waded across the room through all the people, bags of dance shoes, and binders of music.

"Thanks," I said as I sat down in the chair.

"No problem. I think the person who had this chair has already auditioned and left."

That smiling face was Ginger. We chatted all day long. I waited until 5:45pm before my name was even called. I was told while waiting in line that they only wanted us to sing eight bars, or about fifteen seconds of music. All my audition cuts were four times that long. I was flummoxed and in more of a panic. What part of my song did I sing? Was it enough to hear me for only a few moments? Did I sing the high note, or the part where I could achieve a tear in my eye? In the room they looked at my resume the whole time and chatted with each other. I felt like I would have more success singing to a wall in an empty room and worried about my purse being stolen. I was so disappointed. I was also sure that my purse was probably stolen. Ginger waited for me, even though she had auditioned almost an hour before me. She said she wanted to make sure someone was there for me at the end of my first New York audition. And when I came out, she gave me a knowing look and said, "Eh, I heard they're not looking for anyone today, and that this is just a union required audition anyway. But I'm sure you were great!"

Smiling at the memory that faded as I got out of the shower and toweled off, the need for coffee and the rush to get dressed took over. And a hangover headache came pounding back.

Chapter Seven

Thirty-five minutes later, I ran out the door and down the four flights of stairs to the subway. Ecstatic to see the train in the station was the express, I jumped through the doors as they were closing. Now I would get to the office a little earlier than planned. Zella was upset if I was not sitting and ready to take notes on the hour.

My train arrived twenty minutes early, hooray for small miracles. Because my head was pounding, a bagel and coffee from the bodega around the corner were needed.

Even with a stop for breakfast, I was still ten minutes early. I walked into Zella's building. Dominic, my least favorite doorman of all time, was working. Luck seemed to be with me today, as this time he didn't ignore me. But he didn't recognize me and had to call up. I looked around the minimal lobby. Even though this was my fifth time here I hadn't noticed it was a twelve-foot-wide hallway with a doorman's desk off to the left as you walked in. They had a small package office with a door behind them. To the right were the rows of keyed mailboxes, and straight ahead in the shiny obsidian-marbled hall was the elevator bank. It was all black or dark gray, even the trim on the elevators. To most it probably looked chic. The longer I worked for her, the more it felt cold and desolate.

Dominic cleared his throat and then motioned to the elevator, "Fourteenth floor, take two lefts out of the elevator. 1402." This was his only line. I'm glad he didn't do stand-up comedy; it would be such a boring set. On the elevator, I hit the button for the fourteenth floor. The elevator was unlocked by either the doorman or a fob. So, unfortunately, I had to talk to Dominic almost every day.

Arriving at 1402, I removed my shoes and placed them next to another pair I didn't recognize. Jimmy Choo heels. Wondering who they belonged to, I was a little embarrassed that my beat-up Me-Too ballet flats would sit here in such glorious company. I rapped on the door three times, waited a moment, and then opened it and walked in. Even though I had been told to enter when I arrived, I was still hesitant to just walk into the space.

Zella and another blonde were sitting at the giant farm table together with their backs to the door, both looking at several magazines and an iPad. I knew it wasn't Amanda, she and I would no longer be scheduled on the same day in the office. Per Zella, she didn't want us overlapping in work and she didn't want us both in the office at the same time. Although years later, I wonder if this was less to have noise in the office, as she had originally stated, and more to yell at us individually, although I don't have proof, and early on I didn't know. Amanda had trained me to take over the office work as she was transitioning to be a full-time yoga teacher. Now I was the main office helper. Amanda would only be in when we needed extra help with gift bags or invitation stuffing and would be working at events. This made me feel even more inadequate.

My routine, such that it was on my fifth day, was to start immediately, whether Zella was in or not. If I didn't have a previous task to tackle, I worked on logging the mountain of receipts in a crazy triple system. Then I would go through the clipboard of "to-do items." However, there was rarely anything on the clipboard. Zella would rarely write anything down, instead she would just start spouting things that would send me scrambling for something to take notes with thirty seconds after stepping through the door.

Setting down my bag on the floor and my bagel and coffee on the counter, I immediately grabbed pens and notebook. My bagel and coffee would probably serve as both breakfast and lunch, so I would wait a little before I ate. I had not yet gotten into the rhythm of packing a lunch, and Zella didn't like me to leave the office, if possible since I was only scheduled to be there two days a week. Two days ago, I had survived an almost eight-hour day on an apple, a very smashed up and almost not recognizable granola bar, and a bag of almonds. Amanda had told me that Zella didn't mind if I ordered food in, but by the time I actually had time to order, it was almost time for me to leave so it didn't make sense. With a lack of funds in my bank account and dollars in my wallet, ordering food that day was not an option. Even this morning's four dollars for a bagel and coffee was a splurge.

After digging out a second pen I moved over to set up my normal spot in the office. Two pens were now the norm at all times. Only one pen wasn't safe. On the third day in the office, my first without Amanda, one of my pens stopped working. I missed two items while I tried to get the pen to work again. I missed about four while digging through my bag, I missed another two realizing that pen didn't work either, I missed an addendum and another item when I looked around the room in an almost cartoonish manner to see if there was another I could use. After I realized Zella's voice had stopped, and that I was also repeating the things she had said out loud so I could remember them, I turned to find her looking at me.

"Amanda, what is wrong?"

Shocked to be caught without office supplies, not knowing if I should correct her for calling me by the wrong name and trying to keep all of the items in my head that she had rattled off, I just confessed to my misdemeanor.

"I, uh—my pens aren't... working."

"Here, Amanda," she said as she walked back to her desk and grabbed one of twenty black and silver ballpoint pens she had in a horn and silver cup on her desk. "Make sure I get it back, and tomorrow make sure that you have your own," she buttoned her scolding with a sigh. She had said this as if I were a fourth grader who never seemed to bring a pencil to class.

She continued to rattle off tasks as she handed me the pen. Even though I started to write the moment I got the cap off of the pen, I still missed about half of the items. When I had to ask her to repeat herself, she replied, "Amanda, I have told you several times, you have to listen with your complete attention as I'm talking," as if she hadn't even witnessed my pen catastrophe. She stared at me for a moment and sighed. "All right, what tasks are you missing?"

Later when I told this story to Sam, he laughed and said, "She asked you what you were missing? Isn't that what you were asking her? How did you finally get the information?"

"Seriously! Sam, it was like I was playing that Pyramid game show. I was trying to describe things that I remembered from each item. I still missed a few, and at the end of the day, she was pissed that I had 'forgotten' to do certain things when I didn't know they needed to be done in the first place because they weren't on the list. It was my fault. I will always have twenty pens at the ready from now on."

This morning, my pens were ready although Zella and the blonde were still in their own huddle and hadn't noticed me. I crossed to her desk and picked up the pile of receipts that had accrued in the day since my last bookkeeping round. I grabbed the notebook where we recorded them and walked over to the computer. I brought up the spreadsheet, sorted the receipts into the categories that Amanda taught me, and the moment I started to write the first entry, Zella's voice stopped me.

"NAH-tuh-Lee." Every time she said my name it had an affected-British-meets-Massachusetts sound. Shock washed over me as she said my name again. Both from hearing my actual name, and that my notebook and pen were on the other side of the counter. I jumped up and dashed over to my neglected stationery and turned back toward the table.

A couple of barking laughs came from the table, and Zella stood up, and crossed behind me. She put her hands on my shoulders—I was confused because this hadn't happened before. In fact, I don't think Zella and I had exchanged any kind of touch at all. Her hands were warm and comforting. I was so surprised.

"Kelly, I want you to meet my assistant, NAH-tuh-Lee. She is going to be great for your event. We will be able to find her in Cipriani very easily. Because she is so tall." I felt like I was an item on a home shopping channel that was being demonstrated to the viewing audience. I really hoped she wouldn't make me stand up and twirl around. "NAH-tuh-Lee," she turned her attention to me as she walked to my side so she could look me in the eye. I was at least a foot taller than her, but her personality was so large it seemed like there was no lack of height between us. She always seemed to look at me straight on. "Kelly is a new client, and she and her very handsome fiancée, Carl, are getting married at Cipriani 42nd

71

Street in October. She decided that stopping by earlier than our 9am meeting time would be better for her."

Uh oh, Zella's voice was overly cheerful and happy with a squeak that usually came out of teenage girls. She wasn't too happy about our client coming early, I could tell. Zella's kind voice put me on edge. It felt so unnatural. I knew something was wrong, and I knew it had nothing to do with me. This flip of emotions I would come to know very well in my tenure with Tremaine Events, and I even got to the point where I could tune it out. However, at the beginning of my time with her, it was very disconcerting.

"Why don't you come over and sit with us?" she purred.

You know that moment in a scary movie where you know something is going to happen to the main character, but you aren't sure what, and you aren't quite sure who to trust? And you want to scream at the character to make good choices. I had that feeling, but I shooed it away and took the seat beside Zella anyway.

We sat with Kelly for the next two hours. My thoughts kept going to my neglected coffee and bagel on the counter. Kelly meandered through all of the ideas and gave a detailed description of all twelve hundred pins on her Pinterest board. I took notes. Pages of to do items. At one point I chirped in an idea, and Zella just stared at me but said nothing, leaving an awkward silence hanging over the table in front of us. She turned back to Kelly and mentioned a great décor person Zella thought would be perfect.

At one point I had to pee. I didn't know whether it was ok to leave the table to go or not. Amanda had told me that I had to always be ready to take notes. After twenty more minutes passed into Kelly's third hour sitting at the table with Zella and me, I decided my bladder was more important.

"Where are you going?" Zella asked as I stood up.

"I, uh, need to… powder my nose."

Zella looked down her nose at me as if I had said something really ridiculous and then she looked at the clock. Turning back to Kelly, she said in her best Mary Poppins voice, "Oh my goodness, we've been chatting for two and a half hours. Kelly, you make the time fly!" Zella gushed. "We have taken enough of your valuable time," Zella continued as she floated out of her seat and started to gather the things on the table.

My bladder moaned again. I didn't know whether to go or stay. We had never had a client visit before. I didn't know the protocol, just that I was to always be ready to take notes. Maybe I should just wait? Maybe I should run to the restroom, leave the door open and take my pen and notebook with me so I could take notes, if needed? Even though I was a strong and intelligent human, I had an overwhelming terror of doing something wrong in this job every day. I decided to wait. Kelly would be gone soon. Instead, I started to grab the papers and swatches on the table, only to hand them to Zella in a weird relay cleanup, as Zella was dividing all of the items into two piles. She scooped some of them into the plastic oversized envelope, what Zella called "folders" we had for each individual client. She then went to a box beside her desk and pulled out a slim silvery, white-handled bag embossed with Tremaine Events on the side. With a flick of both wrists, while holding on to the satin ribbon, Zella opened the bag. "NAH-tuh-Lee, grab those papers and put them in here," she held out the bag with only two fingers. I wasn't sure if I was meant to just take the bag or if I was to put the papers into it while Zella held it. My mind raced and shamed me: I should have known better at this point.

But I didn't. I zealously picked up the pile of delicate papers and aimed for the bag with them. Zella had turned her attention back to the bride-to-be. She didn't have a firm grasp on the bag. I started to gently move the loose sheets into the bag, and in one motion Zella let go of the bag as I let go of the papers.

Like falling leaves twirling and swirling all over the highly polished wooden floor the papers and swatches went all over. I felt my career flying off with the scattered documents.

Chapter Eight

I dropped to my knees as fast as I could, even though I was in a pencil skirt and a tighter-than-comfortable Banana Republic peplum top that barely let my arms move to shoulder height and made it difficult to do more than type or write. Scampering to pick up every paper, I swore quietly to myself that I wouldn't get fired from this amazing job that I barely had for two weeks just because papers had dropped on the floor. It seemed like I had been gathering the fallen sheets for five minutes. In a messy pile, I placed them on the table with the idea to delicately rearrange them and then put them into the bag.

They were snatched away as soon as I stood. Zella, like one of those people who is a whiz at a Rubik's Cube, flipped and twirled them in about three moves, put them in the bag, glared at me then flipped to a smile as she turned and handed the bag to Kelly assuring her that if anything was missing, we would messenger it to her office right away. They both walked to the door. My bladder screamed, but my feet refused to budge; I stayed glued to the floor. I willed my Kegels to hold.

After the door closed behind Kelly, Zella wheeled around and went from a smiling matriarchal angel to a writhing and unsmiling beast. She marched over to me. It was all I could do to not throw my arms up to cover my face, as I was sure a slap was coming. I was sure she was going to rip me to shreds. Or worse, fire me. Instead, she said calmly but through gritted teeth, "Sit down and get your notebook."

In an attempt to hide my wide-eyed panic and the pain in my abdomen, I grabbed pens and paper and cast my eyes downward. She rattled off list item upon list item. I could swear she was talking faster than she ever had before. My dull hangover headache wasn't helping. I had almost two full pages of notes of things that needed to get done.

My stomach felt bloated and stretched to its limit, and I felt if I moved just the tiniest bit in the wrong way, the floodgates would open. Silence fell. I waited a few more moments for her to continue. When she didn't, I looked up to see that she was texting. Halfway through a text, her phone rang, and she answered it. Her conversations were lengthy, and I knew I probably had enough time to get to the restroom and back.

Standing, I lurched toward the bathroom. I took a few steps but stopped. I worried that I might need my notebook. Just in case she started giving me more instructions. Pausing mid-step to consider my ridiculousness, and then heading back to the table to grab the notebook felt like it cost me valuable time. Sweat broke out on my forehead as I grabbed the notebook and pen, and sprinted, sort of bounced bowlegged, to the bathroom.

My notebook was tossed on the counter as I slammed the door shut and ripped my skirt down from my waist. Finally, relief. I glanced at the notebook that was open to the pages I had taken my notes. Half of the list was errands. The other half was organizing things or research. Mentally I organized the things I had to do. I would be in again tomorrow, so I could try to get as much done today as possible, and then the rest tomorrow.

When I came out of the bathroom Zella was still on the phone. I grabbed my cold coffee and warm bagel and carried them to the computer where I had set up the receipts. I figured I would get those out of the way and then start on the list.

"NAH-tuh-Lee," Zella said with a purr, right as I started to work. I turned my head to face her. "All of your list needs to be done. Today."

"Right. Zella, I have the receipts and—"

"I don't need to hear your problems. Don't give me a reason to fire you. You're a grown adult and you won't drop any of it," she said condescendingly and twisting the embarrassing knife that was already causing me pain, then stood and walked into another room to continue her phone conversation.

Crap. How was I going to get all of this done? I looked at the clock. It was almost noon. I had five hours to accomplish two days of work. Gathering up the returns and deliveries from all over the office, I mentally mapped the route to the different shops and locations. Delicate note cards were to go to the printer and a few extra invitations to get hand stamped and mailed. Both I wrapped in a plastic bag and carefully placed in my Longchamp shoulder bag. It was a hand-me-down, but it was a label. Zella was big on labels, no matter if she knew them or not. She thrived on conversations about weight, designer labels and gossip.

There was also a large box of leftover items from last week's wedding that needed to be dropped off at a past client's apartment, a list of gifts to buy, a list of items to pick up for the wedding in two weeks that included Polaroid cameras and film, and a thank you gift to be delivered to a photography studio. There were also three bags of returns to Bloomingdales, Anthropologie, and Barney's. I finished loading myself up and tossed my coffee and untouched bagel into the trash. The best part about this rash of errands was getting out for lunch. I could grab something fresh and at an edible temperature to eat while I was dashing from location to location. It would have to be cheap and I'd put it on my credit card. Which I swore I'd pay off as soon as I got paid.

"NAH-tuh-Lee, don't forget to take the cleaning too."

GAH! My mind cringed with frustration. I had just gotten balanced. With a deep breath, I convinced myself I could do this. Adding the cleaning wouldn't be a problem. I've hauled more than this to theater contracts through subway stations. The bag of cleaning went out weekly, but it always was a huge laundry bag full. If it were Santa's Pack, I would assume that every child within a ten-block radius was "nice." It only took two tries to balance it with the rest of the bags I had of stationary samples, ribbons, vases, and clothes to be returned.

Zella had a closet at the office where 99% of her professional wardrobe lived. She would usually go to a workout class from home, or have a private teacher at her apartment, and would come to the office to shower and get dressed. The loft was actually a residential location and had two other rooms and a second bathroom. One of the rooms even had a bed in it. I had still yet to learn why. I surmised that Zella would sleep here sometimes because she was married to her work—at least that was my glamorous version of it. I also wondered if she had a bed around for obscene affairs. Zella would have her dry cleaning go out and come into the office for ease—probably also to hide a lot of the expensive designer clothing from her husband, I would assume. I had yet to meet him, and Zella had yet to mention Mr. Tremaine at all. I had only heard Amanda talk about him. A mystery man. Well, it was something to think about as I did inane chores like Zella's returns and dropping off dry cleaning.

Magically, I dashed all around the Flatiron, Chelsea and Union Square areas, delivering all of the returnable items, arguing with the dry cleaner and the stationary store clerks, grabbing a sandwich, gobbling it down, and still able to do a little of the research for the checklist on my way back to the office. When I got there, Zella was out.

Checking her calendar I found she had an appointment but would be back after 4pm. So, I started on the receipts. Zella didn't like to be bothered about receipts after she discarded them in the folder to be noted and filed away for the bookkeeper. Instead, I was to check her calendar for each receipt and match it with an appointment that was around the approximate time. Each client was to be noted or billed later for every meeting expense, be it a single lemonade, or a steak and bottle of Veuve Clicquot for everyone in attendance.

I would come to loathe this triple system, as I had to hand write out every expense on a paper that got stapled to the slip, write out a second slip that was put in a file for each client, then each receipt had to be handwritten on a clipboard and then typed into an Excel spreadsheet. I then had to log each purchase onto a separate sheet for each client, and and file the receipts. It was a ridiculous number of steps for logging a simple receipt. My eyes rolled so much while I was preparing the receipts, they were getting a workout and if eyes had skinny jeans, mine would fit into theirs by now.

I wanted nothing more than to prove myself a worthy assistant. Curtailing my eye-rolling, I would mentally remind myself of this and I would learn everything and adapt. Since Zella had been in the business for over twenty years, I was sure that there truly was a method to her madness. Emphasis on madness. I strived to have the best knowledge of the entire event world and I would learn all she had to teach me. Even her weird organizational and bookkeeping ways.

Often when I start a project or something new, my brain literally storms with ideas on how to make the process streamlined, more efficient, or more effective. I'm far from lazy; I would rather be efficient so I can use my time more effectively. My brain hummed with ideas of what could be overhauled and streamlined at Tremaine Events. But after offering my ideas, they were quickly shot down. Turns out things were not streamlined for a reason.

Chapter Nine

Zella loved to bring on interns. She always hated the interns but loved the fresh blood. Amanda's off-the-record analysis of this was that Zella didn't like to invest in new hires. Interns were inexpensive to pay, and they would do anything so they could gain experience in the event world. They never lasted long. Sometimes because they didn't acclimatize their skills fast enough. Sometimes because Zella couldn't stand them. And almost always because their fear of the woman scared them away.

The official story to anyone outside the office about an intern leaving was always the same: they had gone in a different direction. This covered all nature of sins for Zella. There was only one intern whoever had made it, a golden goddess of interns. Because she maintained her cool while at Tremaine Events, Anne Marie was given a glowing recommendation and had a job for life at the continually in demand and always groundbreaking Floral Elegance, one of the go-to décor companies for elite events in New York City. Proof that the job opened doors.

Zella believed "A person with Tremaine Events experience from her company could open doors," so much that she spoke these words at least once weekly to me or to the interns or anyone who would listen. The experience she talked of was the insanity of her ways. She once even admitted that all office procedures were kept exactly the same so she could groom all of the interns in the same way. I suggested streamlining the receipts process because it was time consuming, redundant, and very overwhelming for a newcomer.

Her eyes twinkled, the corner of her mouth lifted just enough so as to not disturb the new Botox and looking me directly in the eye she said, "Exactly, Natalie." In other words, Zella purposefully maintained an elaborate amount of pain to inflict on anyone new as a form of initiation. If you could hack it through the ludicrous speed note taking, the massively insane number of errands, and the absurd pseudo-bookkeeping, you could actually survive at Tremaine Events. This was if you didn't have another job or school as well. In other words, the algorithm for staying in this job was a psychotic labyrinth that very few people could withstand and survive.

Unfortunately, this understanding and view of the job would come much later for me. After a great amount of anxiety and fear of losing the job. If they would have only come sooner to relieve a great deal of my early onset anxiety. But no matter.

From my first day I was determined not only to keep my job at Tremaine Events, but I was out to impress Zella. I would conquer this entire torturous list brought on by the paper waterfall today.

Diligently, I worked, organized, texted, researched, printed, and at 3:45pm I looked at my list. I had about five items left to accomplish. There were a couple of things I needed clarification on, so I texted Amanda to see if she could chat—Zella now assumed that I knew how to do everything or made it my responsibility to learn what I didn't know. I realized in my first week that even though Zella said to ask her as many questions as needed, she rarely liked to be bothered with "things you should know, NAH-tuh-Lee." Amanda became my own personal Zell-o-pedia.

Whenever I texted Amanda in a panic that I was about to lose my job and that I was an idiot that must have missed when I learned that specific task, Amanda reminded me that Zella tended to make an amalgam of the interns and people who worked for her. No one was an individual in her brain anymore. It was rare that she singled people out and remembered them.

While I was waiting for Amanda to text, I sent Sam a quick message:

Sammo—why did we drink SO MUCH last night? Love you.

I knew he was in the middle of a class, so I didn't expect a response.

No response from Amanda. It was now 3:50pm. Zella was going to be back in ten minutes, and I really wanted to get the list done. My need was great to prove my worth, even though I made a dreadful mistake and dropped a bunch of papers in front of a client. This wouldn't stop me, it just meant the mountain of success today was a higher climb. I looked at the list again. I had yet to accomplish:

1) Reserve heart umbrellas (I didn't know when, who, or where to get them.)

2) Revise menu copy for Robinson (This one was deceptively simple—but there were three possibilities of "Robinson." We had a bride whose last name was Robinson, a groom whose first name was Robinson and a restaurant down the street called Rob and Son that was the location for a rehearsal dinner) and since it was a verbal note from Zella at a speedy pace, I had no idea which one it was.

3) Call AM and revise regular delivery (What was "AM"? I felt like I should know this one. Where would I find the number, and what was the revision? And what was the "regular delivery" for that matter?)

4) Ask Angela to up the output and add anniversaries. (Who was Angela? What anniversaries?)

5) Add peonies (To what? For whom? From where? What color? Generally had no clue on this one.)

The clock now said 3:53pm. More than wanting to accomplish the list before Zella returned, which was seemingly impossible at this moment, I wanted to do something so I looked busy. I looked around the office. It was immaculately clean—Zella never liked a mess left behind, with the exception of her desk, which was so often heaped with things I never understood how Zella found anything there. The only thing I could do now was sit and wait. And try not to panic. I looked at my phone and it was now 3:54pm. No reply from Amanda.

Amanda had previously assured me Zella liked us to dive into her email and answer our own questions. This bothered me a little—I was trained in so many other jobs not to look at my superior's email account. But at this point I didn't have another choice. Zella would be back soon. I almost felt like this was a trap; I trusted Amanda, but I'd seen so many movies where a plot twist happened when someone looked in another person's email and got caught. Did I chance it?

I only had five minutes. What was more important, accomplishing the list, or keeping up a privacy that I had already been told was all right to break? After pacing the floor for a few laps, and checking my phone continually, I made the decision.

It felt incredibly wrong, but I grabbed my notebook and sat down in her chair at Zella's desk. I felt myself watching the door to the office out of my periphery. I knew I could totally jump up at any moment, and pretend to be doing something, anything else if it started to open. However, I couldn't make it all the way back to the computer on the counter, but I could make it to a different location. As I pulled up her email, I thought about pulling open a drawer of the filing cabinet that sat next to her desk that had every client's folder and information in it. My plan morphed into the idea that if she came in, I would jump up and pretend to file a client file back in the drawer. It would work. A little voice in the back of my head calmly reminded me that Zella said had given me permission to look in her email, but I pushed the rational thought away. The conspiracy voice in my head didn't trust anyone and reminded me that Zella could have set a trap.

There were five things to find. There was no rational organization to the remaining tasks, and normally I liked to go for the easiest first. Take care of the simpler tasks and leave more time and brain power for the harder things. Also, you could psych yourself up by getting more accomplished in the beginning. Psychology 101. Or maybe it was one of those women's magazines I had a subscription to. Either way, it worked.

My fingers tapped the keys. I searched "Angela" and came up with two choices. Pulling up the first email, I found in the signature Angela Parkinson, Angel Web Design with an email and a cell number. Score. I wrote these down in my notebook and then thought to forward myself the email so I could have her information. 3:56pm. Still no text reply from Amanda.

Feeling adventurous, I searched emails for "peonies" and low and behold the first email that popped up was to Zella from AnneMarie of Floral Elegance. Bingo—two with one search. I forwarded myself that email as well. As soon as I had collected all of the info, I'd email from my email account, so I could follow up. Why had I waited so long to search Zella's email, I wondered. This was like the Wikipedia of my job.

Feeling super lucky now, I searched for heart umbrellas. Nothing. I searched for umbrellas. Nothing. I searched for rain—because if there was a conversation with a client about rain, I could assume it might be that client. Nothing. Bad weather: nothing. Inclement weather: nothing. Snow: nothing. 3:58pm. I sighed trying to think of other terms to search, but my creative thinking dried up. Pun intended. I decided to move on.

I searched Robinson next but came up with a ton of emails. I opened the first five to find nothing about a menu. I revised the search to be "Robinson menu." Still a ton, and nothing recent that discussed a menu change. 3:59pm and my phone chimed. Thank goodness I thought! Finally, Amanda responded.

But it wasn't. It was my Sam. My heart went zing when I saw his name, but panic took over and told me that I wasn't allowed to waste time replying. Or even spend time thinking about him right now. My job was on the line. I looked at the door that Zella would be walking through and would soon wrap me in a giant blanket of my disappointment for the second time that day.

My eyes sank to the floor. Out of my periphery, I saw the filing cabinet. Of course! I could look through client files. They were filed by month of event, so upcoming events were at the front. I grabbed the first one and took it to the table. Opening the file, I gently pulled out everything inside. Leaving it all in order, I gently turned each piece of paper over on top of the other one, scanning each paper full of scribbles and notes trying to see something about umbrellas.

I got through the first file for the bride whose wedding was in two weeks. Nothing. Putting the papers back in the folder, and replacing it in the drawer, I grabbed for the one behind it that would be in four weeks. Using the same procedure, I got through about half of the pile of papers, and my phone made a sound. I grabbed it, and my mind scanned the phone and saw the time. How was it already 4:07pm? My stomach flipped as I saw that it said there was a message waiting from Zella.

Chapter Ten

I looked at my phone more closely. Amanda also texted—Hooray! I went to Amanda's text first, figuring that Zella's would be something about her returning. Swiping my finger across the screen as quickly as I could, I unlocked my screen and tapped away until Amanda's message was open. It read:

Sure. I can talk now! I was in a class.

I flipped over to the phone app and pulled up her phone number and hit the call button.

"Hey, Natalie how's it—"

"No time," I interrupted Amanda's pleasantries. "Zella is on her way back from a client meeting. I totally screwed up and dropped papers in front of a bride and she gave me a two-page list to complete today, and she will be back any minute. What client needed heart umbrellas?"

"Breathe, Natalie."

"No TIME!" I shouted back a little more vehemently than I had intended.

"Natalie, I—"

"Amanda! Please stop trying to calm me down and just let me know who needs umbrellas," rapidly I yelled into the phone. My voice was crazed as I cradled the phone on my shoulder as I continued sifting through the papers in the file. My desire to do this job overrode everything else at the moment. Even our friendship. And common courtesy.

"NATALIE!" Amanda yelled through the phone. It was so jarring, I stopped everything I was doing, even breathing, for a moment. I stood up straight. "Natalie, are you still there?"

"Yes," I answered sheepishly.

"Natalie. You have to keep it together. Breathe—"

"But I—"

"No, Natalie. You cannot let this get to you. Don't talk. Set whatever you're holding down." I looked around thinking that maybe she slipped in while I wasn't looking. I put the papers neatly in the pile and started to pack them up.

"No. Put it all down."

Seriously—could she see me? I looked around again.

"Okay," I said in a drawn-out, spooked way.

"Now take a breath," she said a little forcefully.

"Do you talk this way to your yoga classes," I asked, trying to lighten the mood.

"Are you breathing?"

"Yes, but I don't see—"

"Natalie. Breathe. Are you breathing?" She paused to listen. "I can't hear it," I blew out a large dramatic breath into the phone making it sound like I was out in a windstorm. She continued, "Good. Ok. The umbrellas are for the McCallen wedding—"

"But," I cut her off, "that isn't—"

"Natalie! Let me finish. You just keep breathing." I took a deep breath while she continued. "Now, I put the umbrellas on hold at Event Elegance last week," Amanda spoke slowly and in a hushed tone. I didn't know if it was so I would absorb the information or if she was doing it to calm me down. She continued, "We will let Event Elegance know a week before if we need them. Are you writing this down?" I dashed to get my notebook, so I could make a note next to my umbrella notes.

"Yes. How many umbrellas did you reserve and in what colors?"

"Natalie, I don't think—"

"Amanda, I got in trouble last week for not knowing the color of the socks that we ordered. Zella made me feel like I was so idiotic. I was in a stupor for days because of it. I'm not going to make the mistake of not knowing a detail again. Ever."

Amanda's chuckle came through the phone. "Fair," she said through her laughter. "They are the ones we always get, the white with the scalloped edge, with hearts that say 'his' or 'hers' in script. They will make sure that we have sixty-five reserved."

"But there are two hundred people invited."

"Yup. Intro to Wedding Math: You always lose about twenty percent of the invited guests. At least fifty percent of the guests will bring umbrellas or will borrow them from their hotels. Sixty-five umbrellas will cover about a hundred and thirty guests, including the bride and the groom. We always over-order, and we can always return. Betty over at Event Elegance is always happy to take our unused returns back—and she has been known to purchase the used ones that we keep in storage if she has another client that needs them immediately."

Amanda went on to tell me more about the Event Elegance, including giving me Betty's phone number and email for next time. I smartly started a list of important numbers on the back cover of my notebook with Zella and Amanda's numbers at the top. I put Amanda on speaker as she continued to talk. I reviewed the rest of the items left on my checklist and gasped when I looked up at the clock and saw it was almost 5pm.

I flipped to my text messages to tell Sam that I would probably be late to meet him and saw that Zella had sent me a text at 3:58pm.

Natalie—if you didn't finish your list, plan to be back at the office at 9am tomorrow. If you finished, please let me know, and I might just have you meet me at the walk-through instead.

"Amanda?" I asked, sure I was cutting her off, but not sure what she was in the middle of saying as I had given my full attention to Zella's text.

"Yeah?"

"Um, she's not coming back today and said that if I got everything done, I could just meet her at the walk-through."

"Oh wow," Amanda replied. "That is great! This is big Natalie. You're going to a walk-through already!"

"I guess so. I mean I got everything done today that she gave me to do, as well as the bookkeeping. I have a couple of my ongoing projects to work on, but nothing that is immediate."

"You're totally fine. You were emailing and working on things as we were talking, weren't you?"

"Yeah, I copied you on the emails."

"Make sure you start copying Zella on emails, although it is silly. She rarely reads them, but she likes to know that you're doing things and completing tasks. Also, there are rare times when she will search her email before bellowing 'Amanda' and will get her answer," she chortled.

"Great. Then yeah, I got it all done," I said with intrepid pride. "Um, Amanda, what do I do at the walk-through?"

"Dress up. Look neat and tidy. Wear all black. Dress like you're going to a fancy dinner after church— you can funk up your outfit with jewelry but stay on the conservative side. Comfortable, but designer shoes if you have them. Take your notebook and plenty of pens—she told me to remind you to have plenty of pens all the time—"

My eyes rolled in embarrassment; this was worse than the feeling of climbing the rope in gym class. Would I be continually reminded of my pen mishap? "I will," I groaned back at her as if I were a moody teenager.

"—and try not to speak unless you are giving a response to a question asked directly to you. Make sure you write down everything you think might be important."

"Amanda?"

"Yes?"

"Why do I feel terrified?"

Amanda laughed again, "Natalie! You'll be fine." Lowering her voice, as if conveying a secret, she said, "But she lightly drills the terror into us. One reason I started to work from home is so I can cower in a corner," Amanda laughed again. It was infectious, so I joined her. It felt good to laugh. And Amanda couldn't have been serious, could she? No one intentionally drilled terror into other humans, at least not in a happy, romantic world of brides and fantastic parties. Right?

Chapter Eleven

With a 10am site visit I got to sleep in a little later. I was up and dressed, with enough time not only to enjoy both cups of coffee I preferred in the morning, but I actually got to eat a bowl of oatmeal as well.

When I dressed, I didn't second guess my first choice. My sleek Calvin Klein dress hit me just above the knee and had an asymmetrical waist that really flattered. My mother had gotten me the dress in her last visit to the city, "just in case." I had found a pair of used but good condition Tarina Turk flats online, purchased them, and they arrived yesterday. They were classy and felt comfortable as I walked around my apartment. I pulled my hair back in a ponytail and sprayed it with hairspray to keep all the fly-aways under control.

A light blush graced my cheeks. Extra time allowed two coats of mascara and even a swipe of eyeliner on both eyes. I topped it off with a lovely natural lip shade. Feeling the need for a little pop of color, I added a blue Tarina Tarantino cameo necklace and some pearl studs to punk and class up my LBD a little more.

Before leaving, I made sure I had at least ten pens that worked and at the last minute, threw in a sharpened pencil, just in case. I triple checked that I had my notebook. I checked that my phone was fully charged, that my lipstick made it into my bag and that I had a bottle of water.

After all of this, I was still ahead by five minutes. I had decided to take the subway to the location. I was to meet Zella at Gotham Hall, which was in the Herald Square area, very close to Macy's. I had even planned to stop for a cup of coffee at Cafe Grumpy, a very exciting treat. Excited for my third cup of coffee, I headed out the door with a smile on my face.

Unfortunately, my good day ended there.

After waiting for almost twenty minutes, a train finally arrived, only to go out of service three stations later. After everyone got off the train and allowed it to depart, another train arrived seven minutes after that. My five-minute pocket: gone. My coffee time was now gone. My extra fifteen-minute cushion that I now added to anything where I was meeting Zella: gone. I would be lucky if I made it on time.

Reaching for my phone in my pocket, I debated texting Zella to let her know that I would be late. I had learned once if I didn't point out that I was late, that she didn't notice. However, another time when I was responsible and sent a text to give a heads up that I might be late, even when I made it on time Zella still logged it in her brain as if I was late. It was a terrible catch-22. Not that there were any good catch-22s. But this one was a continual debate. I come from the theater world where if you think you have an inkling that you might be even thirty seconds late, you contact your stage manager or your director. Was it better to risk arriving a minute or two late, and maybe even beat Zella?

Well, Zella was never late, as she would always have some glamorous excuse why she was late. My favorite excuse of hers over the next few years was that she "was on the phone with Martha, and you just can't hang up on Martha." Every client knew she was name-dropping, and most ate it up that their planner was on the phone with The Martha! However, it was never true. Zella had met Martha at a few very prestigious industry events, but in reality, Martha couldn't pick Zella out in a lineup—sure she had heard the name, who didn't remember a name like Zella, but honestly wasn't as prominent in Zella's life as she suggested she was.

I, however, couldn't use Martha as an excuse—although remember in this moment I wished I had a jaw dropping excuse that would let me off the hook. I doubted that Zella would believe it if I said I had Angelina on the phone. In fact, I would come to learn that Zella would not take any excuse from me. Or she would but would forget that she had and would only see the "I'm going to be late" text in her mind's eye. If I had a dollar for every time I got the "Natalie, you have to plan your time better and you have to start being on time" speech, I probably could have afforded a pair of Manolo's. Cheap ones, probably used, but still...

None of this was helpful, or even knowledge that I had yet. Currently I was still trying to make her think I was the best employee she had ever had and do anything to please my boss. Who, by the way, didn't like me calling her boss in front of the clients, because "it made me seem like I was there to serve her." And honestly because I think it made her feel old and no longer in with the hip crowd.

It was mornings like today that gave me so much hope and then dashed them on the rocks. I typed out "I'm stuck on a delayed 6 train, and I might be late." I took deep breaths, willing the train to go faster or even better, to go express. The time was ticking away. I was getting closer and closer, but time seemed to be going faster. I had to be at Gotham Hall at 10am. If I sprinted, I could get there exactly on time, if the train didn't lag any more than it had.

All was against me: the train stopped for an extra amount of time in the station. My time was ticking away even faster. My thumb felt heavy as my mind was at war trying to decide whether or not to hit send. If she arrived before me, Zella would be pissed that I didn't reach out. If I got there before her, then she would never know. But, if I reached out, and was on time or late, she would just add it to my continual list of tardies. Looking back, I remember feeling like I knew I would be fired for being late. It was a cardinal sin in Zella's book. She always had a threatening manner about how she scolded me about being late. However, all those times I felt in complete terror were in vain. I was never fired for being late. This fact never sunk in. I was always panicked about being on time. Today was no exception.

Three stops to go and twenty minutes before I had to be there. I really did hate being late. I missed having a car for the reason that you could show up to a place early, park and wait in your car. Two stops and fifteen minutes. I could make it. Deleting the text, I was taking my life into my own hands. One stop away. I had twelve minutes. I was just going to make it. If the doors would only close.

"We are being held in the station," the nasal voice of the conductor crackled over the loudspeaker.

"Gah!!!" I guess I bellowed out loud, almost every passenger on the train looked my way, and then pretended to ignore me. But I knew they felt the exact same way.

Five minutes seemed to drag by. I contemplated jumping from the train and hoofing it from here. We were currently at Grand Central, so it would just be eight blocks and a couple of avenues—I might be able to make it. Contemplating this and also berating myself for not jumping on the NQR subway line to Herald Square the moment my painfully slow train pulled in, I decided to jump just as the announcement was made, "We will be moving shortly." I held this announcement with such promise—but we still waited for what seemed like another five minutes.

Panic rose within me as time ticked away. The decision not to text Zella seemed like my biggest mistake ever.

A sweat bead fell down my neck. I was overwhelmingly upset that a slow train would be the end of a career that I had suddenly become so passionate about keeping. I knew it had only been a couple weeks, but I had fallen madly for this crazy business, and I was desperately striving to prove myself worthy. In other words, I was adding pressure to an already pressured situation, most of which I put on myself. I should have been a diamond, there was so much pressure.

Suddenly, the train doors closed, and I let out the breath that I had been holding. The next thing I knew, the train doors opened at my stop, and I dashed like I was running an Olympic race. I tore up the subway stairs. Elbowing almost everyone, I booked down the street not caring that I might have pushed someone over. I was in full panic. Streets passed and anytime I had to stop at a red light, my panic rose. I was so late. The frustration and terror were so high, I went a block past Gotham Hall, and I had to double back to get to the entrance.

The front door was locked. I ran around the building trying to find another entrance. The second door was also locked. I had run around the building almost twice when I noticed a staircase going down. Having no luck with other options, I tried the door to find it open. A long hallway stretched in front of me. Feeling a bit like Alice when she is about to fall down the rabbit hole, both scared and afraid that I'm in the wrong place and I am about to walk into trouble, I fear my employer more, and foray on. Eventually, I found a set of stairs that ascended. I followed them to find myself in a cavernous oval room made of marble. It was a sight to behold. Glancing around in awe, my eyes landed on two people on the other side of the room. I made my way over to them and introduced myself.

"Hi, I'm Natalie from Tremaine Events. We are doing a walk-through today."

"Oh hey, Natalie. I'm Erica Benz, and I work for Gotham Hall. This is Kent Abrams, and he is another event sales manager here. We were just discussing an event that will be this weekend. Feel free to relax," she pointed to another room that was just out of view as the walls curved. "I'll be with you in a few!"

She was certainly chipper. It was very irritating in the state I was in. I took another breath.

"Great, thank you," I said, trying to unclench my jaw, and started to walk toward the room. "Oh, where is the restroom?"

"Just past the room you are headed towards," said Kent who looked like a mousey hipster librarian, styling horn rimmed glasses and ironic sweater vest.

I walked into the anteroom. This must be coat check, as there were some pipe and drape off to the side, and about twenty racks with hangers on them. No one else was in the room. I looked at my phone to make sure that I wasn't having a delusion. Nope, no texts, and it was now 10:17am. This was odd. I flipped my phone to the camera feature and put it on selfie mode to double check my lipstick. It was now non-existent, and my hair was disheveled. My deodorant had given up on me a few blocks back.

As no one else was around, I slipped quickly into the bathroom with the gigantic wooden sliding door. Even the bathroom was stunning. It was all a creamy vanilla marble. The mirror looked antique, the toilet had a faux wooden water chamber above with a pull chain, and a little table held linen-like paper towels and an assortment of lotions next to the pedestal sink. I wanted to just stay in there but went right to work on myself. I didn't want to dally just in case, by fluke the entire group was late, and I had made it before them, I wanted to keep up that appearance. I rushed through reapplication of my lipstick, brushed my hair, and reapplied deodorant—I continually carried these deodorant wipes with me that refreshed and reapplied deodorant at the same time—they were a godsend. As an actor, I never knew what a dance call would do to me, and never wanted to smell.

Upon exiting the bathroom, I returned to the anteroom to find myself still alone. It was now 10:21am and I sent Amanda a concerned text.

At Gotham. No one here. Not sure what to do. Am I in the right place?

I waited impatiently for a response, or someone to appear, panicked that I was in the wrong place. Seven minutes later, after I had checked my phone probably fifty times, I heard chipper voices. I heard Erica introducing herself, and I made my way out to the main room again.

A trio had entered, a younger brunette whose hair was so shiny it looked like it was from a hair color commercial, and an older couple had just entered. I assumed this to be my bride and parents of the bride. Unsure of protocol, I just stood back and waited to be introduced or approached. A few more people trickled in and greeted each other. And then, as if choreographed, Zella came in, fashionably late, and her voice, edged with so much sugar it could have been sold at a bakery, greeted everyone with apologies and an excuse about being on the phone with Martha. And then her eyes landed on me.

Zella sized me up slowly from head to toe. I felt like I could see in her eyes the mental checklist of everything wrong with my person. She pursed her lips and narrowed her eyes at me. With a turn back to everyone else she gave a blanket instruction and handed outlines to everyone from a clipboard.

Erica walked back over and handed me the extras. "I'm so sorry you were here so long, and I didn't get back to chat with you—"

"Oh, you don't need to chat with her, I've got all of the information you will need, Erica," Zella waltzed into our conversation and snatched the outlines from my hand, holding one back out to me with two fingers.

"She has been here for about half an hour—I felt bad to just leave her, but Kent and I were finishing up for this weekend. I meant to find you and ask if you needed water or anything."

"Amanda, why were you here so early?" Zella cut Erica off and looked at me as if I had made a huge mistake and was the most inane human. "I told you that the meeting had changed to 10:30. Why didn't you read your texts?"

I tapped the button on my phone to wake it up, and unlocked it to find no texts from Zella, only one from the actual Amanda at 10:27 saying:

Zella just texted me that the meeting is moved to 10:30. I just got out of teaching a class and just saw it now. Get yourself a coffee and hang out, I guess!

Rage flooded my brain. Having Zella mix up our names was one thing. But to text the actual Amanda who was not scheduled to be here and to forget to text me was crazy making. I panicked and ran all the way here for no reason. GAH! My frustration flickered but I pushed it all down, knowing that what mattered was that I was here. Breathing, as Amanda had reminded me to do the day prior, I got myself ready to take notes.

Notebook and pen in hand, one behind my ear, ready to go, and my bag slung over my shoulder, with my coat over it, through the straps so I didn't have to worry about all of it.

Slapping on a smile, I caught up with the group that was assembling. Zella was introducing everyone. Taking my role as self-elected secretary, I wrote it all down, even though I knew this info was already notated somewhere back at the office. Renee, the bride and her parents Kathy and Carl. Mitchell Whist was décor. Erica Benz was the representative for the space and would also be helping with catering. Joe Vivanti was from the band. Elizabeth Kirk was our lighting designer.

I'm not good with names. At all. I was trying to memorize names and faces and write it all down when Zella came to me.

"And this is my new superstar assistant, Natalie." I stood for a moment in shock. Wait, now she knew my name, and said I was a superstar? I unfroze as I heard, "If you need anything, don't hesitate to let Natalie know and she will get me the message."

I was inundated with business cards. Everyone was handing them to me. Trying to balance my notebook and pen, and trying to gracefully accept one after the next, and also trying to explain that I didn't have one, and after the second attempt, I just said I would email everyone so they would have each other's contact information, including mine. As the party moved forward into the cavernous, converted marble bank that looked like a set for a 1920s bank heist, I stopped to juggle everything so I could put the business cards into my purse in a place where they wouldn't get harmed.

"Natalie." Zella's slightly shrill echoing beckon made my head snap. Everyone was so far ahead of me. I started to run toward the group while trying to shrug my purse back on my shoulder and get my notebook and pen at the ready. Three steps forward and my coat dropped off of my bag. Bending to get it, I heard a tear and felt air on my side—my dress had ripped.

My mind raced. I had to be here for this walk-through, it was a big deal for me. Enough had already gone wrong today, I couldn't let this stupid dress problem get in my way too. Suddenly I had an idea. In one graceful motion, I stood up, sat my purse on the floor, whipped my coat on, in hopes that it would cover the hole, picked back up my purse, and opened up my notebook ready for notes.

"Natalie, I have forgotten something at the office. I need you to go get the swatches for the tablecloths. They're sitting on my desk. Here," she handed me keys with a black fob that would unlock the elevator to me with two fingers, like they were something that smelled. "Be back as quickly as you can, chop-chop."

Unfortunately, I had gotten all the way to the subway and was called back.

"Natalie," Zella exclaimed when I entered Gotham Hall and was within eyesight, "It shouldn't have taken you that long. I sent you a text as soon as I found the samples in my bag."

I didn't want to correct her and tell her that she actually sent a text to Amanda again, who was in the middle of something and couldn't text me back right away, let alone text messages don't mean instant results, contrary to popular belief. Consciously reminding myself to breathe was becoming a mantra. I even have sticky notes inside my notebook and on my laptop with the written reminder.

Instead of reinventing the wheel, I stood back, took notes, and tried to learn who this woman was. Maybe if I could understand her, I could do my job better.

But it was easier said than done. The way she behaved and treated people was totally the opposite of how I worked. Although she stated boldly that she was organized, she just wasn't. She was messy and unorganized and blamed it on the interns or me when we couldn't find something.

Micromanagement was a way of life. She liked people to do things for her but in her way or not at all. And she would make us redo anything that wasn't done her way. High standards were a low bar for her. Nothing was ever good enough, cheap enough, expensive looking enough, lush enough, or done fast enough.

She had these infuriating traits that I would soon come to know, like interrupting when anyone was speaking. She also loved slapping my notebook while it was open in my hand, like a seal asking for a treat, when she wanted something. She also loved standing directly in front of me as if she didn't want anyone to actually look at me. At this Gotham Hall meeting was where I witnessed a lot of her irritating habits for the first time. I didn't know how to handle it—it was my first time out in public with a woman who was one of the most stylish I had ever met.

At the end of the meeting, I was still trying to feel my way around the situation and this event world. I had figured the "seen and not heard" was probably a good way to be, as when I tried to add something to a conversation about where to put the wedding cake during the ceremony, I got a handful of dead stares and complete silence for about five seconds—apparently my suggestion of putting the cake in the alcove by the front door for it to be displayed was not the way it was done.

Chapter Twelve

Walking into the door of our apartment, I ripped off my shoes and chucked them on the floor. I was so angry. Sam stuck his head out from around one of the two screens we had set up in our small apartment to make it seem like we had a separate kitchen.

"Hi babe, what's wrong?" He asked as he stepped out from behind the screen with a wooden spoon in his hand. He must be meal prepping.

"Oh, Sammo. I totally screwed up. I might have lost my job today."

"I'm sorry, babe. I'm sure you didn't do anything so terrible as to lose your job. Besides you've been saying that almost every day," I shot him a look. "Sorry. Not helping. I get it. Come here," he said, raising his arms toward me.

Continuing to frown, I did my best zombie impression as I dragged my feet and walked toward him and buried my face in his chest.

"Breathe, Natalie," he whispered as he wrapped his arms around me, wooden spoon, and all.

I mumbled into his chest.

"What's that?" he asked, pulling back a little, trying to see my face.

Turning my face, I repeated, sighing heavily, "A lot of people have been telling me that lately. I don't know that I'm breathing any less than I normally do."

"Okay," Sam said, drawing out the word, both as a question and an assessment as he stroked my back with his free hand. "I mean, maybe I want to step back and look at it all with perspective."

I pushed back from him, but he wouldn't unwrap his arms. So, we were still pressed chest to chest, but I looked up at him, my face scrunched in frustration, "Sam, I don't need a lecture on perspective." I let my arms dangle limply at my sides, refusing to hug him and hoping I would shrink and could slip out of his clutches. "Perspective is one of the things I'm the best at," I said with emphasis and voice rising.

"Of course, you are, but maybe you have forgotten that." He punctuated his thought by kissing me in the middle of my forehead—my third eye—Sam was into chakras, and I knew was being very pointed in his display of affection.

I sighed deeply and wandered to the sofa. Sam disappeared around the screen that hid the kitchen only to reappear a few moments later with a very full glass of Malbec and handed it to me.

"Tell me about it," he said, handing me the glass and turning back toward the kitchen. He collapsed the screen so he could see from the kitchen to where I was sitting on the sofa.

Dramatically I took a giant swig of my wine and threw my head back over the back of the sofa in a Peanuts character way. "Uhhhhhhhhhhhgggggggg! I don't think I'll ever get this job right."

"Natalie, stop being like that. Remove the negativity and self-flagellation and just tell me what happened."

Righting my head I took another swig of wine, breathing through my nose and enjoying all of the flavors and sensations dancing on my tongue from the wine.

"Today started out well," I began recalling the day. I recounted the ridiculousness from the different starting time, to Amanda being the one she texted, and sending me away only to be mad when I returned.

"Noooo. No WAY! She actually said 'chop-chop'?" Sam interjected into the story as he walked over to me to refill my wine glass.

"Yup. And I can't believe she actually had the swatches with her, and I got a call from Amanda as I was about to step onto a train to go to the office, saying I needed to go back to Gotham to take notes."

"Well, at least you hadn't gotten on the train yet," Sam pointed out. "That would have been irritating."

"Oh, Sam," I said with eyes widening with my next thought, "and it got worse from there. When I got back to Gotham, she wondered what took me so long—as if I had just walked out the door and gotten two feet away."

"I felt like such an idiot, Sam. I have good ideas, and all these people just stared at me like I was in a sandwich costume and said something blasphemous. Like maybe they should invite strippers to the reception to stand on the tables and that they could save on flowers that way." I was now curled up like a ball on the sofa cuddling my head into a pillow but still propped up so I could sip my wine.

"Babe, it couldn't have been that bad."

Giving him a less harsh version of the look, I was inundated with earlier that day, Sam stopped in his tracks as he brought two plates over to the sofa.

"Oh, I see," he said, setting the plates down and returning to the kitchen for the wine bottle. "Ok, so you were stuck on a train but early for your meeting, you had to run an errand but didn't really, your dress tore, and you were made to feel stupid. Is that all?"

"Nope," I said, barely moving while reaching for my plate. "The meeting ended, and she had me get in a cab with her back to the office. We reviewed the notes on the way. At her building she criticized my outfit, saying that next time I should wear a dress that won't rip, a jacket that is black, not navy, and a lipstick that doesn't make me look like a corpse."

I paused to put a fork full of ravioli in my mouth to punctuate the next bit. After chewing and my dramatic pause I continued. "She then proceeded to ask me about the entire list of things she gave me yesterday, and then told me that the only reason she gave me the list was so I would never be clumsy in front of a client again.' Like I was five years old, and I took something without asking, and got reprimanded. I dropped a pile of papers!" A deep sigh left me. "The kicker is, as we entered the office, she turned to me as she was taking off her coat and said was starting a new diet and told me I could join her to lose some of the extra weight on my body." My voice rose as I ended, and I punctuated the whole thing by shoving more ravioli into my mouth, and then sank into the sofa with a gigantic sigh.

Sam put his hand on my thigh and patted it. "Wow. I can't believe that about the weight stuff. That bothers me. But the rest of it, it's all going to be ok," he said rubbing my shin. "It always is. You'll figure this out. Every job always has the boss throwing way too much at the newbies, and they sink or swim and then move on. You'll be fine. You'll get through this too."

Turning only my head, I gave Sam a blank stare.

"I'm serious, babe. You are great at organizing and managing, and you love parties. You'll be fine once you figure her out. Just keep—"

"Breathing," I cut him off. "I know."

He leaned over after letting me stew quietly for a moment, and then kissed me on the temple. "Now, what should we watch?" he asked, clicking on the television. "*The Wedding Planner* with JLo is on, so is *Four Weddings and a Funeral*—one of your faves, babe! No wait, I have it! *So I*

107

Married an Ax Murderer." I turned to see the cheesy grin on his face, and I couldn't help but smile back. Setting my plate down, I snuggled into him, and he put his arms around me. He started the movie, and I heard him mumble into my hair, "It's all going to be ok."

Chapter Thirteen

After working for Zella Tremaine for almost eight excruciating weeks, I finally felt I had a good grasp on how to do my job. I had been learning her style. The panic of the first few weeks faded away like bruises: now gone but with a leftover tender spot reminding me not to do it again. Finally making the connections of why I did one task and how it was related to everything else, I was learning better and faster now.

Organizing social events requires a lot of planning because the people throwing the parties aren't used to the amount of logistics required. The truth was wedding season was upon us and even with the workload increasing, I was surprised I kept up. Even though I had watched tons of shows and movies about wedding planning over the years, I was always on edge, terrified at making mistakes. In the office I was a gopher, a glorified-doormat-meets-personal assistant. Everything Zella said made me question my strengths and capabilities. She even made me question all my personal choices from nail color to my clothing to my body weight.

Shamed into working out more, I was now taking two of Sam's classes each week, took Amanda's class, and lowered my caloric intake to eighteen hundred calories per day. Feeling like I couldn't lose weight fast enough, I even cut out the magic of my life: flavored creamer. Determined to impress Zella with my speed and competence at everything she threw at me. Even losing weight.

Working to show her that I was capable of doing tasks in half of the time only proved to her I could do double the work. She gave me more and asked for more. Mentally I took on more responsibility and stress. This led me to fail more and then was verbally slapped on the wrist over and over.

I was a terrified, people pleaser, striving to maintain an insane pace while failing at perfection. I cringe just thinking about it. But this was the job that "would open doors." Honestly, I didn't know what that alluded to, but the ever-receding carrot felt exactly like what I needed in my life. And I kept striving for it.

I had no idea what I wanted, but I knew it was just over the horizon and when I got to it, I'd recognize it. So, I kept my head down and tried harder and harder to appease and please.

This also made me spend much more time on the phone with my friends in distress and frustration. For every hour I worked on something for Zella, I spent two complaining or in fear that I had done it incorrectly somehow and would be fired. There was always a note when I wasn't good enough. Her flip-flop of emotions was never helpful.

Interestingly, Zella rarely threatened to fire me. Which is the crazy thing. She only actually said it a few times early on, but I always felt an underlying pulse of it.

These last two weeks I had been assigned to work on itineraries for all the upcoming weddings. Everything was timed out and given a spot on the Excel spreadsheet from the opening of the venue, to loading out the last vase of flowers, to the first dance and cake cutting. Zella liked to be thorough. Everyone in the industry raved to her onsite how they loved her itineraries. But the rule with something that seems well done and flawless: the process is time-consuming. Timings for every moment of every event were to be double and triple confirmed with anyone and everyone stepping foot in the venue.

Zella preferred confirmation phone calls to emails, reminding me that "no one can hide from a phone call, NAH-tuh-Lee, and you get the information so much faster."

This annoyed me because I could shoot off five emails in the time it took to make one call. And I could go back and search emails for proof of the information, or attest to my attempt. Phone calls, although lightly documented, paled in comparison—at least in my mind—to an email. But, I was so tired of getting yelled at. So, I called. Every. Vendor.

Also, to cover my ass, I often shot off an email first, and if they didn't follow up within a few hours or overnight, I would follow up with a call to each vendor or their assistants. I also would compile in a separate document the names and phone numbers of every vendor or assistant who would be at the event, per Zella. Getting cell phones was always a challenge. It took almost a year to perfect my bullshit line about needing to have an emergency number for everyone on the day of the event. Just in case anything was to go wrong. It was a little thing, but I quietly celebrated with myself every time I got all of the phone numbers.

My first set of these documents I had so much pride in making and couldn't wait to show Zella. I had worked diligently but creatively and felt that my version of the itinerary and phone sheets were the best I could make them. And were maybe even better than past versions because they were easier to read and didn't have unneeded information in them.

When I started working on the documents, Zella reminded me repeatedly that she wasn't good at training people. So, I would have to rely on Amanda to teach me, or I could look through old documents that we had used in the past. Zella also told me that there was a definite learning curve in this business, and I would be continually

111

familiarizing myself with these documents. Amanda gave me a brief overview of The Tremaine Itinerary early on. But to be honest she wasn't the best at teaching either, and she also told me that they weren't something that she generally worked on. Because I learn well on my own, I tried to piece together all of the parts.

So, I did what any innovative and exuberant new employee would do; I took the old and added some updates that I thought would help. To my version, color and different spacing was added so movement of the bride and groom was a little more visible. I added highlights to guest timing like father daughter dance and maid of honor speech. I created a pack list of all of the items we would need to take with us at the bottom.

One morning, after I'd been in the office for about an hour and double-checking all of the documents, I proudly announced to Zella that I had completed the documents for our next wedding. A whole three weeks in advance. Zella had continually complained to me that no intern ever got the itinerary finished before the week of the wedding. This might have been her way of telling me that it didn't have to be perfect the first time. However, I was bound and determined to be way ahead of the curve. Much to my chagrin, she ignored the documents and me. It wasn't until two days later she asked to see my work.

Proudly I said, "The documents are in our company folder, and I also emailed both the itinerary and contact sheet to you two days ago."

She looked at me like I had three heads.

After pulling up the email and squinting at the screen Zella said, "How am I supposed to look at this Natalie? Print. It. Out."

By the time I had a printed copy, Zella was typing another email and told me, " I don't have time right now. It's your job to remind me to go over the documents."

As the main reason I came into the office that day was to go over the itinerary with her, as it was the first one I prepared solo, and I wanted to learn and make any corrections, I had asked about going over the itinerary three times. Sure, there were other things that were my responsibility for Tremaine Events, but nothing seemed as pressing as the itinerary. And I had been working a bit from home to get ahead on my other projects.

Zella, frustrated by the third reminder said, "Natalie, since this is so important for you, I'll give you ten minutes."

thrown by her irritation, I wanted to remind her that she was the one who kept telling me that she wanted to go over it. However, this didn't seem like the time. Nor did I want to earn one of her, patent-pending, "you're an idiot," stares.

She told me to come sit with her at the large table in the office and she brought out a stunning Mont Blanc pen, a gift from some suck-up vendor we never used that was probably worth three weeks of my salary and sat in front of the single copy.

I knew she would look at it and find a few minor things wrong, things I wasn't seeing, but other than that she would think that it was brilliant. I was finally going to impress her today, and maybe, just maybe, I might get a rare and elusive "Thank you."

However, the first thing she said to me as she was sitting down and hadn't even looked over it yet was, "Natalie, in the future, I expect to get the itinerary in my hands sooner so I can edit it."

Really? I thought. I wanted to remind her that I had finished it two days before, but she was too busy. But it was

113

probably a moot point. Besides, the date was up in the corner of the last revision.

"Why are you giving me an old copy?" Zella asked.

"It's not old, I—" Zella cut me off.

"Yes, it is. It has the date from two days ago on it."

Sitting upright more, I said, "Yes, that is when I had it done."

Zella looked at me. "You have made no updates or changes?"

"Nope," I said confidently.

"Nothing needed to be added or updated since two days ago?" Zella asked in disbelief.

"Not a thing," I responded, still confident.

"There wasn't anything that came over in my email this morning that wasn't added in?"

My confidence started to wane, and my posture slumped a little. "Well, I—"

"Natalie. I'm not paying you to waste my time. I'm paying you to be better than me at all of the details."

Jumping up, I went over to her computer. "Right, Zella, I'll pull up the email now. What is it that you're referring to?"

She was silent.

"Zella?" I asked, looking over my shoulder back to the table.

"Oh, you already have it here. It's a note about the new best man's speech timing."

As I walked back to the table, I smiled in self-satisfaction. But wiped the smile from my face as I was taking my seat, for good measure. I waited for praise that didn't come.

"Now you need to move the timing of the photographer arriving, Natalie, you should know better. The photographer needs at least an hour at the beginning of the day—", she turned and saw me just sitting next to her, taking notes in my notebook. This was new information for me about the photographer arrival, so I was making sure I would know for the future. When she didn't continue, I looked up at her.

"Natalie," she continued, "why aren't you taking notes on your copy of the itinerary? Didn't you print a copy for yourself?"

I like to save paper. Trees are our friends. Besides, printing when unnecessary was one of the things that Zella liked to bellow about. I had gotten to have a pretty good collection of scratch paper that consisted of things I had printed by accident.

"Oh, um, I didn't think—"

"That is right, you didn't think. Print another." When I didn't move, she commanded, "Now."

After working together for a while, most people become accustomed to each other, walls come down and familiarity increases. With Zella, her rage and irritation for me became bigger and deeper. She always thought that I had worked with her for ages and should know everything. But the truth was, there were many times and many things that were firsts for me. Even though I am an amazing trouble-shooter, I am still human in a job learning the job and I would and still make mistakes. But sometimes I did things for a reason. Either way, Zella would always slap me on the wrist if it wasn't her way.

"I thought we should save paper, so I didn't print a second."

"Why do we need to save paper? It's only a few sheets and you will need it to learn. Really, Natalie. You should know this by now. You need to be better about thinking ahead."

"Oh. Well, I, um. I thought I was doing that, uh, Zella. We are low on paper—you only have about a quarter of a ream left, and I heard you say that you were printing all of the contracts today, so I wanted to make sure you had enough to print."

Running out of paper was one of Zella's many pet peeves. Amanda had warned me, but like most things with Zella, it wasn't truly believable until I experienced the tempest that followed when something went wrong. Zella also hated having excess of anything around. Although the office was large there was minimal storage space.

There were never more than two reams of paper in the office. This was difficult when signing a new client or during the week before a wedding—it was nonstop printing at those times. When we ran out of paper, or toner, or other supplies, I would get an earful of how I hadn't paid attention. This was a tricky thing to manage for a few reasons. I wasn't in the office daily and could only keep tabs on supplies when I was in. Amanda was the only one allowed to order paper or toner because she was the one who opened and started the account with ProClips, the online stationery store that was supposedly cheaper than any other stationery or office supply store. It was an infuriating way of working, but I became accustomed to it. Eventually. Later in my tenure I became the RainMan of paper reams. But not yet.

Apparently, Zella, thinking about my forward thinking to not print to save paper for contracts, approved of my action just as I hit print on the computer.

"Natalie, don't print. I'll make the notes. This time. Next time you should remember to print yourself a copy. Or better yet, print on both sides, save paper and give yourself a copy."

Ah, the one-up. Classic Zella. I could have a good idea, but then Zella would always one-up me for the next time or would explain in detail how it wouldn't work or how a previous intern had tried and failed when they attempted something. If she wasn't a woman, this would totally be "mansplaining."

I scrambled to hit cancel, but the printer charged ahead and spit out two of the three pages of the itinerary.

"Sorry, Zella," I said as I dashed to the printer to pull out the paper tray to hopefully get it to stop printing faster.

Her irritation rose. As I grabbed the paper from the tray and started to sit down, Zella rose from her seat.

"Well, Natalie, you're obviously not ready to go over this today. You will have to come in tomorrow and we can go over it then. I don't have time now." Zella gathered her purse and headed toward the main office door.

"Zella, could you maybe take it with you and mark it up and then leave it for me or send me pictures of what to change."

Irritated, she stepped back into the doorway. "No, Natalie, I could not. I am headed to my weekly manicure appointment, and I allow myself the time to do nothing, so I can relax for a moment in my week. I can hardly expect you to understand. You should have gotten me the itinerary sooner if you wanted me to look at it sooner." And with that she swept out of the room and slammed the door behind her.

Chapter Fourteen

It was a whole three minutes after the door shut before I felt the tears roll down my cheeks. Although it was ridiculous, I sat there and cried in the office. I beat myself up that my learning curve was halted because I wasn't, what… more proactive? Faster? More efficient? I had no one to ask about what I was doing incorrectly and how to make Zella love me more. That was a big part of it, I realized way too late in working for her: I constantly was striving for Zella's love and approval.

I sat there and was devastated for a whole twenty minutes until my phone alarm went off. I always set it for thirty minutes before I had to leave, especially on days I had Levi. This was to allow me to "tidy my mess" as Zella deemed it. I was to make sure anything, even folders, papers, pens, etc. that I hadn't touched or looked at, got put away before I left for the day. "An immaculate workspace is a productive one," Zella squawked over and over. It never failed that I would give myself plenty of time, and I would even tell Zella I was leaving in half an hour, but something would always come up in the last five minutes that needed more than five minutes to accomplish, but needed to be done in that moment, or else. I was never on time for Levi anymore. And every audition I tried to go to, I never actually made.

Sniffling, I pulled myself out of the chair. I went to the bathroom, a fruitless effort to clean up my face before cleaning the office. When I stepped out of the bathroom, I was still crying and berating myself. A problem solver to the core, I was trying to figure out how to be better at this job. Sam continually had to tell me that I didn't need to continually excel, but instead I should just live in the moment.

My phone alarm went off again. Five minutes until I needed to leave if I were going to be anywhere close to on time for Levi. I looked around and sighed in frustration and disappointment. I had hoped that tomorrow would be my day off. Sam was teaching a cycling class that I wanted to take. And I had an audition tomorrow I had been preparing a song for a couple of weeks now. The audition was for a big regional theater company. They were doing Cinderella and I had dreamt of playing one of the evil stepsisters, but now it looked like I wouldn't make it.

I guess I would have to come in for Zella to go over this paperwork. I probably wouldn't make it past the first round of auditions anyway, and Sam would understand if I didn't make it to his class. This job had great potential. Right? It would open doors. Maybe it was time to have a more "grown up" career plan. Sacrificing my acting dream for a career like this was worth it.

Sam said later that night when we were snuggled in bed if I had to miss his class, it was no biggie but, I shouldn't give up an audition. But I could swear I felt his disappointment. I knew he was letting me off the hook. I felt guilty for putting work first. But wasn't that what Sam was doing that lately, too.

When I arrived the next day, Zella looked at me like I was an alien. "What are you doing here?" she asked.

"Um, you said that you wanted to go over the itinerary for the Pearson's wedding…" I trailed off waiting for her to remember.

"Oh, Natalie. You must learn when I'm joking. Seriously." And with that she turned back to clicking on the keyboard of her computer.

Dumbfounded, I didn't know what to do and sort of just stood frozen in the entryway. I was unsure whether I should set down my bags and take off my coat so I could get to work, or if I was about to do an about-face and I would have the rest of the day to myself.

"Well? Are you staying or are you going?" She said this as if I actually had a choice. Because I was sure the right answer, the *only* answer, was staying. That is what she told me she wanted yesterday, and I altered all my plans for her. So of course, I stayed.

And then the words came out of my mouth before I could stop them, "Well, actually Zella, I had a cycling class and an audition I wanted to attend today. As you had insisted yesterday that I come in today, I decided not to attend either one and I made this my priority."

Clicking stopped on her keyboard and she turned in my direction with a concerned look on her face. "Natalie, Audition whenever you choose. And I wouldn't want to stop you ever from taking a workout class. Heaven knows they're needed." She said this eyeing my middle.

I was again struck dumbfounded. Was she insulting me and letting me off the hook all at the same time?

"But since you're here," she continued, "I do have a pile of returns and cleaning that need to go out. Unless you want to wait until you're back again." Even though she said it was up to me, she gave me a look that I read as I needed to comply or to find another job. Of course, the menial tasks needed to be done, and not the itinerary.

Although I vowed to be stronger, and uphold boundaries, I said, "Sure, Zella. Anything to help you out." I said hiding my disappointment and frustration.

With a tiny smile, as not to upset the Botox, her nostrils flared in satisfaction. Then she turned back to the email she was working on. Thinking back, I could have sworn I heard a whip crack.

"I'll be with you in a moment," Zella said.

"Great," I started to take off my coat, and set down my bags, "I think I can still make the audition and the class, so if I can be done by 1pm, that would be great."

"Mmmm hmm…" Zella replied.

A few minutes later she rattled off a list to me and piled me high with packages and bags. "Oh and, Natalie, we have a final walk through today at 2pm with our client for next week. It's a good thing you came in today; you can go too, so you can get the final details to put on your itinerary. I'll go over it and you can make the changes when you get back."

"Zella," I said in matter-of-fact way, "I have—"

"I have told you a hundred times, that if I'm not looking at you, I'm not listening. If you have personal things to do you don't have to work. You just needed to let me know yesterday that you weren't coming in. Today, I have too many things to get done to deal with your dilemma. So, you need to make a decision. In fact, I thought you already had, Natalie. At least it seemed as such when you walked through my door."

Confusion like this happened daily.

"I, uh, well… Yes. Fine. I suppose it will be good for me to be at the walk through. I'll just um, reschedule my…things." I put weight on my words, hoping they would sink in. That I was being flexible with my personal things for the job. It didn't seem to make a difference.

"Wonderful," she stretched the word out, sounding a bit like a Disney villain. "I'll see you in a bit," she said and walked back to her desk, picked up her phone and dialed. "Chrissy!" I heard her exclaim as I waddled out the door with my burdens.

I ran all the errands and made it back to the office. I got the itinerary changes—she had made so many, the papers looked like they were bleeding ink. Updates made; we went to the walk through. I kept my mouth shut and my dress from ripping this time. It was actually pleasant and almost a fun outing.

Our bride was delightful. She and her fiancée were golf enthusiasts, so everything had a bright green and white theme to imply the golf idea. The slogan "made fore each other" was their hashtag, and was on cocktail napkins, and stickers on the cookie favor to be given away at the end of the night. We were also going to make golf the theme for the welcome boxes full of treats for the out-of-town guests that we would create and deliver to hotels the day before the wedding. Zella even offered to drop me off in a cab at a subway stop that would take me home. I was slightly in shock through it all. Especially when she was nice to me when no one else was around.

When I got home, I was so upbeat and happy. I made dinner. Sam usually did the shopping and had a recipe plan— So, I found today's and started to cook. I think, even if it's soup from a can, or something that isn't hard to make, it's always nice to come home to a warm smell of food.

"What is this for, babe? You didn't have to cook," Sam said, coming up behind me and planting a kiss on my cheek.

"I actually had a good day today." I said as I stirred the pot of sauce. "And I hate that I missed your class."

Sam gently took the spoon out of my hand, tasted the sauce, and smiled. He set the spoon down, and turned me to him, taking me in his arms, "This is great, babe."

Hugging him back, I said, "My workday or the sauce?"

"Well, both," he grinned. "But mostly your day!"

"What?" he asked as he opened the refrigerator and got out vegetables to chop up for a salad as I turned back to the sauce to put on the chicken that was baking in the oven.

"You are always so positive, how do you do it?"

"Endorphins, babe. And if those don't work," he said, reaching for a wine glass, "liquor."

I laughed as he poured me a glass of wine. We finished making dinner together and went and snuggled on the sofa to eat together. I continued to tell Sam about my day, and how even though I was still afraid to stand up and offer my opinion or say no to Zella, I thought things were starting to move in a good direction. At the time, I hadn't realized it, but I went to bed happy for the first time in weeks.

Chapter Fifteen

The next week went by without much insanity. I was learning a lot, both about wedding preparation and about Zella. We made welcome bags complete with city maps, personalized golf balls, different candies and treats and personalized water bottles Thursday before the wedding. Friday morning was a whirlwind of messengers taking them to the hotels.

This is a ballet in itself. Zella had a certain way she liked things to travel a certain way and wanted to make sure that the tissue paper and the presentation was the same upon arrival as when it left her office. Every messenger that came to the door got the lecture.

"Now, listen to me. I want you to make sure that the tissue paper looks exactly like this when you arrive." The messenger would nod and start to take the package. She would pull it back. "When you arrive at the hotel, I want a picture of this bag on the counter of the hotel with the logo in the background texted to me. You have my number here," Zella would point to the paperwork accompanying the bag that had the hotel name, address, phone number and contact name at the hotel, as well as her cell phone number and the note that said text this number with a picture.

If they didn't send a text message within a certain amount of time, she got on the phone with the dispatch office and would holler until she got the picture texted to her. Or she would call the hotel and check in for them to send the picture of the bag that arrived. Gift bags are serious business. Almost as serious as the actual event.

Friday was the rehearsal dinner, which was at the restaurant in the Museum of Modern Art. Zella had told me I would help her run the event.

It was a very warm March evening, and the dinner was held in the sculpture garden. MoMA's in-house restaurant did all the setup for the evening, and we were there as a backup. Square tables were scattered down the middle with eight people sitting at each one. Candles were all over, floating in the water and on the tables. Unlike the first wedding I helped with there were no seating charts, and I was there to... actually, I didn't know.

We had gone through the run of the evening, and Zella had mentioned that I should attend in case the family needed anything. I didn't realize that Zella had intended for me, and only me, to be the babysitter. She only mentioned this after I arrived in a nice black dress. And although she had told me about the ring bearer and flower girl upon our arrival, I still don't know if she knew that there would be six children, all under the age of seven, at this dinner.

"They probably won't be here long, as they're children. So just do what you can. Take them into the gallery or whatever," Zella said, flipping her hand over her shoulder motioning toward the rest of the museum.

Parents of the children swore that they were happy to watch their children, but when Zella said that it was no problem and volunteered me, the children were handed over to me faster than you can say, "go." I was shooed out, feeling a bit like Mother Goose leading a line of small children, all holding hands, out into the gallery where priceless art hung on the walls. Which was a mistake.

Small children are tactile. And don't know they aren't allowed to touch things in museums. Even with large security guards all around and ropes at waist height to keep them back from the paintings. More than once a gallery security guard came over to tell me to make sure the children weren't touching things. Mortified and pulled in seven different directions, I did the best I could until the three-year-old flower girl punched the six-year-old ring bearer and I had to carry him back to his parents, dragging the chain of hand holding children behind me. His father took him and announced apologetically to the entire dinner party of thirty that his child was usually well behaved and seemed to accuse that I made his child cry. This evening was going spectacularly.

The rest of the children decided to run squealing around the sculpture garden. Parents didn't seem to care. At one point, I gave up and hid, um I mean, went and used the bathroom.

When I emerged, Zella suggested that I might want to take the children out into the lobby while speeches were given. I sighed.

"Aren't you a nanny? Don't you take care of children all the time?" she asked with a tone of motherly scorn.

"Yes, but he's—"

"I don't care. We are here to assist the client. You take those children. Keep them quiet while we have toasts. Then you can come back."

Taking all but the crying ring bearer out to the lobby, the only place we were now allowed, I sat down and sighed while the children played a dizzying game of tag.

"Hey, Natalie," a voice I recognized cut through the dervish of children screaming.

Looking up, I saw the curly haired, handsome caterwaiter from my first wedding.

"Hey…" I was totally blanking on his name, plus I was in a daze from watching all of these children. I never had this many around unless it was a birthday party and even then, I wasn't alone.

"It's me, Matt. We worked the event at The Dance Lab together?"

"Right, Matt. Hey. Nice to see you." One of the kids had laid down and was rolling back and forth on the floor. "Hey, kiddo, maybe don't roll on the floor," I started to walk over to him and tried to pick him up. But he screamed like I was trying to kill him.

"Eh, let him stay down there. Dirt won't kill him."

"Right," I said, looking up at Matt. He was just a little taller than me. Not Sam tall, but he was a good height. And his eyes were a grayish blue. Wait. Why was I looking at his eyes? "What are you doing here?" I asked.

"I was helping with the bar tonight. I've worked at so many places around town, a lot of them will call me in if they're short or need extra people for an event."

"Ah. So, you're here for the–"

"Rehearsal dinner," he said, grabbing a kid who had just tried to run past him. "Where are you going, princess?" he asked the little girl who was now in his arms wearing a fluffy pink dress.

"I want to see my mommy," the little girl said.

"Well, did you know that Miss Natalie was just going to tell us a story? You don't want to miss story time, do you?"

Glaring at him like he was insane, I started to shake my head like I couldn't do it. Levi was an older kid. I wasn't used to little ones.

"Why don't you get all of your friends to sit down in a circle right by the bench over there, and Miss Natalie will be there just as soon as everyone is sitting." He put her down and she raced off. "Just think of a plot of a movie and tell

127

them that story. I'd leave out anything super gory, though. Kids never react well to that, plus they'll tell their parents."

"Right. Thanks?"

"I have to get going, I'm headed to serve for another party. But I just wanted to say hi. And your hair looks great," he raised his arm bent at the elbow with his hand up and waved it slightly even though he was only two feet from me.

"Hi," I said and grinned a goofy grin at him. What was I doing? I had a boyfriend. But grinning wasn't flirting. I was fine. "Well, I'll get back to the kids. Thanks."

"Sure. See you around." He started to walk back out of the lobby toward the restaurant, but then turned back. "Oh hey, they're just serving dessert now, so if you can keep these guys occupied for about twenty more minutes, you should be fine to go back in then."

"Thanks," I said. Which didn't seem to be enough.

I shook my head and went to tell the kids a story. It lasted for all of three minutes. Then one little girl got wiggly, so the little boy next to her told her to stop, and all the others turned. They all then started asking me questions about the story, and then were up and running around again. I tried to get them to play Simon Says. Then tried getting them to all pretend to be airplanes or dinosaurs.

And then tragedy struck.

Someone found the rack of pamphlets. At first, they were just pulling them out of the rack and pretending to read them. I really tried to stop it, but give the child a piece of paper, and they'll make it a toy and then destroy it. Trying to divert them, I told them they could choose one each and they had to treat the pamphlets like books. But then one child "accidentally" ripped one of the pages and wanted another one. Like dominos falling, they all started ripping theirs, so they could have another. Two of them started squatting on the floor and ripping up the torn pieces and throwing them in the air pretending it was snowing. Then all of the children were shredding paper as much as they could and tossing it in the air. On the other hand, it was good we weren't still trying to touch every painting. One parent came looking for her daughter.

"Wow looks like you all are having fun," the mom who looked to be about my age said.

"We are," I said, trying to sound positive through gritted teeth.

"Well, dinner is over, so I think you can probably start to head back now if you want. I think most people are starting to wind down, and head out. Big day tomorrow."

"Don't I know it," I said.

I couldn't be sure, but I think she tsked when she turned around and walked away. Looking around, I was glad I could get away without cleaning this up.

"Come on everyone, grab hands, and let's be a snake back to find your parents," I said, sounding like I should be on a children's television show.

Following my suggestion, they all ran around shrieking and then eventually all linked hands and we left the area. Glancing back, my eyes grew wide. It looked like it had snowed all over the lobby. There wasn't an intact pamphlet to be seen.

When the last of the children was reclaimed, I realized I was exhausted Running around in a tight black dress after children isn't easy. I didn't even want to know how my hair looked, but I knew it was atrocious, because Zella looked at me once and pursed her lips in a dissatisfied way. But Matt would have said something about it, wouldn't he. Wait, why was I thinking of Matt? And why would he have said anything about my hair. I shook my head as one of the dads walked over to me. He had one of the biggest mischief makers slung over his shoulder, fast asleep. Of course, why is it that they fall asleep and are perfect angels when their parents are near, but terrors when they're not in sight.

"Natalie, right? You watched the kids?"

"Yes, and it looks like someone had a really good time." I nodded to the lump on his shoulder and hoped to reinforce that I took good care of the children tonight.

"I hope he wasn't too much trouble. He's at the age where he will just destroy anything," the dad said and chuckled, a knowing look crossed his eyes. So, he knew that his kid was the one who started the war on the pamphlets.

I could play this in so many ways. If I complained, he might take pity on me and then give a good review to Zella. I could also tell him exactly what happened, that his angelic son was the one who made a gigantic mess in the lobby of one of the most prestigious museums in the world and tried to touch several Picassos and a Monet. But really, what good would that do. Or if I said his child was an angel, and I enjoyed taking care of him, you know, lied to his face, then this dad could have a little bit of relief from the pain that raising this kid was already.

I took the high road. "It's always an adventure with kids his age."

"Adventure," he repeated. "That is a nice way to put it. Here," he said, handing me something hidden in his palm between his thumb and fingers. "Thanks again and have a great night." He turned and walked away and back to his wife and put his arm around her waist as she finished a conversation.

Thinking that Sam and I would be like that someday a smile lifted the corner of my mouth. We had recently started talking about the future and kids. It was a long way off but couldn't be too long. We were both getting older. Oof, and I felt old after running after six children for the last four hours. I shook my head. Then I looked down at my hand. A fifty-dollar bill.

Suddenly I was nervous. I looked all around, and no one was looking at me. Maybe no one noticed. Was this allowed? I didn't know. But I also wanted the money. Heaven knows I could use it. Looking around again, standing in a dark corner, I was generally unnoticed. Zella was talking to the father of the bride, probably confirming any details for tomorrow, or possibly just schmoozing. I slipped the money in the pocket of my dress and said nothing to anyone.

After all the guests had left, I ran into Zella at the coat check.

"Everyone is gone," I said, stating the obvious in a similar chipper voice I had used to get the children to follow me earlier.

"Yes," she purred. "And what a lovely gathering, don't you think? I always love the food here."

"Oh, well I–"

"Spit it out, Natalie," Zella said as she shrugged on a fur collared tan coat.

"I didn't have a chance to eat. I was with the children the entire evening."

"And you didn't eat with them?"

Zella didn't have children, or if she did, they were grown and out of the house and she hadn't been around young children in a very long time. "I was watching six children. And by the time I got to the same nuggets and fries as the kids, they were cold, and the kids were up and running around."

"Well, it's a good thing I made sure they wrapped this up for you," she raised a clear bag with a white box in it.

131

My confused look spurred her to roll her eyes and explain, "I had a meal boxed for you. It won't be the same, as it's now cold, but you'll make it work." Zella dismissed me with, "Make sure your hair is fixed for tomorrow, and don't forget to wear comfortable shoes. The tuxedo arrived for you, right?"

"Right. It did and it fits perfectly." I felt the desire to fawn thanks all over her but thought better of it when I saw her pinched face and said, "Thanks, Zella. I'll see you tomorrow."

"Oh, and Natalie, how much did he tip you?"

"What?" I asked, knowing exactly what she was referring to, but playing dumb, unsure if I should admit I got a tip or not.

"I saw the father put something in your hand, and then your hand went in your pocket."

"Oh, well, um…" I sheepishly trailed off. I made a split-second decision that the job was worth more than the tip in my pocket, so I reached my hand in, pulled out the bill, and unfolding it, handed it to Zella thinking it was not mine to keep. She pursed her lips and then looked me in the eyes.

"It's yours. You earned it. I just wanted to know how much they gave you."

"Really?" I squeaked like I did nothing to deserve it, and still held the bill out in front of me.

"Yes, dear. Put it in your pocket and go home. Treat yourself to something." She started to walk away. "By the way, you handled that well," she looked approvingly at me. Her phone beeped, "My car is here, I'm leaving. Can I drop you anywhere?"

"I'm in the other direction," I stumbled over my words as I refolded the bill and put it in my pocket.

"Well, then maybe you should treat yourself to a cab home with that money." And with that, she swept out of the room and left the building.

Grabbing my coat, I contemplated the cab, but decided to take the subway instead. It wasn't that late, and I was already on the east side. The train might even be faster than a cab. Curious, I lifted the top of the box of food and grinned. I got out my phone and texted Sam.

On my way home. I have a surprise.

I peered into the bag again. It was probably enough food to feed all of the people who lived on the floor of my building. I had planned to share it with Sam.

He quickly responded:

Sorry babe, out with Nick and some other people from work. Need me?

Feeling sad but proud that he was out again networking, I responded:

Nah! I was just bringing home yummy food and wanted to share. I'll leave it for you in the fridge.

We texted some more back and forth as I rode the train home. I told him about the insane kids and how beautiful the evening was. I left out the part about running into Matt, because I hadn't mentioned him before, plus, it was probably random that I saw him again. Sam reminded me that he had to be up early the next day, and I reminded him that I would probably be home super late again, with a wedding the next day. I decided that I would make a point to see Sam in the morning. Once inside our door and my shoes were kicked off, I told him I was safe at home. He wished me a good night and the texting ceased. I gorged myself on my MoMA feast and contemplated what to do with my fifty dollars.

Chapter Sixteen

When Sam's alarm went off, I was up like I was an early bird. He had early morning classes on Saturdays, and in the afternoon, he led a cycling group on long bike trips out in the Berkshires. Usually, I didn't see him on Saturdays at all, unless I got up with him. Both the motivation to see Sam and my nerves for today's wedding had me up and going early.

He was already in the shower. I zipped to the kitchen, started coffee, and got out some eggs, cheese and spinach to make omelets. I wasn't the best cook, but I knew my way around eggs. I meant that to sound a lot cooler than it came out. And speaking of coming out, by the time Sam had gotten out of the shower and gotten dressed, I had coffee and omelets on the table, and a green smoothie in a to-go mug for Sam to take to the gym.

"Babe, this smells great," he said as he came over and gave me a kiss on the forehead. I had leaned my face up for a kiss on the lips but didn't let it bother me that he opted differently.

"I figured, you do so much of the cooking, I thought I would this morning," I said with a note of flirtation in my voice. Even though I was still in my pajamas, a tank top with spaghetti straps and sleep shorts, I did a bit of a sassy walk to my chair.

"Well look who is feeling herself today," Sam said. "And I appreciate the repayment, but you know you don't have to do that." He smiled at me. And then he said, "I know you're probably nervous about today, but you're going to be great."

Air seemed to leave my chest as I sat, and he said this. "Do you really think so?"

"You've got this," he said as he dug into his omelet.

"It just feels like there's so much pressure. These people spend a lot of money, Sam. A lot. And I feel like I don't fit in."

"Well, that makes sense, because you don't," he said, and then looked up from his plate to see my appalled face. "I mean we're the people that get paid to help these people to live the vision of their lives that they want. We are the people who make dreams come true. We're not supposed to fit in." I frowned again. "But someday, we'll rise above where they are and people like us will help us to be bigger and greater."

"I think I follow that," I said. "But I would still like to be a part of it. Like this dinner last night. I felt like I was not only an outsider for the people who are attending the wedding, but also outside of even our team. I was off with these little kids the whole time–"

"I love kids. I can't wait to have some of my own," Sam said, looking off dreamily as if he could see a picket fence and children running around inside it.

"Yeah," I said. After last night, I didn't want to think about children. It was a lot to deal with so many at once. I had forgotten how wonderful Levi was now that he was a teenager. After last night, I was a little terrified to have children of my own. That wasn't a conversation to have with Sam now, especially since he was shoving the last bite in his mouth as he stood. "Do you have to go already?" I asked leaning back in my chair to see the clock on the microwave.

"Nick and I are meeting up before class."

"You're seeing a lot of each other lately," I said.

He pursed his lips and looked like he was going to say something, but then walked over to grab his bag and slung it over his head to have it cross his body.

"Not that I mind," I said quickly jumping up and grabbing the smoothie bottle that was still on the table. "I'm sure it's good for you. And your career." Smiling brightly, I held out the bottle.

"Yeah. Yeah, it is." He smiled but rubbed the back of his neck as he reached out and took the smoothie. Something was going through his mind, but he didn't like to share anything until he was good and ready, so I just smiled back. I'm sure he was just going through some work pressure like I was.

"Have a great day. I love you."

He reached for the door handle and opened the door. "Love you, too. You'll be amazing." He said as he walked through the door, "Even if you don't feel like you fit in," he winked as he closed the door behind him.

Thinking through what just happened, I walked back to the table and took a bite of my omelet. My phone dinged. Zella.

Natalie make sure you've got printed out copies of the itinerary when you arrive today.

It was not even 8am and already she was texting about today. I wasn't due to report to the hotel until 1pm, so I finished my omelet while reviewing the itinerary for today one more time and then took a shower.

Thursday Zella had messengered over one of her signature suits. She had me send in my measurements, and her tailor made me a black suit with a tuxedo stripe down the pants. The jacket was fitted, but then also had sort of a peplum flare to it that made it very flattering. It fit like a glove. I hoped the tux made me fit in more. Accompanying the suit were several different colored pocket squares that looked like ruffles of color. There were some traditional wedding colors, white, blush pink, gold, and silver. All of the girls from Tremaine Events would wear a pocket square that was in the color scheme of the wedding to designate who we were. This week we would all wear the green to match with the green and white golf theme of the wedding.

I watched a little TV and tried to relax for a bit. But ended up pacing my apartment and reading the itinerary over a few more times until I couldn't even see it anymore, I got dressed in the suit with my green pocket ruffle and went off to one of the fanciest hotels in town to wine and dine the New York Elite.

All the rags to riches movies where a girl meets a millionaire and is whisked off Cinderella style, fed my intrigue to see inside one of the most magnificent hotels on Fifth Avenue. One that only millionaires and celebrities could actually afford on a nightly basis. But here I was, on the subway in a pseudo-tuxedo with hair, makeup and nails lacquered more than ever before. I was more nervous about this than any opening night of a show I could remember, probably because more than anything tonight I wanted to prove to Zella that I could do this job, I could fit in. Despite my low bank balance, my cheap clothing, and the fact that I wasn't born into an elite class. More than anything, I needed to prove that I was the right choice.

Chapter Seventeen

Y ou know those times where you try to remember everything, so you recall it later? I attempted to do that. In the movies when a main character walks into a beautiful setting, the music swells, possibly a choir sings reverently, and the camera turns to the main character who pauses to take it all in and to regain her breath, that was me stepping into the hotel. The beauty was slightly hazy and sparkly with wonder as people rushed around.

Honestly, I expected people to break out in a musical number. And was disappointed they hadn't by the time I crossed the hotel lobby. But no matter. This majesty. This day. It was better than the first wedding I worked, because the reality set in. My job is to make the beauty happen for a bride making her wedding day a magical reality. Well, technically it's Zella's job. And lighting and decor designers translate the ideas of the bride and Zella to their crew of at least forty people. And the band and the catering team make it all a delight of the senses. And the hotel staff for keeping up the beauty of the—well, you know what I mean.

Today was more of a rush than the first wedding I worked just a few weeks ago. From the moment I stepped into The Pierre Hotel until the end of the night, I didn't stop moving. The whole day was a whirlwind.

My first stop when I arrived at the hotel was The Cotillion Room, and it was a work of art. It looked like heaven had been recreated in a frothy display of flowers and candles. If you look it up on the internet, you'll see a picture of what I mean. It was stunning. No one else was in the room. So I just stood there taking it all in. I took a few pictures of this fairytale of a room. Social media required it.

Feeling a little self-conscious, standing alone in the beautiful room, I moved on. I took a quick self-tour, viewing the Garden Foyer where the massive, mirrored cocktail bar was being set up with ice sculptures to hold shrimp as large as a small child's fist would reside. I also saw the opulence of The Grand Ballroom. The decor in this room was a work in progress. It was meant to look like large trees were popping up from the tables. Slightly worried that not all of the tables were popped open yet, let alone set with tableware and floral decor, I mentioned something to a passing designer.

"Don't worry ma'am. We have plenty of time. No one is in here until eight." He pointed to a few tables. "We did a few to start to experiment and give the team examples to work from. Plenty of time to get it all together."

"Right," I said, still unsure that all the work that needed to be done would get finished on time.

My phone buzzed with a message from Zella.

Natalie come to bridal suite when you arrive.

I texted back:

On my way. Was just checking on what was happening in The Grand Ballroom.

When I arrived in the suite, the bride was incredibly relaxed and happy. One of her bridesmaids was not. Apparently, she thought she was on the marriage track but had a breakup two weeks ago. She was disgruntled and drinking heavily. Her irrational behavior flared when I entered the room. I called the front desk and had coffee and some pastries sent up. Sneaking off to the second bathroom with the sloppy bridesmaid, I let her cry on my shoulder until I got a text from Zella.

Did you order coffee and pastries?!?

The angry tone from Zella terrified me, but I knew I needed to get this gal in the right headspace. Not only so the bride could have her perfect day, but for this gal, too. I had been in her spot too many times, rejected and feeling like I was unloved.

As I went out to grab the sobering foods, I texted Zella back.

I have a drunk bridesmaid in the bathroom.

Only focused on my mission to help this bridesmaid, I didn't look at my phone for the next twenty minutes. I fed her coffee, two pastries and some aspirin. A knock on the door just as we were about to leave made both of us jump.

"Just a minute," I hollered.

"Natalie, it's me. I'm missing a bridesmaid and I'm wondering if she's in there?" Zella's voice was sweet and motherly.

Looking at the bridesmaid, I gave her a look and raised my eyebrows in a question. She shook her head and stood up, with a small bobble.

"I'm in here," the bridesmaid said as she started to walk to the door. She turned back toward me. "Thank you," she said in a whisper as she opened the door and walked out.

Watching the bridesmaid walk into the other room then turning back to me with one eyebrow raised, Zella sized me up. Gathering the coffee mug and the remnants of the pastries, I stood up and walked toward Zella.

"Well," she said, crossing her arms and giving me a look like a crocodile, "I see you're good to have around. Why don't you get all of these women rounded up and down for photos."

Smiling, I nodded as I passed her and walked into the room where the bridesmaids were getting ready. "Alright ladies," I said, "Who's ready for photographs?"

After zipping up a few dresses, and buckling a few shoes, I assisted in getting all of the ladies, their flowers, purses, and personal items downstairs to The Rotunda for photos.

During pictures before the ceremony, the flower girl had to go to the bathroom, so I was elected to assist as we had become best friends the night before in the art gallery.

The night previous, none of the children had to go to the bathroom with my assistance. I didn't realize that I had to do everything for her, including pulling down and pulling up the tights. Putting on the shoes, which she kicked off to sit on the potty. Helping her wash her hands. Helping her dry off her dress once she decided to play in the water. Halting her tears when I turned off the water. Somehow distracting her from the water and getting her in a joyful, clean, and dressed state before leaving the bathroom. And then returning a happy and empty child back for photos. Between the bridesmaid and the flower girl, I felt like I was really making a difference in this day.

The ceremony apparently went off without a hitch—we didn't watch it. Instead we were sent to check on the reception setup progress. I would come to learn that reception setup was never entirely ready, and we would eventually build into the itinerary that the room had to be ready half an hour before the reception was to start—as to allow the bride and groom to get an advanced look, or to allow them to practice their first dance, or just to make sure that if anything went wrong, we had a half an hour cushion to fix it. Panicked but trying to control it when I told AM as everyone called her, that the room wasn't ready.

She laughed. "The room is never ready until right before we need it to be. Breathe, Natalie. All will work out."

AM had started out as an intern for Zella, and now worked during the week for Floral Elegance as one of their sales and design department team. AM was the same AM of my to do list a few weeks prior—and we had briefly chatted on the phone a couple of times, but I had only met her today. She was a lovely calming force and seemed to own the earth mother aura she exuded. It truly made sense that she worked in flowers. AM had worked "what seemed like a zillion events" with Zella over the last few years. When she wanted something more full time, and on the other side of the event world, Zella introduced AM to Katarina the owner of Floral Elegance. They apparently hit it off, and the rest was history. Wanting to earn extra money and to keep on Zella's good side, AM worked occasionally for Tremaine Events as she was needed.

I was truly glad she was at the event today to hold my hand through the wilderness that was a wedding since Amanda wasn't. When that much money is at stake, it puts so much more pressure on things—and this wedding had over half a million in pressure and dollars weighing on it.

Zella wasn't surprised or concerned that the ballroom wasn't ready. She went off to flirt with the Maître'd, a lovely man named Michael who was most definitely not interested, but flirting was the same as networking in this business.

Another lesson I learned, we, Tremaine Events, were the official client. I messed this up a few times before I understood it. I kept being asked if I wanted anything or if I needed anything—and was asked if everything was "to the client's satisfaction." Thinking that everyone was referring to the bride and her parents, I kept trying to figure this out and was unsure what they liked or wanted because I had only met a week prior.

Thankfully later, the magical Maître'd Michael cleared that up. He came over to ask if the client needed anything. From my corner of the ballroom, I looked at the bride and groom happily dancing in the middle of all of their friends and family. I turned to Michael and told him that the bride and groom looked happy and fine.

He chuckled, "No, my dear," he winked at me. I thought that maybe I had wrongly thought of Zella before and maybe it was Michael who was the flirt and not her. "You are 'the client', well you and Tremaine Events. We work for you for the bride and the groom. So, anything you wish, is my command." He smiled a sterling smile at me.

"Well, I am a bit hungry," I admitted. It had been almost twelve hours since I ate—because of nerves, breakfast didn't go down so well, so I didn't stop for anything else along the way. I had some almonds in my purse downstairs in coat check, but I didn't want to leave to go get them.

"Ah, well," he said, "We will be serving all vendors in The Regency Room shortly. Just as soon as we finish serving out dinner here. Should only be about five more minutes."

"Great, thanks!" I said with a little too much exuberance. Michael winked again as he walked away. Somehow, he managed to be caring and schmoozy at the same time. Michael would come to be one of my all-time favorite people in the wedding world.

Zella came to me almost exactly five minutes later. AM was with her. I was scanning the room, watching the bridesmaid who was still drinking too much, and the rest of the crowd, just in case anything tragic happened.

"Ok, girls, who wants to go eat?" Zella asked both of us.

"I'm ok for now, if you want to go first," AM said to both of us.

"Great. Natalie, let's go chat." I don't know why I felt like I was in trouble as Zella led us to a wood paneled Regency Room, to find that under silver rounded covers there were choices of a Branzino or a Filet Mignon. I went for the Filet.

"Good choice," Zella said as she sat down in front of another Filet. "Oh, and before I forget, here is your gratuity for the night from the client," she said as she handed me seventy-five dollars. "Put it away, and don't talk about it."

Folding the bills, I slipped them into my pocket, and marveled. I looked down at my plate and at the table and wondered how life could get better? Cash in my pocket and I was about to eat one of the most beautifully presented pieces of meat I had ever seen.

The table was beautifully set for eight, with a bottle of red wine, a bottle of white wine and two water bottles in front of us. Currently we were the only ones in the room. I started to reach for a bottle that was in the middle of the table.

"Natalie, I don't allow my people to drink at a wedding. Ever." With the last word she caught my eye, and her look seared into me.

"Noted, Zella." I said soberly. To try to cut the tension that I felt, I prattled, "I don't know that I would ever want to drink at a wedding anyway. There is too much to be ready for. I just don't want to put myself in a position where I wouldn't be ready. Even though I can totally hold my liquor—"

"Albert—" Zella oozed in interruption as the photographer came through the door by himself. "Who is your delightful assistant this evening?" I went back to my filet and shoved a bite in my mouth. I guess our conversation was over. As they chatted, I filled my glass with water, and continued to eat awkwardly.

"Oh, that is Violet. We are trying her out. She is an Ohio transplant and has a lot of promise. Owned her own company back in Ohio, but I'm trying to get her up to speed with the New York feel," Albert said both jovially and condescendingly at the same time. Violet and I had briefly met earlier in the evening during the family photos with the whole flower girl restroom situation, and she seemed lovely. I guess we would see what kind of photos she turned out.

They continued to shoot the breeze, and I had finished all of the food on my plate and threw down three glasses of water—I had not had anything to drink all day either, and was parched. AM came rushing into the room, just as I was tipping back the last of my water.

"Zella—oh Albert! There you are. They're about to do toasts—do you want me to tell the band to go ahead, or hold them so you can finish dinner?"

Zella looked at Albert and said, "No, we are done here AM, you can tell them to start." Albert gave Zella an accepting look even though his plate was only half finished. Apparently, I wasn't the only one Zella moved around like a chess piece.

"Sure, I'm finished. Thank you AM," Albert said as he stood and walked toward the door back to the ballroom. "No food for the wicked," I heard him mumble just before he walked out the door.

"AM," I called after her as she was starting to follow Albert, "I'll go. You can stay and eat. I am finished." As I started to stand, I suddenly became very aware of Zella's presence again. I turned to her and sheepishly said, "If that's ok with you Zella."

"Fine, do what you will," she stretched out the words.

Feeling relief, I started to sprint to the door and was reminded I didn't have to run by AM's look as we crossed paths.

"I saved a Branzino for you because I know how hard you're trying to lose weight on that special diet," I heard Zella ooze to AM with the same amount of schmooze as she gave Albert when he walked in the door. They were chattering in seconds of AM sitting down.

The rest of the night flew. Speeches and cake cutting went off without a hitch, and before I knew it the photographers were saying goodbye, and the band was playing it's last song. Guests were streaming out of the ballroom toward coat check, and by the time I ran a handful of gifts and envelopes up to the bridal suite, it was a ghost town.

Back in the ballroom AM and Zella were talking. Zella gave her a hug, and AM said goodnight to me as she walked out of the room. Members of the décor crew were starting to strip the room of the large vases. Zella started walking around and taking all of the green and white Parrot Tulips out of the arrangements and had a pile as large as a pageant queen's award by the time I reached her.

"Natalie," Zella trilled, "is everything done? Did you collect everything? And is everyone gone?"

"Um, yup," I said not so confidentially, even though I knew that I had collected everything, finished my tasks and all of the guests had left. Then, as if my self-doubt willed it to happen, a befuddled guest returned to the ballroom— apparently his wife had misplaced a wrap, and he was sent back to find it.

"Not a problem, my assistant Natalie will help you," Zella said. "I am headed out, but if you have any problems, text me." And with that, she departed.

Searching for almost thirty minutes, with the help of the décor crew and Michael, we finally found the wrap in a corner where the photo booth was. The guest must have taken it off for a photo and never went back for it. The gentleman not only thanked me but also slipped me ten dollars. Michael winked at me.

"Well deserved. You are great at this."

"Really? Thanks, I was worried," I replied, still stunned at the ten dollars in my hand. "Here," I offered the bill to Michael.

"No! You don't have to do that."

"Ok, well, I have a five, if you want to split it," I said reaching in my pocket for the other tip I had received that evening.

"Nah," Michael said walking over towards the bar. "You keep it. They took good care of me tonight." Michael reached over the bar, grabbed two glasses and the open bottle of red that was sitting there. "Drink?"

Zella's searing look and warning that we don't drink on the job flew into my mind. "Um, we… aren't supposed to drink on the job. So, even though I'd love a drink, I think I— no thank you. Not tonight."

"Are you sure? She's gone," he offered the bottle again, but I shook my head. "Well, maybe another time," Michael said over his shoulder as he walked away with the bottle toward his office.

It was probably a $400 dollar bottle of wine that I was missing out on, but my job was more important to me. I'd rather have almost a hundred dollars cash in my pocket, and my stomach full of delicious food, then tempt fate with a taste of an expensive wine, I reasoned with myself.

"Meees. Meees."

I turned to find a short Hispanic man standing next to me with a huge bunch of white hydrangeas and roses. He handed them to me.

"Meees. AnnaMaria said to give-a-you some flowers. I have to go to de truck now but wanted to geeve them to you before I go." He smiled a huge grin at me.

"Thank you." I was taken aback. No, I was stunned. They were heavy, and there must have been at least thirty stems in my hand. Fresh flowers have always meant a lot to me. When I was little and stayed home sick, sniffling on the sofa in the living room, I watched soap operas with my mother. The fancy, rich people whose homes we got to see always had fresh flowers. I had told myself when I got rich enough, I would have fresh flowers in my house every day. So, whenever I could I always loved to have them around. And I was just chased down to be given probably five hundred dollars worth of stems. I was giddy. I was literally high on flowers.

Taking one last look around, I said a quiet goodbye to The Pierre, and its strong opulence. I said a quiet prayer that I would be back here soon and headed to the street. A doorman not only opened the door for me but waved his hand and as if he conjured a magic spell, a cab suddenly appeared at the curb for me. I climbed inside, protective of all of the buds in my hand. I settled my takeaway box of cake next to me and stretched back in the seat while I gave the cross streets to my apartment. I laid my head back and closed my eyes, wanting to be in my own bed. I lifted my head, and looked at my lap, and took a deep whiff of the flowers laying in my lap. Smiling, I texted AM.

Thanks for the flowers.

I sat back in the cab and relished my joy. It was as if I was somehow queen, and a movie star, and it was my birthday, and I had just solved world hunger. My feet were tired, and I was exhausted. My eyes burned from being in my contacts for so long. And I was starving. But I felt on top of the world. If this was how I would be spending my weekends, all of Zella's torment during the week would definitely be worth it. Or so I thought.

Chapter Eighteen

About a month after the golf wedding, I finally got a bat mitzvah. I mean it wasn't mine—we worked one. However, working on this event, I feel like I was the one who became a woman.

Apparently, this bat mitzvah was for the youngest child of a family that Zella had worked with several times. Not only had she planned the wedding for the parents, but she had planned the mitzvahs for the other children. They were allegedly masterful creations. This family came from old money, so nothing was off limits. The catch was they wanted something more creative than all their friends.

And if you know anything about bar mitzvah season, all of the kids go to all of the mitzvahs. They compare them. And thirteen-year-olds are mean. Zella had to not only outdo what she had done for them in the past, but she had to go above and beyond anything seen in the entire current New York mitzvah community. Every year mitzvahs got fancier and more extensive. There was a degree of one-upmanship that was just insane.

How she came up with a circus and hip-hop-themed bat mitzvah was beyond me. And I think up some crazy ideas. It was also top secret. Planning for this event had begun before I joined Zella's team, but I got the joy of the entire thing. Not only did I need to sign a non-disclosure agreement for this event, but Zella told me I couldn't share any of the details with anyone. Not even Sam.

The event was held at The Rainbow Room and was to be spectacular. They had rigged ropes and hoops up on the ceiling to allow silk dancers to drop from the ceiling and spin above everyone's heads throughout the night. Acrobats were hired to be waiters. They would do handstands or balancing tricks while holding trays of food.

There were also human tables: people dressed in costumes with large round flat surfaces at their midsection with food placed all around them. A DJ was hired to play music, but at some point during the night, about an hour in, the guest of honor would walk down the Rainbow Room stairs to surprise the guests.

There was a B-list hip-hop singer named Jazzmin we had contracted to perform. A surprise for the girl-who-was-becoming-a-woman. Jazzmin was a difficult person to procure, even though she wasn't even that well known around the world. She was apparently in high demand. The whole thing was a pain in the ass. There were so many contracts and liability waivers. Not to mention the needs of the singer. She wanted five black hand towels, tropical Skittles and Cool Ranch Doritos in her dressing room.

Zella had put me in charge of the talent because she said that I would be able to communicate best because of my theatrical background. Basically, she didn't want to have to deal with their managers, and if something went wrong, I would be the scapegoat.

My confidence was high coming from the Pierre wedding, so I told myself I could handle this. I could book an obscure musician who was already on tour. But the managers were a pain to get in touch with. They weren't brick-and-mortar managers, apparently, and didn't keep office hours. Or have assistants to help them. Or reply to anything. I emailed... I called and left messages... I sent texts... no response. Days went by and I was getting no results. Sam suggested I reach out to them via social media, and it wasn't until I slid into her DMs that I finally got a

151

response. Once I had made official contact with all of the managers, I realized I could totally do this.

Zella was handling all of the décor and food. She had hired an outside company for the circus performers. Things seemed to be progressing smoothly and we had even started working on other events that were upcoming. Ten days before the event, things started to fall apart.

A blizzard hit Colorado, a day before the bat mitzvah. Jazzmin had to delay her tour because she was snowbound, and of course, she was in Denver before flying to New York to do this gig. They were hoping to get her out but weren't sure if she would still be able to make her appearance for us because she needed two days of rest between each show.

"Tell them that she can rest while trapped in the blizzard," Zella shouted at me. "I don't care what she needs, I have a contract with her, and she will be here for this bat mitzvah if I have to pull strings and get her flown out myself."

Having almost three months now under my belt working with Zella, my skin had thickened a bit, and at times I could turn off her tone. It was like calluses had formed around my nervous system. Although she still scared me, I had become more accustomed to the yelling and complete shifts of personality in mere seconds. The Grinch and Miranda Priestly had nothing on Zella.

Although the snowed-in songstress was a terror, it wasn't the biggest frustration for this event. Four days before the event, Victoria, the mother of the bat mitzvah girl, decided that the cake wasn't right. If they were having a hip-hop circus theme, the cake needed to be more than just a five-tier, five-flavored creation with elaborate designs on it. It needed to hold the singer.

The cake already cost seventeen dollars a slice and was planned to feed four hundred of their closest friends and relatives—don't do the math, just know it was already a seven-thousand-dollar cake. The thing was a colossus of ridiculous proportions. I was morbidly curious how much more it would cost to have it large enough to envelop a person.

When Zella got off the phone after talking Victoria down from the edge about Jazzmin being snowed in but that we had it under control, she sat back and took a deep breath. It was rare that I saw Zella in a mode of self-calming. And it wasn't even a Monday. I took the moment to imagine her in a yoga class, which she swore she took three times a week. That yogi had to be the most patient person in the world. I was sure Zella micromanaged him.

After a few deep breaths, her phone buzzed.

"Shit! I was supposed to be at a tasting for the Marshalls," Zella jumped up and ran into the other room. She ripped off her workout clothing that she was still in from her yoga practice as she went. Muffled yelling was coming from her direction, so I grabbed my notebook and walked to the door, turning myself out to face the office. She had converted the room into one large walk-in closet. Tons of clothes hung from racks in the small room.

I had learned to get close so I could hear her and take notes. But I also learned to face out. I had seen her now naked or semi-dressed multiple times. She hadn't ever cared but would launch into stories about her different plastic surgeries, or issues with her latest wax or procedure, as she stood there in a see-through lace bra with her nipples winking at me, or with her thong-clad ass pointed in my direction. Although I wasn't a prude, I just didn't need to watch her change. I wasn't super comfortable with the nudity

153

of my boss let alone the conversations it would spark. Turning my back avoided so much.

"Natalie! I need you to call Denise at Beauty In Cake. I wrote notes on my desk that Victoria gave me. She wants a donut cake so someone can stand in the middle. Who needs to fucking stand in the middle of a cake? It's a fucking cake!"

Zella swore like a sailor when she was really upset. She spit directions out at me, and then suddenly pushed past me, she sprayed perfume and some of the spray hit me. I now too smelled of Coco Chanel. Snatching her purse from the desk she walked barefoot to the door. As she opened it, she slid her heels on gracefully and then lifted her phone to her mouth to demand the phone call a car.

"Natalie, I expect this all will be fixed this afternoon," she said as if I were the cause of all of the issues.

The door clicked behind her, and I felt my shoulders relax. I picked up my phone and started to text Amanda about the craziness but saw that Sam had sent a text.

Hey babe! How is your day going?

I sighed. My heart leapt a little.

Eh. I am still having blizzard issues. And now I have to have a cake with a hole in the middle the size of a person.

I waited for a few moments hoping he wasn't in a class and would respond right away. Nothing happened, so I flipped over the screen to dial for Beauty In Cake. As autodial took over, I walked to the desk for the notes Zella took. Her writing was atrocious and wasn't easy to read.

"Beauty In Cake, this is Denise."

"Hey, Denise. It's Natalie."

"Who?"

"Oh, it's NAH-tuh-Lee," I said, drawing out my own name in the way that Zella always pronounces it.

"Ohhhhhhh, I must have misunderstood your pronunciation the first time," Denise said sarcastically and then laughed. We had now had at least four discussions about this cake, and two of those were Zella handing the phone to me after dialing, and then telling me to handle it. Denise and I had bonded via telephone because her boss had done the exact same thing. Twice.

In the months to come, Denise and I would bond over many things, and she would become one of my best friends. An amazing person who was disgustingly talented in many areas, Denise not only could handle a highly stressful work environment, and knew her way around a dessert, but she was also a gifted photographer, a social media marketing guru, and used to work for a large off-Broadway theater company. We spoke the same language.

When Denise wasn't doing a million jobs, she was volunteering her time with the Kids Wish Network—a group dedicated to helping make wishes come true for children who have life-threatening illnesses. If I didn't adore her so much, I would loathe her. But loathing Denise was impossible. She was just so darn good at making me laugh. When I finally met her in person, she was the opposite of her larger-than-life persona as she was "fun-sized." A petite curvaceous brunette who had a deep laugh and a twinkle in her eye, she wasn't afraid of a little mischief. But Denise would always hold my admiration because she was a strong woman who would always remind others of their strength.

However, at this moment, Denise and I had only known each other through the phone but spent enough time we knew we could tease each other.

"So, Victoria wants a donut-shaped cake with a hole large enough in the middle for Jazzmin, the hip-hop performer, to jump out through and ultimately perform.

Jazzmin has a twenty-seven-inch waist and a thirty-two inch chest according to her manager."

There was silence for a second, and then a deep throaty laugh issued through the phone.

"Denise. I'm sorry to say, but I'm totally serious."

"What?" Denise shrieked on an upward scale. "Come on Nat—you can't be. How the fu—how are we going to get it loaded into The Rainbow Room? You know the size of that loading dock? Hold on."

Irritated, Denise threw me on hold. I chuckled at how much she swore while *The Girl From Ipanema* ushered through the phone. I was starting to hum along when my phone buzzed.

Sam:

I'm sorry, babe. I want to hear all about it. Running to class now, and then headed out with Nick for dinner, but I'll catch you later. I know you're swamped.

He was right. I uttered a sigh as I looked over at my list of things to do. I really didn't want to eat dinner alone. I had seen Sam less than normal lately. He was just working on his new program at work and was really focused on it. I was really glad he had Nick to be there for him.

Have a good class. Love you.

I was staring at my phone waiting for a response. None came, which meant he had already stepped into class. Oh well.

The Bossa Nova music stopped and Denise's voice over the speakerphone jerked me out of my stupor.

"Ugh. I have to call over there to see when we can get in, we will assemble it there," she said. "It will take my guy an hour to put it together and he will have to do the icing onsite."

"Oh, let me check with the venue if we can get in early and where you can build the cake. Their kitchen is small, so it will be a miracle if we can find someplace. I'll copy you on the email. I have to check in with them anyway to see about placement of it on the rotating floor anyway."

"Great. Thanks, girl!" she perked up. "Hey, what are you doing tonight?" she asked, her voice encouraging me to answer.

Shooting off an email to my Rainbow Room people, I distractedly told her too much information. "Oh, nothing. My boyfriend is headed off to have dinner with his bestie, so I'm probably on for a Romcom and some takeout at home."

"That sounds fantastic—but how committed to it are you?"

"Not very," I replied. In all honesty, I was not looking forward to another night home alone. Sam had been super busy these last few weeks. I felt like we were more ships that passed in the night, and I really didn't want to go home only to be reminded that I hadn't seen him in a week. Nor that it had been ages since we'd had sex.

Denise had been talking, and parts of what she said came through my own thoughts. Event. Free. Food. Tonight. Industry people.

"Sure! I've never been to an industry event. Do you think I need to let Zella know?"

"I think she's supposed to be here," Denise said.

"Oh, I—"

"I just shot her a text saying that Greg wants her to bring anyone she wants, and that he is curious to meet her new assistant."

My phone buzzed.

Industry party at the Beauty In Cake showroom at 7pm—can you make it?

157

My phone buzzed again.

Greg the owner wants to meet you.

My phone buzzed again.

You will go to all of these with me.

My phone buzzed again. Zella often hit send before she was finished with a thought. It slightly annoyed me.

Remember all these experiences can open doors for you.

I laughed out loud. "Wow, you're good."

"What? What just happened?" Denise asked.

"Zella just texted a mild guilt trip to get me to go tonight." She barked a laugh, and I continued. "You know, you could really be a menace if you used your powers for evil."

"Great. I can't wait to actually meet you! The other line is ringing, and I have to go figure out a donut-shaped cake that someone can perform out of," Denise said sarcastically. "Catch you tonight, NAH-tuh-Lee."

Laughing again, I said goodbye and hung up the phone. I shot Zella back a text.

Sure. I've rearranged my plans tonight so I can go.

It was good to make her think that I made this job a priority. She replied again almost instantly:

Good. Be on time and wear something chic.

A second text followed almost immediately.

I'll meet you there—I won't be back to the office today.

I looked at my outfit. Today I had donned a gray t-shirt dress over printed leggings with floral paisleys exploding with purples and pinks up and down my legs. Zella had told me after the first wedding day I worked that in the office I could relax a little more and could wear comfortable clothing unless a client was coming to the office. She even told me I could bring a chic outfit to the office to change into in case of emergencies. Unfortunately, I had yet to bring one in.

My list today needed me to pick up Zella's tailoring at Bloomingdales. An idea formed in my head. I could get her tailoring and express shop for myself. It took them about fifteen minutes to find her tailoring anyway. I could find an outfit in fifteen minutes. Perfect. And even if it took a bit longer, Zella wouldn't be back. And with most of my other tasks done or waiting for someone to reply to me, I felt like this plan would work.

I jumped up and grabbed my jacket. Glancing through the list in my notebook I confirmed I didn't have a lot to do. A few emails to send which I could do on the commute. Zella wanted some organizing done, but I could finish that when I got back. I could change and leave for the party from here. Beauty In Cake was only a ten-minute walk from the office.

Excitement tickled my skin.

Chapter Nineteen

Nodding at Ben on my way out of the lobby, I headed to Soho. I smiled—the afternoon doorman was much more pleasant than demented Dominic was in the mornings.

A lovely spring day, so pleasant that New Yorkers actually smiled at each other. With a bounce in my step, I sauntered into the beauty of Bloomingdales. While wandering back to the counter where alterations were picked up, I found three dresses, a skirt, a flowy blouse, and a pair of slacks. At the counter, I asked for Zella's alterations and asked to be shown to a dressing room.

The woman at the counter recognized me and put me in a dressing room, letting me know that she would bring the alterations out, and winked at me when she let me know it might be a few minutes more than normal. I dived into the clothes. The pants and flowy blouse were, sadly, cuter on the hangers than on me. One of the dresses fit perfectly and was Zella's favorite color: black. After trying them on, I passed on the other two dresses. They were not as flattering as I would wish, and one was very expensive. The A-line skirt was probably my favorite because it hugged and accentuated my curves in all the right ways.

I have the other Scandinavian body type: Tall and round in the lower middle. Sort of a pear on stilts. Not the tall and rail-thin model-esque type. Zella is also on the curvier side and often points out all of my body flaws. Most of which she has now had surgery to fix. So, I try to either magnify them to the point of not caring at all, or some days I come in wearing a zinger of an outfit, and she asks what diet I'm currently on.

This A-line skirt would be a zinger. I just had to find the right top.

"Natalie?" I heard the lovely sales associate who was in her fifties and with her snowy white hair and lovely demeanor reminded me of my grandmother.

"Down here," I said as I cracked open the dressing room stall door covering my chest with my dress, with the skirt still on.

"Oh perfect," she said. I wished I could remember her name. Bonnie, Bunny, Betty? None seemed right. "I brought this top to go with the very skirt you're wearing. And I'm so glad I grabbed it because that skirt looks amazing on you! "And," lowering her voice to a conspiratorial whisper as she leaned toward me while handing me the hunter green blouse, "I have a friends and family discount I can give you."

"Amazing. Thank you so much!"

"Bernice?" another voice called from outside the dressing room. Right! — her name was Bernice.

"Coming," she started to walk away from me, "Natalie, let me know how you like the top, and if I'm not back, your alterations are at my register."

"Thanks, Bernice," I called after her.

The blouse was stunning. A flowy poly-silk blend with a puffed sleeve that was boxy but feminine. The skirt was high-waisted with sailor button trim on the front, and it had a raised swirling flower damask pattern that was only apparent if you were close. From a distance, it just looked luxe. My auburn hair popped with the dark green, and the boxyness made my waist look smaller, as the skirt accentuated my hips and bottom, which were white-girl-non-existent. This was the outfit. I changed back into my own clothes and was delighted that I had worn my black biker boots. They would give the whole outfit a little more edge.

Deciding to get the dress as well as the skirt and blouse, I made my way to the register. Bernice was there, and she smiled at me.

"It worked. Good," she purred with the air of knowing that she had once again, selected the right item for the right client. "Oh, and you're getting the dress, too?"

"Yeah, it will be a good basic to have ready. And it fits like it was made for me."

"Don't you love it when that happens?" Bernice said as she started to scan my selections, remove the sensors, and put them in a garment bag for me. "I steamed the blouse for you already, so I'm going to hang it, so you can just take it off the hanger and wear it." She flashed a piece of paper in front of the scanner and popped it back in her pocket. "Oooh, I didn't notice that the skirt and the dress are on sale, and with the discount, you're making out like a bandit." She winked at me and said in a low voice as if we shared a huge secret.

"Thank you so much," I replied, handing over my credit card trying not to cringe. I didn't want to know how much I was spending even with the discounts it was more than I could afford. But I reasoned with myself, they were work expenses and I needed them. My continual need to impress Zella always hung over me like a smoky haze. Plus, I didn't want Zella to look me up and down like I was an uninvited homeless person. Her praise was like a rainbow, I knew it existed, I had seen it, but I had yet to catch it. I had never felt this about anyone else in my life before, it was very strange. Even though I continually tried, I always felt that I failed. Miserably.

Signing the receipt, I popped my copy and my credit card into my wallet. Maybe I could write it off. I grabbed my garment bag and Zella's alterations. Thanking Bernice, I headed back to the office.

Chapter Twenty

P ulling out my phone as I walked, I saw a few email responses to the ones I sent while on route, I started to reply to the first one and noticed that I had made it in and out of Bloomingdales with two new outfits, in twenty-five minutes. Amazement held me for a moment before I went back to emails as I walked back to the office.

Hanging Zella's alterations out of the bag, I placed them in the front of the closet so she could see them. Then I wrote my name on the front of my garment bag and waded into the back of the closet and hung the black dress there. Although Zella had offered to leave an outfit here, I didn't want my dress to attract attention. She forgot she offered things and when I took her up on them, got upset at me. I didn't want my forward thinking to be the contention of another tongue-lashing.

Hurrying through my tasks, I found that I was finished with everything by quarter to six. I went downstairs for a bite to eat, as I wasn't sure what kind of fare would be at this party, and I wanted more than cake for dinner.

By 6:30pm I was back in the apartment, fed, and dressed. I decided to put my hair up in one of those poofy, ballerina buns. I had started to always carry blush and lipstick with me in case a client decided to stop by—which had happened twice already, and both times Zella was frustrated that I didn't have any of my own. She shoved some of her Tom Ford Scarlet Rouge on me. She approved, but I felt like it made me look a little too ready to walk the street. Plus, I don't know why but I felt weird putting on fifty-dollar lipstick. In my makeup bag, I also found a pair of Labradorite teardrop earrings that Sam's mom had given me. They completed the outfit. By 6:45pm I was leaving the office and walking to my first industry event. I was terrified.

As I walked in at five 'til seven I saw a curvaceous woman humming while arranging mini cupcakes on several trays. I watched her for a few moments, while she got them just right and then picked up a camera with a pretty long lens for a short distance, and she snapped a few shots. After completing her task and her focus decreased, she sensed she was not alone, and looked up to meet my eyes.

"Killer outfit," she said as she raised the camera lens at me and took a few shots. Making my best model poses, I smiled. "Natalie?" she asked, almost sure, but not wanting to assume. As she walked toward me, she continued, "I mean NAH-tuh-Lee. Sorry, I got the pronunciation wrong the first time. I was just so excited to see you in the flesh."

"Ha! Well, I suppose I'll let it pass. This time," I said in my best Zella impersonation as I waltzed into the room and filled it. "You must be Denise!"

"That I am, but don't say it too loudly, people might hear and need something!"

Laughing with me Denise walked me around the offices giving me a tour and introduced me to those who were still working or prepping for the party. We heard a few raucous voices and returned to the main showroom where a very flamboyant man with the curliest black hair stood dressed in a midnight blue velvet jacket. Denise walked me over to him,

"Greg, this is Natalie, Zella's new assistant. I'm sure Zella will want to introduce her to you, but I wanted to let you know who she is since she might be one of the only faces in the room you won't know."

Jovially, Greg's face lit up. "Zella's new girl? Well, this job will open doors for you!" Again, that reminder!

"How do you like working for Zella?" and then looked over my shoulder, waving a silent hello at someone.

"Well, it is… an experience—"

"Jimmy!" Greg exclaimed to someone over my right shoulder. "Excuse me, ladies."

As soon as he was two steps past us, not even out of earshot, "Aaand he's gone. Don't worry, you'll get asked that question a lot, how you like working with Madame." Her smile went from rueful to sly. She leaned into me conspiratorially and said "Most people won't even care about the answer. Let's get a drink." Denise led me to the bar. As we waited in line, she pointed out important people, and introduced me to a few more as we all waited together.

When we were one person away from the bar, Zella magically appeared at my side.

"Are you enjoying yourself, Natalie? Who have you met so far?"

"Well," I stammered, slightly unhinged that she just materialized next to me. I had to review my last few thoughts to make sure I hadn't said anything negative about her or the business—I was pretty sure I was safe. "I, uh, met Denise, and Greg, and—"

"Natalie, we really have to work on your timidity. You should have been all over this party and meeting everyone. You've only met two people? And do you know you always stammer when talking to me." We moved forward. "Get me a chardonnay, while you're getting your drink," Zella flicked her wrist toward the bar and replied in a way that made me wonder if she only came up to me so she didn't have to wait in the line, which was now about twenty people deep.

Denise ordered her drink and turned to Zella. When I turned to order her Chardonnay, I saw a face I recognized.

"Hey, it's you," I said to the wavy-haired handsome bartender. "Matt, right?"

"Good memory, Natalie," he said and winked. "What can I get for you?

"A glass of Chardonnay. And–"

"Is the wine for you?"

"No, it's for Zella," I motioned behind me.

"Ah." He said and then leaned in. "Can I make you something special?"

"Umm," I said, giving him a squinty look as he poured Zella's wine.

"You can trust me," he said and handed the wine glass to me.

"Fine. Make me something special."

"I'll make the drink. But you, I believe already are something special," he said as he turned away. Wait. Was he flirting with me? I didn't have a chance to think about it because Denise tugged my arm as I heard her tell Zella about our evening so far.

"Oh, no Zella! I have been introducing Natalie to everyone. She met Greg, of course, and I introduced her to Stan and Emily, Carol, Mark, and Melinda. I steered her clear of Alexander, since he seems to like the fresh meat, and—"

Zella reached across Denise to grab her wine glass from my hand, and waved Denise off, "Yes, yes. Good." She turned to me, "Natalie, make sure you get business cards, and we will review who you met when you are back in the office." Looking my outfit up and down, she pursed her lips and turned on her heel. Over her shoulder she said, "Satisfactory outfit. Needs a better bag." And we both watched her recede into the crowd.

167

I turned back to the bar, but Matt had disappeared, and my drink was sitting there. I took a taste and the bright but smokey flavor crossed my tongue. It was something with Bourbon and Prosecco and something I couldn't place. It was delicious. Taking another sip, I savored it. Then Denise led me away from the bar.

"I can't believe that 'get business cards for us to review.' Like you're going to be tested on who you met at this party. And what does she mean by 'satisfactory?' Your outfit is rocking. Who made your bag, by the way?"

"Min and Mon made it." I petted the bag. "Yeah. Who knows. I tune it out now," I shrugged. "I find myself always wanting to please her, but at the same time, I have started to take everything with a grain of salt. Somedays the entire shaker." I took a sip of my drink and looked out over the crowd. "Who is that?" I said pointing at a very tall man in his late thirties, with clipped blonde hair and a slim, but rounded face.

"Ah, that would be Alexander. From one friend to another," she turned toward me and looked me directly in the eyes to over-emphasize the point, "Stay. Away."

As if he heard her say that, and urged me to disobey, he turned, and our eyes met. He looked me up and down, pursed his lips and then smiled. I quickly looked away.

"Come on, let's do something fun."

Apparently "fun" meant hopping into the photo booth, where we took multiple pictures together. She also introduced me to many more people. Another trip to the bar, I was mildly sad when I didn't see Matt, but was revived when we got two drinks each and a handful of canapés. I was barely through one of my two drinks and was confused when the party had emptied out. In only sixty minutes, a party blossomed, and started to wilt. Only a few people were still

168

hanging around, and they looked deep in conversations or wasted.

I would come to learn, at industry parties, attendees would go hard and heavy, then would schmooze and depart quickly. Most parties were only two hours long, and people also wanted to get home to their families. Or expensive dogs.

Zella would always insist that I be on time to industry events and stay until I met enough people. What amount that was, I still don't know. She would always arrive fashionably late, make two loops, and would leave. Sometimes with a great deal of fanfare. Sometimes with an Irish Goodbye. She never said goodbye to me at these events. In fact, she would seem surprised to see me, if she even came up to me at all. Most times I would find her, say a quick hello, and be waved off.

Although I was always reminded to get business cards, we never 'went over who I met' the next day. I would name drop when I was in the office next to see who she approved of and who she didn't. There was always at least one person she had gossip on.

All of this I would come to learn. But at my first party, I was just blissfully naive. The party was empty by quarter after eight. So, I took my cue. Denise hugged me then gave me a box of canapés, and a box that contained a small cake. She told me to share it with my boyfriend. We promised we would go out for drinks once the season was over.

Chapter Twenty-One

A blissful feeling fell over me as I walked out of the party and out onto the street. Although it might just have been three heavily poured drinks and very little food. And that compliment from Matt. It was weird that he was popping up everywhere, and then disappearing. He was my own personal White Rabbit. Did that mean I was Alice? I was in Wonderland.

I paused my train of thought and looked up and down the street trying to reclaim my bearings after my third drink and tried to remember which direction the subway was.

"Well, hello," I heard a man say from behind me and I froze, not knowing what to do. Chills ran down my spine. I wasn't in a terrible neighborhood, but it was dark and deserted. I took a deep breath while trying to remember what my self-defense class taught me in college. I wheeled around.

"Leave me—," I cut myself off the moment I recognized who it was. "I know you," I said. My eyes narrowing and my lips forming a snarl. "I'm supposed to stay away from you," I said, not understanding why my voice was so cold and angry. Denise said he was bad news but didn't elaborate. I felt I could trust her. But I was also not one to make snap judgements on people, so why was I being so defensive.

"It's nice to meet you too, Zella's-new-girl." He smiled at me. To be honest, I couldn't tell through all of the alcohol currently swimming in my brain, but his smile seemed genuine. "Did they tell you why you were supposed to stay away from the big bad wolf?"

"Nope. Just that you like fresh meat. Hey—that's funny. Big bad wolf, fresh meat." As I was busy mulling over the hilarity of this in my head, Alexander had moved closer and was only about eight inches away from me. He was much more handsome up close, and I could smell the woodsy ginger and musk of his Burberry Brit waft to my nose. Tall and handsome in a well-cut suit, he was totally my type. What was happening? He held out his card. It read *Alexander Milford: Events.*

Ungracefully, I reached for it, tripped over my own feet, and somehow landed in one of his arms and while my food care packages landed in the other. Somehow his business card was the only thing in my hands.

"Whoa there. We just met. Do you think it's right to be throwing yourself at me so soon?" he asked in a very cocky way. Righting myself and snatching my packages out of his hands, I gave him a snide look. I had been warned about this man, and I was wary about smarmy men in general. Especially those men who smelled good and knew how handsome they were.

"Ha. Ha." I sarcastically replied, shoving his business card in my pocket. Then I said with a disgusted tone, "I'm probably not your type anyway."

"And what type is that?"

"Curves. Boobs. A girl." The alcohol made me more sassy than normal.

He looked at me with a questioning glance. "I'm not quite sure what you mean."

"Well look at you. Handsome. Well dressed. In events." I waved my hand at him with a floppy wrist. "You're obviously gay."

"Actually, I'm not. Thank you." His politeness was unnerving. There was just something about this man that made my skin crawl and made me want to spit all kinds of obscenities at him. I didn't know why.

Even though I felt so many things in this moment, a drunken "Oh," was all I could say. I was dumbfounded. Both at my incredulity and at his honesty.

"And," he continued, "Aside from your vocabulary, you are lovely, and I would ask you out, *if* I were dating right now."

Stupefied, I stared at him. I didn't know what to say. I finally said, "Thank you for helping me. It was nice meeting you."

"It was nice meeting you, too." He took a step toward me. "So," he said with a devilish smile and a rumbly low voice, "I hear Zella is trying to top herself, or should I say big top herself, with the Kellerman Mitzvah."

My eyes snapped up to his. This was the event I wasn't supposed to talk about with anyone. "I..."

"So, what is the plan," he asked, his voice was now a purr as he took another step close to me his eyes flicking from my lips to my chest.

What was happening. Was he flirting? This was the second man in the evening. Was this top and skirt that good? Maybe I should never shop at Bloomies again. Or maybe I should always shop there. "I know it's a circus theme. What is she going to do to top the mermaid theme she did for the older sister at the Natural History Museum?"

"Mermaid theme?"

"Yes. They were in the whale room, and she had actual mermaids swimming across the ceiling. Or they were swinging acrobats. I'm sure the pictures didn't do it justice." Giving me a caring smile, he said, "Come on, you can tell me. I won't say a thing. To anyone." He was ridiculously close. Like almost kissing distance. I didn't know how I felt about that.

Finding a non-existent fuzz on my skirt, I picked at it. Then looking up at him to see he was staring at me, I took a step back and politely said, "Good night." I walked a few steps and felt very confident that I didn't give in to either his tempting closeness or telling him about the event. I felt good and let out the breath I had been holding and felt like I had just escaped with my life. And then he spoke.

"If you're trying to get to the subway, it's the other direction."

Taking a deep breath, I halted. Feeling incredibly stupid, I did an about face. I looked at Alexander who was looking right back at me. A warm smile crept over his face as he stuffed his hands into his pockets. If I didn't know any better and was more sober, I would have guessed he was wishing we had met under different circumstances. But at this moment, I was buzzed, indignant, was not single, and warned that he was someone to stay away from, so I did my best not to notice. I walked past him, grumbling a very ungracious, "Thank you."

"Oh, and New Girl," he said to my retreating back, "keep my card in case you need a friend. But if I were you, I wouldn't mention this meeting to Madame." And. He. Winked.

It didn't connect in my brain until I had righteously stomped all the way to the subway, that he had referred to her by "Madame." So had Denise. I wondered what they meant by that nickname. Although, I probably could guess. Filing it away to ask Denise about when we finally made our wine plans, I popped in my earbuds and drowned everything out with a random musical theater song that popped up on my playlist. I even forgot about Alexander.

A dangerous thing to do. But I wouldn't realize that until later.

Chapter Twenty-Two

Bridezillas are at times dangerous, and rightly feared. But Zella on a bad day was a horror show. And I never knew when either would suddenly appear.

Wedding weeks I was still a bit of a wreck even with side encouragement from AM, Amanda, Violet, and Denise. There were always too many things to accomplish, the tiniest of details to hone, and Zella and I alone didn't seem to be enough of a work crew to do everything from wedding invitation and welcome stuffing, to welcoming all vendor meetings and timing each event down to the minute. We did so many weddings over the next few months, they were a blur of cake, Prosecco, and expensive designer sequined tulle. But, with long hours in the office, and even more when I got home, we seemed to get through everything.

A few of those days I even took my laptop and would work on things for Zella while with Levi. Suzanne said that as long as Levi was happy and not watching television, she was fine with it. He was at the age where he loved to read or chat on the phone with his buddies. So often there wasn't much for me to monitor or assist with anyway.

And, if you're wondering how the bar mitzvah circus went: everything was smooth. There was a bit of an incident with the DJ booth being larger than the décor designer knew, so the logistics of some of the displays had to be dismantled and shifted and rehung and of course I got a lecture about not having gotten the dimensions to the designer. Even though the measurements I got from the DJ and gave to the décor team were wrong.

Then when the party started the three-foot helium balloons, we got to cover the dance floor wouldn't stop popping. The designer's crew had to stay on site and kept inflating balloons all evening. Now when I hear a balloon pop, I feel the PTSD. We must have gone through one thousand balloons.

Other than that, the event was flawless, and the client was very happy. So was Jazzmin as she hopped over the side of the cake, getting frosting on her butt, and then waggling it in a thirteen-year-old boy's face. It would be a night he would live in infamy in his mind—and probably a few wet dreams.

After that we had a succession of events at Cipriani 42nd Street, a beautiful, converted bank that had high ceilings and marble columns. The cavernous feel of the room was a great site for the spectacle. For the ceremony they would cut the room in half and put up pipe and drape so the tables for the reception were set and hidden behind. They would make this very dramatic ceremony space, most of the time with a chuppah—even if the couple wasn't Jewish—to create a beautiful dramatic effect.

One of the more memorable weddings we had was for Eli and Ruth. Memorable, more for what happened before their wedding than during it. Although their friends were huge partiers. He worked on Wall Street. There were so many nose jobs at this party, of all kinds, if you catch my drift. Ruth worked for the family business, a company that made designer handbags. She headed the marketing department and was very Type A about everything. Ruth had known what her dream wedding would look like and was not afraid to let anyone know that they were not in the realm of her perfect concept. Nine months before her wedding, she came to us with two wedding binders full of pictures, clippings, and swatches—and don't get me started on her Pinterest board.

Zella was also adamant about not retaining items in the office for any wedding more than a week before the big day. She would never explain why, although in the large loft space there actually was very little storage space that was out of view. Understandably, I wouldn't want my creative space to be congested with boxes of sugared almonds, place cards, and personalized wine bottles for five to six weddings at a time either. Most brides were respectful, but some would just ship to our address anyway. Ruth was one of these brides.

Three weeks before their wedding the boxes started to arrive with various items. Personalized bags of potato chips shared when they met had theirn name and wedding date on the front. A cartoon map of New York that folded up to fit in a pocket noted with landmarks special to the couple. There were water bottles, his and hers: "His" had Eli's face on them, "hers" had Ruth's. Eli's favorite candy was Peppermint Patties, so there were twelve pounds of those in the office and mint hung in the air.

Zella started to complain the week before the wedding when the boxes hit three rows wide and were about my height when the Ring Pops arrived. I don't know if it was the sugary smell of all of the candy or the amount of boxes in the office, but Zella snapped.

Through the towers of boxes Zella turned and shouted at me as I was loading in the last box from the hallway—she didn't want any of the doormen actually in her office for some reason.

"Natalie! How could you let this happen?" Every word had a harsh emphasis, and I felt like I had just done something massively disappointing like give the launch codes to our enemy. As I turned around to her, the rant continued. Zella yelled from her desk. "How could you let the bride just send all this here? What could have possessed you to go against my instructions. You know I like a clean workspace."

My mind reeled through rebuttals and thoughts including: It would only be a week, it wasn't that bad; and Zella's desk faced the opposite way so she could just ignore it. Why was I being blamed for this? I'm getting fired. Wait, why would I get fired for this? Nope, she's still yelling. I'm going to get fired—I'm such a disappointment.

"I'm…. sorry Zella," I spoke timidly during a break in the rant. She wasn't looking at me, which meant she probably didn't hear me, but I said it anyway. "Um, what can I do to make it better?" I wiggled my way through the boxes and began frantically looking at all of them, as if one of them held the answer. "I could put a sheet to cover it and—"

Her head whipped up from her cell phone where she was tapping away. "A sheet? A SHEET? Natalie. Don't be ridiculous."

In eight words her tone went from condescending to irritated to calm. I could feel something was still wrong. She went back to texting.

Like a child hiding behind a too-skinny tree during hide-n-seek, I stood in an awkward position trying to pretend I was invisible and staying as quiet as I could, in hopes I would not be seen, but also, in a ready-to-dash stance. Zella didn't move or say anything. It seemed like five minutes I spent waiting. I was afraid to move. She sighed and turned to her computer, while chewing on a cuticle. She did this on wedding weeks that were very tense, which is why manicures were on Thursdays before we had rehearsal dinner. She could nibble all week, and then look fabulous on Friday. I slunk over to the table where I had been putting the personalized menus in order of table.

The week of the wedding we always manufacture all the paper goods—as you never know what your final numbers will be of a wedding, realistically until then. So, all napkins, menus, place cards, table numbers, and escort cards are printed with short notice. Which meant we had to organize them all a day or two before the wedding. And since these were what people noticed most because they were personalized, everything had to be double-checked and in order.

Hairs on the back of my neck suddenly stuck up. I was so focused; I hadn't noticed Zella had come to stand right beside me. "Natalie," my name curled out of her mouth, the likes of a Disney Villain with a plan questioning the abilities of her second.

I tossed the menu cards that were in my hand, and like a tossed deck of cards they scattered all over the table.

My eyes felt like they popped out of my head, I turned slowly to face her. She whipped her phone up, putting it right in my face. A text message conversation between Zella and Ruth was on display. I looked at her questioningly.

"Read," was all she said.

Zella: *Hi Ruth! So excited about your wedding over here. We are getting ALL of your boxes. Didn't know there would be so many!*

Ruth: *Hi Zella! Busy day! Yes, you should be getting another shipment or two today and tomorrow.*

Zella: *Wow! These are going to be some great favors and welcome gift bags. Did we know that all of this was being sent here?*

Ruth: *Your assistant told me that it was ok.*

I tried scrolling up, but that was the end of the conversation. I looked up into Zella's waiting eyes.

"Why in the hell did you tell Ruth that it was alright to send her shit here?"

Jarred by both the feeling of a New York City bus rolling over my body, and the sensation that I didn't remember telling Ruth she could store things here, I assumed Zella had offered. By Zella's sudden slinging of swear words, I knew she hadn't.

Zella swore all the time now, but mostly it was under her breath or in a general outburst to a room. Until now it hadn't been directed at me. I had the sensation her words were flaying wide open, because I was roadkill, just before she was about to put me on a spit and roast me.

My brain churned. There were so many details piled up in my brain like the boxes in this room. I tried to mentally scroll through all of my correspondence with Ruth as Zella burned me with her stare. I started to get a niggle of something, and I turned to my computer.

"I, uh, think there was an email about it—"

"I don't want 'you think.' I want that you know," Zella hissed.

Sweat beads started to form on my forehead. I felt like I was trying to disarm a bomb with how quickly my brain and my fingers were working in tandem. My fingers tapped out a search word then used the mouse to quickly click in and out of emails. My eyes scanned through the text faster than the Roadrunner.

Zella breathed down my neck as I read as many emails as possible. Ruth was a huge email person, and she sent anywhere from twenty to fifty emails and responses a week to us. Twice that many had been sent in the last two days alone. There was a lot of correspondence. Finally, I found it. At first, I was in disbelief, because my eyes had to be exhausted at scanning over a hundred emails in the span of just a few minutes. I read it three times.

There it was. In a long chain, probably twenty-five deep, Amanda had emailed Ruth letting her know if she needed a place to ship things to let us know. Amanda and I copied each other on everything, so at moments like this we could help each other out. I both cringed and took a deep breath. I didn't want to throw Amanda under the bus, but I also wanted to keep my job and prove I was not to blame. I'm slightly ashamed to tell you in this moment of terror, while I was in the office and Amanda was safely not, I handed her over on a platter.

"I found it," I proclaimed in a proud shout. I turned to Zella with bleary eyes.

She had hopped back on to her phone and was texting. So focused on what she was doing, she didn't hear me. While I waited for her to stop texting, I thought about my decision. Not that there was much to decide. It was there in black and white. Amanda had left the door wide open for the client.

Although, I should probably stick up for Amanda for many reasons. But mostly because the bride had taken this tiny offer as an invitation to move into the Tremaine Events office. As Zella kept texting, and her focus was off of me, I sighed wondering how to combat this. And wishing she would stop texting and focus on this goose chase fire drill she made me stop everything for.

Some days I wished for a flag I could raise, or a flashing light when I needed her attention. Maybe one of those things people use for their cats with the pointer light to chase around the floor. While she was typing, she went to her desk, sat down and then went to her computer. Feeling like I had already lost momentum from this craziness, I went back to my menu card sorting and cleaned up the ones I had tossed, trying to remember what order they were in and inwardly groaned.

"Natalie." I jumped hearing my name just over my shoulder. Zella had somehow crept up behind me again. I almost fell out of my chair trying to hold onto all the cards this time.

I took a deep breath. "Yes, Zella?" I felt slightly annoyed that she was interrupting me while I was trying to match table numbers and first names from the invitation list.

"What did you find out? You were going to show me how you messed up."

Irritation raged inside me with this comment, but I pushed it down into my stomach. Why did she always assume I messed up? I took a labored breath in through my nose and walked over to the computer. Clicking over to the tab that contained the email from Amanda, I turned my laptop toward Zella. "Nope, Zella, I'm not to blame." There. That was open ended. Zella could choose to blame Amanda or Ruth. Her choice.

She read the email; her nostrils flared. "Natalie, you are my office manager. Amanda works from home. It is your job to tell me when things come in, and if they are going to clutter my office space."

My mind took a moment to follow her down the crazy path she skipped down. Wait a minute—she wasn't upset at Amanda for leaving an open door to the client to ship things to the office. She wasn't upset at the client for just taking her own initiative.

Zella was upset at me because I didn't tell her about the boxes piling up in a corner of her office, most of which came the day before. When I wasn't even here.

Looking back, I think a lot of our issues would have been solved had I just stood up for myself more. Zella really did respect people who stood up for themselves. But at this moment, I was just dumbfounded that I was getting blamed for something I had no control over. It's like I was being yelled at for getting hit by a bus while I walked on a sidewalk. Yeah, I should have moved out of the way, but who expects a bus to suddenly jump onto the sidewalk?

Instead, I took the high road. Mostly because when she was like this, there was no use in trying to defend myself.

"Alright, Zella." I tightened my jaw and squared my shoulders. "I know for next time to let you know when your office will be crowded with boxes." I was into taking responsibility for things lately. And I figured it was best to just stay under the bus that jumped the sidewalk and hope that help would come soon.

"Do that." I wasn't sure if she needed to have the last word or if she just didn't know what to say and wanted to maintain power. She made a call to Ruth as she walked back to her desk and sat languorously.

Taking a deep breath in, I went back to the menu cards. Five minutes later, Zella was still on the phone, so I got up and went to the bathroom. Staring at my reflection, I willed myself to have more courage and also to have less fear of this woman. Although I had taken my phone with me into the bathroom, I hadn't checked it. It wasn't that I had developed the Fear of Missing Out. Sadly, there were no longer boundaries in my world. If Zella couldn't reach me immediately, she would fly off the handle. In the last week alone, I had answered the phone twice while using the bathroom. Once she came to the bathroom and shouted at me through the door, which was just weird.

Seven text messages waited for me. All from Zella.

Get rid of the boxes.

Then:

Today.

The next followed two minutes later:

You'll find a place.

A minute after that:

Never mind. Leave them.

Then immediately:

I *don't want to be responsible for damaging a bride's things.*

A minute later:

I'm going out to lunch.

Then immediately after:

Have those menu cards finished and, on my desk, before you leave. I'm going to spot check them. There had better not be any mistakes.

I inwardly groaned, at her massive amount of text messages, threats, and micromanaging. Her blatant micromanaging was getting worse. Always multiple text messages about one thing. I was a capable woman in my thirties who held many demanding jobs. However, she felt it necessary to continually remind me to work on things that I was currently working on. It irritated me to no end.

The menu cards weren't going to organize themselves. I dragged myself back to the table and finished. After checking every table for the correct order, for the third time, my cell phone rang. My entire body tensed. Relaxing when I saw it wasn't Zella, I reached for it.

"Hey, Denise!"

"Hey girl! What's shakin?"

I moaned into the phone.

"Uh oh. You sound like I feel."

"Yeah," I responded. "I don't know what it is that I'm doing, or not doing, but I feel like there is more hand holding going on now in my job then when I first began.

183

Micromanaging is Zella's favorite hobby. She has to look at, and review everything I do these days."

"Wow. Did you do something wrong?"

Wracking my brain again for an inkling of a reason, I answered, "Not that I can think of."

"Well, who knows. Most of the people in this industry are absolutely crazy." Denise's reply made me feel a little better. "I should know, I've been in it for eight years. I'm thinking of getting out of it. Some days the frustration of it all just isn't worth the hassle."

"Yeah," I distantly replied. Past jobs I've had were irritating, but none came close to the glamour and the excitement that this job held. "But this job will open a lot of doors for me," I repeated the saying that was tattooed on my brain. Almost everyone said it when I mentioned I worked for Zella. And yes, I was still collecting business cards, but we still hadn't reviewed them. "And speaking of opening doors…"

There had been seventeen industry events over the last month and a half, and Zella had sent me to most of them so I could network and meet people. Networking was almost a full-time job. The first two I went all alone. I got all dressed up in fancy clothes and walked in like the weird girl at prom who knew no one. Most of the time I would do a lap of the room, look at the displays while chugging a couple glasses of free wine and trying to chase down the waiters who had scant trays of snacks.

Within twenty minutes I was bored-out-of-my-mind while awkwardly trying to talk to people who had no interest in talking to me trying to get business cards. And also skulking in dark corners trying to avoid Alexander Milford. I thought I caught sight of him once and ducked into a group of giggling blondes who were from some big marketing company. It wasn't him, but because of my awkward dive, I found out from this gaggle most of the reason people went to the parties was to see each other. Because there isn't really time at events to chat with each other, they came to industry events to trade gossip and drink.

I tried to bop in and out of groups but ended up being the weirdo that took pictures of each canapé as it was served to me. You know, just in case Zella wanted my notes on the party. Although they seemed fun at first, I would rather go to the dentist and have my teeth pulled than go to another industry party alone. Sadly, I had three more this week.

Smith and Spencer were giving a party the next day. I had forgotten that I had texted Denise earlier when I got to the office. The towers of boxes had absorbed the day. Apparently, this team was a new catering company in town showing off their skills. Zella had RSVP'd for two and had decided not to go when she found out no one she wanted to rub elbows with was going. I wasn't sure if this was a snub or not. She said her husband had tickets to the opera. Which was a legitimate answer, but I think it was more for show if anyone asked about her.

"Do you want to go with me to the Smith and Spencer event tonight?"

"Sure girl, I'll go. Meet you there?" Denise asked.

"Oh good. I am so tired of going to these things alone. Promise me we will get in and get out if it's bad?

She giggled. "Sure, peaches. Whatever you want."

"See you tomorrow." I said.

I started to pack up to leave, but because I felt Zella's watchful eye, even though she wasn't around, I went back to the menu cards. I checked them a fourth time just to be safe.

Chapter Twenty-Three

Denise and I met in the lobby of the office building that was home to Smith and Spencer. We both were about an hour late to the party that started at five. When we reached the small loft space on the fourth floor, we realized we were the only two people under fifty years old, and the only two women under sixty.

There have been many things that have shocked or stunned me in this line of work. None more than when I walked into this party. Not five people deep when I walked off the elevator was the mysterious Matt, who looked stunning in his well-cut navy suit, light blue button up with no tie, and shoes that looked like chocolate was used to shine them.

"Hey, stranger," I walked over to him.

"Hey, you look familiar," he said with a joke twinkling in his eye. "Nancy? Norah? Oh wait, it's NAH-tuh-Lee." He smiled as he did Zella's pronunciation of my name.

"Right, right." I rolled my eyes. I turned to Denise who was at my side. "Matt, I think you might know Denise. She's from—"

"Baked In Love" Matt finished my sentence.

"So, my reputation precedes me?" Denise said, succumbing to Matt's charms. Or just shamelessly flirting. He gave her an appreciative glance, that I think was more for show.

Denise was dressed casually in jeans that were lightly covered with flour, heels that she kept under her desk for emergencies, and a silk Ralph Lauren blouse that she randomly found at the Goodwill on the way to the event. I was dressed to impress, in a tight A-line skirt and a sapphire knit blouse with tiny, pleated cap sleeves. I even had on a pair of patent kitten heels. Zella had instructed me that I had to be dressed to impress from now on if I was going anywhere that event industry people would see me. I needed to be in all black or dressed like I owned the room. Earlier, her voice was in my head as I got ready, I rolled my eyes as I finished my mascara. Making myself look done up, but like I hadn't tried very hard wasn't an easy task. I tossed my hair up in a French twist and wasn't very happy with it. Why couldn't I just look like Rachel in Friends when I did my hair and makeup like this?

Now seeing Matt, I was glad I took the time to look this good.

It turns out the mystery guy who had been popping into my life at events was Matt Spencer, executive chef and the creative side of Smith and Spencer. His friend and business partner, Jack Smith was the operations and sales side. He called over his partner, Jack and we did a round of introductions. Chatting for a bit, we were told stories of how they met in college, and were rivals, but then got stuck as lab partners and then they were inseparable. Both were very handsome and very straight—a rare commodity in the event world.

Because we arrived late, most of the glamorous gay men were finishing their vodka and diet tonics realizing their canapé tasting plates were now empty, and that they didn't have a chance for more with either of the hosts. I felt every jealous eye on us as they sized me up and said a little too loudly just as the jazz trio paused to change songs that I needed a stiff drink. Not a minute later, Matt was at my side with two low-ball glasses filled with amber liquid in his hand. One had rocks, a pick filled with cranberries, and a floating mint leaf. The other was just amber liquid.

187

"Pick your poison," he said, lifting both drinks to his face and making a cheesy grin.

"Um, I'll take the straight whisky."

"It's rye."

"Even better," I said, holding my hand palm up for the glass, waiting for the treat.

"Good girl. I knew I liked you," Matt said as he sat the glass gently on my hand and looked into my eyes.

"I, uh, see someone over there that I need to talk to," Denise pointed to a wall with no one near it. "Hey Jack, why don't you come with me, and I'll introduce you." The two scuttled away as if they had planned it.

He slammed half of the cranberry mint concoction in his mouth. "So, how's it going with Zella? That job can open doors, or so says the word on the street." He smiled at me. We were close to the same height, he only had two inches on me. He leaned closer as if he had a secret and said in a low voice, "Speaking of which, everyone is talking about you."

"Oh no. Why?" I asked and looked at him like he had two heads.

"Well, you've already lasted longer than her last few interns. You've also turned some heads during events."

"Uh oh." I hung my head. My mind flashed to our event two weeks ago, where Zella dragged me out of the reception to give me a verbal lashing. She was mad because a couple of names were spelled wrong—but after the wedding when I went back to check, I had spelled them exactly as I was given them. Nothing could be proven during the event, and the client was upset with Zella because of the embarrassment of the misspellings. Zella was mad at me because, well, because. It was the true version of passing the buck. Unfortunately, the buck stopped with me. In that moment, I took the criticism. Her micromanaging in the office came from little moments like this where I wasn't exactly in the wrong, but my hands were the last that they went through before the event. What was I to do.

"Actually," Matt continued, "the reviews I'm hearing are that you're good at thinking on your feet, and you're a fast runner."

Ah! He was referring to the incident where the father of the bride hadn't brought his reading glasses to read his speech, and I was told moments before. Immediately upon hearing this, I sent the Maître'd off to ask his staff if they had anything he could borrow, Zella went up to father of the bride's room to look to see if he had left them up there, and I dashed to the drugstore around the corner, with the thought that we could return the purchased pair if we found another. Within minutes, I was back from the store, and the proud father of the bride sported the new reading glasses I had for him. Later that night he had tipped me really well. It was a nice feeling to be rewarded for helping. I told him that I was glad to be able to make his night go smoothly.

"How do you know so much?" I asked.

"I know people. You forget, I have connections all over and work at a lot of places."

"Ah yes, that. So, were you just working all the side jobs before you could start your own?"

"Something like that," he half smiled, with only one corner of his mouth raising, "So what did you do with the money?" Matt asked, changing the subject.

"I'm saving it. I'm going to take my boyfriend on a Caribbean vacation once I've saved enough. Which, if they're all generous like this last weekend, won't take much longer. Fingers crossed"

"Well, that's too bad," Matt said.

In confusion, I scrunched my nose and forehead. "What's too bad," I asked.

"That you have a boyfriend." Matt winked. "So... tell me about him,"

"Impressive segue." I smiled. "Well, he is a fitness guy, and he is working to make the world a better place."

As if on cue, the phone in my hand rang. It was Sam. I smiled an even bigger stupid grin.

"That's him, isn't it?"

"Yup. Excuse me. I just have to answer this. We have been playing phone tag for days. I'll be back." I stepped away to find a quiet spot in a corner.

"Hello, handsome stranger," I said, feeling flirty and saucy from the drink and the evening.

"Hey!" Sam chuckled at my response. "I think somebody's been drinking!"

"You know I always drink at work!" The words came out more heated than I wanted them to. "I have to in order to keep my cool around Madame."

"Aww, babe. I know you're frustrated. I'm so sorry we haven't seen each other lately. Or talk more than just on text in the past four days."

"It's ok, Sam," I said. "We're both building careers. This choice sometimes makes things hard." I sighed and leaned against the wall. "I feel guilty. Ginger wanted me to see a play tonight, Jordan told me she stopped texting me because I never respond, and Bennett is just angry at me. And I don't know how long it's been since we've kissed."

"Babe," his voice was soft like a caress through the phone. "I kiss you every morning. Twice if I remember to make it back to the bed before I run out the door." I smiled, and a tear started to form in my eye.

"I know. And I kiss you when I get home. But it's not the same. I want to make out with you like we're a couple of horny teenagers."

Sam laughed again. "Well, how long will you be out tonight?" He said, turning on his propositioning voice.

"I shouldn't be that long. Zella isn't at this one, so I can leave whenever. The guys who own this company are really nice, though. I think one of them is flirting with me."

"Is he cute? And could he give you a discount on something?" Sam asked, in more of a girlfriend prodding way, than the expected jealous boyfriend way. "Maybe that would help with the Zella situation."

I laughed and then was a little confused at his query. I was cautious when I said, "He's kinda cute." Feeling I needed to recover as I was in unknown territory here. I tried to rebound with, "But you know my type. I like the tall, snuggly, gym bunny types. Not these schmoozy, angle seeking event people who ply you with alcohol just to get you to hire them."

Out of the corner of my eye, I caught a movement. I turned around to see Matt storming back toward what was left of the party.

"Crap. Um, Sam, love," I said distractedly watching Matt's hunched shoulders retreat. "My sarcasm was just overheard and I might have offended someone important. I should go and see if I need to fix it."

"Oh, those event people," he said jokingly. "They have such delicate egos!"

"Sam, I know you think you're joking, but you have no idea how right you are," I said, taking a deep breath and bracing myself. All I needed was a rumor to get back to Zella that I was rude to someone at a party, and wham! I'd be fired.

191

I was so distracted, I barely heard him say, "I love you."

Removing the phone from my ear while trying to catch up with Matt, I moved my thumb to the screen and hung up the call. I quickly held the phone to my mouth and shouted, "I love you, too!" with the hope that I had said it before the call disconnected.

Pausing for a moment to consider if I might be a callous girlfriend or a more callous colleague. I quickly dismissed the thought as I walked faster to find Matt. I knew that Sam would forgive me. But Zella would not. I walked all around, surprised that with just a few people left, I couldn't find Matt. I made a quick trip around the room and scanned it twice with no luck. I grabbed Denise and unleashed my worry.

"Oh Natalie, I'm sure it's all fine. Matt can't expect anything from a three-minute conversation with you. People in this business are super catty, so I'm sure he's used to the snarky and bitchy comments. And more importantly Zella isn't going to fire you. You're paranoid."

"Are you sure?" I asked.

"No, nothing is for sure. However, you've been with Zella for a while now and she doesn't have anyone else working for her. I'm not saying you're not replaceable, but we're in wedding season, and if your roster is anything close to ours, she can't afford to fire you at the moment."

With a deep sigh I looked at her. A movement over her shoulder caught my eye, and I looked up to see Matt walking toward us.

"Hey! Welcome back!" He said jubilantly.

"Wow, what put you in a good mood? I'll have what he's having." Denise asked suggestively. "Did one of the gay and fabulous corner you in a back room and do you a favor."

"Denise!" I shrieked quietly and smacked her across the shoulder with my clutch purse.

"Ha-ha!" Matt chuckled. "Nope. No sexual acts have been committed here tonight. The health department wouldn't allow it." Matt continued with the joke.

"Ah good. I saw one of the Beverly Brothers eyeing you and I was wondering."

"No, they left a while ago," Matt continued to banter in an overly happy way. He was almost bouncing on his toes. "Actually, we just booked a big client. I went in the back to call my girlfriend and tell her about it."

I couldn't be sure, but he seemed to put emphasis on the word girlfriend. I found myself both curious and disappointed at the same time. As I was shaking it off, and reminding myself I had a boyfriend, I felt a hand on my shoulder.

"Why hello, New Girl Natalie. It is Natalie, right?"

"Hello, Alexander," Denise said to him in a stay-away voice. "What brings you out with the little people?"

"I think what my friend Denise is trying to say is," I whipped her a look, and then turned back to Alexander while brushing his hand off my shoulder and starting a handshake, making it seem like he just missed my hand, "How are you finding the party?" I was always polite and tried to leave a good impression. Especially after Matt overhearing my phone call with Sam. I still wasn't sure I was in the clear there, but one thing at a time.

"Denise, it's always a pleasure," Alexander said in a tone that made me think he didn't really mean what he said. "And Natalie, it's so nice to see you out again. I always come out to meet and greet the talent that is worth meeting," he said, giving me the tiniest of winks and then turning to Matt. "I'm so glad we came to an agreement about my party."

"Party?" Denise asked.

"Yes," Alexander said with a grin and turned toward Denise. "Smith and Spencer are going to be the hottest new company to work with. I'm doing an industry event with a few of my colleagues and Smith and Spencer agreed to cater it. Anyone who is anyone will be there. I'll send the invitations soon, but until then, try not to get too excited, Denise. I'm not sure if there will be room for all of the Beauty In Cake crew."

"I'll try not to Alexander," she said with an extra heavy emphasis on the last two syllables of his name.

"Well then, with that done, I have more work to do, so I will see you all later. Matt, make sure you email me that contract first thing tomorrow. We have to create the menu, as soon as possible." He turned toward me and lowered his voice just enough to make it seem nefarious to any who heard, "Natalie, don't forget our conversation," and Alexander turned on his heel and started out the door.

While Alexander was still in hearing range, Denise hissed at me, "What was that about? I thought I told you to stay away from him."

As I watched Alexander Milford walk away, even though all I saw was his back, I could have sworn I saw him smile. That was a man who loved to see people wriggle like a worms on hooks. Until Denise grabbed my arm and turned me toward her, I couldn't tear my eyes away from him. I was starting to understand why he was dangerous.

"Earth to Natalie. Why is Alexander Milford reminding you about a conversation?"

"Oh no reason other than to make you ask I'd assume." I waved it off then saw her face scrunched in an angry confusion. "It wasn't anything. I ran into him outside of your Beauty In Cake party and he was trying to poach me, I think."

"Oooh, girl, stay away," she reminded me.

194

"Denise," I looked into her eyes questioningly, "Why exactly should I stay away from him?"

We stared at each other for a minute. She broke first, looking at her feet then over my shoulder. "At an event, that man—" she stopped herself, and looked around with paranoia, "well let's just say, he can ruin a reputation in a second. And it can't be confirmed, but he might have broken up an engagement and helped cancel a wedding that a planner who currently employs you had booked."

"Yikes," I replied, looking over my shoulder as if to check that he hadn't crept back to our group. "So, he did something to you and to Zella? Ok, I get it. I'll steer clear. Although in this business you know how hard it is. Just know that you've been heard, and if you see me talking to him it's just niceties."

"Good. Now back to more important things. Matt, I believe my glass is empty," Denise said while grabbing his arm and taking him over to the bar.

As they walked away, I felt conflicted. On the one hand, I wanted to go home and see Sam. Snuggle in bed with him and maybe have that make out session. On the other, I just wanted another drink and to talk to friends.

Four cocktails and two hours flew by. We were all sitting around in rented chairs, I was wearing Matt's blazer and had taken off my shoes. Denise had left, and Jack was turning off the lights signaling he was about to leave.

"Night, Matt. Lock up when you," he gave Matt a knowing look, "leave."

"Alright brother. We're not long behind you." He smiled at me. "Can I get you anything else?"

"No, I shouldn't." I started to move, but then just sat back in the chair. "Well maybe a few more minutes just sitting here. Who knew kitten heels could make your feet

195

hurt just as much as tall heels?" I said, feeling very wise, but it probably came out very sloppily, with how thick my head and lips felt.

"Well, it's almost two. I don't have to be anywhere in the morning, so you can sit here as long as you'd like." He smiled at me. "It's nice talking to you."

Two in the morning. What had we talked about for so long. I couldn't even remember. But I had to agree, it was nice to sit here and just talk with someone who understood. About the business. About the hours. About how crazy my boss was. As I looked at him, I had an inkling of why some people cheat. It is nice to be seen and recognized. My dangerous mooning at him was interrupted by a hiccup, which made me jump. It also made me realize I was thinking about sloppily making out with Matt. While Sam was in our bed at home sleeping.

"Well, I think that was enough sitting," I said, reaching for my shoes, and slapping them on my feet as quickly as possible, while trying to dial a car at the same time. The car would be outside in two minutes. Wow, that was fast. "My car will be here in two minutes. I have to go," I said as I darted toward the elevator. Stopping just short of it, realizing I was wearing his jacket, I jogged back to him while whipping it off my shoulders and held it on one finger from my extended arm. "Thank you for a great… party," I said.

I could feel the blush rising in my cheeks. What was I thinking? My phone chimed telling me my driver had arrived. I jogged to the elevator and pressed the button. It opened immediately, and I hit the button on my phone to call the driver to tell him I was on my way. Just as the doors were closing the last few inches I looked up to see Matt smiling at me with a dopey grin. And he winked.

It was a good thing I left when I did. I could have gotten into a lot of trouble. And I certainly didn't want anyone to accuse me of cheating.

Chapter Twenty-Four

" Just what exactly are you accusing me of?" I asked.

"Not being in this relationship." Sam put his hands on his hips and gave me a death glare.

"What are you getting at?" I mirrored his stance.

"I took out the trash two days ago! You could take it out once in a while on your way into work!" Sam yelled at me.

"Sam, I can't possibly get drippy trash on my outfit while I'm walking out to work. Besides, you are the one who makes all the trash!" I screamed back at him.

"I'm the one who makes the trash, because I'm the only one who is ever home and does any of the cooking."

We rarely fought but were both sour from terrible days. We also hadn't seen each other awake in over a week. Spark Gym kept dangling Sam's promotion over his head. He was working almost seventy hours a week with his classes and all the extra things to "prove" he was worthy of a coordinator position at one of the club locations. He had started to tell me about all of this to catch me up on everything that I'd missed. I told him to pause for a second while I checked my phone, as it had bleeped at me four times since I walked in the door and in case it was Zella, I needed to look. Sam sighed with irritation and muttered something like, "of course you're checking for her message," as he galumphed back into the kitchen with the spatula in his hand like a wounded hero who failed at saving the day. He started to empty something into the trash when it fell over, causing this current exchange about taking out the trash.

I didn't need to feel like my relationship was in jeopardy on top of work nonsense where Zella railed at me from the moment I walked into the office—actually it had started with a barrage of ten text messages around 7am that were in response to an email that I sent her at almost 3am when I had finished working on one of her organizing documents for the wedding in two weeks. My head was pounding from the continual shrieking she did all day and reading these text messages. I had brought home another pile of work to do, which would probably keep me up very late again. I was cowering with my shoulders at my ears. Not equipped to take Sam's crabbiness in addition to all that Zella had tossed my way today, I snapped back at him.

"You're not the only one doing important things—"

"Oh, and finding the perfect ribbon and the perfect font for an invitation are saving the fucking world," he retorted with his back to me.

And so, it began. We started tearing each other apart for every infinitesimal detail bothering us the last few months. The fight jumped from our jobs, to how we weren't home for each other, to our mothers calling the other one to ask why we hadn't called lately, to Sam accusing me of having something going on with Matt. Sam swore there was something going on between Matt and me even though I'd only seen a couple of random times.

We continued down a rabbit hole of complaints from not cleaning the apartment, to a time I was late giving him rent, to how I was tired of hearing that he was at the bar with Nick, Kate, and Fiona all the time. How would things be like if we got married, how he wanted kids, and I maybe didn't. How if I couldn't even help around our apartment a little, how would we even take care of kids. He hated that I was out all the time at industry events. I was sick of him saying he couldn't see me in the middle of the day to have lunch together. He was pissed that I had stopped coming to his classes when I used to go at least once a week.

The fight went on for hours. It was a good thing we lived in Harlem—sadly fights of the high volume of ours were a common occurrence.

We picked on every little thing about each other. My headache raged. I drank two bottles of red wine by myself and ate nothing. Finally, Sam brought up the trash, and how he does all the cooking. And I'd had it. Feeling tears start to fall. I slammed down my wine glass so hard I'm surprised it didn't shatter. I walked over to him about to slap him. But instead, let out a guttural scream then stomped into the bathroom slamming the door.

Bracing my arms on the sides of the sink, I stared into my own eyes. What was happening? My amazing job that should open doors was creating so much unrest in my life. I had just screamed because I didn't want to take the garbage out. Whoever this was that I was becoming, I didn't like. The girl in the reflection pitied me.

Tears streamed down my face. I erupted in sobs. Sam and theater were my greatest loves, and I was neglecting both. I hadn't seen Sam in a week; I hadn't auditioned for anything in months. I was captivated by the event world. Kept on a leash by my boss, who was driving me insane, I was missing out on my life.

I didn't know how to sort out, let alone fix any of my problems. I just wanted to keep crying. I wanted Sam to bust down the bathroom door, pull me into his lap and hold me. I wanted to be told everything was going to be alright. Deep down, I knew that was what Sam needed, too. He needed someone to burst into the kitchen and hug him until he stopped hurting. Many times I tried to get myself up from my sitting position, but I didn't have the strength to leave the bathroom.

Footsteps came to the door, but nothing else happened. I started to say Sam's name out loud, but suddenly the urge to vomit was more important. The next few hours were spent on the bathroom floor, sleeping and vomiting into the toilet. Who knows if it was from the stress of my life, the fight with Sam, or the two bottles of Pinot Noir and nothing else in my stomach.

I was in a much-needed reassessment moment in my life. How had my glamorous life become so full of pressure, lacking authenticity, and become devoid of love itself? Well, maybe I'm being a bit dramatic. I was laying on the bathroom floor while having these thoughts.

The next morning, I tried to call in sick. Feeling like death, I tried to convince Zella that I had caught a stomach bug that I was sure was going around. But she wouldn't have it. She said she "just needed me for a few hours," and in a tone that said if I didn't get myself to the office today, I wouldn't need to get myself there again. I threw on leggings, flip-flops, a sports bra, a see-through t-shirt, and my Yale sweatshirt that I got on a trip with my mom.

My abandoned wine glass sat on the table. Picking it up, and feeling nauseated at the waft of wine, I walked to the kitchen and reached for aspirin. The rattling pills sounded like a jackhammer. First only one came out, then I had five in my hand. I tried to scoop them back up, but all went back in. I shook again. Three this time. Fine, who cared, I tossed all three back. Overdosing on aspirin was the least of my issues at the moment. I put the wine glass up to my lips, thinking Hair of the Dog might help me a little, but the waft of the wine went up my nose and made my stomach turn. I dumped the contents of the glass into the sink and went to the fridge. There were a few boxes of coconut water in there. Perfect. I pulled out one and chugged it to take the aspirin.

I started to place it on top of the recycling pile, and I remembered the end of the fight last night. The trash. Both it and the recycling were disgustingly high. I decided that it might be an olive branch to take them out. This was a big feat because the smell was enough to make me heave. I got both bags, tied them up and walked them the four feet to the front door and placed them in the hall while I sprayed both empty bins with Lysol, then put new bags in. Grabbing my phone, charger, computer, another coconut water, and a sleeve of saltines, I left the apartment with the trash in tow.

Walking to the subway, I started to text Sam a cute message about how I miraculously woke up this morning as an adult and took out the trash. But I deleted it. Looking around the street I took a deep breath. The fresh air was nice, so I decided to walk to the next subway stop and called my mom.

"Hi, pumpkin!" She trilled. "To what do I owe this pleasure?" Ugh. She was so darn chipper.

"Mom, I love ya, but I'm so fucking hungover. I had a fight with Sam last night, drank too much, and I'm headed into the office because Zella can't seem to let me have a day to recover from Wine Flu."

Slightly dumbfounded, my mother floundered a little. "Well, um… honey… I… don't quite know where to start on this one. Uh—"

"It's ok, mama." I sighed. "I just needed to be told that I was loved, and that I'm not a terrible person."

"Oh, honey. You're far from a terrible person. I'm sure your boss will change her mind, or you will deal with work and go home. And as for Sam—"

"Oh, mom! I'm totally fucking up my life." I cut her off, trying to get to the heart of the issue.

"Honey, I'm sure you're not fucking up your life."

My mom knew almost everything about me. I swore and drank around her. She knew a decent amount about my sex life. Sam and she chatted regularly too—I assume about things other than our sex life, but who knows. I would just get updates about both of them from each other. My mother and I celebrate Call Your Mother Sunday every week. Generally, she was the first person I called when my life needed a readjustment.

"I haven't auditioned for anything in over six months because every time I actually book one, Zella always needs me and have to cancel. I live with my boyfriend, but never see him. And I'm in a job that could open doors, but are they even doors I want opened? And to top it all off Sam and I fought about taking out the trash."

A loud guffaw came through the phone. "I'm sorry! I'm sorry," she said, trying to contain herself. One more big laugh came through the phone. "I'm sorry. Ok. I'm done. I think." She breathed out a big sigh. "Well. Honey, everyone fights about taking out the trash. It's like religion and politics: everyone has an opinion, but sometimes you just have to be the one doing the work behind the scenes."

Puzzled I answered, "I don't think that analogy works, but—"

Mom rolled right over me. "It's never really about the trash. I'm sure you will figure it all out. He loves you. Very much. I see it, so don't you worry. Nick at work is helping him to climb the corporate ladder, but Sam is concerned he might be getting the wrong advice."

"Wow, Sam is telling you more than he is telling me."

"Well. Honey. I pick up the phone."

"Mom, I pick up the—"

"I'm not going to argue with you," she cut me off and continued. "I just know what he tells me. And what I see. And what I see is that you two have something very special. It's different. You'll figure it all out."

"Yeah. I hope so," I sighed.

"And as for the auditioning, and the working: wasn't part of the reason this job was so great was because you were supposed to have more free time to audition?"

"Well—" it was useless to try to explain the logistics of my life to my mother at this moment. I didn't have the headspace or the patience. Plus, I was about a block away from the subway entrance now. "Mom, I just don't know what to do. My boss is demanding. But I think the money is decent, and the events are amazing. I can see myself with a career in it. But I hate that I am neglecting Sam and theater."

"Honey," my mom's tone made me stop walking. "It's a good job. Stick with it for a bit. Just remind your boss that you need to go back to the original agreement and take the time for yourself."

My mom was partially right. I needed to start taking time for myself. But, if I were to admit, I really liked the prestige of the job. And it felt more grown up than the dream of theater that felt so difficult at times.

"Mom, I've gotta go, I'm at the subway station and I've got to hop on the train. And I'm getting texts from Zella I should answer."

"All right honey. You take care. I love you." I could hear concern in her voice.

"I love you, too, mom."

"And stop thinking you're a bad person."

"Thank you," I sighed.

"Such a heavy sigh. Oh, my love. You will figure it all out. Remember what I always say: Keep breathing, and everything will work out."

"Thanks, mom. Talk to you Sunday."

"Ok, honey. Good luck." Hanging up, I dashed down the subway steps. I read Zella's twelve texts.

Of course, she needed me to run errands. Ten things to get at four different stores, and I needed to stop at the printer and pick up some invitations. Goody, I thought to myself, we were stuffing invitations today. Sarcastically I thought, what a perfect activity to do while hungover and in a fog of self-loathing. Zella is going to be crasser and more irritated at me today than yesterday, I surmised.

Chapter Twenty-Five

An hour later I had run all her errands and texted Zella that I was on my way. She responded that she needed me to stop by the post office. Not only did I need to weigh an invitation, but I needed to buy the special rose stamps she had promised the client.

For a short time, the post office offered this bouquet of flowers that were a forever stamp. Zella loved to use these on wedding invitations if we weren't making custom stamps, because they were much more romantic than most designs. I rolled my eyes as I stood in line.

Why is everything much more difficult and painful when suffering a hangover? The line in the post office was intolerable. The long, slow line allowed me to stop and revisit all the frustrations of last night. I kept wincing to myself. Anyone who was watching probably thought I had a facial tic. In fact, a familiar face commented on it.

"What's happening there, Zella's New Girl? Are you allergic to something here?"

My eyes attempted to focus on the voice that made me cringe a little. Alexander Milford. Without thinking I looked down through my sunglasses at what I was wearing. I looked homeless, or like a college student. Great.

And of course, he looked perfect from his shined loafers, without socks, to his tailored pants, and he was making a sweater vest look good with his muscular torso. I could see why Zella might have gone for him. I told myself to stop thinking that. It was just a rumor. Changing tactics, I decided if I was cheerful, he wouldn't notice my slip up.

"Hey. There. You. How are things?"

"It's Alexander, if you're forgetting my name."

"Right. Alexander."

"Tough night? Zella keeping you up at all hours? Ooh! Or did you have a slumber party, braiding each other's hair and swapping secrets?"

I laughed out loud at that comment.

"See, Natalie, I'm not so bad." Then he winked at me. "Unless you want me to be."

"Gross. Does that line actually work?" Wow, my filter was totally gone today.

"You tell me," he said.

I sneered. He chuckled and put his hands in his pants pockets. "Sorry. Occupational hazard."

Shaking my head, I asked, "So what are you doing here, Alexander?"

"Last time I checked the post office was a public place."

"Fair."

"No need to be rude or think I'm following you. Or trying to steal you away from the clutches of Madame, although I know you would be better working for me than for her." I rolled my eyes, but he chuckled and then continued. "I needed to mail some wedding invitations for a client."

As I lifted my sunglasses and set them atop my head I made an overly appalled face, "Don't you have assistants to do that for you?"

"I do, but it's nice to get out sometimes." A slow smile crept up his face. Then he winked at me. "And you never know who you're going to run into."

My mouth dropped open. I didn't know what to say.

"So, New Girl. Zella doesn't want you looking nicer than her?"

"What are you talking about?"

"Well, I don't know how to put this without sounding totally condescending, but your choice of clothing today is not what I've ever seen her girls wear. Even to a workout class she has dragged them to."

"Thanks. I don't need your opinion or observation of my life." I crossed my arms. He crossed his and watched me. "Well, if you must know, my boyfriend and I had a big fight."

"About?"

"Why should I tell you? From what I hear you'll pass the gossip along to all of your friends and then Zella will fire me from my incompetence because I can't keep a man."

"That's just ridiculous," he said with no indication of which part he thought ridiculous. Alexander Milford was annoying. Hot, but annoying. I started to wonder about his age, especially since there was the rumor that he slept with Zella, and he seemed very interested in me. How old was this man? He looked to be in his late 40s or early 50s.

Rolling my eyes, I asked, "Will you promise not to spread this around?" After he nodded, I continued. "My boyfriend, Sam, thinks I work too much. And with his schedule being mostly mornings and mine being mostly nights, we never seem to see each other awake anymore."

"Ah, the Event Planner Widow Syndrome."

"What? That is just ridiculous."

"Is it?" Alexander lifted an eyebrow in question. "We are always out, and always working, leaving our significant others home alone while we go to parties where we are out with the most beautiful people. They can get into all kinds of trouble without us."

"Trouble?"

He gave me a knowing glance. With disbelief, I squinted back at him waiting for him to elaborate. He didn't.

"Come work for me, New Girl. I'll make sure you get all the time off you need for good behavior."

Now come on. There was a total double entendre in that. Probably more than two. Ugh, I was not in the mood or the outfit to be flirted with shamelessly in this way.

"I would never work for you," I said, spitting with more venom than a velociraptor.

"We'll see."

"What does that mean?" I put my hand on my hip and waited for an answer.

He didn't give one. Instead, he turned on his heel and said over his shoulder, "Just make sure you know what's important, New Girl. And know I'm a friend when you need one."

By the time I got to the office, I had berated myself so much for my fight with Sam, and for talking to that slime Alexander, that Zella's demands were going to be a welcome relief. But I was walking in as she was walking out.

"You took too long, Natalie. I have an appointment, so you'll have to do these alone." She sighed as she did an about face. Dropped her bag on the counter. Quickly flew through putting together a sample. Looked at my nails to confirm I had no polish on them that would rub off on the envelopes. Reminded me five times not to screw anything up, and then left.

Chapter Twenty-Six

I was alone with my headache, my bad choices and five hundred wedding invitations to be stuffed. Wedding invitations are deceptively hard and require a good deal of concentration.

First the reply card needs to be numbered and noted on a spreadsheet next to the invitee. This is to make sure upon return if someone doesn't put their name on it, or it's illegible, you know who sent it. Then a double check of the addressed outer envelope address matches the address on the spreadsheet. You know, the spreadsheet that this week alone, the bride changed three times, and although I asked her to proof each time, she still didn't. Errors were found. I was blamed. But not bitter, moving on.

Then there was the matchup of all of the inserts. This invitation had so many different pieces. It had the standard invitation, the reply envelope, different reply cards for those attending the wedding and rehearsal. Different invitation cards for wedding, rehearsal, and brunch. Different cards for just the wedding. A different card for wedding and brunch.

And finally, a wedding website velum, because it is gauche to put one's wedding registry in an invitation, but not the website guests can go to that will direct them to your Le Creuset wish list. The invitation list had to be cross-referenced to see who got which reply card. And then there were the different inserts for the rehearsal dinner and the brunch.

My eyes were crossing already. And then, if that all wasn't enough, stamps had to be placed perfectly squarely on the reply envelopes. And three on the outer envelopes. It's an intricate puzzle and focus and attention are needed the whole time. My afternoon consisted of five hundred and forty-one invitations.

If there is a purgatory, it is stuffing wedding invitations.

I laid my head down in a whimper on the table. It felt like fire trucks with judgmental mini versions of me holding rubber mallets and gongs were running back and forth through my head making all kinds of loud noise and hypercritical comments about my life choices. I wanted to get up, walk away from the table and never come back. I wanted to call Sam and sob and apologize. I wanted to crawl into my mother's lap and just have her hug me and pet my head until I felt better. I wanted to throw a cold beverage at Alexander and his perfect outfit in the post office. I was borderline going postal. Always wondered what that felt like.

Wishing at this moment, I had all of the disposable income I wished for—like the clients we served—I would take off to Brazil or someplace warm and sunny and just tune out the world.

A thought slithered into my mind. Zella kept cash in the office. A good deal of cash. Enough cash to live on for a long time. Especially in a foreign country. This struck me for a tiny opportunistic moment. I knew exactly where it was. She was going to be gone for a few hours. I could easily get the cash, get back up to my apartment, book a flight to a foreign country and skip town before she even knew the cash was missing. And wouldn't realize anything was wrong until I didn't text her back the next day. She would probably not even put it together because I was so trustworthy.

As I dreamt about running away, I knew I had to eat first. I called for delivery. I got a greasy hamburger, extra fries, and a blue sports drink. I figured the grease and carbs would soak up anything left in my stomach, and the sports drink would replenish my electrolytes. And color my tongue blue, which would annoy Zella when she returned. If she returned. Then I numbered the return cards and stamped their envelopes.

The doorman called up and I stood at the door expecting a delivery man with my food, but in walked Violet instead. Two paper bags in her hands.

"Hey girl!" She exclaimed, letting herself into the office, "Do we still take off our shoes upon entering?" Zella had a rug she claimed was one of a kind. Only clients were allowed to walk on it with shoes. Everyone else was required to go shoeless. I was pretty sure this was a power play. Today I had half forgotten, and half refused to remove mine. Zella hadn't noticed.

"We should," I said, tucking my sneakers under the table. "I'm so glad to see you, but could you only talk to me in a whisper," I half joked, half wheedled at her.

"Uh oh, what is wrong?"

"So many things, but the most prevalent is that I'm hung over… I mean, I have a 'stomach bug.' You're carrying my salvation." I lifted myself from the table and took the bag that she held out to me, then sat down at the bar away from the invitations. Without even blinking I dove into my burger and wolfed it down. Maybe I shouldn't eat so quickly with a tender tummy, but I kept eating. I was ravenous, and a bit masochistic.

Violet sat down next to me. "So… how are… things?" She said looking around the office.

"Zella isn't here. She is out at a meeting and who knows when she will be back, but it won't be before four this afternoon."

As if on cue, my cell phone rang.

"I'll get it for you." Violet jumped up and grabbed my phone. "Ha! It's Zella."

212

As if I had done something wrong and needed to hide the evidence, I jumped from my seat, wiped my mouth, swallowed quickly, and answered the call on speakerphone. "Hello, Zella." My voice was a bit garbled from my last bite.

"Natalie, what is going on there?"

"Um, nothing. I mean. I'm stuffing the invitations. Oh, I was drinking a sports drink—" she cut me off while I was putting her on speaker phone.

"You'd better not have it near the invitations."

"No, ma'am. I mean Zella." Whoops, I thought, trying to correct myself.

"Natalie, I told you not to call me that. Also, Violet from Albert Barnes Studio is going to stop by. She has a zip drive for me and probably some ridiculous present from Albert." She said his name like it was a French disease she didn't want.

Violet and I made aghast faces at each other while Zella continued. "Make sure you put the zip drive on my desk," she said the last three words incredibly slowly like I spoke a different language or was a child. I rolled my eyes at Violet, who got up and tiptoed over to Zella's desk, and moved things so the zip drive was in plain sight and in a prominent place.

"After you get done with the invitations, and this is very important, Natalie. Make sure you're writing it down."

"Yes, Zella," I replied even though she just kept speaking.

"I need you to call down to Dominic and get him to have the landlord come up tomorrow at 10am to look at the spot on the ceiling. I need you to call my nail place and make an appointment for me and a guest for manicures at 11:30am tomorrow. Let the nail place know it's me and I want my regular girl. And let them know that if Georgina isn't available for the second person, I want Ken. Call Christopher and let him know that I'm working on a proposal and ask if he's thought about The Plaza. Actually, never mind, I'll text him right now."

The phone went silent for a moment, and Violet thought it was safe, that Zella had hung up.

"Wow, that wom—"

Whipping around so Violet, my eyes wide, I put my finger to my lips with one hand and pointed at my phone with the other.

"Oh, she's still there?" Violet whispered.

I nodded yes.

Through the phone we heard Zella screech angrily at the driver. She then remembered I was on the line. "Natalie, are you still there? I swear some of these drivers are terrible."

"Yes, Zella. I can hear you. I'm sure the driver can hear you, too."

"Right. Well, what else. I need you to pick up the dry cleaning, or have it delivered. I need you to get the card on my desk for my doctor and call him and tell him I can't do a follow-up until next week, and figure something out, you have access to my calendar. I have to go now, I'm here." Click.

There was a moment of silence in the room. I shook my head while reviewing my notes.

"She's officially gone now," I said and turned to Violet.

"Can I speak frankly?"

"I mean," I said timidly, "I'm always a tad bit paranoid talking about her in her own office, but sure. Go ahead."

"Wow! Are you always doing personal things for her like that?" Violet asked.

"Yeah. It's part of the job. You do personal things from time to time for Albert, right?"

"Nope. Not my job description," she said, making a face of disdain.

"Well," I reasoned unconvincingly, "maybe it's because you work for a photographer, and I work for a planner. She is used to providing these services for other people that pay her, so she expects it from the people she pays."

"That doesn't sound right," Violet mused. "In my experience, anyway. I feel like there are too many boundaries that can be crossed."

"Do you mean like text messages or phone calls at any time day or night?" I asked. "Or when I get reamed out because I didn't prioritize correctly—you would assume that the clients we service would be first priority, right?"

"They're not?"

"Nope," I said. "Sometimes not even the week of their own wedding," I said. "Last week I thought referring to picking up paper stock for reserved seating was more important than picking up Zella's tailoring. Nope." I took a deep breath and readjusted my salty tone. "But I keep breathing. I get paid well, and this job will open a lot of doors…"

"Wow. Are you sure this is the right job for you?" Violet asked. "I mean, I know that Albert gets under my skin sometimes, and I work way too many hours, but at least I can turn it off."

My head snapped around to Violet. "Everyone has to pay dues, right? In every career? I have only worked for Zella now for about eight months. I've learned a lot, but with no prior industry experience, I just have to suck it up and keep doing what I'm told. Besides, she is a prominent woman in this town. Yeah, I do a lot of grunt work, but I get to work from home. If I ever book a play, she says she would be flexible with performances. And I really am meeting a lot of people in the field."

"Yeah, but is she treating you well? Are you sure this is all worth the stress you're going through? I don't know you that well, and maybe you're just having a tough day."

I let out a loud humph in response.

"Guess who I ran into at the post office." I didn't wait to let her guess. "Alexander Milford."

She gasped. "No."

"Yup. And he offered me a job. Again."

"Well, if that weren't career suicide, I would tell you to entertain the offer. Plus, he's so handsome."

"I know."

"Maybe it wouldn't be such a bad thing. I mean he did horrible things to Zella apparently."

"Do you know what?"

"No, do you?"

"Well," I said, my shoulders drooping with the weight of a thousand worlds on them. "There was the alleged affair, and he did something heinous to her apparently. I could never work for a man like that."

"Right. Because he's a very horrible person. I swear he sits at hotels to bag clients." She twisted her mouth to the side then kept speaking, "but it sounds like you're really frustrated with working here."

Honestly, I didn't know if the pain was real or if I was just being dramatic.

"I'm just having a day. I had a fight last night with Sam, my boyfriend, about how much I'm working. I drank and cried too much last night, and I didn't want to come in and deal with any of this nonsense today. Stuffing wedding invitations is such a pain. I feel like I'm doing the work of three people."

"Maybe you should tell Zella."

"I tried. She wouldn't hear it," I said.

"What happened to the other assistant?" Violet asked.

"Amanda? She works from home only and is busy with all of her personal projects. I'm actually pretty jealous of her, she auditions so much. I haven't seen her at all since I've been working here." I sighed again. "Truth be told, I thought I'd get to see her more."

"What do you really want?" Violet looked into my eyes.

Without a beat, I solemnly replied, "A handsome and caring sugar daddy."

After a moment we both laughed.

Jumping up to throw away my lunch trash and wash my hands I said, "I have to get back to stuffing these invitations." I also didn't want to talk about my situation anymore. This job might just be sucking my life away. But I didn't want to admit it because I wanted it to work out. I wanted to be an event planner.

"Right. Well, Albert did send over a 'ridiculous present' for Zella," Vi said, copying Zella's outrageousness. "He sent this photo book and a box of chocolates. If I were you, I'd keep the chocolate. She never has to know. And it sounds like you deserve it."

"Ha, yeah, but I'd know. Want to hear something crazy? I contemplated stealing money and running away to a desert island right before you came in."

"It's not the same thing. It's chocolate." Her mouth twisted as if she were sizing me up. "Plus, you'd never actually take money. Here, I'm handing it to you. I think it's for you."

"I can't. I don't want to lose my job over chocolates," I said, putting both hands up. "Plus, she is guilting me into losing more weight. Thank you, though. I'll make sure she gets it."

Violet headed for the door. "Natalie, not for nothing, but you're doing great at this stuff. If this is truly what you want, keep up what you're doing." She stopped and turned back to me. "I heard Zella say you're one of the best assistants she's ever had."

My head snapped up from the invitation I was currently stuffing. "What?" I exclaimed.

"Yup. Interesting, huh? When they were on the phone yesterday talking about this zip drive, she told Albert that there wasn't anything you couldn't do. That you are one of the best assistants ever."

"You're making that up to make me feel better. I swear she is going to fire me any day now," I said, my face stormy with derision. "Zella gets so upset with me about the tiniest things. Some days I don't even know which way is up because she is continually mad at me. Then I keep making more mistakes because I'm terrified that she'll be upset about the next thing—which she usually is."

"Nope, she was on speaker phone. I heard it with my own ears. Girl, with all you do for her, if you're not making at least twenty dollars an hour, you're not making enough." She smiled a devious smile. "And I think you could thrive on your own. If you wanted to." She opened the door while sliding on her shoes. "Just think about it. She couldn't do all she does without you. No matter how much crap she puts you through." And on that note, she left.

Was Violet right? Was I worth more than this? I knew I had worked for other companies with larger responsibilities and had been compensated accordingly. But I had never worked in this industry before, and thought I had to pay my dues. Other traditional jobs, I had company-instated reviews and then got a raise. I had never actually asked for more money. Ever. This thought took over the hangover and pounded in my head.

While the thoughts rolled over in my head, my hands were busy at work. Before I knew it, all of the invitations were done. Frustration put a fire under me. I was in such a trance I was actually terrified when I finished the last invitation and reached to the box of envelopes for the next to find only blanks left. I spot-checked, opening up every third envelope to check their contents were correct to make sure that I had done everything right.

Zella returned just as I was finishing my inspection.

"How are the invitations coming?" she asked as she walked in and partially disrobed.

"I haven't sealed them yet, but all are stuffed." I wanted to wait to seal the invitations until she gave the okay. Zella did a random spot check of thirty invitations. Satisfied, she sat with me, and we sealed them together.

"Aren't you glad you came in today?" Zella asked.

Maybe it was the residuals of the fight with Sam, the remainder of my headache, or the frustration of not knowing if I was worth more. Or maybe it was just my irritation at stuffing over five hundred invitations alone.

"Humph. Sure."

"What is the matter? You're not yourself today. Are you ok?" Zella asked. Shocked into silence, I gaped at her, mouth open, unable to speak.

"What, Natalie?"

Finally finding my voice I said, "You've never actually asked me about myself before."

"Oh, Natalie. Don't be ridiculous. I'm sure I—"

"Nope. You haven't," I said, cutting her off with the abruptness of a meat cleaver in a butcher shop.

Zella whipped her head around. "I—well. You've never—" she cleared her voice and her accusatory train of thought and the polished veneer she worked so hard to keep up, fell away for a moment. "Would you like to tell me what is going on?"

For a moment I sat amazed, wondering if it was a trap. Zella got more than personal with all of her clients and truly cared about each bride she worked for. It hadn't been apparent that she had a heart toward anyone that worked for her. Maybe that was an unfair view, but it was the view I had.

A heavy sigh escaped. I decided to take a chance. "Huge fight with my boyfriend last night. I haven't heard from him today, and I spent most of the night crying in the bathroom. Which I know sounds pathetic." I decided to leave out that I had a good amount to drink and was insanely hung over. "I'm also frustrated about my job." I had made a split-second decision to share that I was disgruntled, but I would make it about my nanny gig, not about this one, and see what her view was. It seemed like a good plan.

"Men come and go. The right one will stick with you and won't be afraid to show you the truth." Zella looked out the window absently. There was a deep silence for a moment.

I knew Zella was married, but I didn't know much about the relationship. I knew he did something in commercial real estate. There was gossip that floated around that her husband was so focused on his job that their marriage was suffering. It was ironic that the woman who made magical weddings for people was suffering in her own union. Looking at her in this moment, I saw a glimmer of a real woman there. I had always assumed that she was just a work machine because she never showed much emotion. Now, I wasn't so sure.

She continued to look out the window as she said, "In college I was head over heels for a man. We were engaged, and so in love. And then one day he just… disappeared." Her tone was soft and reflective. Suddenly it came matter of fact and in the voice I was used to as she turned back toward me. "But then I met my husband and the real magic happened." Zella's wall was back up. I didn't believe all the rumors, but something told me that she didn't have a magical relationship with her husband. Zella continued, "If it is truly meant to be, it will. That is what I tell all our brides." She had resumed her normal voice and was back in business mode. "And I don't want to meddle in your affairs with other employers, but if you think that you're worth more, I can help you figure out a way to negotiate. A woman should know her own worth."

Slightly stunned, and just in a swirl of emotions and confusion, I told Zella maybe another time to deflect the conversation of worth and a pay raise. What can I say, I am a chicken. We sealed all the envelopes, and I took them to the post office to be hand canceled so they wouldn't get stuck in the sorting machines.

Sam hadn't texted. I went home to our empty apartment. Feeling sorry for myself, and not knowing what to say to Sam, I ordered Chinese food and snuggled on the sofa watching some ridiculous and mushy Hallmark movie. I fell asleep on the sofa, and I woke to my phone alarm going off the next morning. Sam was nowhere to be seen. A dirty protein shake cup in the sink was the only clue he had been here. Still no text or contact of any kind from Sam. We had never been this upset at each other before. I felt abysmal and I didn't know what to do to make any of it better.

Chapter Twenty-Seven

Zella didn't require my presence in the office the next day. It was unfortunate that I didn't have some mind-numbing tasks to work on so I didn't have to think about my personal predicaments. Instead, I lounged around in my pajamas and self-pity all morning.

Why is it that when one is neck deep in personal questioning that every movie and television program, every song, and every magazine article seem to be pointing fingers directly, making the situation unavoidable but not revealing solutions to the issues?

Around 2pm I took a quick shower to try to rinse off the stupor before I went to pick up Levi. I still didn't understand the last forty-eight hours. Sam and I had fought about a bunch of tiny insignificant things, Zella showed that she was somewhat human, and I obviously didn't know my worth.

Levi was his normal tween-brooding self, and we chatted on the way to the trumpet lesson. Just as soon as he walked in, my phone rang. It was his mother.

"Hi, Suzanne!" I answered, trying to cover up any low and sad tones my voice might contain.

"Well, aren't you chipper today?"

Apparently, my acting was still pretty good. "Yup. No reason. How are you, Suzanne?"

"I'm all right. Listen, do you have time for a chat?"

As far as I was concerned, I was on her dime anyway. "Yeah, I have no plans right now. What's up?"

"Well, I'm around the corner at the museum. Can you come over? Would you mind?"

"Not at all. I'm on my way now."

"Oh, no need to rush," Suzanne said with a tiny bit of rising panic in her voice. "In fact, if you want to stop for a coffee on your way, it's on me."

"Ok. I'll do that. Do you want anything, Suzanne?"

"Sure, I'll take a coffee with a bit of milk in it."

"Got it," I said.

"Great. I'll see you soon. Take care!"

About ten minutes later I walked into the museum with two coffees. As I started to tell the security guard that I was there to see Suzanne, she came out of a room, waving at me.

"That's her, sir," I said to the guard.

Suzanne walked me back to an office behind a heavy wooden museum door that had "staff only" written on it. The kind I always had wondered what was behind. We sat down in a cozy wood-paneled room that looked like it might be the model for a gentleman's club or a hunting lodge.

"How are things going with you? I feel like I need a Natalie update," Suzanne said as she was settling in and taking a sip of her coffee."

"Things are... well, they're interesting at the moment," I replied.

"How so?" she asked.

"Well, Sam and I are having a disagreement at the moment. And although wedding planning is a great career, I feel like I'm failing my dream by not auditioning enough at the moment. I might be focusing on the wrong things—which is what Sam and I are fighting about."

"Well, Natalie, do you want my advice?"

Advice from employers seemed to be a trend. Since I was feeling vulnerable and figured it couldn't hurt. "Sure," I shrugged.

"Well, I think you should focus on the event work. You're a great actress. You know that we support you.

Maybe it's time to focus on a career. I have a feeling that would help your relationship as well," she said in a very motherly tone.

Unconvinced, but not wanting to be rude, I replied, "Yeah, you're probably right."

There was a moment of silence between us as Suzanne let her thoughts sink in.

"There was something else I wanted to discuss with you," Suzanne said.

Tensing up, I replied, "Oh? What is that?"

"Well, Levi is getting older, and next year he is transferring to a different school. And although we love you, I think that maybe for next semester, we probably... well, definitely won't be needing a nanny for him anymore."

I chuckled. Suzanne read it the wrong way and said, "We love you, and you're family. So, we still want to see you. Don't think that I'm trying to pawn you off on your other job. In fact, if you want, we could set up an arrangement where you can come over once a week to meal prep for the week."

"Suzanne, I've been gearing up Levi to not have a nanny for a while now. You are a wonderful family, but it's definitely time for me to move on," I said as caring as I could.

Suzanne let out a breath and laughed a little. "Oh good. I was afraid to do this. But since the event job is going so well, I felt like we could finally have this conversation."

I couldn't help feeling both released and trapped. But I didn't want to deal with these feelings now. So, I exchanged pleasantries with Suzanne and showed photos of our events I had taken on my phone. Her cell phone rang, and she answered it. While listening to the person on the other line, she whispered to me, "This is going to take a while. I'll let you go! Have a great day, and I'll see you at home," and she waved me out of the room.

I slowly meandered back to get Levi. When I briefed him on my meeting with his mother, he whooped with glee at hearing that I would not be his nanny much longer.

"Gee, thanks kid," I said in response to his pleasure.

"Aww, Natalie, you know what I mean. I just don't need you anymore."

"Yeah, I know. Now you know that means next semester, not today, right?"

"Yeah, I do. Let's go home, I have homework and I want to call Jessica."

"Oooh, Jessica," I said, drawing out her name. "So that is still going on, huh?"

"Ugh, fine! Jessica is my girlfriend, okay?"

I threw my arm around his neck as we were walking down the street to the subway. "Yeah, I know, kid. I wish you all the luck. Girls are crazy. You know that, right?"

He looked at me with confusion. "But Natalie, you're a girl."

"Yup. So, I know for a fact we're all crazy."

We both laughed. I would miss this kid. I had spent so many years watching him grow up.

On the train, I marveled at so many conversations about my future within days of each other. By the time we had reached Levi's apartment, I had made the decision that if Levi was growing up, maybe I should be too. I was going to put my theater career on hold. For a time. I would focus on this career as an event planner. I was also going to put more time and effort into my relationship with Sam. Maybe our own kids were in the future. We really loved each other, and we just needed to make time to be with each other. Together we would figure it out.

While Levi dashed to his room to call Jessica—he said he was going to start his homework, but I knew the news was too good to wait, but I didn't mind. I took out my own phone and composed a text to Sam.

Hey. I love you. I've made some big decisions and am ready to work on us. Are you home tonight?

He answered back almost immediately:

Hi. I love you, too. Yes, home tonight, and can't wait to hear about the big decisions.

I smiled. A huge weight felt like it was being lifted from my chest. I was going to figure out how to make my life work with a career in events. I was going to be the best assistant. My brain started forming a plan to pitch myself to Zella, maybe I could even be her partner someday.

Little did I know there was a bigger storm brewing on the horizon.

Chapter Twenty-Eight

"**B**itch," Zella spat at her computer screen. I was curious, but at the same time I had also learned that 'don't speak unless spoken to' was a rule in this office. Therefore, I kept at my task: reviewing the details for the upcoming wedding weekend.

I knew Zella was reading an email from Genevieve Cross, our full-service bridezilla from a couple of weeks ago. Yesterday in an email, Genevieve stated she refused to pay the remainder of her balance because she was unhappy with the services provided, including that didn't think she needed to pay for Zella's transportation to and from meetings and the wedding. She also complained that our service wasn't the best.

Basically, she was trying not to pay, and coming up with ridiculous reasons for it. This was her second email to Zella. Her first, I had read and given Zella a rebuttal to everything that was mentioned.

"What?!? Genevieve Cross says that you were drinking at her wedding. Natalie? Is this true?"

I froze.

Zella's first rule, well there were a lot of number one rules, but she always said this was number one: do not drink at a wedding. She was also pretty adamant that her vendors didn't drink at her events either. Upon her instruction, I would hide the wine bottles at vendor meal, just so they weren't even a thought. There was still drinking, of course, but at least this way it seemed non-existent to Zella.

Knowing the drinking rule was a priority, and remembering what I did, my heart stopped, as I scanned through my memory of the Cross wedding.

At this point we had done fifteen events together and I was good at running them. Every detail of every wedding was being executed to each bride's satisfaction, if not better. More importantly they met Zella's standards.

We had gotten into a rhythm. I would cover the reception and she would handle the bride and the family, including all of the ceremony activity. I had become very adept at problem solving and being quick to fix things that were wrong and made it look smooth and effortless. We really were a great team. Or so I had come to believe.

Seemingly certifiable the month before the wedding. she was incredibly picky about every detail in every call and email. Which came in at any hour of the day or night with the expectation of a response within thirty minutes. An improbable task during a busy weekday and an impossible task at 2am

Genevieve Cross wanted to impress her Swiss in-laws, so she was micromanaging every minuscule detail. And was driving us insane in the process.

The Swiss believe in eco-friendly weddings with traditional live pine trees as decorations, and pine branches to walk on during the ceremony. With her wedding in the month of May, the flora she demanded was difficult to get. Although evergreens are evergreen, they're not in abundance in spring. Our micromanaging first-time bride had been throwing the grown-up version of temper tantrums for a month because of this. And this was only one detail of at least seventy she was crazy about.

Another was the imported fancy Swiss Rolls set up before the reception started to be given out at the end of the reception as the parting favor. Genevieve had emailed multiple pictures of traditional displays along with diagrams and pages of instruction. But the favors in the picture came in gorgeous plastic boxes that showed the contents and could be stacked like building blocks. The less expensive ones she ordered came individually wrapped in paper tied with a ribbon, were very, very soft, and didn't stack easily.

Honestly, they looked terrible when I stacked them up in a three-dimensional pyramid shape to try to echo the photos she sent even with Sylvia from the venue providing a tiered tray for them to sit. Feeling comfortable in my role managing the party and knowing that Zella preferred things to look elegant and not like a child attempted their display, I decided to set the favors out in a triangle, stacked two high and continued adjusting and rearranging as people took them. Everyone leaving was drunk and loved that they had a snack for the ride home. I even remember Genevieve approving of the displayed favors as she walked by the favor table. I told her in passing that I tried to emulate her photos, but the favors wouldn't stack because they were in different packaging. She seemed fine then.

It was all going smoothly, so Zella left me with the last hour by myself to manage the reception. Which went by impossibly fast. My time was spent restacking favors, chasing down the disappearing photographer and searching for a lost cell phone.

Every time I turned around Genevieve would have me dashing for the photographer who wasn't taking enough photos for her tastes. I think the photographer was just there for the food—she was a referral from a friend of the groom. I continually found her with a plate of food in her hand, barely taking photos at all. And to top it off she turned out terrible photos of the wedding.

If searching for the photographer wasn't enough, I was looking in every nook and cranny of the party space to help a guest locate her cell phone, which she swore was in the tiny ballroom somewhere because her boyfriend could ping its location with his phone.

A new intern was with me until the last half hour of the wedding. And was driving me crazy. With thirty minutes to go, Zella sent us both a text.

If everything is smooth, Molly can go home.

With half an hour left, even if it was total chaos, it was probably easier for me to handle it alone, instead of Molly asking me how to do something when I assigned her a task. I shrugged at Molly. "I'm fine if you want to leave now."

"I think I might. This crowd is very mellow. I'll take off and I'll see you at the next one!"

Molly was a very sweet girl, but not the best at initiative. I had not worked with her before this evening, but I could see why Zella liked her. She blended in, was quiet, and acquiesced to anything you wanted her to do. The problem with Molly is that she just stood there until you gave her a task. It was almost easier to just do it all myself. Cleanup would all be handled by the hotel, so I would be out the door as soon as the last of the guests left. I wasn't expecting to be around much longer anyway.

Just as Molly was turning to leave, the cell phone couple came back and wanted one of us to look for the phone. Again. I asked Molly if she would be a fresh set of eyes on the room. I promised she could go home after they did a loop. She said yes, and off they went.

I texted Zella back:

Molly is assisting with one more task and will head out after that. All is well here. Happy guests.

Accompanying the text, I sent a picture of all of the guests on the dance floor having a great time.

I went and stood by the bar. Oh, and I forgot to tell you who was behind the bar all evening. Matt. Even though I hadn't seen him since his party we hit it off like we had just seen each other a day before. I visited often during the evening. But not for either reason you're thinking. I am committed to Sam. And Zella's rule: no drinking.

At our previous event I was supposed to be the beck-and-call girl for the parents of the bride, but after the wedding they complained to Zella that they could never see me. Even though I had stood behind them the entire night. Anytime they seemed to need something I would send someone over to them to take care of their needs. My job was to make things happen, not to be seen.

I was determined not to be accused of this infraction again. So, at the Cross wedding I made sure to introduce myself to everyone in the wedding party. Also, to ensure my visibility, I became a personal waitress to the bride, groom, and both sets of parents. During the evening, I must have made over twenty runs to the bar, where Matt would pause in his service to whomever he was helping, or would transfer them to the other bartender, help me, and then resume service. I could get drinks faster than anyone else in the room and would deliver them directly. He even asked me a couple times if he could pour something for me. I would reply with a flirty "maybe later" or "not while I'm working."

This time when I went to the bar, Matt was busy pouring Vodka shots. He had twenty-five on a tray. Then like ants to a picnic, all the remaining guests came and picked up a shot glass and went back to the dance floor for a final toast. There were two shot glasses left on the tray when a bridesmaid, who had been drunk since she walked into the hotel, slunk to the bar. Grabbing both she lunged toward me and shoved one in my face.

"This is for you," she aggressively slurred in a European accent.

"Oh, thank you," I replied with my hands up, palms outward as if being arrested, "but I think it's for you."

"No! It's for you!" She became more aggressive and raised both of her hands full with a shot glass each in my face. "See, I have one. This one is yours." She stumbled over her words and her feet, losing her balance. I reached out and grabbed her elbow to stop her descent towards the floor.

"Thank you so much, but I think maybe we both shouldn't have one," I said. My sarcasm unfortunately didn't penetrate her drunkenness.

"No. It's a party. I want you to have one," she insisted.

Realizing that she wasn't giving up, I took one of the shots from the drunken girl and lifted it toward my face. I touched the glass to my tightly clenched shut lips because she continued to watch me as if she knew I was just going to put the drink down on the bar. Instead, I raised the glass close to my lips, pretended to drink, and quickly slammed the full glass down onto the bar and stood between the drunken bridesmaid and my obviously full glass.

She downed hers and I took the glass from her flaccid wrist just before she dropped her arm in a fluid drunken motion. Then she went back to the dance floor and threw herself into the willing arms of a groomsman who had unbuttoned his tuxedo shirt all the way open and was wolfishly looking at her. I hoped they knew each other, because I was pretty sure they were going to be keeping each other company for the rest of the night.

Over my shoulder Matt asked if I still wanted the drink. I moved away from the full glass and shook my hands again like I was trying to prove my innocence.

"I want nothing to do with that drink. I just took it so she wouldn't spill it on me or drink it herself."

Matt snickered as he took the bridesmaid's empty glass away. My full glass remained, mocking me. Honestly, I wanted a drink, but I respected Zella's rules. But since Vodka really isn't my drink, I told myself to wait until I got home and could have a glass of wine or maybe whisky. I looked over at the bride and thought that she looked very happy. I smiled. All of her harassing emails, texts, and late-night phone calls were worth it if she was this blissful.

The last five minutes passed, and I returned to the favor table to bid goodbye to guests and ensure no one left without one of the precious Swiss Rolls. The bride and groom came around the corner and chatted with their guests as they were leaving. Staying in the background, I made sure to press Swiss Rolls into everyone's hand as they were leaving. There were still thirty left on the table at the end. When the last of the guests had departed, Genevieve seemed blissful as she and her husband danced into the elevator and sloppily kissed her new husband.

Chapter Twenty-Nine

After the doors closed behind them, I let out a huge sigh. Thinking the agony of the Cross wedding was over, and a wave of relief washed over me. Collapsing in one of the large leather armchairs just around the corner from the elevator bank, I contemplated removing my shoes that were pinching my toes. Matt came over with a glass filled with amber liquid and handed it to me. I really wanted a drink. I deserved a drink. If nothing else, to wash away the chaos that this wedding was out of my brain.

Looking up at Matt I asked, "Is everyone gone?"

He looked all around the room and said, "All guests left the bar and I see no one here. You're safe, our staff won't tell." He winked at me.

"Maybe you should disguise it with something. Coke?"

"If you'd like, I can."

I thought about it for a second. I really didn't like soda with whiskey. "Nah. I'll take it as is. What is it?"

"Angel's Envy. Cask Strength."

"Wow," I replied in great surprise.

Angel's Envy Cask Strength was something like 126 proof and only made in limited quantities. I had only ever had a sip of it, but it was delicious.

"Just trying to help you forget the evening. Ooh and I saved you the last piece of wedding cake. I know you tried to get one earlier but didn't. And if anyone deserves a slice, you do."

A blush crawled up my neck and I deflected, saying "Yeah, thanks. I was trying to pass out the stupid Swiss Rolls which no one wanted. I said standing and took the glass and plate. "To all your help this evening," I said, raising the glass but setting it down without taking a drink. Instead, I took a bite of the sweet vanilla cake. The waft of the liquid had a beautiful smell and I wanted the drink more than the over-sweet confection.

"Thanks," he said and walked away.

I set the plate down after a second bite, I just couldn't eat anymore. Instead, I carried the glass as I f it were my prize for the evening. As I motivated myself to leave for the evening, I took a last look around. I did this at the end of every party to ensure nothing was left behind, including guests. Confirming the coast was clear, I took another inhalation of the bourbon. The DJ, packing up his equipment, was sipping a beer. Most of the staff had drinks in their hands as well. Technically, I was off the clock. It couldn't hurt to take one sip. And this was amazing bourbon, it would be a shame to waste it.

Throwing caution to the wind I took a tiny sip to relish the amazing flavor and rolled the half-teaspoon on my tongue. With my eyes closed in bliss, I heard the footsteps, and turned to see Sylvia, the head of events. I felt like I had been caught and thought about spitting the bourbon back into the glass. Since that would have only implicated me more, I gently swallowed. Quickly I picked up some of the other glasses on the table to make it look like I was clearing. Hoping she hadn't noticed.

"Oh, you don't have to do that," Sylvia replied. Like everyone else I had worked with on events, Sylvia and I had become fast friends.

"Ok," I said, thinking on my feet. "I just wanted to be helpful."

"I was talking about hiding your drink. Matt told me that he set you up. I can't believe you can get through these things without drinking," she chuckled conspiratorially. "I had one

235

already tonight the moment the bride walked into the building. Go ahead, no one here will say a thing to Madame."

"I don't really want it—I mean I didn't really have—I mean, I don't need to, I—" stammering I set down all the glasses in my hand. I looked at the one that was painfully obvious that it was mine. It was the only full glass; the rest only had a drop or two of liquid in each. I really did want this glass of bourbon, but I felt like my guilt was a blatant sign that I shouldn't drink it. "Thank you for all of your help," I said, once again composed. "Is there anything left for me to do?"

"No, I think my crew will cover it all. Did they find the cell phone?"

"Yeah, turns out it was in their room all along," I replied. "Oh, and tell your crew that they can take flowers, but not vases The florist will come pick those up in the morning. And to help themselves to the Swiss Rolls that are left on the table. There are tons. I guess if you're from Switzerland you don't really want a Swiss Roll as a favor at a wedding!"

Just then we both heard a crash of glass, and both of our heads turned toward the sound.

"Ugh. We have a new waiter tonight. I hope that wasn't him. Gotta go. Let's go out for a drink soon and decompress!" Sylvia hollered the last line over her shoulder as she walked toward the kitchen.

Forlorn, I looked back at my glass. I really didn't need it. I lifted it to my nose and took a sniff and one more small sip. I rationalized again: two sips weren't enough to make anyone drunk, and that was the point of her rule, I'd assumed. And it wasn't like I asked for it or drank during the wedding. It was given to me after my shift was over in front of no one. But I still felt guilty. Taking one more look around the entire area, I made my way to the elevator and took a couple of Swiss Rolls. I figured maybe Sam would want one.

On the short elevator trip to the first floor, I took out my phone to text Zella that the event had ended, and the bride seemed happy. I hit send. At ground level as I walked out of the elevator, I had a thought that I should send another text telling the story of the crazy drunk bridesmaid who shoved alcohol into my hand. But just as I was about to start typing, I heard, "Wedding Planner!" Looking up from my phone, I found three of the groomsmen looking at me.

"Hey, guys. What's up?" I asked as I walked over to them and instinctively shut off my phone's screen.

"We are trying to get into the club, but they say that they can't let us in. That they're at capacity," one of the very attractive men said. A tuxedo makes every man look attractive, no matter his size or shape, but this one was particularly handsome and turned on his charm.

"Let me see what I can do," I looked at him back with a devilish grin. I walked over to the host and asked the hulking man at the door if there was any way I could get the three men into the club.

"Like, I told them lady, we are at capacity."

"Dude, I hear you. But they were just at the wedding upstairs. Is there nothing you can do for me? My clients just dropped so much money to throw their party here."

"Nope. Like I said, we're at capacity," he said glaring at me long and hard before he crossed his arms and turned away to pretend I wasn't there.

Turning back toward my hopeful groomsmen, who were probably looking to get laid tonight. Their original viable candidates, the bridesmaids, were hopefully sleeping off the substantial levels of consumed alcohol in their rooms. My brain raced. I grabbed my phone and called Sylvia.

"Didn't you leave?" she answered without a hello.

"I did," I laughed, "But, I got caught by some eager groomsmen who want to get into the club. Apparently, they're at capacity, and won't let my boys in."

"Ugh! Carl is the doorman tonight and he is such a stickler for those things. How many groomsmen are there?"

"Three."

"I'm texting him now," Sylvia said. I glanced back toward the club. The doorman took his phone in his hand and after a moment, he looked up directly at me, sighed and motioned me over.

"I think he got it," I said, and walked over to him.

"Lady, get your boys over here. Sylvia says I'm to get them in, no matter what."

"Thanks," I said to him and started walking toward the groomsmen. "Sylvia," I said into the phone, "you heard?"

"Yup. You're welcome."

"Thanks! I hope they tipped you well!"

"Girl, don't you worry your pretty head about me. Talk soon." She squeaked a kiss into the phone and then hung up.

"Well boys, you're in luck. I think if you tip him, you'll get in now," I said to the awaiting groomsmen. They all scrambled for their wallets. They each had ten dollars in their hand, which they pooled together. The first one in gave Carl a thirty-dollar handshake. Pausing a moment, I made sure my boys got into the club, then I walked to the front door and walked outside into the night. It was a beautiful spring evening in New York. One of those beautiful nights that they make movies about.

"You look like you just worked an all-nighter," a warm voice said a few feet away from me.

I nodded like a bobble head as I slowly turned my head toward the voice. "Were you waiting for me, Matt?" I asked and raised an eyebrow.

"No," he said with such audacity, I didn't believe him.

"You seem to pop up everywhere."

"That I do. I know a lot of people in this town." He grinned so big that his eyes twinkled.

"Wait, don't you own your own company now?"

"I do." He shrugged revealing nothing, then looked over at me. "You hungry?"

"Starved," I said before I could stop myself.

"There's a great diner just around the corner. Open all night. We could go get a bite."

I looked at him. Really looked at him for the first time. I knew he was handsome. But at two feet away, with no one else around, no party to attend to, or drink to order, I was able to focus on him. His eyes were so earnest, and his smile so inviting. Matt had that aura about him that made me feel like I had both known him forever and I wanted to get to know him. He had become my own personal guardian angel.

Feeling pulled in two directions, one that I should go home and rest and see Sam if he magically happened to be awake, which was a very slim chance, or to go out and have a greasy spoon meal with this handsome guy with whom nothing could happen because I had a boyfriend. My lips pursed together in a frown.

"I have to get home, I'm afraid. Early morning." It wasn't really a lie. I would most likely get up with Sam before he went to teach a class. My stomach growled, protesting.

"Ah, the boyfriend, right? You know I mean no harm. I just want scrambled eggs." He shoved his hands in his pockets and kicked at a pebble on the sidewalk.

"Yeah. Well," I waved at the solitary cab that had turned down the street. When it stopped, I walked over to it. "I'll see you at the next one."

"You might not see me for a while. Work is picking up," he said just as my door was closing. I tried to roll down the window to ask him why, but the cab pulled away, as Matt bowed at the waist to wave at me through the window.

As we turned the corner, I had the feeling I had forgotten to do something. I pulled out my phone to check it trying to remember. My brain lulled into a meditative calm, and I thought nothing about the evening once we were above 14th Street.

Chapter Thirty

Zella's squawk about the Cross bride's accusation that I drank brought it all back. Even two weeks later, Bourbon-colored guilt flooded my mind. Trying to keep my wits, I quietly rationalized I had very little, and it was after hours. Not in front of guests.

My face burned. Paranoia surged. My shoulders tensed. The groomsmen wouldn't have smelled anything, would they? They were liquored up themselves and wouldn't have smelled anything on me. Figuring Sylvia and Matt hadn't thrown me under the bus, especially not to the client, I suddenly remembered the bridesmaid with the vodka. Crap! I had planned to text Zella on my way home. That was the nagging thought I had forgotten. Truthfully, I felt more guilty about the two sips of bourbon after the event than faking a shot. One that witnesses could prove I didn't take.

The thing is, I couldn't just plead Mia culpa with Zella. She would rip me to shreds as if I were dressed in bacon and her, a dog with a ravenous hunger. Zella would remember remnants of any sin. For all time. Many times, I had taken blame for something I didn't do, just to move on and have her stop screeching. But it always came back to haunt me.

As an actress, and a damn good one, I was ready to plead my way out of the guillotine today. Slowly turning in my chair towards an angry boss, I formed the words in my head.

"What exactly is she saying now?" I asked, figuring with more information, I could buy myself a little more time to work out my innocence.

"Read it!" Zella shrieked again, as she violently pointed toward her computer. As to not excite her more, I slowly

241

rose, and quickly walked to her computer and leaned over the desk to read out loud.

"…the favors were not as shown in the picture. No one was at the table at the end of the night making sure that they were all handed out because there were incredible amounts left, after I did all the work to have an exact amount of favors. Someone obviously was not doing her job.

"The photos we got back from the photographer are ghastly, and I refuse to pay her. You need to discuss this with her, as our planner.

"A cell phone was lost, and no one could find it. How is this possible when so many staff were on hand the entire night standing around doing nothing?

"And I didn't want to say anything because it was a party and we all were having a good time, but both the groom and I found it very despicable that Natalie was drinking during the party. We refuse to pay for that drink.

"In fact, we refuse to pay for any of the services we have yet to pay the balance on."

"Wow, so she's trying not to pay for anything." I stood and said with a chuckle, "Did she run out of money?" I thought I should be lighthearted about the whole thing.

"That is possible," Zella had felt the joke, and lightened up a bit. For a moment this gave me hope. "But, Natalie," the guillotine tone was back, "What is my number one rule?"

Trying the joking angle again, "Besides 'Always have your hair and nails impeccable; five minutes early is late; and bring a snack as we should never ask the venue for food until the vendor meal?" She glared, and I sighed. Then spoke in the monotone recitation voice used by students everywhere, "Never drink during an event, ever. Ever."

Before the judge and jury, I would not perjure myself because technically I did not have a drink during the event. I turned and looked her straight in the eye, "I assure you, Zella, I did not drink during this event."

Ok, you and I both know this was a way around the truth. But I had also learned, don't go down with the ship, if there is another way off the boat.

We stood facing each other in a standoff. If I moved first, I was sure she would know I was bending the truth, not far, but I was still bending it. If she moved, it would mean that she believed me. Time froze. The only thing in the room that moved were her eyes which traced over every pore on my face as she surveyed me, waiting for a quiver or a sign I wasn't telling the truth. Her phone buzzed with a text, and she snapped her eyes down and her phone up to see who had written.

Not entirely sure if I was in the clear, I stayed exactly where I was. I didn't move a muscle. I don't know if I took a breath. If I didn't move, didn't shift, the blade might not fall today.

It felt like an eternity as Zella read her text. Her eyes zigzagged back and forth reading the lines at least twelve times. It was a long text message. Zella chuckled and I inaudibly sighed. The tiny movement of my breath reminded her of my presence in the room.

"Natalie," she trilled like a jackhammer, "Are you sure there isn't anything you want to tell me?"

Shit. I really was caught. Two of the tiniest sips of bourbon were the end of my career as a wedding planner. Zella would ruin my reputation in the industry in this town, and possibly all over the world by a tiny piece of gossip, and I would never work again. A hint of this job could open doors, but if Zella were to speak of my screw up would blaze through the industry like wildfire and could totally end me. All because a cranky bride didn't want to pay the infinitesimal amount that was the last of her bill. Crap. How was I going to get through this with my entrails still intact? Wait. The bridesmaid suddenly flipped into my head.

"Shoot. Sorry, Zella," I sputtered like an old car coming to life.

"Spit it out, Natalie," she huffed, starting to tap her foot on the new leather rug that was made of the hides of interns, I was starting to assume.

"At the end of the party—everything got so crazy—and I meant to text you on my way home about this and—"

"This better be good. I've let go of people for things more offensive than drinking. OUT WITH IT!" The foot tapping was becoming more rapid. I could hear the blade of an invisible guillotine being sharpened.

With all the confidence I could muster, I said, as rapidly as the words would spill out of my mouth, "One of the bridesmaids handed me a shot at the end of the night. She was drunk and relentless about me taking it. I tried to just set it down, but she wouldn't let me. So, I pretended to take the shot, but set the thing completely full down on the bar. Ask Matt, the bartender. He will vouch for me. He even asked me if I wanted to drink it. I promise I didn't touch it to my lips or anything."

Moments passed and we stood there looking at each other again. A bead of sweat rolled down my neck as she stared at me. Her foot stopped tapping, and she blinked,

"Fine," Zella finally said and clicked on the screen of her phone and put it up to her ear.

"SIIL-VEE-uh, darling, how are you?"

Feeling incredibly guilty and like I was still head down in the stocks, I stood still. I took a breath before I slowly walked back to my workspace. Zella turned and walked to one of the windows and looked out at the park as she loudly spoke into the phone. Making sure I could hear everything she said.

"Wonderful, wonderful," she chuckled, a totally different person on the phone than the viper who was out for my blood only seconds before. Not knowing my immediate future, I quietly gathered my things together in a neat pile on the table, so if I needed to, I could scoop and go.

Trying to keep my movement minimal like a gazelle hiding from the cheetah, I kept going with my work. If this was it for me, I wanted to make sure I finished everything I was assigned today. Partially, because my people pleasing nature and the Zeigarnik effect keep me from leaving things unfinished, and I remembered things better.

And partly because I knew Zella would hunt me down, ask me why I left something unfinished, tell me that it was "wrong" and shame me into finishing even after I was dead to her and not on the payroll anymore. And probably send me twenty text messages about it in the interim starting at 5am.

Through my work blinders, I heard Zella's conversation. When I listened in, which she never seemed to mind, I would be a step or two ahead when she came to me with instructions.

"Silvia, what did you think of Natalie?" Zella's voice was the purring of a jungle cat luring its prey.

In anticipation I had stopped typing then quickly clattered my fingers over random keys and typing nonsense to fill the silence.

Zella's voice seemed to get nearer. Peripherally, I could see she was facing me watching me type. I hoped she wouldn't get near enough to see the gibberish. Daringly, I glanced over my shoulder and seeing that she turned back to the window, I let out a breath and in one click deleted the nonsense.

"Well, I'm glad you like her. I like her too. Listen. I'm having a little issue with the Cross bride, I—"

Zella's voice stopped as Sylvia cut her off. My shoulders tensed.

"Oh, she copied you on the email. I didn't see your name on it. You know drinking at events by my crew is something I don't tolerate. I've fired people—"

Sylvia cut her off again. I was in wonder that Zella wasn't angry from being cut off so much. Anytime I looked like I was about to interrupt, she became infuriated. Probably keeping up appearances with Sylvia, I thought. If no one knew how crazy Zella was in the office, everyone would continue to love her. Maybe…no it couldn't be. Maybe it was just me that made her this crazy? My thoughts were cut off by Zella's sigh.

"Well, that makes me feel so much better. Although I would love to talk to your bartender Matt." My shoulders relaxed.

Pause.

"Oh, he doesn't work for you anymore. Why is that?"

Pause.

"Where did he go?"

Pause. Her intensity rose.

"How is it you don't know?"

Pause.

"Well, that seems odd," she said in blatant disbelief. Even though I was only hearing half of the conversation, I felt like Sylvia was keeping information from Zella. And could tell she did, too. I also wondered why Sylvia wasn't telling Zella that Matt owned his own company.

Pause. I felt Zella's eyes on me, and I confirmed she was by looking through my periphery again.

"Do you have video of the floor?"

Wait. What? My body tensed. Why would she need video? Was she serious?

"Ah. Really, it all gets erased within a week. I find that hard to believe—"

Pause.

"I do take your word for it, but I would feel so much better reasoning with the client if I could talk to the bartender or see the video."

Pause.

"Well, that is great news that you saw Natalie on the way out and she didn't seem or smell like she had any alcohol—"

Pause. Zella glared in my direction.

"I would love it if you put it in writing." Zella smiled and her voice took on a Cheshire Cat quality. Somehow, I felt off the hook, but still like I was going to have to answer something.

"Wonderful," Zella continued after a pause. "And if you hear from Matt, was it? I would love his observations as well. I'll take care of the rest. Thank you, Sylvia."

Silence fell, and I couldn't tell if the phone call had ended. My need to turned me into a sacrificial lamb. I hit print and crossed the room for the paper. On the way back I noticed Zella eying me.

With blinking eyes, I asked as chipper as an ingenue at her first audition, "So, what did Sylvia say?" And I averted my eyes, waiting for the guillotine blade to fall.

Chapter Thirty-One

I would miss this job. Don't get me wrong. The insanity I could live without. But I had really found my groove here. The ability to create spectacular events and work immersed in a world of flowers, cake and dreams that people didn't even dare to fantasize about, I knew I was lucky.

My love of this industry was the only reason I put up with the crazy from Zella, the demands of drunken groomsmen to get them into clubs, and the advances of the sleazy Alexander Milford. Who had left me a few messages to call him. As if. Things were getting good here. I could see myself sharing this company with Zella someday. Maybe then she would let down her guard all the time like she did the day we stuffed the invitations, and we could actually collaborate. I'm sure she wouldn't want it to be a fifty-fifty partnership, but honestly, I didn't think I would mind.

Then, on the brink of what felt like I could be fired, I realized I wanted to run this company with her. This company. Not join Alexander or anyone else. But Tremaine Events. Even with the unrelenting need for excellence, the overwhelming amount of personal tasks I was asked to do, and the limited time I was being asked to carry it all out, I loved the mission of our company. Ours.

Thinking back about it now, I wish I had not been so scared. I wish I had stood up and said the things about partnership and how I wished we could collaborate. Zella might not have taken it well, or even pretended not to hear it. But I think the fact that I thought of Tremaine Events as ours would have pleased her. It might have been on a deep internal level that she wouldn't have shown the light of day, surrounded with Botox. But I think it would have made things going forward a little better.

It would be great if I could tell you that here, everything changed. I became inspired and created a plan to pitch myself to Zella. Instead, I sat quietly panicking. Did I had enough in my bank account to at least pay rent this month? I was fired about five years ago. That day felt like my heart and lungs were being ripped from my chest while it was happening. And that was a job I actually hated and was glad to leave. Crossing fingers, I tried to generate hope that Zella wouldn't be as painful.

"Well, Natalie," Zella's voice cut through the room. She was right behind me. "Either you are making friends in this industry, or you're telling the truth. Something tells me," she paused to eye me, "it's the friends. Which is almost as important. If Sylvia of all people is backing you up, I suppose that is good enough for me." She strode to her desk. I scuttled out of her way. "Interesting though. That Matt fellow apparently no longer works for the hotel. He mysteriously quit and disappeared. Which doesn't sit right with me," she sat and flicked her wrist. "But no matter." And I thought the conversation was over until a moment later she asked, "Did we have his contact information on our sheet?"

"No, Zella. You've never had me get the waitstaff information, only the managers," I said with a bit of deflection back to her.

For a split second I thought about telling her he was a freelancer who had worked at other events of ours and he owned his own company. But I thought better about it. There wasn't a good outcome. Either she would have me scour old contact lists which was additional work I didn't need. Or would have me track him down via my industry business card pile, which we still hadn't reviewed.

Fear of her talking to him didn't bother me, I didn't want Matt dragged into this, with his new company just taking off. Instead, I kept my thoughts to myself and focused back on my computer screen.

The air between us sizzled with her lack of information. Zella stood and tapped her phone against her palm, her eyes in a piercing squint. Her phone buzzed. She looked at it, sighed, huffed to her desk, and began to click away at the computer keyboard. Her newly manicured nails seemed to tap the keys louder than normal.

An email dropped in my inbox from Zella. From across the room. Great. This was it. I was being executed electronically.

Embracing fate, I opened the email. I was floored. The email was to Genoveve Cross, and I was copied. Zella refuted everything the bride had said.

I had to read the section where she defended me three times. Zella wrote there was "Zero chance Natalie could have been drinking," and that if I had been, it would have been cause for dismissal. Not dwelling on that threat directed at me, I kept reading. Zella recounted the phone call she just had with Sylvia, mentioning, "the hotel staff have been questioned as well," about both my imbibing and the cell phone issues. On both counts, Zella found "no lack in responsibility from her event crew" and the phone was said to have been found in the hotel room of the guest, according to the hotel staff. The email went on to say that she refused to discuss payment with the photographer, as the bride had gone against Zella's recommendation, and we had nothing to do with that final payment. Especially if the bride was refusing to pay her balance to Tremaine Events.

After reading the whole email from Zella twice, I clicked back to my inbox to find an email from Sylvia. All it said was:

RE: Cross

I hope you're surviving. It will all be ok. And I won't tell where Matt is if you won't.

-S

I was stunned by Sylvia's cryptic note. It was, glad to have a friend. Even more, I was stunned that Zella stood up for me. After telling me hundreds of times I had done something wrong. Sometimes in front of other people. It didn't seem like a Zella thing to defend me. I glanced over at her, clacking away at something on her computer. Maybe I was completely wrong about this woman. Maybe she didn't hate me as much as I assumed. She trusted me, of course, but trust and hate are two completely different things.

Confused at the thoughts swirling around my brain in a competitive dance number, I refocused and reviewed my checklist for the day. Doing a double take I saw I had completed everything. Clicking through emails, I checked that I hadn't missed anything. Nope, I was done, and even ahead. Letting the air in the office settle a little more, I spent another thirty minutes clicking around on the computer.

Gathering my courage, I called out "Zella?" I looked up to see that she was still focused on her computer. It was almost eerie that she hadn't moved in the last half hour. Normally she moved every five minutes unable to focus as she was continually interrupted by some phone call or text.

A whole minute passed before she responded. "Yes?" she asked distractedly and still not looking away.

"Zella, I'm finished."

I walked over to her desk with a few piles of papers for her to see.

"Fine." She looked up. "What are those?"

"On the top is the timing for the Amberly wedding, and the second is the contract for—"

"Never mind," she said, her voice dripping with sarcasm. I didn't understand where her general malaise stemmed. She was so hot and irritated not forty-five minutes prior. She sighed, pointed to the door and said, "Get your things and go." I was shocked.

"Wait... am I.... fired?" I asked meekly, still holding the papers that I had worked on.

Zella whipped around to me and said, "Don't be ridiculous Natalie. If I were firing you, you'd know it. Leave the papers. It will remind me to look at them in a bit." Her tone sounded a bit defeated. Tired even. She turned back and added, "Enjoy your evening. I'll see you tomorrow. We have the Bloomfield invitations to stuff and mail. Go home. Have a glass of wine," she said, but I didn't quite trust where she was going until she continued, "Where you're allowed to have one," she added.

And there it was. The Zella Tremaine scorpion attack.

Chapter Thirty-Two

When I arrived home, early, I relayed the entire day to Sam as he prepared meals and cooked dinner. A moment hit me where I realized it had been exactly a month since we had our big fight. Then it felt like my life was over, and now it felt right.

We didn't just click back together right away. It had taken us at least a week of conversations, some of them borderline fights to resolve our differences. In the end, Sam agreed he would not stay out late or network every night. I promised to leave work alone when we were together. I also promised that I wouldn't look at emails or text Zella back immediately when we were together. I promised to take out the trash at least twice a month. And coincidentally both Sam and I agreed to drink less. Sam was also trying to get me to second guess myself less, but that was a work in progress. And part of tonight's conversation.

"Maybe I should tell her the truth, what I really did. That would probably be best, right? For her to know the truth. And by telling her and coming clean she will trust me more. I mean it was two sips. She wouldn't fire me for two sips, right?"

"Babe, you have to go with your gut," Sam said over his shoulder as he browned the hamburger in the pan. He was making a high protein chili. He started to tell me the ingredients, but I told him to stop, because I knew I wouldn't eat it if I knew too much more about it.

"Well, maybe that isn't the answer. I don't know if it would make it worse or better. Besides, it was after the wedding was over. People drink after work with their colleagues." I sighed and flopped to find a more comfortable position on the couch. "This will come back to haunt me later." I sighed. "Maybe I'll just wait it out and see. Move on to the next wedding and be as amazing as possible."

"Great idea, babe," Sam mumbled as he tasted the sauce in an adjacent pan.

"The worst part," I slid back into bitching. Sadly, for me deciding wasn't enough. To walk through it all again. See every angle. I needed to air it all out. Talk everything out over and over and over until I could find some glimmer of closure or information that might help me understand my predicament more. Slap it on rocks until it died. "I worked harder for this bride than I have any other client. She barely tipped me. And then accused me of drinking."

"The worst, babe," Sam said, echoing me. I knew he was listening, however when he got into his cooking zone, his replies were minimal. He came out to the sofa and refilled my water glass. "Speaking of your tips, not that it's any of my business, but what are you going to do with that fat envelope of cash sitting in your sock drawer?"

I blushed and looked up at him. "Well, it was going to be a surprise. But," I hopped up onto my knees and looked at him with a big smile on my face. "I was going to take you on a vacation!" Throwing my arms up in the air like I won something, I said, "I have seven hundred dollars now. So, a few more weddings and we might be able to take a cheap trip to the Caribbean. I keep getting emails from travel sites that have deals that include everything." I meekly looked up at him as he stood over me. "Would you…" I paused and cocked my head to one side. "Would you want to do something like that?"

His face gave away nothing for the longest five seconds of my life. He just stared impassively. Usually, I could see a glimmer of something, whether it be for or against the idea, but he was giving me nothing. I thought this would make him happy. He had been working so much lately. Always out with Nick. And the other people from work. And his boss was putting him through his paces. Rest would do him good. It would do us both good. Sitting on a beach somewhere with nothing to do or nowhere to be. Tropical drink in hand as the waves lapped at the shore and the palm trees shook in the breeze. I would have jumped in at someone offering me a vacation. He didn't. It wasn't like I asked him to marry me, or anything. Or to rob a bank. It was just a vacation.

Sam rubbed the back of his neck and looked down at the floor. "Sure babe."

With a puzzled look on my face, I said, "It's not a punishment. I don't have to take you on vacation." My forehead crumpled like my spirit. "I know I should pay bills with it, but since it was unexpected income, I thought why not use it for fun? And with our rough patch…" I rambled to fill the silence. Something was off. But what? What was I missing?

"Sure babe. A vacation sounds great. It's just work and all—"

"Oh! Work!" Of course. He was stressed. That must be the reason for his less-than-ecstatic answer.

"For a second there, I thought it was me," I said and shrugged. "I'm so sorry all I've done tonight is vent about work. I just wish—" I cut myself off. "Nope. Not going to talk about it anymore."

"It's ok, babe," Sam brought me a plate. He sat next to me and started to eat. There was silence I didn't know how to break. Finally he did. "So, this vacation—"

"It's just an idea. I can do something more responsible with my money." My shoulders slumped in defeat. "I just thought since it was unexpected, why not use it for something exciting. Live a little," I said, then ate, ignoring the thing hanging between us. I looked over. Sam looked at me like he had something to say. "What is it?" I asked and smiled at him.

"Nothing," he said, shaking his head and focusing on shoving the chili into his mouth. After he chewed a double spoonful, he continued, "Babe, if you really want to go on vacation, we just have to talk about it."

"I wasn't going to just blindfold you and take you to the airport! I was going to get the rest of the money and find a few affordable options. Then let you pick one."

"Good," he sighed deeply.

"Sammo, I love you so much. I know how dedicated you are to your career and I support you ten thousand percent." I stared at him to drive my point home and tried not to cry. "And if this isn't a good time to escape together, I understand." My eyes started to water, and I quickly looked into my bowl and I moved chili beans from one side of the bowl to the other. In a very low voice I said, "I'm so very sorry that I've been self-absorbed."

Sam looked up and smiled at me, patting my feet that curled on the sofa next to him.

"I love you. You know that, right?"

"You'd better." I said with a joking bravado. "You're totally stuck with me for life. Especially when you make chili like this." I shoved a spoonful in my mouth to emphasize the point, and after I finished, I said, "Now, fill me in on what is going on at Spark Gym."

"Nah, babe. You'd be bored. It's nothing exciting anyway."

"No? What happened to the promotion? And the gal who wanted you to create a class? And what about the thing you and Nick were planning together?"

"All on the back burner for the moment. I don't want to talk about it. Do you mind if we watch TV?"

Something was wrong. But whatever it was that it was hidden like the vegetables in this chili. If he wasn't going to tell me I couldn't pry it out of him. My feelings were a bit hurt that he didn't want to share but I tried not to show it. So I said, "No problem! Pick whatever you want to watch."

Turning to me he asked me seriously, "Babe, are you mad at me?" He asked.

Uh oh. I over acquiesced. I always put up a fight or had some heavy suggestion as to what to watch.

"No, love. I just… I want you to be happy."

"Oh, ok." Sam said, making a confused face and picked up the remote. "Are you sure you don't want to pick?"

"I mean… if there is a RomCom or a quirky comedy on, I'm totally in."

"So, you don't want to watch the big fight?"

"No!" I squealed and flipped my legs to the other side of the couch so I could snuggle into Sam more. It was a little more difficult to snuggle while eating chili as both arms were required. But I made it work as Sam flipped around stopping on a reality show where brides-to-be pick their wedding dresses. When he set the remote down, I snatched it up and flipped the channel.

"Hey! I was watching that!" he said in fake irritation.

"No, you weren't. You stinker!" I flipped to find some sort of explosion and Gerry Butler running from it in a suit. Perfect. Cute guy for me; shoot-em-up movie for Sam. We were staying right here. After we emptied our bowls, we snuggled closer. Everything was fine.

Chapter Thirty-Three

The movie ended and Sam went to bed. I wasn't tired. My brain was still running in circles from the day. Checking my phone, I saw that there were emails from brides that had come through after I left work. Feeling guilty about breaking my promise to Sam that I would "leave work at the office," I threw my phone on the sofa cushions across from me. Ignoring both the brides and my feelings, I got up and washed the dishes. I scrubbed down the stove and the entire kitchen until it sparkled. I even mopped the floor. I could be good at this cleanliness thing.

Thirty minutes later I walked back into our little living space and felt how tiny it was. I picked up the remote and turned off the television. Nothing woke Sam after he fell asleep, so I turned it off for my sake. I didn't want the extra noise right now. Stillness fell over the room. I meandered looking at everything we owned.

Framed photos of us were all around. There were two Brooklyn Bridge paintings right next to each other on the wall that we did at a wine-and-paint night. Neither were good, but the memories from that night were. I smiled as I reached up and adjusted mine on the wall, it was crooked. There was a dead orchid from an event that I picked up and tossed in the trash. We had piles and piles of books and scripts. I picked up a play that I had started to read a lifetime ago, but never finished reading. I took it over to the sofa and read the same page over about four times before I finally gave in and picked up my phone to check my emails. I really tried to keep to my word and not work this evening.

If I just spent an hour tonight, I rationalized, I could hack out a lot of these details and have them ready for tomorrow. We were stuffing envelopes tomorrow, which sucked up a lot of time. Besides, Sam was asleep so he wouldn't know, and I wasn't taking attention away from him. I still wasn't tired, so what was I supposed to do, watch him sleep? Even working in the office four days a week, work was never finished.

Getting up and walking over to my bag that was resting against the wall by the door, I took out my laptop. I had started taking my personal computer with me to the office because it was a whole lot easier to work from my computer and upload the documents to the internet-hosted company folder rather than to start something on the work computer only to find that I hadn't uploaded it or forgot to email it to myself to finish at home.

Around 3am, I hauled myself to bed. I wasn't sure if it was the guilt or the need to be great at this job that kept me working so late. It was probably some of both. These started as survival and were now my workaholic habits. Sam was right that I was working too much. But then that was the pot calling the kettle black, wasn't it? Determined not to fight with myself, or with Sam when he wasn't even awake, I made myself go to bed.

When I crawled under the sheets, Sam snuggled close, throwing an arm over my waist, and snuggling his nose into my neck, mumbling something. He would be up in two hours. I lay staring at the ceiling, overwhelmed with guilt, hoping sleep would take me. It was a while before it did.

When I woke up, my phone was ringing incessantly, and Sam was gone.

"Hello?" I groggily answered.

"Natalie, what time are you planning on coming in today?"

Zella. I hadn't set my alarm. My brain slammed into awake mode. I jumped out of bed and started to panic dress. Hopping around the room I grabbed underwear from yesterday, it didn't smell, and grabbed a pair of pants from my closet that seemed less wrinkly. I put Zella on speakerphone as I was looking around for my bra. As I was turning everything in the room over, I said, "I thought you said I could come in at ten today. But if I had that wrong—"

"Calm down, Natalie. It's only 7:30."

"What? What do you mean it's only 7:30?"

"In the morning. It's only 7:30am. Calm down. You're not late."

I didn't understand. My brain didn't compute. I clicked the home button on the screen of my phone to see the clock and confirm that Zella was right. She was. It was only 8am. There were also ten text messages from her starting at 5am on my screen.

"I don't—Zella what—I—"

"Natalie, focus. If you're going to come in so late, I'm going to have you stop to pick up a payment for me."

"Yup," part of me realized I wasn't coherent. I need at least two cups of coffee before I can comprehend anything. I also think I'm extremely funny before I have coffee, but it usually comes out as really rude. In other words, it's best for me not to speak or be spoken to before coffee.

"…Are you writing this down?"

"Zella," I said in an irritated voice, "I just woke up. Your call woke me up." Sass dripped from my mouth, but I couldn't shut myself up. "My alarm hasn't even gone off yet, and you're calling me." Wincing at my confession that I didn't set my alarm this morning, I continued, "I'm stumbling around my bedroom looking for a bra so I can come into the office, so of course I'm not writing this down. I don't even have contacts in to see anything yet." I had started to shuffle toward the kitchen. Maybe if I made coffee this would all go away. That would be nice if I made coffee. Maybe Zella would go away. Probably not. Before I could stop myself, I prattled on. "I was up until 3am working on things for you," a loud yawn involuntarily came out as if to prove my point. "If you want me to pick something up, fine. Text me the info—"

"But, Natalie, I'm—"

"Zella," I cut her off very abruptly, "most times of the day I care, but as I'm still supposed to be sleeping at this moment, I don't." I set the phone on the counter as I started to make coffee and continued on speakerphone mode. "If it's important, text me where I'm supposed to go, and what time I'm supposed to be there. I'm going to make coffee now. If I don't understand, I'll call you back."

Silence plagued the line. I suppose any other time of day, I would have worried, but at this point I was too busy putting water into the coffee maker and scooping coffee grounds.

"Zella?" Getting no response, I leaned down close to the speaker on the phone to ask, "You still there?"

"Fine. I just texted you. I'll see you at 10:30. The Bloomfield invitations are already there, so feel free to start on them. Goodbye." And the phone clicked off.

If I wasn't still trying to wake myself up, I would be stunned at my moxie right now. After standing up for myself against the accusation yesterday, did I find I had a backbone? Warmth started to fill me, and I sat straight up with hope. My phone buzzed again. Zella.

Nope, guilt started to pour in. I was wondering if I should call her back or text to apologize. No. No, Natalie. Just make the coffee. My head fell back, and I stared at the ceiling. My phone buzzed five more times.

Shuffling out to the kitchen, I held my phone in my hand not wanting to look at the dreaded messages. If I didn't look at them, I still had a job, right? Sighing, I lifted the phone to look at it, but just couldn't allow myself to unlock it without a little more courage. Percolation finished. I took it as a sign to have coffee first. I set the phone down on the kitchen counter and I grabbed a mug and the 1% milk.

Sigh, I missed cream. My beautiful, full of fat and chemicals, Amaretto flavored creamer. The guilt from not going to Sam's class regularly and Zella constantly asking if I was still trying to lose weight made me stop buying it. Plus, it was an expense that I didn't need, especially since I was down to one job.

Even though the guilt of the texts sitting unread on my phone clawed at me, I knew better than to look at my phone as I was still at an incoherent level. So, I left it on the kitchen counter and ignored it while I snuggled on the sofa and clicked on the television to a talk show. Curling up in my rebellion, I drank my coffee.

Five minutes later, I got up and poured a second cup and then returned to the sofa. This cup was a slower sip, as this was the one I enjoyed and not just fuel to get myself moving and it took me about seven minutes to drink it. My phone buzzed a few more times while I was sitting. As my phone chirped away, my third cup of coffee was enjoyed. Resettling on the sofa with my fourth cup, I was interrupted when my phone started ringing. Great. I wasn't answering the texts, so Zella was calling again. Probably to scold me, or worse, fire me for my attitude. Petulantly, I let it ring. It stopped and then started again. Take that Zella. New Natalie has a backbone and won't jump to take your call. The ringing went on and kept getting louder. That was odd. I listened to it for a moment before I realized that I had put my phone to silent mode. Realizing it was my alarm, I grabbed it from the kitchen counter to turn it off. I shouldn't have picked up my phone.

Sixteen text messages and it was only 8am. It was going to take a lot more than backbone. Zella was driving me crazy.

If only I made more money or a guarantee off job security this would be much easier to deal with. A dreamy thought floated through my head: maybe I should ask. For job security, for more money, heck why not pitch to her to share the business like I had dreamt of a few days ago?

I sighed and chugged my cup of coffee. Asking for a raise, who was I kidding? That would take quite a bit more backbone. Especially after telling off Zella. But time to get up. I needed this job. It was the only one I had now. And if I lost it, I would have nothing.

Chapter Thirty-Four

Honestly, I have no idea what made it happen, but Zella started trusting me a lot more. Maybe it was stepping up my moxie. Maybe she liked how I had friends in the business that stood up for me. Or maybe it was that she found that I was a capable cash mule allowing her to stay away from the Upper East Side.

It sounds illegal, and it probably was a little, but I must have carried in total close to two million dollars in cash while I was working for Zella. Not all of this went to Tremaine Events by the way. A lot of companies that we worked with and in the business in general offer a cash discount: if you paid in cash, you got a discount. Which was always funny to me, because someone kept that much cash lying around, why did they need a discount?

Although I was sweating from my nervousness for my first pickup, over the coming months I found the routine was generally the same. I would arrive in the building at the scheduled time and the doorman would call up. I would wait a dollop of time in the lobby watching dry cleaners, mail carriers, and nannies deliver their care packages before I was allowed up to the actual apartment. When I arrived on the floor, I would either be asked to wait outside or asked to step into the foyer while the mother or father of the bride stepped to the safe to get the cash.

It was always the weirdest feeling to be stopped just before entering these magnificent homes. It was as if they didn't want me to see what they really had, on the chance I might be casing the joint. Either that or didn't want me to track mud on the carpet. Moments later they would hand over tens of thousands of dollars without counting it and usually in an unsealed mailing envelope.

Maybe it was just my paranoia or maybe I've seen too many movies, but I would always have them seal the envelope and sign their name across the seal, so when it was broken it was obvious. Every single one thought I was odd for asking them to do such a thing and would repeat—sign the envelope? How would they not let a stranger not even a few steps into their home, if at all, but would hand her a ton of cash. I will never understand.

Every single time I would explain the broken seal to them, and clients were still confused. I told them that if they knew how much money was in the envelope and so did Zella, this way it got to her or to whomever I was dropping it off to would be assured all the money was there. I tried to be tactical about telling them I wanted to assure them and Zella that I wasn't taking any money from the envelopes and pocketing it. But there is no good way to say, "I want to prove I'm not stealing by having you seal and sign the envelope so I can verify I didn't steal any money." Since I'd been accused of being dishonest by one bride, I was going above and beyond to do everything in my power to prove the opposite.

Twenty or more of these cash money drops happened in my time with Zella. It never got less stressful. Of all the things that were weird in my job, that was probably the top five. Walking hundreds of thousands of dollars around Manhattan. Bizarre. Remember before when I thought about taking the money from the stash? Now I had tons of cash given to me and I didn't want to be anywhere near it. I really hated being responsible for so much money.

A few times I would take the cash straight from their apartments directly to the décor or catering companies. Most times I would bring the cash back to the office, which made me even more nervous. To have all of that cash just sitting around made me crazy. I was having a hard time with my minimal cash tips sitting in an envelope in my sock drawer at home, let alone having client's cash sitting around the office.

Although I was always paranoid about the money, Zella was never phased. The only time she was ever upset was when I took the subway instead of taking a cab. Once I rationalized that I had a very heavy umbrella and the cab from 93rd and Park would have cost almost forty dollars and would have taken triple the time in the rain, she agreed with my decision.

As I look back now, I can't say that anything in my event planning career was smooth. Although the few months after the drink accusation flowed by easier. Neither my job, nor my life were easy, but I seemed to be juggling it all better. Weddings came and went. All had some hitch or difficulty the day of the wedding, but I handled the problems with a flare. I could tell you about the bride who misplaced her underwear and refused to walk down the aisle without it, the groom who went missing and showed up five minutes before the ceremony, or the flower girl who tore up an entire set of bouquets, but you can use your imagination.

I was no longer scared or needed approval to act on things while in the moment. It was only back at the office where I questioned myself. Maybe it was because she yelled so much more behind closed doors.

A year had gone by for me working at Tremaine Events. Miraculously, I found myself alive, still with the job, and with the gumption to ask for a raise. Apparently, my backbone grew like the Grinch's heart on Christmas morning. Without planning, I just asked.

Well, I think by this time you know me well enough to know there was *some* planning. There was a lot of planning in fact. I rehearsed what I was going to say with Ginger, Bennett, and Jordan when we met last week for brunch. I had texted my mom a lot for pointers. As she and Zella were close to the same age, I wanted to get her point of view. I also tried to talk to Sam about it, but he always seemed preoccupied with something, or would get frustrated when I talked about money. I think work was getting even harder for him, so I didn't pry. Instead, I met for coffee with Violet one day, and for drinks with Denise. Both were incredibly insightful about the industry and Zella. The only thing I didn't plan was when.

This was decided by the universe the day I had to count out six dollars in change to pay for my breakfast. Shame is a powerful thing. It was exacerbated by Alexander Milford. As I was walking out of the bodega, I almost lost my coin-bought-coffee when we collided.

"Why Natalie, if you want to get physical, you'll have to buy me a drink first. And coffee isn't strong enough," he said, catching my coffee and righting it in my hand.

"You always say the worst things, Alexander."

He bent down to pick up my empty wallet that was lying on the sidewalk. And then poked around inside. "Hmm, interesting. Does your wardrobe," he looked me up and down, "make you into a pauper both on the street and in your bank account?"

Today I was wearing an acid burnout shirt that had a floral pattern, with a bright pink blazer and torn Armani jeans I found at A thrift store. I rolled my eyes at him. "Oh

Alexander, there is more to fashion than LL Bean and Vineyard Vines." I tried to push past him.

"Listen, I'm sorry for offending your outfit… but it looks like I've caught you at a good time."

"It's terrible, actually. I need to get up to the office."

"Oh, how quaint. She calls her auxiliary apartment her office, now? Has she told you about the fun times we had in that apartment? Fun times that if you were willing," he winked, "we could have."

I didn't like what he was insinuating, and I tried to walk away from him, a look of annoyance on my face. The way he kept stepping in front of me, it was clear he wasn't going to leave me alone until he told me what he came for. I sighed and put my free hand on my hip. "What do you want? You have thirty seconds. My egg sandwich is getting cold." See, backbone.

"Well, well, well. I like this. Who is this and where have you been keeping her?"

I tapped my foot.

"Fine. Fine." He waved a hand in the air as if my mood could be fanned away. "I was wondering if you had reconsidered yet."

My face scrunched into a mix of perplexed and revolted.

"Of coming to work for me. I will make it worth your while. Whatever she is paying you. I'll double it."

I sqinted at him.

"Why do you want me so badly, Alexander?"

"Well, that should be obvious," he looked me up and down again. I felt like I had been splashed by a bus with cold muddy sewer water.

"No, Alexander," I said as I pushed past him. "Final answer," I said over my shoulder as I walked away.

As Dominic and I now were on friendlier terms, I nodded and kept walking to the elevator. He sometimes pretended to pick up the phone and call Zella, but always would unlock the elevator, and we did this all without talking. Which was just fine for me. I held my wallet in my hand, knowing what was in it. Nothing. I threw my head back like a cartoon character. This was it. If I just turned down money on the street, I needed to ask for it. Today. Now.

"Morning, Zella," I said walking into the office zipping up my empty wallet. "I would like to talk to you about something important to me when you have a chance, please."

Maybe it was the please. Maybe my hunger was more than just for the egg sandwich I bought even though I knew I barely had enough to pay rent this month. Maybe she had gotten laid the night before or landed a big client and was in a rare, good mood. Who knew, but the stars aligned.

"Yes, Natalie, what can I do for you?" Zella said as she turned to look at me.

"Well, Zella, we've done seventeen events together. I feel like my work was good on the last few events, and although I'm not perfect, I'm leaps and bounds from where I was a year ago." I took a deep breath to ground myself and seeing that she was still looking at me, I kept going. "When I started here, you said that I was starting out at a rate of fifteen an hour and we would discuss a raise later. I had hoped you would mention it. But since it's been a while, I decided to bring it to your attention." She looked at me blankly. Could I really say it? I took a deep breath and said in what felt like slow motion, "I would like a raise. Please."

She looked at me with a stone face. Then her smile bloomed into appreciation. Pursing her lips, she repeated,

"You would like a raise. I can't believe it's really been a year."

"Yes, Zella. It is a year next week," I said, reporting the facts.

"Well, it is high time that my Production Manager gets a raise and an official title. I'll raise your daily salary by three dollars an hour. At events you'll make twenty-five. When I'm not onsite and you're in charge and you'll make twenty-eight."

It felt too easy. I looked back at Zella for what seemed like a long time. She blinked at me. I realized it was my cue and so I finally said, "Thank you, Zella!" Then I tried to stop myself from hopping up and down like I had just spun the wheel on a game show.

"And what the hell, your new rate will start today. You have been working hard. I know you have." She turned back to her computer, and moments later she asked for the Matheson file, which was not a foot from her, but I walked over and handed it to her anyway.

Trying to play it cool as I walked over to a seat at her big table and took out my laptop, I first pretended to type something but then I quickly texted Denise, Violet, my mom, Ginger, Bennett, and Jordan.

I asked for a raise and got it!

I started to text Sam, but instead opted to tell him when I saw him at home. It was better to tell him in person, I convinced myself. There was a distance between us. It was like we didn't heal properly. The whole vacation thing still hung in the air, undecided. But honestly, it was one of those things that didn't seem big enough to distract me at the time. I loved Sam and he loved me, and everyone went through bumpy moments in relationships.

Everything seemed great. A career and a man of my dreams. I was finally headed in the right direction. And I only missed theater every once in a while sometimes as I was falling asleep I thought I should really go to an audition soon.

Chapter Thirty-Five

But my life left no time for auditions. I was soon distracted more than ever from the dream I set out to have. I told myself weddings were a great exchange for the dreams I left behind. We did twenty-one events in my second year. The glitz and glamor of each one blended into the next, especially since my world and work consisted of contracts, itineraries, researching and shopping for details, and collecting phone numbers. Growth doesn't hurt as much when it sparkles.

Winter rolled into spring, and we had another slew of characters and catastrophes. Half-way through wedding season, Sarah arrived. Just out of college, Sarah was a cousin of a friend of Zella's and needed a job. Sarah was half Jewish, half Grecian goddess. She was curvy and cute. Zella loved her from the moment she walked in the door. And although she annoyed me at first, just like all the other interns Zella chewed up and spit out before her, there was something about Sarah that I quickly grew fond of.

Sarah caught the wedding fever early on, just like I had. And her first few months were similar to my experience. She loved the glamor of the business, but always was coming to me looking like she was just about to cry and worried that she was going to get fired. Perspective allowed me to see how much I'd really grown, and because I knew how to navigate the waters I could help guide and protect Sarah. I liked her a lot and wanted to make sure she stuck around.

We would still have one or two additional people with us on the Tremaine Events team, but it was a revolving door of mostly past interns. None of them were amazing. Amanda and AM both had other jobs, making Sarah and me the staple at most weddings. Sarah was someone I could count on in the insanity of the wedding day.

By this point we had a whole system. Zella would schmooze with the bride during the morning, and I would oversee the setup of the reception. The entire team would be on standby to help get the bridal party down the aisle, then we would scatter back to our missions of anything from escort cards, double checking the place settings, and confirming cake arrival. Zella was the face of the company and was among guests during the happy hour, as the minions scurried around.

Although it sounds like I'm disgruntled, I thrived in it. Production Manager was the perfect title for me. Because I was elbow deep in the planning, it was easy for me to make sure everything looked flawless and ran smoothly. A few weddings into the season Zella started departing after the speeches, letting me run the last few hours on my own. This was bliss. Especially since there was always something that Zella thought went wrong at every wedding. With her not around to micromanage, things went a lot smoother. But sometimes she came in full force, no matter how much she said she trusted me.

One wedding had an outdoor space to be used for a late-night party after the reception. We had rented all this white furniture that glowed. And of course, Zella and I had a passive aggressive disagreement over it. Actually, it was more like a Laurel and Hardy routine. Before the wedding, she handed me a floor plan, which was just a bunch of boxes drawn with no kind of notation indicating which items were which. I knew from ordering the furniture a few weeks ago that there were love seats, chairs, side tables, and a few ottomans. We hadn't discussed it previously, and when I asked her, she said the rental company was handling it. I was only handed the paper, not given any kind of instruction.

When the rental company delivered during the ceremony and I couldn't find Zella to help, I attempted to put the furniture in some sort of semblance as it was on the paper. After getting most of it in place, I was called into the kitchen by the Maître'd to answer a question about dinner service. When I came back to finish the job, the furniture moved all around, scattered in what looked like a mess.

In a confused huff, I went back to putting the pieces how I had originally arranged them. Then the bandleader asked me to confirm with the band about the order of the evening, so I went to the dance floor to go over it with him. When I came back to put the finishing touches on the furniture, I saw it was once again in disarray. I was just starting to move the furniture again when I heard a shrill, "Hey, stop that!" I looked up to see Zella zooming at me from the hallway. "I put the furniture as it is supposed to go, why are you changing it, Natalie?"

"It was you?" I asked, putting my hands on my hips.

"Of course. It was wrong twice." Zella came toward me at a fast pace. "This is right. Leave it alone," Zella snapped at me and slapped me on the wrist.

"What? But this doesn't look like anything on the floor plan you gave me," I said holding up my paper.

"Of course, it does," she said, snatching it from me. She turned the page ninety degrees and started pointing out what the different shapes were, and I started to see how the boxes on the paper looked like her arrangement in front of me.

I snapped back at her, "Well next time, please go over it with me beforehand, so I don't make this mistake of wasting valuable time again." And I walked off. The best part was I wasn't terrified that she would fire me that night,

I now knew she needed me to run things for her so she could focus on the client.

One of our nightmares was a spring wedding that not only was on St. Patrick's Day but had an outdoor element to it. If you've ever been to New York on St. Paddy's, you know the mayhem the streets become. And, yes, it's Paddy with a D not a T; Patty is short for Patricia. Enough trivia. Back to our event.

Add to the insanity of the holiday, streets filled with people drinking from early hours of the day, all wearing green and usually yelling obscenities, we might have the threat of rain. If I haven't mentioned it before, whenever we have a wedding that has even a part of it outside, we check weather updates two weeks in advance and try to plan for any possible weather. Since I've lived in New York, weather on St. Paddy's has ranged from hail and snow to rain to eighty-degree weather. Spring in New York is a crazy time.

We were to have the ceremony at St. Patrick's Cathedral on Fifth Avenue, and then we were having the reception at The Rainbow Room inside Rockefeller Center. It was a three-block walk. However, because of the possibility of rain and snow, three blocks became a possible calamity. We had umbrellas to purchase and cars on standby. Luckily, at the last minute, the weather report cleared, and we canceled all alternate plans.

And a three-block walk couldn't just be a walk for Zella. Nope. A wedding on Saint Patrick's Day had to have bagpipers lead the guests from the cathedral where the ceremony took place down Fifth Avenue to the venue in midtown where the reception was happening. It was both a pain in the ass and an amazing sight to get three hundred guests outside the cathedral and not have them wander off before the group photo and literally follow the piper down the street.

This was a true feat. The ceremony took place, and just afterwards we had all three hundred guests meet on the front steps of the cathedral for a group picture. We weren't allowed to yell in the church, and they didn't want anything said during the ceremony or in the program. So, we had to corral everyone as they came out of the church, explaining and begging everyone to wait for the photo. That took almost thirty minutes. Strays wandered. People wanted to see the bride. Someone wanted water. Someone else wandered to the hotdog cart on the corner and was treating a whole slew of guests. Some people went over to the reception early and we had to have them sent back. Finally, we got everyone in place, and brought out the bride and groom to stand in the middle of their guests. It was a really neat picture; one I highly encourage if you can get it.

After that, five men came around the north corner of St. Patrick's in full regalia, the entire crowd including the groom was stunned. It was a surprise the bride had planned for her new husband. The pipers walked up to the group and serenaded as people pointed and watched. As soon as the groom figured out that this was a serenaded walk, he started the parade down Fifth Avenue toward their reception. Following the pipers as they crossed the busy street, we stopped traffic. It was an amazing photo that I am so glad the photographer was ready for. Pipers then the bride and groom followed by their wedding party and gaggles of guests zig zagging through the streets of Manhattan.

Because it was New York, and a beautiful spring day, we had tons of people on the street asking what was going on, taking photos, or joining in. I kept running from the front to the back of the group, which was about two blocks long, to either slow down the bagpipers or to speed up the tail end of the group. No one was going to be left behind. They continued to play outside of the doors to the entrance to the Rainbow Room and the congestion on the street was also a sight to see. New Yorkers ignore everything unless there is a large group, and then they have to join it and ask all the questions. We had to turn so many people away. It's a good thing it was a black-tie event, and any wedding crasher wearing green and asking for a kiss because they were Irish, was adeptly turned away.

Speaking of photos. Another crazy bride held her wedding for almost two hours late because she swore up and down that the photographer hadn't gotten all of the photos she requested. During our lead-up to the wedding, we would always send out a suggested photo list a month before the wedding. We would ask the bride and groom to provide us with the list of shots they wanted, and the names of the people in the shots, so we could make the photo session go as quickly as possible. It takes a good amount of time before but saves tons of time on the wedding day.

The tricky thing is, some photographers also do this, and then don't share the list that the bride and groom give them. I had sent out at least four reminders to the bride and groom, and her mother asking for the photo list. I told Zella about not receiving it. The day before the wedding the bride said that she had given the list to the photographer. I reached out to the photographer to get a copy of the list but never heard back. I never understood why photographers don't relinquish their list. Planners can help corral all the people. Why not use all the help you can get?

Although this seems extreme, believe me, when it comes to the day of a wedding you want to have as much of the paperwork done ahead of time. It takes time. It is a pain.

But believe me, when you only have eight hours to get everything you want out of a party, you need to be well prepared. And those hours go by so fast.

I had gone so far as to have phone calls with the bride and groom to ask for names of their attendees so I could write them all out for them on the photo list. But this one time I didn't get a photo list in advance, although I tried. The photographer came back with two thousand photos, and a list that he swore he checked off the day of the wedding. He showed us his wrinkled copies of what the bride had sent over. Although I agreed with him and trusted that he got all the photos and more, I didn't hear the end of that one for weeks. The conversation went something like this:

"Natalie, you should have followed up."

"Oh, believe me, Zella I did. I copied you on all the emails if you want to look them up, and I asked her for it on the phone three days ago and at the rehearsal last night."

"Unacceptable, Natalie. Next time try harder and get the list."

Sigh. So helpful. I remembered back to the time I asked her how to get the un-gettable information for a wedding.

Her response: "Natalie, just do it." Great, I thought to myself, a running shoe slogan from the nineties was how I was supposed to do my job.

Every moment like this was a learning experience. I became more resilient and honed my skills. When we were doing any of the paperwork, I would from then on place names in the photo list for people to approve or add to, instead of filling in themselves. And at least now I made more money and the insanity of it all phased me less.

Chapter Thirty-Six

There was a food standoff at another wedding. The bride and groom kept walking all around the reception talking to their guests as dinner was being served. The entire room had their dinner, and the bride and groom were still chatting. Then toasts were given, and the bride and groom were on the dance floor with their toasters. Later in the evening, the mother of the bride came over to me saying her daughter was complaining that they never got served dinner. I went immediately to the Maître'd to solve the issue.

"My waiter was holding their dinners until they sat down," he explained.

Like a kid playing telephone, I relayed the message to mother of the bride. It turns out the newlyweds were waiting for their food to come before they sat. I got their waiter to rush food out to them. But by that time, they were dancing like crazy and wouldn't stop. I even wiggled my way onto the dance floor through gobs of people to let them know that food was waiting for them, only to be told they didn't want it anymore. I relayed the message back to the Maître'd who had the plates removed.

Mother of the bride went after the waiter after he returned from taking away the plates. He then went back into the kitchen to get the plates, only the food had been given away to the kitchen staff, as it was cold. So, the chef fired two new entrees. They came out again, and I told the waiter to take them back. Mother of the Bride bent the ear of the waiter again as he came back from the kitchen.

Luckily this time I intervened and explained that the bride and groom no longer wanted food. She went and got her husband, father of the bride, who emphatically stated to me that his daughter would eat the food at her own wedding, especially since he was paying over four hundred dollars for every meal in the room. Finally, the Maître'd came over to save me, and stated that we would fire two meals around 11:45pm and then we would take them to the bridal suite for the couple.

At the same wedding, AM was working for the first time in a long while. She was feeling like Zella didn't use her as often as she should, and somehow AM and I got into a conversation about pay rates. AM hadn't gotten a pay raise from Zella in over six years. Everything came to a head for her at this wedding, as Zella kept giving her orders and then she would get a different order from the client just as she was about to execute it. AM was running around and around and around the venue to try to figure out what was the right answer. She had been stepped on three times, had her vendor meal eaten by someone else, and then had a tray of desserts spilled on her pants. AM was just about to leave, and Zella marched in the room.

"AM, I need you to stay late. Why aren't you answering texts?"

"I don't know if you've noticed Zella, but there are desserts all over my pants, and Natalie was just helping me try to salvage them," AM quipped back. "In fact, I was about to tell you that I'm done with this evening, and I'm going home."

As I was kneeling on the floor helping AM wipe her pants off, I was truly in between them.

"Zella, I can stay late," I offered.

"Not good enough, I need you both. They're extending and you both need to stay." Zella looked sour and started to walk out of the room.

AM looked downtrodden. I knew she wanted to get home to her husband and new baby.

I looked up at her, "It's now or never," I said hinting.

"What?" AM looked puzzled.

"Why not ask her now?" I suggested.

"Ask me what?" Zella queried.

"Well—I've been with you for six years, Zella and... oh never mind," AM started, but then fell short of asking for a raise.

"What AM is trying to say, Zella," I jumped in, "Is that she isn't quite sure you value her."

"Why of course I value her. How stupid to think otherwise," Zella punctuated her thought.

"Well," I said, in a rare moment of contradicting her, "truthfully, what you pay AM is less than industry standard, and she deserves more."

Zella whipped around back at both of us. "Oh, really?" she questioned. "Well, why hasn't AM said this for herself."

"Honestly, Zella," I said, boldly honest, "In moments like this, you're not the most approachable. And talking about money with you isn't an easy thing."

"Well, if AM wanted more money," Zella said suddenly, all milk and honey, "All she had to do was ask. I'll give you a three dollar an hour raise at events."

"Oh Zella!" AM gushed and rushed toward her to embrace her. "Thank you. I'm happy to stay late," AM said, her voice muffled into Zella's shoulder.

"Fine, fine. Now get out there and help manage the favors," Zella said smiling.

Grinning to myself, I watched AM go, when I turned to put my messy rag down, when I felt my arm yanked. Zella pulled me toward her and invaded my personal space, her face in mine. With her teeth bared, she said, "Don't ever undermine me again like that."

"What?" I questioned. I wasn't sure what she was talking about. Plus, the flip of mood that was always so weird to witness.

"Don't you ever talk about money with someone else who works for me again."

"I—but Zella, AM just—" I sputtered.

"If you value your job," she said, spitting in my face a little, "do not dare to do that again."

She stared me down for another moment, and then released me and turned to go back to the ballroom. I wasn't sure if she was sincere about her threat, but I never urged another colleague to ask for a raise again.

Chapter Thirty-Seven

*Z*ella was crazy, but some of her clients were worse. One wedding had me sign a non-disclosure agreement that not only would I not talk about anything that happened at the wedding or who I saw there, but that we were specifically not to talk to, make eye contact with, or look at the famous groom. There were so many crazy things that I would like to tell you about that wedding, but I legally can't.

This wasn't my only wedding with famous people. In fact, I did several weddings with famous guests. We planned the wedding for a film producing husband and wife team. They were some of the coolest people I've ever met. Her father is a famous director, too. I remember going to their office one day, trying to maintain my cool on several counts. First, I was there on professional terms as their wedding planner, not as an actress, although I rubbernecked so much that I needed a massage when I left. And, because this was one of my infamous cash pickups, and I was carrying sixty thousand dollars in cash from their cozy, barn-inspired production office. You wouldn't have known they produced two of the top five television shows at the moment. I wanted to slip my acting resume, which was in my backpack that day because I had an audition I was trying to get to, to everyone in the office including their non-existent receptionist. Don't worry, I did not. I remained professional.

Their cozy wedding at a Tribeca hotel included A and B list movie and television stars and a handful of rising stars. The standout moment of that night was when I loaned my phone charger to a television celebrity who shortly after might have donned a cape and a spandex super suit. I was thrilled I kept my cool during our exchange, and that I didn't mention I was an actress too like I felt I wanted to. However, I was heartbroken when she didn't bother to return my charger, but instead just left it randomly on a table, where I found it at the end of the night. I honestly think I was more upset that I could have lost such a good charger. But I can confirm that you shouldn't meet your heroes.

At another wedding I was asked to go up to the groom's suite and help with the tying of bow ties and pinning of boutonnières. This wedding I was just helping out the day of, so wasn't part of any of the planning at all, so I had no idea who any of the bridal party were. When I got to the room, I had my breath knocked out of me at how handsome the groom was. I kept trying not to stare at him as he looked like someone I recognized, but I couldn't put my finger on who he was. After assisting him with his tie and boutonniere I heard a gentle voice of another man behind me ask if I could help him as well. I turned around to find it was a Pulitzer Prize winning author whose work I admired. It took my entire acting prowess to not lose my cool and to quote his book to him verbatim as I pinned on the boutonniere of Madagascar Jasmine. When I finally looked him in the eye, he smiled a knowing smile at me.

But I wasn't the only one. There was a wedding when Zella went a little fangirl overboard. We were notified that one guest was a host on a famous reality show. Before the wedding, as she always did when we were informed that a famous guest would be attending, Zella would remind us to keep our cool and to treat them like any other guest.

We were doing our usual split of the wedding work, where Zella was with the bride and wedding party and dealing with last minute needs and photos, while I was dashing all around the property making sure that all vendors were on track to finish on time and didn't have any questions. I was also fastidious about checking all vendors in, and things like the cake and musicians often didn't arrive until very close to the wedding, so I was also checking to see if they had arrived.

The event manager for the venue found me and said that they had a guest stating they were supposed to have a room, but they couldn't find a room assigned under the guest's name. I went to the front desk to assist. We had been told that the father of the bride had purchased a block of twenty rooms for the evening for family and various guests, but that the front desk had all the names.

When I arrived at the desk, the nonplussed desk clerk was explaining to a very leggy, raven-haired woman that the issue was being solved, but his hands were tied. He sighed with great relief when he saw me walk up.

"This is the planner, she will be able to assist," the clerk said and motioned to me.

I was about to correct him when Zella came from nowhere and stepped in front of me, and said in a loud royal version of herself, "I'm the planner," she said, correcting him and not bothering to mention me. "We will take care of this in an instant," she said with a smile to the celebrity. In the same breath, she turned to the desk clerk, and in a heated fashion through clenched teeth said, "Get our guest a room. Now."

"Well, ma'am," uh oh, I thought to myself. The desk clerk called Zella ma'am. Eeek. He was in for it. "As I was telling your guest—" he continued nervously. I felt like I was watching him shrink from Zella's penetrating gaze. "The father of the bride reserved a block of rooms. We don't have a room with your guest's name on it," Zella pointed a finger so close to his face he was cross-eyed. But before she could interrupt, he plowed through, "There are two rooms that are unclaimed, but the only one who can adjust that would be the person whose credit card is on file."

Without hesitation, I took off running. Actually, it's humorous how much I jog at weddings. And I hate running for sport. Usually, I have done enough steps at a wedding that I've done about six miles. I probably run half of those.

When I last saw him, the father of the bride was in the library drinking a very nice bottle of rum. My money was that he would be there until he walked his daughter down the aisle.

I also knew that he didn't have his phone on him as he had dropped it into the toilet the night of the rehearsal. A last-minute decision was made by the best man who wanted to do a dance at the reception with all the men in the wedding party and needed me to choreograph it. And because the father of the bride put his phone in his back pocket, and at some point during the rehearsal visited the restroom…and you can imagine the rest. It was currently sitting in a Ziploc bag of rice back at his apartment.

My phone buzzed.

Where the fuck are you going?

Although incredibly skilled, I never perfected texting and running at the same time. Besides, Zella could chill for a moment.

As I turned the corner to the library, I found the man in question. Breathlessly, I explained what was happening at the front desk. And then I dialed Zella.

"What is it, Natalie. Where did you go?"

"Zella, hand your phone to the front desk clerk, please."

"Not until you—"

"Zella, I'm here with the father of the bride who would like to speak to the front desk. Please," I said with such a pointed tone, I hoped Zella felt my finger in her ear.

I heard Zella mumbling and then a chipper voice said, "Front desk, this is Chris."

Without even saying hello to Chris, I handed my phone over to the father of the bride, "Here sir, it's the front desk."

Not a minute later, my phone was being handed back to me.

"Everything is ok. The front desk is going to put her name on one of my rooms." I smiled. "Thanks for coming to get me Natalie. You're doing a great job. Anything our VIP guest wants, she gets! Oh, and I'll make sure Zella knows how much I appreciate your work." He started to explain how he did her face lift, but I excused myself before the gory details.

"Anything for the father of the bride. Enjoy the rum!" I said, turning to jog back to the front desk.

At the front desk as I walked up, Zella was taking a selfie with the celebrity who was looking less than pleased. As I got close, Zella grabbed me by the arm and said, "Natalie, show this lovely lady to her room," and then in a whisper she said, "I don't trust these idiots to do it," and then in her normal tone again. "Thank you, Natalie," as she walked off and hid behind a plant so she could post her picture on social media.

"Sorry about that," I said to everyone within hearing range. I turned to the special guest and asked, "Should I show you to your room?"

"Thank you." She smiled. "Natalie, right?"

"Right," I said.

"I should be alright, now that I have a room," she said jokingly.

"Great," I said. Then as a quick afterthought, I dug into my small black cross body bag, and pulled out a Tremaine Events business card. "Here is my card if you run into any other issues. Or need to find the father of the bride before the ceremony. His phone is out of commission, and I seem to have a knack for finding him quickly," I explained, finally feeling nervous that I was in the midst of a celebrity.

She took the card and picked up her garment bag. "Thanks, Natalie. You've been a great help." She walked off toward her room.

With great confidence, I walked back to the ballroom to check on the progress of the setup. It was not lost on me that I gave a celebrity my personal info, and she knew my name. But I let it go and focused on the wedding.

Zella tracked down our VIP later, striking up what I can only imagine was an inappropriate conversation with a celebrity guest who told Zella I gave out my business card. Zella came storming up to me later in the evening. She made sure to drive home how unhappy she was with I had done so and kept grilling me as to what my angle was.

"I just gave her my card in case she had another issue. Father of the bride said to treat her like a VIP." Then I lowered my voice a little, "And since you thought the people running this place are idiots and told me that you didn't even trust them to see her to her room, which is their job, I figured that you would want me to assist her in any way possible."

"Why didn't you give her my card, then?" Zella prodded.

"Because you've told me to handle things. You've told me to take initiative. You also got me my own cards, so I don't carry yours anymore," I said as strongly, and blasé as possible. I didn't want to call attention to special treatment and even buttoned my rebuttal with, "I would have done it for any other guest."

Zella was trying to find some sort of hole in my argument. "Are you sure you didn't give it to her because you're both actresses?"

I let out a huge laugh. Partially because there were moments I felt Zella could read my mind. But mostly because as I told Zella, "There is really nothing she can do to help me. We both are performers, true, but it's not like she could get me a gig. Those come from casting directors and producers. Giving her my card was just to do my job for Tremaine Events, nothing more."

She needed to calm down; this wedding was already trying my patience with so many other little things, the band was plowing through all of the itinerary, and were going too fast, there was too much time between first course and the entrée, and the flower girl was having a fit. I didn't need Zella to have one as well.

"Fine," she acquiesced. I breathed a sigh of relief. Not letting me off the hook too easily, Zella turned and put her finger in my face and said, "But if you ever cross the line again…" and then walked away leaving her threat hanging in the air.

Chapter Thirty-Eight

She threatened me so often, but I always took it as I was expendable, and she would fire me as soon as she thought of it. But with all of the questionable things she accused me of, she herself did. Gotta love double standards. Another double standard of Zella's: Don't befriend brides.

Jamie worked in the industry. Zella handed the reins to me because we had two other weddings the same month, and Zella had her hands full. This meant two first for me: I had direct contact with the bride and Sarah assisted me. Zella was supposed to be completely hands-off.

Originally, Jamie said she only needed day-of-assistance, but two months before the wedding, the pressure was finally getting to her, and I stepped in. We chatted on the phone, texted frequently and sent ten to twenty emails back daily. We built a bond. We had already met previously at industry parties.

In a panic, Jamie called me; she was spending way too much money and needed to cut back. Unbeknownst to Zella, I went and met with Jamie. Besides, Zella had given me permission to take over and I didn't feel like I needed to update Zella on every detail. I'll admit, it was a bit of rebellion. But at the same time, waiting for Zella to approve things could take forever, especially if she were in the crux of two other events.

In three hours we had reconfigured a whole bunch of things, including questions she could ask other vendors, a less expensive route to go on her table numbers, place cards and menus. We reviewed contracts with the photographer and the videographer and realized that she didn't need the full packages she had originally was offered. And we found a few other ways to cut a little bit back. In other words, I was a little more hands on than Jamie was actually paying for. I didn't mind. It was good experience. And I still did all my normal duties like the itinerary and contact sheet, all viewed and approved by Zella.

Zella came to the rehearsal to make sure everything was going well, even though Sarah and I were supposed to be running it and the wedding day. I think she wanted to be a presence as this was a wedding of an industry event person so it was packed with industry people. At the end of rehearsal my heart sank when Zella told me she would be on site to run things the next day. I should have felt some frustration. But I knew how to do my job extremely well, and another person at an event to help is never bad. I mean, I was looking forward to running an event and not getting questioned or scolded by Zella at any moment, but I took it in stride.

Everything went off without a hitch. Well almost everything. The few duties I handed over to Sarah, including the escort cards and helping the bridesmaids Zella had something to correct about each one. She was probably scarred for life even though I had told Sarah later that this was Zella hazing and testing new people. Sarah refused to believe me and was sure she was going to get fired.

The morning after the wedding, as agreed in our contract, I set up Jamie's brunch for her and she actually asked me to stay. A few weeks later I had wine and hors d'oeuvres with my newlyweds after they went to see a show I recommended to them. Months later, I was in my first play in a year, and they came to see me in it. And I saw Jamie several times at industry parties after her wedding. It's not like we were insta-besties who braided each other's hair, but we were friends and colleagues.

Somehow Zella got wind of this and scolded me. I wasn't allowed to befriend the brides after their weddings. I reminded Zella that Jamie was in the industry and I was keeping in contact with her because of that. Zella put her foot down and didn't want me to see any of the brides after their weddings. Sometimes she even hovered at weddings now, to make sure I wasn't getting too close. So, I stopped.

If Zella had been a boyfriend, someone would have alerted me sooner to how she was manipulating me and molding my life to be only about her.

Even after crazy incidents at events, my public humiliation, being blamed for things out of my control, or abuse in the office, I stuck with her. Disillusioned that the schedule was good and that I was being paid well. Truly I was convinced that with my experience with Zella, doors would open. I was sure they were already opening, I just hadn't gotten any offers for jobs elsewhere, other than Alexander. Everyone raved about my management of events. But no glamorous jobs were revealed. And the fabulous life was still more than I could afford.

At some point there was a turning point where my vernacular switched from "she's going to fire me" to "I really should quit." All my friends, especially Sam, were tired of giving support and advice. And to be honest, I was tired of complaining. So, I stopped talking about it, and just absorbed all the abuse and stress. I felt like I had no other choice if I wanted to be something in this business. I was sure I was going places. Doors would open for me if I just waited a little longer.

Until I completely broke down.

Chapter Thirty-Nine

The thing about breakdowns is you never know they're coming. This isn't even the day where you came in. It only gets worse from here.

The day started like any other. Sam was up and out of the apartment before me. I snoozed twice before dragging myself out of bed already hating the day ahead. Honestly, this was a clue things weren't right. Because if anyone is at the point where hiding in bed is the best option of the day, a life examination needs to happen.

Instead, I pulled myself out of bed and pulled on some clothing. I didn't even register lately I had been starting to just grab whatever black was easiest. When I wore black, Zella was less likely to talk about dieting, and since my only workouts were running around the city doing errands and weddings, I was thin but not toned. But the thing was, I was depressed wearing black daily. I thought this as I looked around at all of the people in rush hour traffic. They all looked as melancholic as I felt.

At the office, Zella was hurling accusations about research on veils. And she was upset at me that I was one minute late. I didn't even bother to mention Sarah was doing that research, it just wasn't worth it. Tongue lashings were more like a bee buzzing around my head at this point, slightly bothersome, but if I stood still, the stinger flew away and I would be unscathed.

Sarah was still timid around Zella. Although I didn't appreciate the mistaken blame, it was easier to tolerate five minutes of Zella than a couple of hours of scraping Sarah's wilted, boneless mental state off of the floor.

These days I was only in the office two days a week and Sarah was in daily. Most days I could work from home and get via phone or email. It was much easier to get yelled at while in pajamas.

Today my presence was demanded in the office via text message late last night. "The Tucker wedding is a mess," Sarah whispered as Zella was distracted from screaming at me by the buzzing of her phone and she walked into another room to take the call.

"What's going on?" I asked in a low voice. Whispering always seems more conspicuous, so I learned to talk in a lower voice instead. If caught, I could blame it on vocal rest, or something that sounded like an actor's excuse.

"Did you see the email?" Sarah looked over her shoulder towards the room where Zella was shouting on the phone.

"No. What email? From whom? What did it say?" I said, simultaneously opening my laptop and opening the email on my phone trying to get to the information faster.

"Just read the Simpkins email," Sarah whispered as she scampered around the room. "I have to run errands for Zella."

Most of the time Sarah and I stood up for or protected each other from the wrath of Zella. I couldn't figure out what was wrong, and I didn't know what I had done, or what anyone had done to put Zella in such a continually foul mood.

"Don't leave me," I pleaded in a fake sad voice, although I really meant it. I did not want to be left alone with Zella today as her anger grew.

"I won't be gone long," she said as she loaded herself up with four different store bags, and the dry cleaning. "I'll bring you a coffee!"

As she scuttled out the door, I read the email. It obliterated Zella.

Honestly, I can't say that I was shocked. Andrea Simpkins, our bride, decided to toss out all the original designs and ideas two months before the wedding. Six months of planning was down the drain. Instead of luscious white flowers and candles, she stated she wanted a tropical vibrant feel. She also stated that she didn't feel like she had been heard in any of the design meetings.

Her words rang true to me. I had felt exactly like this every moment of every day I had worked Zella. She ran over my thoughts and ideas like a truck barreling down a highway. I completely related to this bride. In every line of this email, I felt Andrea's vehemence. She was saying things I always felt I couldn't. When I read the last line, I almost threw up. "I don't know if we should continue to move forward together." Woah. I looked up to see Zella standing over me to one side.

"Zella, um," I said, the words not wanting to form in my mouth as I wondered if I had projected my feelings onto our bride.

"What Natalie," she yelled.

"What can I do?" I asked as calmly as I could.

"I want to look at everything. Get out every contract, every note, and every email we have on this client. Piece it all together about what she agreed on and what she originally wanted." Zella started to text as she loudly muttered, "I have no idea what this girl is talking about, do you?"

The words were right there. This was one of those moments where a strong human or a heroine of a story should speak out with truth and feeling. I wanted to just tell Zella exactly what I should have. But I froze. Things might have been different if I had just spoken up. Stood up for myself.

Stood up for a bride who felt trampled. I wished I could channel any number of heroines I was dying to play in a play.

From my vantage, everything the bride called Zella out for in her email was true. I had been there. At every meeting the bride was continually bulldozed into picking things she didn't want. Every time she brought up an idea that was creative or colorful, she would get shoved back into the prim and proper white wedding box.

I knew what it was like. I was boxed in, too. Both of us badly wanted to fit in, but also wanted our own personality to shine. I wanted to stand up for her, a woman after my own color palette. A woman strong enough to say eight weeks before her own wedding that it was someone else's dream and she wanted her own, or she would go elsewhere.

I didn't stand up for her. And although as I think back on that unfortunate moment of me, wearing all black, feeling insignificant and small, knowing that could have been a turning point if I had not been afraid to speak up and take a risk. I did what I thought was right in that moment to fit in. And I was what Zella wanted.

Instead, I said, "Right, Zella. How do you want to handle this?"

Her head whipped up from her phone and she stared like I should have already known. After burning me with her retinas, she said, "We will show her that she is getting everything she wanted. We will fix this. Today."

Heartbreak and burnout slammed together in my chest.

Today's agenda was already full. And now she wanted me to work to prove Zella's vision was what Andrea really wanted. This was in addition to drafting a new client's contracts, building an itinerary for another client Zella just picked up this week whose wedding a month away. Also on today's agenda were in person client meetings at the venue with the band and décor team and then a tasting at Baked in Love. I didn't know how to get it all done. But the ever-present panic of failure and needing to please Zella sat there, in its normal place, hanging over my head like certain death. So much of my life I had now sacrificed for this job, and I had to keep doing it. Numbly, I kept my mouth shut and started to work on the task Zella put me on.

As I tried to get through the mountain of work, everything was wrong. Instead, everything today was a punishment for not brandishing my moxy. When I tried to print out the emails, I got in trouble for using paper. When I tried to show Zella documentation on the computer, she snapped that she needed a better way to read them. When I lined up all the different vendor contracts with all of the notes, she told me everything was in the wrong order. At some point she started yelling for the itinerary. Andrea's wedding was still two months away, and because we had been so busy, I had barely started on it. So of course, I got berated. Which made me start to cry.

Tissues crowded around my computer as I dared not leave my seat to toss them, as I sniffled and my eyes dripped tears. I had nail marks in my palms and had taken up Zella's terrible nail chewing habit, so I had nubs for fingers. Every inch of my body was urging me to scream for help, but I didn't know who to ask, or even how to ask. So I kept working. My brain was tired of being reprimanded and overwhelmed with the amount of work I still had to accomplish, I didn't pay any attention to the time. Then I heard Zella shriek as if she had been branded by a hot iron.

"Holy fuck, Natalie. Our appointment started ten minutes ago. Why didn't you remind me?" Zella dashed around the room grabbing paperwork and tossing things in her purse.

At that point I was so bereft, everything registered at a very slow speed.

"Let's go!" she yelled at the same time she applied her lipstick.

Hopping up, I thrust my feet in my shoes. I had gotten these gorgeous black suede pumps and thought today was a good day to break them in because we usually took cars to all appointments. Sarah who had returned thirty minutes ago, grabbed my notebook and pens for me as I called a car.

"Address?" I shouted.

"What?" both Sarah and Zella said.

"Where are we going? For the car?" I asked with the vehemence of a quickly rising storm.

"Don't talk like that to me," Zella said.

"I wasn't… I just…" I stammered. I turned away as a tear rolled down my cheek.

Zella grabbed my wrist as I wiped away my tear. She hauled me down her hallway to the elevator. I was tripping over my feet as I ran after her. There was no cell service in the elevator. My requests for a car weren't working. When the elevator finally opened on the ground floor, I tried again for a car, as Zella dragged me through the lobby and hailed a cab on the street. I didn't understand what was happening. Zella tapped away at her cell and yelled at the driver. Five minutes later we pulled up to the museum where the wedding was taking place.

"So sorry we are late," Zella oozed in a lovely tone. "I just couldn't get off the phone with Martha—you know you just can't hang up on Martha!"

My stomach churned. It was always freakish how she could change her mood so easily.

During the meeting we walked all over the museum. Then we walked the ten blocks to the office of the wedding band. I took tons of notes, per Zella. I would just have finished writing something down and she would tap my pad and say, "Write that down," as if I were new. My irritation expanded and grew like a bubble in my chest.

On the way from the band to Baked In Love, we paused at a coffee shop. Zella bought coffee and croissants for the bride, her parents and herself, but didn't offer me anything. When the mother of the bride asked if I was having anything, Zella answered for me, "Oh she's on a diet. She is trying to lose about thirty pounds."

Shame filled my face with heat. The black wasn't working. Trying to avoid further embarrassment, as I knew she had told other clients about how she and I talked about different surgery options and disgusting diets she had me try, I just nodded and smiled, trying to hide the tears that were welling up in my eyes.

A reprieve arrived when we got to the bakery, and I saw Denise's smiling face.

"Hey!" She said, happy to see me.

"Hey," I answered back in a tone that would rival that of Eeyore.

"Wow, what's wrong? Why are you—" Denise was cut off by Zella.

"Denise, we need the tasting. Now. Snap snap."

Denise looked at me, and I looked quickly down at my notebook. She dashed to grab the plates for the client, as they all sat around the table. There weren't enough chairs, so I stood. Blisters had formed all over my feet from the shoes, but I was so overcome with everything else, I barely felt them. I didn't realize we were going to be walking all over lower Manhattan today. Every time Denise tried to talk to me, Zella called her away.

My phone buzzed multiple times and Zella snapped at me when she caught me looking at it.

Once was Sarah asking me:

Where are the blank documents located?

The second text was Denise:

I have news to tell you. Also, why is she being like this?

One was Matt the caterer:

Hey. It's been a while.

Then Alexander:

We should talk. I have a great opportunity for you.

Then Matt again:

Dinner?

I answered Sarah. I refused to acknowledge Alexander. I started to reply to Denise but got snapped at. And I was generally confused by the text from Matt. I hadn't heard from him in a while, and he knew I had a boyfriend. Convinced he must have texted the wrong person, I ignored his text.

Meetings concluded at 4pm and Zella sent me on another errand. She took a cab back to the office, and I walked to the flower district for a flower girl's sash ribbon. When I got back to the office, I was accused of taking too long, and I was told I needed to stay until I got all of the work finished that I needed to do, so it could be printed and, on her desk, to review in the morning.

Sarah left at 5:30pm. Zella left at 6:15pm. I was in the office until almost 7:30pm. I don't know why I stayed. Was it guilt? Was it self-flagellation? Honestly looking back, I don't know who was worse to me, Zella or myself.

I could have left and gotten things done at home on the comfort of my own sofa. But for some reason, I was beaten and bruised on the inside and I just wanted everything finished before I went home.

Thoughts of Sam filled my head and warmed my heart when I finally got on the subway, which was severely delayed. I didn't get home until almost nine. As I reached my apartment door and slid the key into the lock, I took a deep sigh of relief knowing that the man I loved was just behind the door. I knew when I walked through it that I could fall into his arms for a few moments and this day would fall off of me like dirty clothing. In one fluid movement, I locked the door, set down my bag, kicked off my shoes and threw my keys in the bowl by the door.

With the hypnotic movement of these actions, I felt safe inside my sanctuary. Finally, I felt my calm and soothed spirit start to rush back into my body. I was still a mess, mind you, but I knew now that I was home everything would be all right. Or at least I could shut it out for the night. With my feet now touching the cool wooden floor, I almost felt a nice deep breath fill me from head to toe. I needed to soak my feet. I needed to soak my heart. Everything hurt inside and out.

Chapter Forty

A s I sighed, I turned and looked into the living room and jumped to see Sam leaning against the couch, watching me. I rushed over to him and threw my arms around his middle, laid my head on his chest, and just hugged him. He hesitated a moment before wrapping his arms around my shoulders. He was hugging me so tightly, as if he just knew what a terrible day I'd had. We took a deep breath together. After a few moments like this he started to pet my hair.

"It's so good to be home," I said. "I had such a terrible day today."

"Oh babe, I'm so sorry," he muttered into my hair. "You really need to quit that job. The woman is a flat-out bitch."

I pushed back from his arms. He had always defended me, but this was different. For some reason, his tone and his cursing made me need to justify her behavior.

"True. But if you—"

"Don't. Don't do that. Don't stand up for someone who mentally beats you up continually."

I shrugged him off and stepped away from him crossing my arms. Shooting defiance daggers from my eyes I looked back at him. He was right, of course. But that meant I had to hate that I was such a doormat today. He tried to reach out to me but I slunk away into the kitchen for wine.

From the cabinet I picked my favorite glass, a Vera Wang with a flowing bow etched into the side. It wasn't until I had opened the refrigerator, reaching for the Chardonnay in the door, the realization hit. Sam's packed suitcase was next to him. I grabbed the wine and shut the door with my foot. I uncorked the bottle, took a breath. As I poured I asked as cool as the bottle of wine in my hand, "What's the suitcase for?"

"Well... I...," Sam said and shuffled his feet like he was doing a soft shoe routine.

Stepping back into the living room, the bottle in one hand, I threw back the glass of wine in one gulp. Then refilled my glass.

He looked painfully over my shoulder and then down at his toes as he continued while I just stared at him. "I've met someone."

Air left the room. The floor disappeared. My ears rang. My heart went into total shutdown. I threw back another large swallow of wine. Then sloshed more from the bottle into my glass.

He continued, less confident, "But it's not what you think," he said in that comforting rich baritone. My mind raced wondering what I'd done lately that would be any kind of deal breaker. I had been trying to take out the trash and clean up more.

Maybe it was that I was being a bad friend, or a bad girlfriend. Was it my job? I had been working a lot, but Sam knew that Zella had been getting nicer, or at least I told him she was. My job was important to me.

Maybe it was because I'd been neglecting my body, clothes had been fighting tighter. But it couldn't be the way I look, could it. Sam wasn't like that. I mean it was his job to help people get skinny. No, his job was to make people healthy, stop bending the truth Natalie.

His voice echoed my own, "Natalie, there is no easy way to tell you this." I looked into his eyes trying to derive the truth. But when it came out of his mouth, I didn't expect him to say, "I'm gay."

I must have blinked forty times in the next ten seconds. Throat dry, and voice gone, I couldn't speak. Having shed so many tears already today, I was sure I had none left. My heart was now in my feet pulsing through every blister I had unrightfully gained today.

To quench the desert that was my throat, I threw down the rest of the wine in my glass. Then I decided in one of my classiest moments to date to cut out the middleman, and just put the bottle to my lips and took a huge swig.

I would like to pause for a second here because the next bit paints me a bit heartless and uncaring. But when humans are weak and scared, we rip others apart. In these moments fear makes lashing out in pain the better option. What I did next wasn't good, or right, but it was what really happened. If time travel were possible, I wish I could go back to that moment and be more thoughtful. More supportive. More sober. Tragically, I wasn't. The wine was gone, and it was the last bottle in the apartment. I finally met his eyes, and I didn't understand how or why he was still there.

My lips quirked to one side, and I took a deep, audible breath through my nose as I found the courage to look into his eyes. "I guess I kinda knew," I said wondering how the words came out. I couldn't breathe, let alone speak. I found myself looking down at his suitcase with the Lady Gaga luggage tag. He said it was a gag gift from another instructor because he used her music in his class a lot when he brought it home.

All the signs along always seem incredibly glaring, bright, and blatant in the worst possible moment, don't they? It's like they appear only to make you feel even more stupid in moments like this.

I felt him start toward me, his need to comfort me was still instinctual. But he stopped himself. I looked at him again, then I was in his arms, sobbing.

"I'm so sorry," he said. "There is never a good time to tell you. Been meaning to tell you for a while. But I've also wanted to be here for you while you struggled with work. This isn't about you. I still love you deeply. I'm just… I'm just not…attracted to you."

That made me cry even harder. This moment wasn't about me, and it was all at the same time. Sam was my best friend, and not only did I not notice something so defining about him, but he had found someone else before telling me. I felt so sorry for myself, and such a terrible person all at the same time. A coming out moment is a big deal. Admitting who you truly are as a person is a milestone. And I, having one of the worst days of my life because I was continually denying who I was to keep my job, didn't see any of the clarity in this moment. I had ignored so much.

My shoulders heaved. He hugged me tighter, thinking I was sobbing. But quickly took me by the shoulders and pulled me away from him as he heard laughter issuing from me.

"Of course. Of course, this is happening today. How could you do this today on the worst day. How could I be so stupid—"

"Stop. Just stop." He stood back, his hands on his hips and one knee popped while his chin jutted out. Wow. He was gay. How did I not see this for so long? He shook his head, "Every day has been the worst day for you for months. Maybe even for the last year or longer. Don't put that on me. I have tried to tell you. I have wanted to tell you. Every time I started to, there was something that happened to you that made me wait to tell you. But this… I just can't pretend

305

anymore. I didn't want you to be alone in your frustration while you figured everything out with your job, but my goodness—there has never been an opening for me to bring this all to a head—poor choice of words, I know."

I guffawed at the entendre. I shook my head in disbelief. I cried at the fact that I couldn't see that my best friend was not only no longer attracted to me but was something completely different than I thought.

Vehemently I walked up to him, I felt like I wanted to slap his face. He winced, bracing for the blow. Instead, I gently put my palm on his cheek. Tears streamed down my face. Breath tried to issue from my aching lungs. My heart stopped beating.

"Oh Sam," I sighed heavily. "I'm so sorry. I am so very sorry that I have been so absorbed in my job that I didn't see you for who you really were and see you hurting."

He covered my hand with his.

"It's ok, babe," he said so quietly, and his voice broke when he said babe. "I am sorry," he paused while catching his breath. A tear fell down his cheek, "That I fell in love with someone else."

This shattered me. My heart broke. Sobs wracked my body. Sam helped me to the sofa and held me for a little while. Eventually, he eased himself off the sofa.

"We will work out the rent later," I heard him say through my sobbing haze as he placed his keys on the tray by the door. "I called Bennett and Ginger. They're on their way. And I made a bunch of food, and put reheating instructions on how to prepare it, so you'll not have to order delivery for a few weeks."

He kept talking, but I couldn't hear it as my sobs filled my own ears. Even as he was leaving, he was taking care of me. I didn't understand any of it.

The broken pieces of my heart shredded even more as I watched him roll his bag out the door. My body was wracked with sobs as I lay pathetically on the sofa for some time. The door buzzer rang. Bennett arrived with three pizzas and gummy bears. Ginger had three bottles of wine and three bottles of coconut water and arrived around the time that Bennett pried me to sit up on the sofa to blow my nose. Ginger made me chug one of the coconut waters as she helped me strip from the depressing black outfit I was in all day into comfy pajamas. Then I was allowed more wine.

My haze had made me uncommunicative, so they both chatted while we all watched some movie. I started to think about my relationship. For the last eight months Sam and I had been roommates who slept in the same bed. We cuddled, but nothing more intimate than that. It had really been eight months since we had sex. And at least two days a week, one of us slept on the sofa, usually me when I had fallen asleep there.

The rest of the night felt like a blurred, slow-motion haze of a drugged character in a movie. I don't remember eating pizza. I don't remember how many glasses of wine or anything else I had. I don't remember when Jordan arrived. And I don't remember calling Zella. Or talking to Alexander.

Chapter Forty-One

When I awoke the next morning, head pounding, mouth thick and dry like a cotton ball, I padded into the living room to see Jordan typing away on her computer.

"Hey, what are you–"

"I hope you don't mind. I told work that I had to work from home for the next few days because of a family emergency. So, I'm here as long as you need me."

"Great," I said, only slightly confused. Still in that blissful state where I could remember nothing that happened over the last day, I started to walk to the kitchen. Jordan jumped up, and steered me to the sofa, then grabbed water, coffee and aspirin.

"Here, start with the water and aspirin, then you can have coffee."

Starting to push myself up, albeit weakly, in protest, I said, "What time is it? I need to get to work. I need to call Zella–"

Her look conveyed that I should remember something. And when nothing registered, she gently sat me back down on the couch. "You took care of that last night," Jordan said.

"What do you mean?" I asked flatly.

"Well, I don't know where your phone is, Bennett hid it from you after you insisted you needed to call Zella back because you thought she might think you were lying to get out of working today."

"Oh, god."

"Yup," Jordan nodded with a knowing look.

"Oh, god," I repeated.

"Yuuup," Jordan kept nodding like a bobble head.

"Oh, fuck," I said jumping up from the sofa and starting to scramble around my apartment looking for my phone. "Where did he hide it?"

As I scampered around my tiny space like a mouse trapped in a maze, Jordan chuckled a little. I looked in the refrigerator; I crawled on the floor looking under the coffee table, the sofa, and the entertainment system. I ran to the bedroom and looked on and under every imaginable surface.

Jordan was now laughing very heartily.

"What?" I yelled from the bedroom. "You could be a little more helpful."

"No, sorry, I will. It's just that Bennett, knowing your love of coffee, figured it would be the last place you'd look for it, but the first place you would go in the morning. He was right." I walked over to the coffee maker and found my phone plugged in, sitting on top of the machine.

"That is the most ridiculous," I ran into the kitchen, "and the most brilliant thing I've ever heard before in my life." My mood started to lift a little. "Points for Bennett!" This good mood lasted only about five more seconds when I clicked the home button to light up the screen. "HOLY FUCK."

"What?" Jordan quickly shoved her laptop onto the coffee table making all sorts of clattering noises and jumped up and ran into the kitchen. "What's going on?"

She looked over my shoulder while I was scrolling through text messages. There were thirty-two text messages. Two from my mom, four from Denise, five from Violet all with various levels of checking in, twelve from Sarah with work questions I couldn't even start to fathom, four from Ginger and two from Bennett with pictures from last night and memes trying to cheer me up. One from Matt Spencer again asking about dinner. Three from Alexander that didn't make sense that asked me if I was serious about leaving, when I could start, and to call him. I seriously wish he would leave me alone. He made my skin crawl.

But if that wasn't enough, at the top was a text that made my stomach churn. From Zella. I swallowed the hard lump in my throat and tapped to read her message. It only read:

Call me.

As if the text message was the key to everything suddenly became clear. Sobriety hit hard. I had drunk dialed my boss.

"Oh god what did I do?" I said as I fell onto the sofa, my body wooden and my eyes refusing to close.

"Not exactly sure." She dragged out the words. "You locked yourself in your room, saying it was the best decision to deal with it right then."

"Why did I feel the need to blow up my entire life last night? Like Sam leaving seemed like a good time to actually do something to lose my job. The entire time I have worked for Zella and I felt like she would fire me at any moment, but now, when I have the least control, I make the biggest mistake, at the worst moment."

Jordan sat next to me, put my coffee mug in my hands and patted my knee. "Drink this. You'll feel better."

"I don't know how, I–" I took a sniff of the coffee mug. "Wait, is this amaretto?"

"Yup. The flavored creamer was in the fridge."

I started to tear up again. Sam.

"Well," I looked at Jordan, and took a sip, trying not to think of Sam and how to fix this mess I made with Zella, "time to face the music."

"After coffee."

"Right after coffee," I echoed Jordan.

After twenty minutes, two cups of coffee, and many text replies to all but Alexander and Matt, I called Zella. And as Jordan suggested I put the phone on speaker. We sat next to each other on the sofa, and Jordan held my hand for the entire time.

As the phone rang, my anxiety grew. I had checked my call log while drinking coffee and I saw that I had called Zella three times around 9:30pm. The phone rang once after I dialed Zella's number. The first two calls were only seconds long, so I must not have talked to her. Two rings. The third was almost four minutes long. Three rings. I had no idea that I had made the call or any recollection of what I had said. Now I completely understand the insanity plea. And then she answered.

"Hello, Natalie, feeling any better?"

"Yes, Zella, thank you," I said, waiting to be devoured. "Zella, I'm so very, very sorry to call you last night," I gushed. "I was having the absolute worst—"

"I know Natalie. You told me."

Silence.

"Oh," I said. "So you know about Sam and me, and–"

"Yes, and you told me everything I needed to know last night."

"Right," I said, wondering about what I said.

"Now, listen Natalie. I've told you this before, men come and go. If you need to take some time, that is fine, but honestly, I think the best thing for you," she paused. Jordan squeezed my hand, and we exchanged looks as Zella continued, "is work. I'm sure that you're in no state to come in today, and at this late hour," it was only 1pm, "you'll be of no use to me today anyway. I know Sarah was trying to get in touch with you—"

"Yes, Zella," I interrupted. "I was answering her texts right before I called you back."

"Oh, good. I'm not in the office at the moment, but that girl was having a panic attack when I told her you weren't coming in for the rest of the week," Jordan and I both whipped our heads and looked at each other again. She held my hand tighter. "Now listen, Natalie, I want you to take the rest of the day off, and I want you to work from home for the next two days. I want you to do nothing this weekend, if you can help it, and then I need you back here on Monday morning, ready to work with your head held high. We have the Mittner wedding next week, and you need to be in the office. I'll also deal with the fiasco that is also the Simpkins Bride. Also when you get back I need you to train Sarah not to panic," Zella continued to rattle on about things she needed done. I let go of Jordan's hand and grabbed the closest pen and the back of an envelope and jotted down notes.

"Thank you, Zella. I'll take care of all these things, and I'll give Sarah a call when we hang up."

"Good. Thank you, Natalie. I have to go," and then the phone clicked, and Zella was gone. I stared at the phone blankly. The air in my apartment stilled and everything went silent.

"Does she not say 'goodbye' like a normal person?" Jordan asked.

"Nope," I replied, being verbally shaken back to life, dialing Sarah's number. "Hey Sarah, it's me."

"Oh my goodness! Thank you so much for calling Natalie, I don't know what to do and Zella got really mad at me for not having a pen that worked, and I forgot the address of the cleaner," Sarah rattled away for a moment about a few things. I said a quiet prayer for Sarah.

312

"Listen, Zella wants me to work from home for the next few days but call or text as much as you need. You're going to be fine. Now get your notebook, and I'll answer your questions one at a time. Oh, and Sarah, you need to start breathing. The job is a lot easier if you don't panic and remember you're not saving lives."

I could hear Jordan chuckle over my shoulder. As I helped Sarah work through all of her questions, I wondered how many times I had this panicked conversation with Amanda, or how many hours I had spent on anxiety-filled calls with my friends, terrified that I wasn't doing my job correctly.

When I got off the phone with Sarah, I looked dumbly at Jordan who had gone back to working on her computer.

"I can't believe I have the day off."

"Great," Jordan said, fanning me up off the sofa. "Go take a shower and get dressed. We're going out."

"Jay, I don't think I can—"

"Nope! I don't want to hear it," Jordan said, pushing me toward the bathroom. "Your ex-man left only healthy food in the fridge, and I want greasy pancakes and bacon."

"Alright, alright," I called out over my shoulder as I went and got into the shower. The rush of the warm steamy water was just what I needed. My body hurt from all of the emotions. I took a nice long shower and cried more.

We went for brunch at a diner nearby. It was great to reconnect. I had been such a distant friend. In fact, I got great one on one time with all of my best friends. After our brunch we went back to the apartment and played board games and watched a movie. Jordan stayed until Ginger came over around 5pm.

Ginger took me out to dinner, and then to get foot massages. She said she would have done full body, but I didn't think I should be in a room by myself and have all of my actual pressure points pushed. That was a recipe for more tears. After stopping at a wine bar and sharing a beautiful charcuterie tray, we had a sleepover. The next morning Bennett joined us for a boozy lunch. He took the afternoon off, and Ginger went on to check on her clients. As we were near Chelsea Piers, we decided to go bowling of all things. After two games, and a combined score of 157, we realized we were both terrible bowlers. Bennett said he would sleepover with me on Friday night, but I told him that I should try to sleep alone for the first time in months. Bennett was only a few stops away on the bus, or a quick seven-minute cab ride from my apartment. He said to call if I needed him.

When returning to my apartment and the door shut behind me, I put my hand on it. In the hope I could keep emotion at bay if I didn't move a muscle, I stayed that way for a few moments. Then I felt the sobs start to bubble from my stomach again, and I pushed myself away from the door. Fighting back tears I walked down the hall to the bedroom, but not wanting to be in that bed, our bed alone just yet, I grabbed the comforter off it and walked back to the sofa and curled up in it.

As I dozed off to sleep, my heart felt it had been beaten with oranges in a sock, having bruises no one could see that would take a long time to heal.

The funny thing was that in the weeks to come the thing I felt most was anger at myself for being so very blind. It was almost as if I had created the pain for myself. Not wanting to

314

be anywhere near the temptation to work for Zella, even just a little bit, nor wanting to refresh my social media fees to see what Sam was up to, I left the house without my cell phone. I had a list of emergency numbers with me to call if I got into a pinch, but I just took my purse and myself.

Exiting the subway at random stops, I wandered neighborhoods I had never fully experienced. I'd flaneur until I found another subway station. When I was up on the street, I'd look all around me. There were so many things I hadn't looked at before; hadn't seen. I looked up at all of the giant buildings and the magnificent architecture. I watched people, animals, trees. It was as if I was seeing it all for the very first time. As I looked at everything, I kept wondering: what else was I blatantly not seeing in my life?

Chapter Forty-Two

Y ou would think after a breakup, I would have been
bitter about going back to making dream weddings
for couples in love. But no, I found a new vigor and
life and threw myself into work. It was as if making couples
happy through their weddings obliterated my pain. I could
have been avoiding my life, or maybe I just went headfirst
toward more suffering. Either way, I seemed to be more
brilliant and more resilient than ever before.

The great part was, I could go to all the industry parties,
flirt my heart out, and not worry about getting home too late.
And speaking of home, I had to move out a month after Sam
left. Which was just fine for me. That apartment had
memories of us, and I needed to start fresh and focus on my
life. I lucked out and found an amazing apartment just off
Central Park North that I shared with two other gals. It was
a beautiful pre-war walk-up, and we were on the third floor.
I was in the park all the time. Working from the park almost
seemed to make me more productive. It made me happier.

Change seemed to be in the air. Denise quit Beauty In
Cake. She said it was because she wanted to work on her own
and start her own business. But really it was because she
couldn't stand being employed by Greg anymore.
Apparently, he was a very demanding person to work for
always needing Denise to work late or come in extra early.
Over celebratory drinks one night we compared notes. It
sounded like Greg and Zella were a lot alike.

"Natalie, the same person shouldn't be writing the
contracts, doing the client tastings, and decorating the
cakes," she said. "I can't be front of house, back of house,

and administration. It's too much for the volume we do. I do the work of at least three people."

Something started to fester in the back of my mind, but it wasn't clear, yet. Denise did the work of many, and wasn't compensated for it. She worked much harder than I did and had been around much longer than I had. Everyone deserves to be valued for what they bring to their jobs. I fully supported her career shift, even though I felt I would miss her. But I knew I would keep her as my plus-one for industry parties, she was just too much fun at the most intolerable ones.

Speaking of the wedding industry, it seemed to burst more into my personal world. Matt texted for a third time about a week after Sam left. Responding, I explained I thought he had sent a message to the wrong person and also told him that I was recently single and might lay low for a while. Apparently, his girlfriend broke up with him a month ago.

He texted: *Must be going around. Let me know if you still want that dinner. As friends.*

A few days later he texted again to check on me and encouraged me to attend an industry event at The Brooklyn Botanical gardens the following week with him. I had never been and heard that the gardens were a gorgeous place. Although he offered to pick me up, I suggested we meet there. And once he found me, Matt took me around all the gardens. It was beautiful, all lit up with candles and fairy lights. It was so romantic.

"You look amazing," he said as he hugged me.

"Thanks, I've lost about twenty or so pounds since you've last seen me." Feeling awkward around Matt, I didn't know what to say, and Zella had made me so self-conscious about how I looked. And as I was fumbling over my words, it struck me that this was the first time we had seen each other since the Cross wedding.

Confusing thoughts bounced through my head. Matt was so attractive, and there was a sort of a pull between us that night. Was this a date? Was I ready for another relationship so soon after Sam? Maybe I was reading way too much into this invitation. Maybe he was just being nice to me and saw me as a safe island in a sea of event barracudas. He was handsome and newly single, and not even one's personal life was off limits in this insane industry.

As we meandered past the jazz band quartet and through the vendors who were showing different options of side entertainments like a husband-and-wife duo who would create a poem on a vintage typewriter for you, a decor team that would allow guests to create their own bouquets out of the leftovers from the evening to take home, and a roll your own sushi spot. We took turns introducing each other to people we knew in the business. Matt gave out tons of business cards and had stopped to show a planner several photos from his last few events to try to get her to take a meeting with him and a client. Their backs were to me a few feet away and I had turned to watch the jazz band. Left alone, I was ambushed by Alexander Milford.

"Why, hello," he said, his voice sliding up my spine like a caress of a snake.

"Alexander," I said.

"Lovely to see you, New Girl."

"You know very well; I've been around for a while." I said, trying to be sassy and light, "You'll have to find a new nickname for me."

"Well, when you come to work for me, you will be new all over again."

Alexander looked at me as if we were both in on a secret. I returned his look with a confused glare. I looked over my shoulder for Matt, who was still schmoozing. "So…" I said awkwardly, "how is business?"

"Fine, Natalie, fine. Thank you for asking," he said smiling like he was up to something. "And how are your last days with Zella?" He really hit the Z hard so her whole name buzzed in his mouth.

"Fine?"

I wondered what his motives were. What was he really asking?

"Is Madame treating you well?"

I must have paused too long before saying, "Sure. Yeah. Why?" because he smiled even bigger like he knew something.

"Ghosts of interns past say she can be extra demanding at the end." End, what did he mean by end? I looked at him with a puzzled expression. When I didn't answer, he continued. "Also, I know you've been told not to trust me, but I wouldn't trust her."

Alexander looked at me again. "Someone as talented as you is wasting your time with someone like Zella." I looked up at him as he stood up and straightened his suit jacket. "Now I will open many things for you, including doors." Was that… an innuendo?

Matt was suddenly at my side. "Alexander, nice to see you."

"And you Matthew. The boy wonder of catering," Alexander said, extending his hand to Matt and brushing my elbow in the process. "Lovely to see you again." He smiled a greasy smile as he winked at me.

"It's just Matt. Thank you for sending so much business my way lately. I hope your clients are happy." Matt said as he took Alexander's hand and looked back and forth between the both of us.

He looked at Alexander and then looked to see the revulsion that was still on my face from the disparaging remark Alexander had made. "What were you two chatting about? You're not still trying to poach Natale from Zella, are you? Be careful, the walls have eyes." Matt looked all around the room.

"Oh I'm not worried, it's a deal that's much as done, isn't that right, Natalie?" Alexander was almost shouting over the band now. People on the other side of the room could probably hear.

What was he talking about? I was just about to ask when Matt jumped in.

"I don't think that will be happening anytime soon," Matt said.

Alexander had stepped in between us and was now taking my arm in his. "Come Natalie, let me introduce you to some people that you will work with when you work with me."

"*When* I work with you?"

"Oh no need to play coy. We're on the same team now."

"Same team?" Matt said the words for me.

"Yes," he said looking to Matt and then back to me, retaking my arm and leaning his head into mine as if we were sharing a confidence, "a couple of weeks ago you texted me, Natalie, very late at night, and said you were done with Zella and you were coming to work for me."

I yanked my arm away from him and I turned abruptly. "I didn't. I wouldn't. I…" the words stammered out of my mouth. I looked from Alexander to Matt trying to piece things together.

"Why, it's all here in black and white," Alexander held up his phone screen to my face. I refused to look at it and instead kept looking at Matt.

"Want me to read it to you?" Alexander said. "It's very interesting." He put the phone back in my face. I blinked and then I read it.

There was a whole conversation where I told him how terrible Zella had treated me, made me walk all over Manhattan running crazy errands, and made me do client interviews all while trying to rectify a wedding that Zella had refused to listen to.

The night of my breakup vividly slammed into my memory. I locked myself in my room and started texting Alexander. I started to blush at the innuendo that was underneath the texts. They were sent at a time when I was broken and sad. And frankly, I just wanted attention from a man. Sam had left me, and Zella had been a horror. I needed a kick of serotonin. Why my drunken broken-hearted brain decided Alexander, I have no idea. No wonder I had deleted most of the text messages from that night.

"There, there." Alexander said. "It will be a bright new future for you. You said you needed a few weeks to finish up with some clients you cared about, and then you would come over." He smiled and opened his arms wide like a preacher accepting new brethren. "She has treated you so terribly, ignored you, browbeaten you, hasn't she?"

Like a wild animal in a cage, I was frightened, and I did the only thing I could in that moment. I retaliated. Something in me snapped like a rubber band.

"Well at least she doesn't ruin reputations, trick people, and break up engagements of other planners."

"What?" Alexander was truly taken aback.

"Oh yeah, I've heard what you do to people," I aggressively stepped toward him. I didn't exactly know the story, no one would tell me the whole thing, but I knew it wasn't good.

"Maybe you, ahem, need to get your story straight," Alexander said.

"Really? Now seems good. Why don't you straighten me out?"

Alexander looked around the room. I was talking loudly; people were pretending not to pay attention. But this gossip would be all over the event world, shortly. "Natalie," he nervously chuckled my name, "why don't we get together and discuss this—"

"Nope, now or never, buster," I said standing my ground.

"Well, if you must know," he spoke in a low somber voice, "The couple in question had come to me first to have their wedding planned, but as they were fighting at every turn, I simply asked them one day if they were sure that they really wanted a big wedding.

"Next thing I know Zella has a contract with them, which I find out from the venue—as no one had the actual decency to tell me that they had broken their contract. And maybe I flew off the handle and smeared Zella's name with a handful of people, but it wasn't anyone who loved her or worked with her often. The couple wasn't bound for the altar. I only called them to let them know that I was keeping the retainer, per our contract. Then I'm getting calls from people applauding me that I stabbed Zella in the back. There was even a rumor that we had slept together, and I was trying to break up her marriage to get back at her. It may or may not be true." A smile crept over his face. "Gossip flies around in this business like germs in the subway. Everyone is always spreading it around."

My head was in a spin with the information. He laid everything out without hesitation.

Alexander broke my silence. "Do you know how many clients Zella has poached from other people?" His nostrils started to flare. He spit the words at me. "She also begs and pleads with almost every vendor she works with and has them cut the costs so much that no one makes a profit. And on top of that, she asks for a big commission." I had seen her do this. I just thought it was a regular business practice.

"Plus," he continued, "with the way she chews up and spits out interns, and so many of them are scarred for life and can't get a job in the industry because they can't be anywhere near her…" Alexander trailed off as another thought showed on his face. "And here you are, without her, at a party. Natalie, how many weddings have you done?"

"Less than a hundred, but—"

"And how many have you managed on your own?"

"About twenty."

"Now be honest." He gave me a knowing look. "How many weddings have you planned?"

"None, Zella—" I was cut off by Alexander.

"Now, now. No need to play the dedicated worker now. We're friends." A smile curled his lips, that didn't feel quite authentic. "How many have you actually planned?"

"Well, I… I really don't want to say, because honestly, I feel like it might come back and bite me." I said, squirming like my underwear were too tight.

"If I had to guess, I'd say that you've been responsible for at least ten of them." He looked around. "And I'm sure that you talked plenty of brides down from the ledge, haven't you," he asked. His smooth voice was back. It was as if he was setting a trap.

"A safe guess," I agreed, not wanting to give away too much. But my ego jumped in and I added, "A low guess, but a safe guess."

"Ah ha. See, there we go. We can talk as friends, Natalie," he said, grabbing a couple of champagne flutes off the tray that passed. "Now, how does she treat you? I want you to say it. Out loud. Not hiding behind a text."

"Well, I..." I really didn't want to say. The air seemed to go out of the room. Silence rang around the room. Did the band stop? I felt all eyes in the room on me.

Everyone knows that the abuse victims mostly stand up for their abusers. This is partially to hide that the abuser is bad, and partially to hide that they, themselves are too stupid or too in love to leave. In this moment, I realized I was both things.

When I didn't say more, Alexander asked, "How much does she pay you?"

"It's competitive," I said, not wanting to give more away.

"Hmm," he said. "If you start with me tomorrow, I'll put you in charge of at least six of your own events, and I'll pay you thirty dollars an hour to start, and forty an hour for the day of events. But this is only if you start with me tomorrow. You said you were leaving and I think you should. Get away from that woman now and come to someone who will use your abilities to the fullest." He held out a champagne glass to me. I looked from the glass to his face and then to Matt. "I need to know now, I'm afraid."

This felt like a bad game show where you knew neither door was a good option. What is the saying about the devil you know is better than the devil you don't? Well, I didn't trust the one standing in front of me. Maybe I should have. But I couldn't. Instead, I threw gasoline onto the already burning pire.

"How dare you! I see what you're doing. You're trying to get back at Zella through me. Well, I won't have it. I'm sure you're telling all kinds of lies about her." I wanted to stop, but for some reason I kept talking. "She is a decent human being, and she and I work well together. I bet I'd work for you for two weeks and you'd just cast me aside. I can't believe you would think I would work for you."

"Are you finished—"

"No, I'm not," I interrupted, wishing I would just shut up. "How dare you try to poach me at a party. Don't try to talk to me again."

Time stood still as he stared at me.

"Well, if that is what you want," he said, smirking and setting down the two glasses of champagne in his hands on the tray of a passing waiter. He put a fingertip to his lips as if trying to suppress a laugh to find the perfect thing to say. His eyes flared. Then, he looked right at me. "Give my regards to Madame." And he turned and walked out of the conservatory and disappeared into the night.

"Ugh, that guy gives me the creeps. I wish I didn't have to work with him, but he brings me so many clients," Matt said. "Natalie, I–"

Shaking my head and putting a hand up to stop what he was about to say, "It's fine. I'm pretty sure he wants revenge on Zella. They have a weird rivalry. And lucky me, I'm in the middle. I don't know if he really wants to hire me, or if he just doesn't want Zella to have me."

"Good. Well if you ever don't feel safe–"

"Thank you," I said. "You don't have to–"

"Do you want me to take you home?" he asked.

"No. Thank you though. You should network more. It seemed like you had a handful of potential clients."

"Yeah," he smiled and rubbed his hand over the back of his neck.

"Good. You need and deserve that." I leaned in, put one of my hands on his shoulder, and gave him air kisses on both cheeks like people in the industry do, "Well, good night. Thank you for the invitation. It was great seeing you." And I turned and walked up the path toward the entrance. Hoping Matt wasn't pitying me as I walked away.

Chapter Forty-Three

Unfortunately, that wasn't what I should have been worried about.

Greg from Baked in Love was suddenly in front of me. Warning bells were going off in my head. He was a gossip, I knew that from Denise and first hand. I had said things to him that had gotten back to Zella.

"Hello, Natalie," Greg purred in a lower version of Zella's voice. "Are you having fun this evening?"

Everything about this felt like a trap. "Well, some." I said looking around, wishing that someone was here to save me. Matt now was across the room handing business cards to a small group of women in their late 50s. "The band is great. A little loud."

"What?" He leaned in. "The band is a little loud."

"Yes, that is what I said." I twisted my mouth, willing myself not to say anything.

"What do you think of the decor?"

"Well, it's nice. The white is classic," I said and turned to look at him. He was sizing me up. "It goes well with your cakes," I pointed to the display his team had set up in the conservatory.

"Yes," he purred. "It gives a very dramatic effect." A smile slowly curled on his lips. "Not as dramatic as your little," he paused, seeming to search for a word, but it was probably for dramatic effect, "tete-a-tete. Lover's quarrel?"

"No, definitely not! I don't have any intention to... I mean I don't like either one of them... I—"

Greg smirked and then started tapping at his phone.

"I didn't mean to cause a scene. But Alexander has been talking to me for months, I—"

Greg's head snapped up and he gave me a glare. His creeping smile returned and he started to chuckle. Then he turned on his heel and swaggered away.

What did any of that mean?

As I walked out of the party with all kinds of regret, I tried to think that Greg had the best intentions, but would he tell Zella about my outburst? Maybe he already had. With my luck, there was probably a video online by now. And maybe even a remix. That would be terrible on so many levels, a remix of me telling off Alexander.

Or maybe it would be good. Maybe Zella would finally see that I had firm solidarity for her and for Tremaine Events. Yes, that was it. I tried to put that thought into the world. Zella would appreciate what I had done. It didn't take long for me to find out what she thought.

The next day, the gossip of how I turned down Alexander for Zella spread like wildfire. Zella even called me to ask me about it.

"I heard you screamed at the party last night," Zella stated.

"What? No. I raised my voice a little, maybe. But the band was loud. Only the people immediately around us heard." I told Zella what happened from my point of view. I didn't mention how much money he offered me, but I mentioned that he offered me a job.

"How much did he offer you?" she asked.

The one question I really didn't want to answer. I tried to be as polite as possible without revealing everything, "It wasn't enough, Zella. That is all that matters."

"Well, fine," she said. "Now, I need you to work on—" and with that she launched into all of the things she needed me to do. There was no thank you, or you made the right decision. There was no back up for my actions. I just told off a man who I had been continually told had hurt Zella's business, and I didn't even get a verbal pat on the head for it. I stuck up for her and proved my solidarity, and it didn't get acknowledged. Showing my team colors, I seemed to only hurt myself.

Why did I keep blaming anything else, when it was Zella who kept setting up the elaborate house of cards? It was only a matter of time before it fell.

I'm stating these things now as much for my own affirmations as I am about to set up the next crazy thing. At the time I felt I was in the right for sticking up for the woman who paid me. And then the pudding incident happened.

Chapter Forty-Four

L abor Day weekend we had a huge tent wedding in the backyard of a beautiful New Jersey home. The bride was a YouTube celebrity. Her parents were real estate magnates with extremely rich friends. They had business deals all over the world. This wedding's theme was "impress our friends," eight of which are in the top fifty of the richest people in America.

Tremaine Events had been contracted for the wedding to do a full-service job, which meant we were there for any and all decisions. We offered service for everything from finding a custom cake topper that looked like the bride and groom, to making life-size replicas of a tent in their backyard for a visual, to replanting the grass. This bride was a dream bride from start to finish. Easygoing and always happy. I was waiting for the shoe to drop the whole time.

Because here is the thing, no matter how great a bride is, she always has a bridezilla moment. And I have gotten to the point where if I have a spare moment with a bride, I tell her this. She will always protest. And I say back, "It's ok. Every bride has one, I just want you to know when you have yours, it will be totally ok and I'll be here to help you through it. I will fix anything on your big day to make it perfect for you."

But for all the loveliness this bride exuded, her parents were high octane obsessive. They wanted her to have the quintessential backyard wedding, with all the glitz and glamor we could achieve. An open-air event with crystal chandeliers hanging from free standing pillars, a seven-tier cake, a white monogrammed dance floor. The glitter of opulence and the essence of home. Her parents had a big concept and a tiny budget. father of the bride had dreamed of a big open-air dinner out on their massive acreage since his little girl was a baby.

Outside events are always a gamble with weather. A tent should always be on reserve, just in case, especially on a holiday weekend. Usually reserving a tent means that you pay a partial amount for the tent, usually about half the total price. This is kept by the company, no matter if you use the tent or not. It's a bit crazy, but just picture if you don't reserve a tent and it does rain; everyone wants a tent for their event.

The previous two years, Labor Day had been dry and hot. So when the topic of the tent came around, the father of the bride decided to go with a—to be polite I'll call them a value tent company—and kept his fingers crossed. Now, I don't mean to brag, but Tremaine Events had great luck with rain. I joked with Zella early in my first year with her that I would do a rain dance before all of our outdoor weddings, and that it was me who kept us from being rained on. All but two of our weddings with outside portions had beautiful weather.

Unfortunately, this was one of the two that we didn't luck out. The week before the wedding, everyone kept refreshing the weather on their phone apps or on their computers. The Weather Channel was constantly streaming in the office. A big storm was to hit, but the date kept dancing around the wedding day. A decision to put up the tent has to be made approximately three days before the event, because of scheduling—if it rains, your tent isn't the only one going up! With all the discussion of the weather and the tent, it felt like we were in a version of Hamlet set in summer camp: To set up the tent, or not to set up the tent, that is the question.

331

Wednesday afternoon, the tent company highly suggested pitching the tent, as there was a seventy percent chance of rain on Saturday. So the tent went up on Thursday to make sure it was in the right spot. It poured, no it dumped rain on Thursday night, and the, ahem, value tent, leaked all over the custom dance floor. Friday we all hopped on a train to New Jersey inspecting the situation and assisting with cleanup. Well, Sarah and I mopped, and Zella yelled at the tent company. It was a long day and I only got five hours of sleep before I had to be up and out for the wedding.

Saturday, I went early to the famed Magnolia Bakery and got two hundred mini cups of their banana pudding, the groom's favorite, to be passed out as favors on the dance floor later in the evening. Since I lived on the Upper West Side, the plan was for me to go to the bakery to make sure the order was correct. Zella would meet me in her car, and we would drive out to New Jersey together.

We preordered the puddings, so when I got there, they were all ready to go in three different boxes. Zella said she was running late and hadn't gotten lunch. She gave me instructions to grab a sandwich. Leaving the twenty-two pounds of pudding at Magnolia, Zella called again while I was getting her sandwich. She started dictating priorities to accomplish when we got to the property. I was still on the phone with her jotting things down as she pulled up.

My hands were full with the sandwich, my phone and my notepad, so I put it all down in the front seat. Zella had double-parked and was making room in the back of her SUV for the puddings, as we had some decor pieces and the bride's wedding dress which I had picked up from the atelier and taken to the office yesterday. As she rearranged, I went back to grab the pudding. I could only carry two of the three boxes at once and maneuvered them into the spot in the back.

"Zella, is the band going to be at the house today?"

"I believe so, why?"

"Well, it's Alyssa the band leader's birthday." I started to walk back into the cupcake store.

"I'll go," Zella said as she dashed into Magnolia.

My phone rang. It was one of our vendors checking on the new timing with the rain plan. My notebook had the itinerary in it, and I jumped in the passenger seat to finish the call. While I was on the phone, I heard Zella close the trunk. And she got in the driver's seat and drove off.

When we arrived in New Jersey, I went to grab the pudding first. It needed to be refrigerated, and I wanted to get it in the fridge before the caterer took over too much space.

"Zella, where is the third box?"

"Third box, Natalie?" she said in her chipper happy voice as we were on the property and vendors or the client might hear her.

"The third box of puddings. You went into Magnolia. Didn't you get the other box? You shut the trunk and drove off. I thought when you said you were running inside, you were grabbing the other box."

"No, Natalie. Why would I grab the other box?"

"Because you went inside."

"Went inside where?"

"Into Magnolia," I said. I started to feel like I was doing an Abbott and Costello routine.

"It was your job Natalie," she said, her voice expanding and growing darker like the rain clouds overhead. "I went in to get a cupcake for Alyssa the band leader, because I remembered it's her birthday," her voice was now as sickeningly sweet as too much cupcake frosting.

Trying not to panic, as Zella smelled fear like she was a shark in chum infested waters, I took a deep breath and tried to keep cool.

"Alright, well, Zella, we are short about a hundred puddings. What should we do?" I started to brainstorm. "You can give me the keys and I can drive back to the store to get them."

"No, that would take too long, and I need you here."

"What about if I went into the town here, and got some cute cups and we divided what we have up?"

"We paid for the ones that you left sitting there, so we need to get those." Of course, the blame went to me for leaving the pudding.

"Well, I'll keep thinking as I put these in the fridge," I had been holding them the entire conversation and my arms were shaking.

"Do that, Natalie," she said after me.

As I waddled inside to the refrigerator, my mind went into overdrive as it muscled out solutions for this predicament. How could I make two hundred puddings into three hundred. Or who did I know who could drive out to New Jersey. I heard my name and went running, to find the band leader and her group, wandering around the property looking for me.

Twenty minutes later after helping the band figure out how to get their car down to the pool house where their dressing room was, I walked back to the SUV to find that Zella hadn't moved from where I left her and was finishing up a call.

"Well, you're in luck, Natalie. The cake delivery truck hasn't left Manhattan yet and can stop by and grab the puddings. I offered the driver an extra forty dollars to stop by Magnolia for you on his way."

I was thrilled with this news. But it was too easy that everything seemed fine. I was still tense. But after a few successes I started breathing again. The cake and the third box of puddings arrived without a major hitch.

The valet team had two shifts, so the same people who parked the early arrivals were partially stranded while we searched the neighborhood for their cars at the end of the wedding. No rain fell during the ceremony which was held in front of the lake that the bride and groom swam in together as kids. The rain started just as the couple was finishing with pictures, not only making some adorable umbrella sharing photos of the couple and helped scoot everyone into the tent for dinner and dancing.

Stragglers are always a problem at a wedding, but when the only dry spot is the reception tent, they were a non-issue. The rain made for a magical evening for the guests, but rough for the vendors. The leaky tent had been fixed, and the rain pattering on the tent made it more romantic. Until a huge gust of wind came up just after the first course was served, blowing out almost all the candles and power to the electric lights that were making the chandeliers twinkle overhead. Even the band lost power but they had a backup generator and were quickly making music again.

In a mad dash, caterwaiters, and the event staff rushed all around lighting and relighting candles as fast as we could accompanied by an acoustic guitar, while guests chatted.

Rain hindered a few of the dramatic effects we had planned, like the trail of lanterns we were to put out that went all around the pool area showcasing the monogram of the bride and groom in candles floating in the pool. A sparkler send-off as the bride and groom rushed to drive off to their honeymoon was canceled due to inability to light the sparklers. Instead we leaned the monogram up against a tree on the front lawn, and had everyone line the front walkway under large golf umbrellas that were held high like a salute of mushrooms and the bride and groom ran through. It was a perfect picture moment, and to this day is one of my most favorite shots I've ever seen taken at a wedding.

Once the bride and groom were off, we set up the puddings on a table for guests to take as they left. Although they were a very well-received parting gift, there were still about a hundred left over. Of course, there was the same amount of pudding left over that had caused drama. But no matter. Zella was genuinely happy the whole night. She complimented me on how far along Sarah was progressing and applauded me on my work. We even took to the dance floor and shook our money makers to a few songs.

During an event we rarely saw each other for more than a few moments, but because of the rain we were trapped in the tent, so we had long casual discussions about owning property and trying to guess who the Gregionaires in the room were. This could have been my favorite wedding to work with Zella.

As we drove back to the city together, it seemed like I truly could be successful in this business. With Zella. I had made the right choice to stay on her team and not to go with that terrible slimeball Alexander Milford. The feeling of this wedding radiated within me for the next few days. The bride was so happy with everything that she sent us individual thank you notes and a little bit of an additional tip.

But what is the saying about not believing that you're on solid ground, because just when you do, the rug is removed from under you? Or maybe it was just that I had forgotten about the Ides of March. Even though it was September, one should always be aware of the Ides.

Chapter Forty-Five

We were so busy that fall, and I remember being happy for the first time ever at Tremaine Events. Everything seemed good. Zella was in a decent mood. Sarah wasn't scuttling around in fear. Things were running smoothly, and I actually had a couple of mornings free, and I went to a few auditions again Ginger begged me to go with her. I was very rusty, but it was fun to dust off the old monologues. I didn't tell Zella about them, of course.

Often in the office, I got a decent amount of work done with minimal distraction or drama. Today was one of those days. So, when Zella spoke, I didn't think anything was amiss.

"Natalie, let me know when you get to a good stopping point," Zella said. "I have some new company policies I want to go over."

The wording she used was very odd, but it didn't register until I thought about it after. Maybe I was just so focused on my work, that I didn't really hear her.

"Sure, Zella."

"Great. Close your computer, and let's all gather around the table," Zella said, picking up some 3x5 cards from her desk and moving to the table. Already sitting at the table, I just closed the lid of my computer and shifted my notebook in front of me. Sarah dashed over and sat a seat away from me at the table. That was strange. She almost always sat right next to me. We were a united front that way.

"First of all, things have been so busy, but I wanted to say great job on the Labor Day wedding." Sarah and I smiled at each other. This was good, I thought to myself. Maybe Zella was giving us raises today.

"Next, I want to say that our filing system is changing a little. I'll have Sarah explain it."

Sarah made a flippant hand gesture at me when I looked over at her as if to tell me it was nothing major.

Zella continued, "Now then Natalie," she said and smiled at me. "I don't know if you noticed, but your paycheck was short last week." Bile started to rise in my stomach. Zella had been questioning my hours a lot lately, especially the ones I worked at home.

The truth was that I often undercharged her for hours worked. I didn't count the hours I probably logged reading and answering emails on the subway. Nor did I count the times I picked up a phone call from a vendor or client when I was walking around town. And I always shorted myself about a quarter of the time when I was working from home, reasoning that I would multitask and take care of things for myself. Like I would run a load of laundry to the basement while I was waiting for Sarah or Zella to respond to an email. Or I would wash dishes while on the phone with a vendor. Or I would get a personal call in the middle of working on a document or something, and I would continue to work while on the phone. Looking back it was horribly wrong to short myself for the work I actually did.

It just didn't feel right to charge for a full hour when I would spend five to fifteen of that time working on something of my own while tackling a Tremaine Events task. Although, to be clear, in hindsight, I was still working the entire time and I should have charged as such.

"What?" was all I could say. My mouth went dry.

"I took the forty-dollar delivery fee from your paycheck," she said.

"Wait. What?"

"When you forgot the pudding and I had to pay for delivery," Zella repeated, getting a little frustrated that I didn't understand. In truth, I was getting the words, but I didn't understand why she was doing it. Zella had not double checked the pudding, and Zella had offered the money to the driver.

"But... I don't understand. I'm sorry—"

"That's right, you're sorry. In fact, if you had just said that you were sorry at the house, this whole thing wouldn't be an issue."

"But, Zella, I did."

"No, you didn't. I would remember."

"I disagree," I said frustrated. "'I'm sorry' are probably the two words I say to you the most. I'm pretty sure that I said it to you, even though it wasn't completely my fault."

"Well, now you'll never forget to say 'I'm sorry' again. In fact—," Zella went on to explain more about the situation and to prove herself right.

I didn't hear most of it. I now understand what it means "to see red" because it was happening. My pulse raced. My ears heard the pounding of my blood. My eyes saw a dark red color. My hands clenched into fists under the table. I did the only thing I could to keep calm; I said a Shakespeare monologue in my head as she continued to talk.

Zella rattled on about how it was only forty dollars, not that much money and I would be able to live without it. Plus, she said, many people she talked to about the issue, including the caterer, the bandleader and Sarah, agreed that the money taken from my paycheck would be a good lesson for me.

I looked at Sarah, whose head was now buried in her notebook, pretending to take notes. I didn't understand this. How could she betray me? I had always stuck up for her. E tu Brute?

At the time, there were so many things going on in my brain, I didn't register it. To take money from an employee's paycheck without telling them or giving them some sort of prior notice wasn't nice. Nor is it legal.

"You should totally get a lawyer and sue her," Denise said after I relayed the story.

"I don't know that it would be worth it to go through all of that red tape for forty bucks," I said in reply.

"Yeah, but is your dignity worth it?"

I laughed, "I don't have dignity anymore. I work for Zella Tremaine."

I had said it as a joke, but it was true. I didn't take legal action and should have. Instead, I kept working for Zella, sliding back into the role of minion. The stunned shock I now felt was worse than ever feeling trapped in the job or worse, the possibility of being fired at any minute.

The worst part was that I stood up to Alexander Milford on her behalf. When it was really her who was terrible. True he was probably just as slimy. But I torched that bridge, and this was all I had. This was the tiny crack in the ice that was about to crumble the entire continent. Before this, I stood by and let her get away with treating me like I was nothing. But when I was monetarily and illegally punished for a mistake that she was part of, and turned Sarah against me I knew I should look elsewhere. I even picked up my phone, scrolled through my contacts and found Alexander's number. I started to call him, but it made me cringe.

Sadly, the addiction I had to this job kept me coming back for more. This codependent relationship I had formed with her, or with wedding planning was something I just didn't want to shake. Once again I told myself it would get better and the job was worth it.

Then we did the wedding at The St. Regis.

Chapter Forty-Six

nd here we are, where you came in. Here I am,
sitting on the marble floor of the St. Regis Hotel.
Alone. Pushed out of an elevator. My knees
throbbing, I thought back through every single moment of
this job. I tried to look for a glimmer; something to hold on
to that would make this moment worth it. I couldn't find
much. So instead, I rationalized the behavior of my bad boss.
This was ok, I thought to myself. It was a mistake, and I
shouldn't have tried to step into the elevator. I pulled myself
up and hobbled down the hall to the office and let myself in.

My phone had quieted, and I knew the programming
would keep everyone busy for the next half hour. Sarah was
in charge of cuing the band tonight, so until the cake-cutting,
I didn't really need to do much. I sat in a chair and relaxed. I
rubbed my knees and the throbbing faded. Mick Anders
walked into the office tall and statuesque but squatted at my
side the moment he saw me.

"Are you ok?"

"I'm fine, Mick. Just a little tumble," I said and smiled.

"You fell pretty hard. Do you need an ice pack or
anything?"

"Nah, the throbbing has lessened. I'll probably have
bruises tomorrow, but nothing major." And stop his
speculation, I said, "It looked worse than it really was."

"Well, it looked," he gave me a look that he knew I was
lying, "like she pushed you. Let's file an incident report."

"No," I scoffed. "No need for a report. We collided, my
forward energy and her hand, and we—"

"No," Mick said, putting his hand on my shoulder, "She
pushed you. I saw it."

Now here is the part where it gets horrific.

I was so gaslit, so bound to this woman and her horrible treatment of me, I said, "It's really ok. I'm ok." To distract him, I said, "I should get upstairs. I don't know if you've noticed but we have a small shindig going on up there," I said as I started to stand. Honestly, I was more worried about what Zella would do if I didn't get upstairs, show a brave face and pretend like nothing happened. I was worried that she was going to fire me. Or worse, make my life more of a hell than the past two years had been.

Mick removed his hand from my shoulder, and said, "Sit. Relax a little." My face must have revealed my fear, as he continued, "Don't worry, they have everything well in hand, and I let them know you're helping with things down here." He winked. "Can we get you anything?"

"Well, if there are any of the jumbo shrimp left…" I trailed off, trying not to push my luck.

"Ha! I meant more like can I get you an aspirin. But I'll go check on the shrimp. Anything else?"

"I mean, if there are more good snacks left, I'll take them. It's two hours until vendor meal."

"A woman after my own heart," Mick said as he slid back out through the office door.

I sat wanting to cry, but the pain in my knees was going away and I didn't want to mess up my makeup. The only thing I brought for touch-ups was lipstick. Instead, to keep my mind off myself while Mick was out, I packed up the personal things in the office. Sarah had left her purse; we had the Tremaine Events emergency kit full of anything you would ever possibly need at a wedding from a sewing kit to super glue to flip flops for people who were tired of wearing heels. I grabbed these things and my coat and put them all in a pile to take up with me. Then I sat back down again, reasoning I should sit as much as possible because it was going to be a long night. Not that my knees still throbbed.

Mick returned and tried to convince me again to file an accident report. I declined as I munched on the treats he brought. After the two plates of canapés, including fourteen beautiful jumbo shrimp, I went upstairs and dropped the Tremaine Events items in the coat check so we could grab them easily at the end of the party. I walked into the ballroom and Sarah and Zella were on the edge of the dance floor chatting and dancing.

"Come dance with us," Zella waved, as if nothing had transpired. I guess for her it hadn't.

"I need to go check in with the photographer about the paper goods, I want to find out where he left the set." It was a blatant lie. The paper goods were in the pile of things I had just put in coat check. But I didn't want to be near the bully anymore.

"Check and then come back."

"No Zella, she needs to go to the kitchen for cake cutting soon," Sarah reminded her. She was calling the shots tonight after all.

A shiver ran down my spine as I faked a smile and turned out of their view. Moving around the room, I surveyed everything and everyone. Things were running smoothly, and the bride and groom seemed very happy. The splendor. The elegance. The joy. It seemed the work I had been doing was something worthwhile and important. As I looked around, I wanted it to be worth all of the criticism and scolding Zella gave me daily. I wanted it to be worth feeling stressed out so much that I wasn't sleeping and was ruining relationships. I wanted it to be worth always dieting and never fitting as well in clothes as I would prefer. I wanted it to be worth getting pushed out of an elevator. But it wasn't. I was worth so much more than this.

A zen washed over me, and, I just watched the wedding flow by. Dinners were served, drinks refilled, songs played, toasts given. Finally, the cake was wheeled onto the dance floor and cut with a saber by the bride and groom. I went down the hall into the kitchen and helped cut the cake—Zella always wanted one of us present to watch over the cake cutting. Mick came into the kitchen about halfway through the cake being sliced.

"Hey, you hanging in there?" he asked me.

He probably meant my knees, but my brain was over processing everything.

"No. I'm not." I stood still for what felt like an eternity as my brain whirred, then came to a stop. "Mick, I can't do this anymore."

"Cake cutting? You don't have to. My guys can take care of—"

"No. I'm talking about working for Zella. I can't do it anymore." Grabbing my jacket which I had removed in the toasty kitchen, I turned on my heel and started back out to the ballroom.

"Hey! What are you going to do? What can I do?" Mick yelled after me.

I stopped at the door and turned to him, "Save me the last piece," I yelled back. "And make it a big one. I deserve it," I said as I walked through the door and smiled.

It took me a few minutes to find Zella. She was off chatting with a guest in a corner. I caught her eye, and patiently waited while she introduced me and did her normal parading me in front of the guests, telling them how together we had made the magic happen and that she couldn't do anything without me. I played along. The guest got distracted

346

a few minutes into the conversation by another guest he knew and walked off.

"Zella we need to talk," I said to her in a soft tone as we stood side by side.

"What is it Natalie?" she sighed at me as if I were an irritating child with an irrational request.

"I can't do this anymore."

"You mean you can't watch over the cake being cut? You know I have you do that to make sure that all of the pieces come out—"

"No, Zella," I said, my voice rising slightly. "I don't want to be told I'm worthless behind closed doors and then paraded like a show pony at events. I don't want to have to wait for you to look at me for you to hear me. I don't want to be hissed at while I'm trying to be helpful." I rolled my shoulders back trying to keep the momentum of courage. "I don't want to be shoved out of an elevator onto the floor."

"Natalie, that was an accident," she said in a cunning voice and starting to put her arm around me.

Keeping my cool, I stepped away from her coiling arm. "I don't think you understand Zella. This is my last wedding with you. I don't want to work for you anymore."

"But Natalie —"

"I'll finish out here tonight, and Sarah can take over for me. We have no events until December, so if you need me to, I can help Sarah with the paperwork—"

"That won't be necessary," Zella snapped. Her face changed from questioning, then to hurt, and then rage. "I knew you said yes to that double-crossing Alexander."

A burst of laughter exploded from my chest that was much louder than I expected.

"No, actually. Not that it's any of your business, but I did not. I told you I stood up for you. Although it wouldn't surprise me if your ego was in the way and blocked your hearing. But after you shoved me onto the floor and laughed it off, it made me think about all the things you've done to me that were wrong."

With a light laugh, I shook my head, seeing this villain for what she actually was, a tiny person whose self-esteem fed on making others small. "In the end, it doesn't matter to you. Tomorrow you'll tell everyone I'm just one in the long line of what you consider idiot interns. But tomorrow, I'll hold my head up high, and you will keep making people's lives miserable."

Her mouth opened and closed a few times, giving the best impression of a fish. "Well then." She stood by my side for another minute watching the dancing, and then walked away.

I don't know what I expected. Especially resigning during a wedding. Probably not my best move.

I should have just hung on for a little while longer, but I couldn't. "A little while longer" is a forever-receding point, until it isn't. It sounds close by, but no one can know the actual timing of "a little while." I should have left this job much sooner.

Sarah came over to where I was standing about ten minutes later.

"Zella says you can go," said Sarah, and handed me an envelope with my name on it. "There is your tip. She told me to tell you that we have it all under control here." Her tone dropped to a whisper, as she was trying to put everything together. "What just happened?"

I smiled and had a tiny chuckle. I turned to her as I said, "I don't know. I'm pretty sure I toppled to the giant." She blinked at me, not understanding, so I clarified, "I just quit working for Zella."

"Oh," Sarah said. A single syllable said so much, commenting on the apocalypse that was about to befall her.

"I'm sorry, I think," I said. And I turned to hug her but stopped myself not wanting to, her traitorous act still hung between us. "I'll be on my way then, unless there is something you need from me."

"No. I don't think so," she said, back to business.

"Good," I said, knowing she was already panicking but didn't want to show it. Sarah would learn. I shouldn't have said it, but before I could stop myself, I said, "My phone will be on, so if you need anything, tonight or in the future, don't hesitate to reach out, ok?"

"Ok." She looked at me with a mix of confusion and disdain.

"Bye, Sarah," I said. Waiting to see if something more came to mind, I found myself at a loss for words for this person who I had once taught and protected, but just a few weeks ago seemed to turn against me. Instead, I turned on my heel and started toward the door. I looked back over my shoulder to take one last look at the elegance of the world I was leaving behind.

"Wait, Natalie," Sarah said jogging the few steps toward me. For a moment I felt touched, maybe she was going to come with me and save herself too. A smile started to spread on my face, but halted as she said, "I need your company credit card back." She held out a hand and put the other on her hip like a mother waiting for her scheming child to return stolen money.

Pursing my lips and nodding, I reached into my purse and hand Sarah my card. Taking her outstretched hand, I said, "Make sure you always stand up for your own worth. This fairyland is beautiful," I gestured an arm around the room, "but it's not worth being mentally beat up and mistreated every day," I said as I looked out around the room with all the fancy décor and food that was making this evening cost half a million dollars. Unsure if I was saying it to her or me, my mouth went sour thinking about Zella's world. Turning and walking out before I feel the need to run and throw myself at Zella's feet, pleading for my job, I head for the doors that lead out of the ballroom.

Chapter Forty-Seven

J ust as I reach the doors I look back. At the small bar to the right, the father of the bride is holding court with a bunch of his cronies. An idea starts to form, but do I have the gumption to follow through?

No, I think to myself. Don't be ridiculous. Just get your things and go. It won't really matter. And as I'm almost out the door the thought rolls through my head: besides Zella might fire you if... But wait. I just quit. I'm nobody to her anymore. And since I torched my chances at working with Alexander, the chances I'll work again in this industry is probably slim to none. The rumor mill was already churning, and tonight's events will turn my actions into a roaring river.

Screw it, I think, and I walk over to the bar.

"Hey, look, it's our wedding planner," the father of the bride says pointing at me with his highball filled halfway with either scotch or rum.

The three men around him give a cheer for me.

My mind clicks into action. "I, uh... I'm just leaving for the night, and I just wanted to say..." I look around the room. Zella sees me, but she's talking with the bride so she doesn't move. "I wanted to say," I keep going, no sense of steering now. "That you're in good hands with Sarah. And Zella, of course."

He reaches out and gives me a big hug while still holding his highball glass. "Why thanks, kiddo. For all you've done. My baby is so happy thanks to you," he points to the bride who is still talking to Zella. The latter is now burning a hole in my forehead.

"You're welcome, sir. It was a pleasure."

"We took care of you right," he says, reaching for his wallet.

"Yes, sir," I pat my own pocket where the tip envelope now crackles.

"Well, here, have some cab money," he says and pulls out a twenty.

I look back to Zella, and this time she's not looking, so I take the bill.

"Thanks so much," I say and pocket it.

"Can we get you a drink," a short balding man asks me and then points to the bartender. "Hey, can you get this gal a drink, she'll have a—what do you want, sweetie," he turns to me.

Without hesitation, I say, "I'll take a bourbon. Best you've got." Moments later, a highball is in my hand, half full. I clink with the men I'm surrounded by then look out at Zella who is now looking at me again. I wink at her, and then down as much of the drink as I can, still leaving some in the glass. I look at my phone, pretending I got a text, say goodbye, and head out.

Feeling like I probably shouldn't waste time hanging around, I let myself into coat check and gather my things that were in the corner then head to the elevator banks and pressed the button and the doors opened immediately. I stepped in. Just as the doors were closing, I hear, "Wait!"

Chapter Forty-Eight

Hitting the doors open button before they closed, I saw Mick Anders standing in front of me. He had a large paper bag. "Here," he said. "Compliments of the chef," as he handed the heavy bag to me.

"What is—"

"Celebration dinner for you and someone else," he winked and smiled a familial, knowing smile at me. "You are a lovely person Natalie, and don't be a stranger, ok?"

"Ok. Thanks, Mick. For everything," I said as I lifted the bag.

When I got to the street, the doorman politely asked me if I wanted a cab as he started to raise his arm to call one. "Thanks, but I just quit, so I should probably save my money," he looked at me with a confused grimace. "No, it's a good thing," I said and then turned to walk to the subway. It was only a few blocks, and honestly at this hour I'd probably get home faster. I pulled out my cell and started to call Sam out of instinct, but then I stopped myself. Instead, I called someone who I knew would appreciate the deliciousness I carried.

"Hey girl! How is the St. Regis tonight?" Denise chirped as I answered the phone.

"Well, I'm not there anymore," I replied.

"What? What happened? If she did—"

"Well, she did. And I quit."

Silence fell over the line and then Denise squawked, "Well it's about time. I'm so proud of you. Tell me everything."

"Oh, I totally will, but where are you now?"

"I'm actually upstate visiting my parents."

"Ah. Well. Can I call you back in twenty minutes?

"Sure, honey! Just tell me that you're ok?"

"Yeah, I think so. I am just walking to the subway, and I think I want to get home and take off this ridiculous suit and get into some pajama pants so I can gorge myself on these steaks while telling you everything. It's a juicy story."

"Ok, call me back when you get home."

My phone buzzed. I ignored it while I said goodbye to Denise as I figured it was probably Zella or Sarah. The group text was probably still active, and I would hear things the rest of the night. After hanging up with Denise, I looked at the text. My mouth dropped open in shock and surprise. It was from Matt.

Hi. How are you doing? I think you have a wedding, but I was just thinking about you.

Shocked to hear from him, I blinked and read the text again. I scrolled up through his texts. He had asked me to dinner or out for a drink a few times and I had responded with desolate non-answers. Groaning audibly on the street, I looked around to make sure no one was around. I was terrible. My heart sank a little. He was so handsome. I had always thought so.

The inaugural night of his catering company's industry party came to mind. We sat for hours after just talking. He always made my heart flutter, and he disappeared from The Gramercy Park Hotel event to protect me. Matt who had stood up to Alexander at the Brooklyn Botanical Gardens, even though he was a good client. How had I not seen this the entire time? He was thinking about me. Tonight, of all nights. A smile slowly crept from ear to ear and I hit the button to call Matt.

"Hey?" he said as he sounded like he didn't expect a call from me.

"Hi," I said smiling. "Hey, so I was at a wedding," I said, drawing out my speech, not quite knowing how to ask Matt if he wanted to eat with me, "but I am no longer there. At the hotel where the wedding was. And I know you keep inviting me to dinner, and I keep saying no. And it's not that I didn't want to, it's just been crazy with Zella, and—" I stopped. I was rambling. "Anyway. The thing is, I was just handed two meals, so I have about a thousand dollar's worth of food in my hands, and I don't know who to share it with. And since you texted right at this moment—"

"Yes."

"Yes, what?" I said not understanding.

"Yes, tell me where and when to meet you and I'll be there in twenty minutes or less."

"I'm at the corner of Fifth Avenue and Fifty-eighth Street," I said looking up at the street sign to make sure of my location.

"Really? I'm just down the street at a bar." I heard some background voices, and Matt's voice said muffled, "Here, keep the change." His voice became clear again, "Hey Nat, I'm coming to find you. Don't move."

Four minutes later, Matt was standing in front of me.

"Food," I said, feeling a bit like a shopping neanderthal holding up the bag. "Where should we go?"

Matt took the bag from my hands, and then took my hand. "Come with me," he said. "Wow this bag is heavy. What is in it?"

"I'm not entirely sure, but I'd guess that it's two filets with spareribs, two slices of cake and a bottle of wine. I haven't looked," I said.

We walked toward Columbus Circle.

"So, how was the wedding?" Matt asked.

"Oh, crap!" I said and stopped. I grabbed my phone.

Matt had gotten a few steps ahead of me when I stopped, and he turned back to face me. "Is everything ok?" he asked with concern. And then added with humor, "Did you forget and leave the wedding early without telling anyone?"

"How did you know I left early?"

"Well, I… it's kind of embarrassing."

Looking up from my phone to his face, I could tell he was blushing even in the dimly lit street.

"I'm sure whatever it is, it's ok," I said reassuringly.

He rubbed the back of his neck with his hand, and he said, "Well, I knew you were at the St. Regis tonight. You said a few weeks ago that you would be there. And I was following the posts you and Zella were putting on Instagram. Is that weird?" He asked but didn't wait for an answer. "She posted something ten minutes ago about a toast. So, I figured the wedding was far from over. But then you called, and—"

"You are adorable," I said, feeling the overwhelming desire to kiss him. Before I could take a step into him, a thought stopped me, "Shoot. I have to call Denise back."

"Sure," he said confused.

"I—well, wow. Do I have a story to tell," I said explaining. "I called her before I called you and told her I would call her back when I got home. And since, well, I want to tell you both the same story, I might as well only tell it once tonight. If that's ok?"

"Why wouldn't it be?" he asked.

"I don't know," I said nervously. "I'll put her on speaker and we can keep walking, ok?"

"Sure," he said and smiled. I hit the call button and then the speaker. Matt took my hand in his again and we started walking as Denise answered.

"Hey, I met up with Matt instead, and—"

"Oooh! Hunky Caterer Matt?" Denise asked in an excited girly way.

"Hey, Denise!" Matt said into the phone.

I laughed nervously. "Yup, he's here and you're on speaker, so keep it clean, lady." I said the last through gritted teeth. Then smiling again, I said, "You won't believe how crazy tonight has been."

And I told them the whole thing.

Matt and I walked the three avenues and arrived in Columbus Circle as I was telling the story. From getting pushed out of the elevator, to the mental highlight reel of my wedding planning career, to being fed up over cake, Sarah asking for my company card back, and my final trip to the bar. We walked over to a large metal door and Matt rang the buzzer as I finished with Mick handing me a bag with dinner for two.

"You just walked up to her and quit," Matt had come to stand in front of me and was slowly rubbing my upper arms. A gesture of pride and comfort.

"Wow! Girl, I'm so proud of you," Denise said.

"Me, too," Matt said as the metal door was opened by a short dark skinned and haired man, "Hey, bro! Is Kevin here?" The two men started chatting and I took Denise off speaker.

"Like I said I was given this amazing food by Mick. Matt texted while I was talking to you, so I figured it was a sign and—"

"Then what are you doing still talking to me?!?" Denise railed. "Get off the phone and go eat with that hunky man. I'll talk to you tomorrow."

"Alright, I will." I looked at Matt talking to his friend. To keep away the tears I felt forming, I shook my head and looked up at the sky. "Denise, I can't believe it," I said.

"I can. Both that you quit, and this Matt thing."

"But what am I going to do?" my voice had fallen to a whisper.

"You're going to go eat delicious food with a delicious man. The rest we will figure out tomorrow. Now go," And without a goodbye, she hung up.

Smiling, I looked down at the phone and then put the phone in my pocket.

"Come on, beautiful," Matt said, reaching his hand out to me. The other man had disappeared, and an elevator was opening down the hall. Of course, another elevator. I took his hand and he squeezed it. "Don't worry. I won't push you out." He smiled a devilish grin and put his arm around my waist.

We went up several flights and when the doors opened, we were in a beautiful restaurant that looked out over Columbus Circle and Central Park.

"Hey, man!" I heard a voice say to our right.

"Hey!" Matt said, dropping my hand and embracing the other man on the shoulder. "Kevin, this is Natalie. She just stood up to her boss, quit her job, and somehow ran out the door with a feast. Natalie," he said turning back to me, "this is Kevin. We have been friends since college. Kevin manages The Robert," Matt said moving his arm wide and motioning to the restaurant.

Kevin chirped in, "We're closed, but I owed Matt a favor, so you can eat here while we finish the nightly cleanup and inventory."

"Thanks. It's nice to meet you," I said.

"Show us to your best table, my good sir," Matt said, flipping into a British accent.

"Pick whatever one you want." Kevin went into a thick Bronx accent and gave his friend a shoulder check. "I'll bring you some wine."

Matt laughed then took my hand once again, and let me to a table right by the window. He set the bag on the floor with one hand and pulled out a chair for me with the other.

"Wow. This is amazing," I said, my breath was taken away with the view. Before I knew it, Matt had set out all the boxes. Two of the boxes each had a filet, spareribs, potatoes, haricots vert. The other two boxes had gigantic slabs of cake in them with a couple of chocolate covered strawberries nestled next to them. The bottle of wine was pinot noir, that I'm sure cost somewhere in the eighty dollar range.

"Wow, that is a nice wine. Almost as nice as mine," Kevin said as he came over and set the bottle on the table with three glasses. He uncorked his bottle first, and then poured a little in one of the glasses and tasted it himself. At the end of his sip, he sighed with an Ahhhh. "Here," he said, pouring three equal glasses and handing the first to me.

"To Natalie," Matt said, raising his glass.

"To Natalie," Kevin echoed as he raised his glass to me as well. I blushed. We all drank. Kevin brought over a chair and sat with us while he drank his glass.

We ate and had a lovely conversation. I heard stories of Matt and Kevin, and the raucous times they had through the years. As he finished his glass, Kevin poured the rest of the bottle into Matt's and my glasses, before he excused himself.

I looked out over Central Park. It was a large dark mass with soft lamplight dotting here and there. Cars swirled below as they went through Columbus Circle. A few pedestrians crossed the street or went down into the subway.

There was a whole world out there that could care less that I was looking down at them.

"How are you doing over there," Matt asked me.

"Pretty good for quitting my job working for the Stalin of the wedding world," I joked.

"Is there anything I can do," Matt said, reaching over and taking my hand in his.

"This right here, right now," I gestured out the window to the view, then around the restaurant and then my eyes landed on him, "is exactly what I needed tonight. Matt, I…" I cleared my throat out of nervousness. I wanted to put the right words together. "I'm not going to say this right, but I just quit my job and I don't have anything else going for me at the moment. I was an actress just trying to survive, and then I was an assistant trying to survive. This is not a brush off, but I will have to do some soul searching and self-seeking for a bit." Matt started to take his hand away, but I set my wine glass down and put my other hand on top of his. "What I'm saying is, I'm a bit of a mess at the moment. But I really like you and I want to see where this goes. So, if you're willing to—"

Before I could finish, Matt was up out of his chair standing over me. He put one hand softly on my cheek and the other on the back of my chair. Looking into my eyes he waited for a moment. Waited for me to say no or to give any reason. I gave no reason for him to stop. Instead, I gave a smile. He leaned in and kissed me. I kissed him back. It started out as a lovely soft kiss, but then gave the promise of something exciting yet to come.

Matt pulled back to look into my eyes. "We can go as fast or as slow as you need."

I leaned in to kiss him again, when Kevin shouted out "Five-minute warning, you lovebirds." We both blushed.

Then seeing each other blush, laughed, and looked into each other's eyes. Minutes, days, years went by, and I didn't care. This felt so right. Why had I taken so long to see it. Matt, quitting Tremaine Events, living my life, my way.

Kevin came over and started to take the empty containers away. We split one of the cake slices, and gave the other to Kevin. After helping clean up, we all went down in the elevator to the ground.

I hugged Kevin around the neck and said, "Thanks for the wine and the view."

"I'm sure you needed both on a night like tonight," he said, inferring all kinds of things. "Oh, you forgot this," he said, holding up the bag with the unopened wine bottle in it. "Maybe you should save it for a special occasion." Kevin gave Matt one of those high-five-bro-hugs and they said goodbye.

Matt offered to see me all the way home, but I told him that I would be fine on the subway. He lived in Brooklyn so his apartment was in the opposite direction.

"Can I call you tomorrow?" he asked.

"You'd better," I said, and I leaned in for another kiss.

Before he kissed me, he smoothed a stray hair behind my ear. "You are an amazing woman, you know that? Who quits a job during a huge event in the ballroom at the St. Regis?" A gigantic smile of admiration beamed across his face and then he kissed me again. A good, long, I'm-totally-here-for-you kiss that you feel all the way to your toes two hours after it happened.

Climbing into my bed that night solo, Matt's words came back.

Who quits during a huge event?

Who indeed.

Chapter Forty-Nine

When I got home, I turned off my ringer and slept for almost sixteen hours. I hadn't plugged in my phone the night before, and it died. After calling Matt, I left it in my room to charge and binge-watched some terrible show until it was dark. Believe it or not, I never heard from Zella or Sarah.

Three days later, I ran into Sam on the subway stairs in midtown. The first two minutes were awkward with neither of us knowing what to say. After a couple of pleasantries, there was silence between us. Then, as if we were still best friends, Sam reached out and pulled me into a giant bear hug. We stood there just hugging in the subway train car for two stops. At the third stop, we decided to get off the train, and we went to get a coffee.

"Sam, I quit," I said.

"Wait, what? You're not with Zella? Tell me everything."

I started with the pudding incident and told him everything that happened the night of the elevator shove. When I got to the part about Mick giving me the bag of food, I stopped talking abruptly.

"You ok, babe?" Sam asked. "I guess I shouldn't call you 'babe' anymore," he said, correcting himself.

"Yeah, I'm fine. Or I will be. And actually, I don't mind what you call me," I said, my mind meandering back to what felt more important. "Sam, you're one of my best friends. And I'd like to try to get back to that—not the romantic side of it, but the part where you are you and I'm me, and we share things."

"Yeah, I'd love to get back to that, too," Sam agreed. "Why, what's up," he said, sensing I was holding something back.

I blinked. "I think… I think I met someone. But I don't know."

"Wow! That is great, Nat… babe…"

"Really, Sammo, call me whatever. I'm comfortable with whatever you're comfortable with."

"So, who is it," Sam asked. "Wait! Is it that food guy?"

"The caterer? Matt. Yes." I went on to explain the night in the restaurant. "It was only a couple of days ago, but I really like him," I looked up at Sam. "Is this weird to talk about with you?"

"I am so happy to have you back in my life again, I'll talk about anything you want to talk about. Actually, I take that back. I don't really want to talk more about Zella. Unless you have a story where you push her off the top of a building."

"Sam!" I exclaimed, "You're terrible."

"I know. But so is she," he joked.

My phone rang and I jumped.

"Sorry, I still haven't let go of the terror that she might be texting to tell me how much of a horrible person I am."

A New York number that looked familiar was on the screen. Not wanting to chance it, I sent the call to voicemail. They called back again almost immediately. My phone chimed letting me know I had a voicemail, when the phone ran again from the same number.

"Maybe you should listen to that. The PTSD will take a while to get over, but I can hold your hand while you listen to the message."

The love he still held for me warmed my heart.

Nodding and taking a deep breath, I squared my shoulders. I had done hard things, crazy things, brave things the last few days. I could do this. As I tapped on the voicemail and held the phone to my ear, Sam reached out his hand for mine. I smiled and shook my head. He nodded acknowledging my need to be strong on my own. My heart pounded and my ears rang as I heard the message. I stayed on for the second message. Blinking with disbelief I took the phone down from my ear, and then looked directly at Sam.

"Sammo, I have to go." I tried to keep my voice steady as I continued. "I just got asked to come in to read a second time for a big role for a Broadway workshop. A couple weeks ago I went to a couple of random auditions with Ginger but they said they'll be making casting decisions based on what happens today, so I have to get there. It might just stay in the workshop phase and not make it to a full production," I started to bounce on my feet as I said the last, "but I really want this role."

"Go babe! I'll call you later this week to see how it went, and to set up brunch for you, Matt, Nick and me."

"I'd love that," I hollered as I was dashing down the street toward the subway.

"I'm proud of you!" I heard him shout as I took the last steps down to the platform.

Less than seventy-two hours ago I'd confessed to Matt that I needed to get my life back to something I recognized. I didn't have a job. I jumped every time my phone rang expecting it to be Zella. But I was happy, and this was New York. I'd figured out how to make it work before, and I'm sure I'll figure it out again.

Yes, my life might never again be as glamorous, going to million-dollar weddings, eating five-hundred-dollar plate dinners, and seeing the inside of the elite worlds of New York.

But I was free. Doors were opening for me, and I didn't need Zella to open them.

The... beginning

Acknowledgements

There is a trend in fiction right now where it dances on the edge of real, but is familiar enough that many people ask if the things in novels if not the whole thing happened.
Fiction is the opposite of real. It is fantasy and healing. So, while yes, I did work in the event industry in New York City for many years, and yes I saw many things, and heard many stories, this book is fiction. Did some of these things happen? Probably. But there is no Zella; I'm not Natalie, and although I worked with some very interesting people, this is a story.

That said, I do want to acknowledge first the folks who were in the trenches with me during my time in the industry. Working sixteen- or twenty-hour days to make a dream wedding was a reality. And there are a handful of folks who I worked with or ran into at industry events that helped make all the event magic happen. It is crazy how passionate and creative people in the industry can be and how they make it happen week in and week out. I will never *not* be amazed at any wedding I go to.

I started writing this book several years ago while I was doing an acting gig out of town, and I want to thank Jessica and Joe Nevins for allowing my broody writing habit on a daily basis while I lived with them. And thank you for always having strong, hot coffee at the ready.

My editors TiMothy Belliveau and Karoline Rayne, I honestly can't thank either of you enough for your eye and suggestions. It is truly amazing how much you ignore details when writing a book, and these two lovely people found most of my errors!

My gorgeous cover was made by one of my best friends, Erin Vivero who took the time to have multiple conversations with me over my terrible hand drawn cover and then added a cat because she knew it would make me giggle until I fell over. I hope you don't throw this book across the room as you read it... or maybe I do.

To Rebecca, who makes me charcuterie and still swaps stories with me from being in the trenches. May you be blessed with cheese and Breeze-once always.

To Eli, Paula and Jeff, thank you for so many things, especially the gift to help raise an awesome young man.

All of my readers who took the time to poke through early stages of this book: Jackie Pepe Greenstone, Jennifer Fanska, Kathryn McLaughlin, Barbara Landin, Kaylin Clinton. This book wouldn't have been the same without your helpful and kind feedback.

To my wonderful friends and family who are always curious about what I'm writing now, and when am I going to be finished with it so they can buy it. To Alex Roth-Bianco, Grace Bennett-Dickash, Michael Keeney, Dr. Gina Grandi, Susan Edyburn, Lesley Logan, Katherine Santeramo-Palmer, Tyler Riley, Josh Jordan, Amy and Colin DePaola, David and Audrey Solly, Cameron Clarke, Patti Veconi, and countless others who are just there for me giving love and support.

To anyone who has ever had an assistant job and talked yourself into staying for whatever reason, I hope that you got what you needed out of it. And to those who are quietly suffering, don't. There are other jobs that are much better. Be brave, take the leap to the better opportunity.

To you the readers, thank you for seeing a book with a cake and a hand on it and realized it might be an interesting story, and reading it.

About Clare Solly

Clare Solly is a modern-day Renaissance woman living in New York City. She is an actress who has performed on stage and screen in many things with a best supporting actress credit to her name and three off-Broadway show credits. She currently passes her days by an amazing executive assistant.

Many crowns live in her apartment including the one that accompanies the title of America's National Elite Natural Queen 2022. Clare has a Masters Degree in Psychology with a focus on nonprofit management.

At the date of this publication, Clare has published other books including *The Time Turner* and *Christmas and Cleats* with more to come. In addition to writing novels, Clare runs two different theatre companies in NYC: The Bechdel Group and Company of Fools Theatre where she loves to foster and challenge new writers.

Clare loves to do anything creative and crafty and can get lost in a puzzle or a book. She loves to cook and bake and is a bit of a seltzer aficionado. A believer that a cup of coffee makes morning better, she also thinks that bacon is better when it's crispy, and pineapple does belong on pizza.

Feel free to find her on Instagram @youwontbesolly or @hiddencatpublishing or email at youwontbesolly@gmail.com

And if you liked this book, feel free to take a photo and tag her in it!

Made in the USA
Middletown, DE
04 December 2025

22753988R00222